Praise for
New York Times **bestselling author**

DICK WOLF

AND THE JEREMY FISK THRILLERS

THE ULTIMATUM

"Wolf's best yet. . . . [His] storytelling skills are on full display in *The Ultimatum*, and readers couldn't ask for a more worthwhile beach read."

San Diego Union-Tribune

"Wolf is the most prescient thriller writer writing today."

The Daily News

"The third incredible book by Dick Wolf featuring Detective Jeremy Fisk . . . [A] very intense and thrilling ride . . . In magnificent Dick Wolf fashion (creator of *Law & Order*), there are shadows and corruption around every corner. . . . The chase scenes are unforgettable."

Suspense Magazine

"Wolf, creator of TV's *Law & Order* franchise, is in complete control. . . . His smartly drawn characters and situations lift the novel, as do the crisp chase scenes and shootouts. And the sniper and drone elements couldn't be timelier. Another solid thriller by Wolf, who is proving as dependable a novelist as a TV producer."

Kirkus Reviews

"[Wolf] is now putting his stamp in the political thriller genre, challenging the likes of Brad Thor and David Baldacci . . . a master storyteller and it shows perfectly in *The Execution*.

Suspense Magazine

"[A] gripping adventure . . . Wolf has moved from strength to strength, from his early success as the creator of TV's *Law & Order* to his more recent incarnation as novelist. Not to be missed!"

BookPage.com

THE INTERCEPT

"Fascinating, tense, and twisty—the real deal."
Lee Child

"The hottest thriller of the year. Superbly written and amazingly intense, Dick Wolf has created an action-packed masterpiece. Picture Robert Ludlum writing for *24* and you're only halfway there. Do not miss this incredible novel. Intercept yours ASAP!"
Brad Thor

"A can-they-stop-him thriller in the manner of *Day of the Jackal*."
Miami Herald

"An adrenaline-fueled, ripped-from-the-headlines suspense novel. *The Intercept* goes where few thrillers have gone before. . . . It does for the NYPD's Intelligence Division what Thomas Harris did for the FBI's Behavioral Science Unit. In this novel, danger is *always* closer than you think."
Lisa Gardner

"Dick Wolf, the brains behind *Law & Order*, brings his considerable talents to *The Intercept*, a thriller that grabs your attention on page one and holds it until the breathtaking ending. Jeremy Fisk of the NYPD's Intelligence Division will enter literature's Great Detectives Hall of Fame. I hope to see more of him. This novel has sharp writing, perfect pacing, and a smart and sophisticated plot. It's a head above most War on Terrorism novels."

Nelson DeMille

"Like *Law & Order*, this book unfolds crisply and intelligently, with a nice mixture of suspense and social observation. . . . Wolf does a shrewd job of setting the stage for his protagonist's next appearance. Storytelling pro Wolf knows how to ratchet up tension and sustain it."

Kirkus

The first novel by the creator of *Law & Order* feels like a *Law & Order* episode. Thank goodness. . . . Like *Law & Order*, *The Intercept* works as well as it does because of its pacing; it's a fast read with a satisfying arc. . . . Its supporting cast members are drawn sharply enough to imagine them being inhabited by New York character actors."

Slate

"Wolf makes it look like he's been writing novels his entire life. The tight prose, great characters and the intense twists are all signs of a master at work. . . . Readers will be clamoring for more adventures with Jeremy Fisk."

Associated Press

Also by Dick Wolf

THE EXECUTION
THE INTERCEPT

THE
ULTIMATUM

A JEREMY FISK NOVEL

DICK WOLF

WILLIAM MORROW
An Imprint of HarperCollinsPublishers

This book is a work of fiction. References to real people, events, establishments, organizations, or locales are intended only to provide a sense of authenticity, and are used fictitiously. All other characters, and all incidents and dialogue, are drawn from the author's imagination and are not to be construed as real.

WILLIAM MORROW
An Imprint of HarperCollins*Publishers*
195 Broadway
New York, New York 10007

Copyright © 2015 by Dick Wolf
ISBN 978-0-06-228686-4

First William Morrow mass market printing: February 2016
First William Morrow hardcover printing: June 2015

To Noelle, Olivia, Serena, Elliot, Zoe, and Rex Wolf. You have all blessed my life.

THE
ULTIMATUM

BOOK ONE

From the *New York Times:*

LEAK EXPOSES QUESTIONABLE NYPD INTEL PRACTICES
By Chay Maryland

Published: May 22, 2015 10:27 P.M. *169 Comments*

NEW YORK—WikiLeaks plans to post a slew of classified documents that amount to a sweeping indictment of the New York Police Department's Intelligence Division.

The NYPD internal electronic communications, obtained by an anonymous source who provided the *New York Times* a preview, detail an extensive effort by the Intelligence Division and Counter-Terrorism Bureau—a CIA-style intelligence-gathering agency within the NYPD—to collect information on New Yorkers with "ancestries of interest." There are 28 such groups, all with origins in Muslim countries.

This information may be released via the WikiLeaks website as early as midnight Friday.

In April 2014, Commissioner William Bratton disbanded the NYPD's much-maligned Demographics Unit that had been created by his predecessor, Raymond Kelly, to spy on law-abiding Muslims in neighborhoods and houses of worship. Bratton publicly stated that the Demographics Unit undermined the fight against terrorism by alienating innocent Muslims who knew full well that they were being singled out for surveillance, not based on illegal activity, but because of religious affiliation. However, the new leak offers evidence that the practice has continued.

Since June 2012, according to one of the operations reports, the Intelligence Division has installed 5,000 Microsoft Domain Awareness CCTV (closed-circuit television) surveillance cameras in Brooklyn and Queens neighborhoods with a high concentration of Muslims, more of the high-tech cameras than in the rest of the five boroughs combined. Many of these cameras include "shot spotter" microphones, intended for the identification of gunshots, but capable of recording conversations.

In addition, Intel has stepped up its use of "rakers"— officers who speak Arabic, Bengali, Hindi, Punjabi, and Urdu—to "rake the coals." More than 1,000 Intelligence Division—or "Intel"—operations reports detail visits by rakers in the guise of customers to gathering-place businesses such as barbershops, diners, and travel agencies. In the course of casually chatting with the owners, rakers asked questions about other patrons no more specific than "Who dresses in the clothing of observant Muslims?" or "Do they like to talk politics?" According to the Handschu Guidelines, the 1985 legal agreement restricting the NYPD from building files on innocent citizens, officers are permitted to engage in such visits only if they relate to potential criminal or terrorist activity. It appears that Intel has taken a very broad view of what qualifies as potential terrorist activity.

The leaked documents also contain troubling details of the most significant terrorist operation thwarted by Intel, Swedish Muslim extremist Magnus Jenssen's attempted assassination of President Obama. An Internal Affairs report offers compelling evidence that the division engaged in an illegal assassination of Jenssen and subsequent cover-up. The same report goes on to relate a possible vendetta by

Detective Jeremy Fisk, the Intel officer who apprehended Jenssen. Jenssen had earlier murdered Fisk's fellow Intel officer, NYPD Detective Krina Gersten, with whom, according to another Internal Affairs memorandum, Fisk had a personal relationship. When interviewed by Internal Affairs officers at his Sutton Place apartment, Fisk admitted to covertly visiting Jenssen at the Metropolitan Correctional Center seven days prior to Jenssen's death. Jenssen died from a previously undetected, rapidly metastasizing cancer commonly caused by massive radiation exposure. Additional documents reveal that Fisk received medical treatment for radiation exposure the same week. Yet the investigation was closed, with no action taken against him.

From his living room couch, Jeremy Fisk glanced up from the *New York Times* article on his iPad to the TV, affording him an angled view of the center-field scoreboard in Dodger Stadium, where his Mets were tied at three with the Dodgers in the bottom of the eighth. The stadium clock read 9:50 P.M., meaning 12:50 A.M. here in New York.

So much, Fisk thought, for his first night off this month. If at midnight WikiLeaks had indeed published the PD-302—the NYPD Internal Affairs record of the interview that was conducted here, at this apartment—then his home address was now available to anyone with Internet access. In a decade and change of police work, he'd crossed paths with more than his share of the sort of characters he wouldn't want dropping by. And since his promotion to Intel, he'd all but had a fatwa issued against him—he was even less popular with Muslim groups than with the Civil Liberties Union. On top of that, a recent Mexican Cartel case here in the city, a win for the good guys, had landed his name on the Cartel hit list. On his way home one night last week, he'd picked up a tail, doubled back on the guy, and invited him, at gunpoint, for a chat at the nearest precinct house. Turned out to be a Cartel cutout tasked with learning where Fisk lived.

With two outs in the top of the ninth, the Mets' third hitter, David Wright, lined a single to center, deep enough for catcher Travis d'Arnaud to lumber from first base to third. Fisk slid to the edge of the couch as cleanup man Curtis Granderson strode to the plate, when the doorbell buzzed.

This was odd, because of the late hour, of course, and because the doorman was required to call residents on the intercom before admitting visitors. Even when a resident from another floor decided to visit your apartment, the elevator man was supposed to give you a heads-up. Only the residents of the four other apartments on this floor had unfettered access, but in the five years Fisk had lived here, a neighbor had spontaneously dropped by a total of zero times—New York was like that. The only neighbor who'd ever visited always phoned ahead: Mrs. Cooper, the octogenarian who lived around the corner and every year at Christmastime delivered homemade menorah-shaped cookies.

Fisk was home alone—as he'd been every night since Krina's death. He clicked the remote control, shifting the image on the TV screen—Granderson digging into the left side of the batter's box—to the digital peephole's view of the hallway. Just outside Fisk's door stood Mrs. Cooper, the platinum hair that ironically emphasized her age peeking from under a head scarf. A large evening bag dangled from a stooped shoulder. Her scarf and her coat were studded with drops from the latest of the April showers that had continued well into May. There was no sign of anyone else in the brightly lit corridor, yet Fisk couldn't rule out the possibility that someone else was there, maybe someone who'd convinced Mrs. Cooper to admit him to the building as her guest, someone who might now be positioned out of sight where the hall doglegged, pointing a gun at her.

Fisk held his breath, cocked an ear toward the outside hallway, and listened for squeaks of the pile carpet resulting from shifting weight. He heard nothing. Then again, between him and the hallway were his living room and a prewar plaster wall meant to ensure that residents heard nothing from the hallway.

His eyes remained glued to the digital peephole's low-res feed from the hall. No shadows. No telltale fluctuations of light. Mrs. Cooper had just been outside, obviously, yet her face was pale.

With a sigh, she looked down the hall, to the point where it turned. Through the door, Fisk heard her ask, her voice quavering, "What if he's not home?"

She looked toward the dogleg, as if taking in a response.

Easiest thing would be to ignore the door. Just pretend to be elsewhere, meanwhile covertly summoning backup.

But Mrs. Cooper was in immediate jeopardy.

If he could get into the hall, he figured he could neutralize the man. Which, taking into account Murphy's Law—a tactical necessity—meant there were two men. Unfortunately, this apartment was practically a tomb, with just one exit route, the front door. Well, and the seventeen-story drop to the street. Fisk hadn't equipped the place with the sort of high-tech defensive measures he was accustomed to at work. Other than the furnishings—all of it acquired in one hour-long visit to a department store that was having a sale that weekend—he hadn't equipped the apartment at all. It was just a place where he crashed between cases and, on occasion, caught a bit of a ball game.

Fisk's chest tightened and his body temperature plummeted. Ignoring both, he reached behind him and into the pile on the back of the couch: suit coat, raincoat, and Glock 17 in a black leather De Santis shoulder holster. Prying free the gun, he tried to formulate a plan of action.

"Hello?" he called out, as if he were battling a yawn. Setting a foot in the foyer risked drawing fire through the front door.

"Jeremy, it's Gladys Cooper from around the corner."

"Everything okay, Mrs. Cooper?" he asked, as if he didn't suspect anything.

She didn't immediately respond. Was she being coached by whoever was around the corner? Finally, she said, "I just need to talk to you about something."

"Sure, but just a sec. I need to find my robe." This would buy him twenty seconds before whoever was in the hall got antsy.

"Uh . . . okay."

He hurried into his bedroom. The casement window was already open, saving him from contending with the handle, whose squeaky hinge invariably scared pigeons into flight—like many New Yorkers, he relied on his bedroom window to counter the steam heat on chilly nights like this one.

He climbed onto the radiator and squeezed out the window, an act of contortion, meanwhile inspecting the ledge. If it could even be called a ledge. The narrow limestone surface, which extended from the base of the window by five inches at most, was slicked by rainwater on top of an accumulation of Manhattan soot.

Securing the Glock inside his waistband, he stepped out tentatively until feeling that the ledge would support his weight, meanwhile taking in his East Fifty-Fifth Street block, seventeen stories below, deserted but for parked cars. The street looked twice as small from this height when there was no window or guardrail between him and it. He thought of the opening sequence of *Mad Men*, when the main character is seen plummeting from a high city building. Best to focus on staying up here, he decided. Unfortunately, wind numbed his hands and face and lashed the rest of him with cold rain.

Clinging to icy bricks, he rotated his feet so that they pointed away from each other. Then he began a variation of a crab walk to the neighboring apartment, from which he hoped to flank Mrs. Cooper's coach.

Seven seconds, he figured, until the hostiles considered dispensing with Mrs. Cooper and coming in after him.

The neighbors' bedroom window was ten feet away. He hoped that the couple who lived here, Larry and Sue Foster, bankers who rose early for work, would be in bed, and thus able to let him in. If indeed the apartment were empty, he would have to utilize the Glock's muzzle like the pointed glass-breaker tool on a Swiss Army knife: when jammed into a pane, it caused vibrations concentrated enough to break the surface tension and separate the glass molecules, shattering the glass. The noise was minimal and brief, but might give him up still.

He reached the Fosters' bedroom window. The bedroom was dark. No sign of the Fosters in bed, in the adjacent living room, or otherwise.

Of course not.

He was in luck, though. The Fosters too employed the "Manhattan thermostat"—their bedroom window was open a crack. With a brief nudge, he opened it enough to fit through. Reflecting that he'd exhausted the one piece of luck he might reasonably expect, he slipped into the bedroom, landing with a muted tap on the pile carpet.

Through the wall between the apartments, he heard a muffled rendition of its buzz and Mrs. Cooper calling out, "Jeremy?"

Right on schedule. He had another ten seconds, tops, to come up with a plan of attack.

Darting out of the bedroom and into the marble-tiled foyer, he formed a mental diagram of the corridor outside. It was shaped like an uppercase L, of which his apartment and this one formed the base.

Hanging on the wall between the two doors was a small framed English countryside print. The lone door other than the apartments' opened to the emergency stairwell, across the hall. The corridor was lit by three recessed fluorescent bulbs in the ceiling. It might be better from a tactical standpoint if he turned them off—the switch was in the emergency stairwell—but even when they were out, the illuminated red exit sign adequately illuminated the hallway. On the uppercase *L*'s ascender, the three other apartments faced the elevator landing, which included a cushioned bench and a mirror.

The old-fashioned analog peephole on the Fosters' door gave Fisk a fish-eye view of Mrs. Cooper stabbing at his door button. A silenced handgun—a SIG Sauer P226, going by the stout black barrel—peeked from around the corner, pointed at her. The gun was gripped by a caramel-colored hand. Two similarly complected, thickset young men stood on this end of the hallway, one gripping a boxy black Taurus 9mm, also fitted with a sound suppressor. Pros didn't use the suppressors for stealth, but, rather, to protect their own ears.

The guy closest to the Fosters' apartment held a steel-handled ax that looked like it had been hand-wrought centuries ago. This explained some things. On the recent Cartel case, Fisk had seen a similar weapon, an Aztec tomahawk. Tomahawks were now in vogue in Cartel assassin circles for dismemberment or decapitation, or both.

He backpedaled, turning in to the small kitchen, where he slid the half-full garbage bag out of the pail. Now he had a way to conceal his gun as well as a convincing prop for the role he intended to play: bystander taking out the trash. Once clear of the door, he would toss the bag to the tomahawk guy. When you throw something into a man's face, he first senses the motion and processes information, then reacts by either catching the object, fending it off, or dodging it. Any of these reactions would occupy him long enough for Fisk to get the drop on the Taurus 9mm guy.

With the trash bag held against his shirtfront, Fisk turned the door handle. Prior to stepping out, he intended to let go of the door handle and slide the gun from his waistband and into hiding behind the bag. Unfortunately the steel door offered extraordinary resistance, which had little to do with its steel plating or considerable weight. A hazard of the "Manhattan thermostat" was the wind tunnel effect an open window could cause within an apartment, with its force directed at the door.

This was a one-second fix, a hard tug. Then Fisk wedged his shoe into the gap between door and jamb. But that one second was enough to draw the full attention of Taurus and Tomahawk as well as the man from around the corner, their leader by virtue of seniority if his graying beard were any indication.

Taurus and Graybeard hid their weapons. Tomahawk let his dangle at his side, as if it were a nothing accessory. None of them appeared to recognize Fisk. But Mrs. Cooper did.

Before Fisk could devise a means of forestalling her, she asked, "What are you doing in the Fosters' apartment, Jeremy?"

Tomahawk reared back to throw his ax at Fisk, Graybeard leveled his SIG, and Taurus aimed his pistol and squeezed the trigger.

Adrenaline compacted Fisk's world into a tunnel between him and them: Mrs. Cooper, the walls, the ceiling, and everything else outside the tunnel snapped into soft focus. He threw himself back into the Fosters' apartment. Not that a door—even a thick steel-plated one—could do much more than slow a bullet traveling at a thousand feet per second. The idea was to remove his body from the gunmen's view.

The bullet snapped through the steel plate and buzzed over his head, spraying wood dust into his eyes before boring into more metal in the kitchen, maybe the fridge. He cracked the door enough to peer into the hallway, and squinting against billowing wood dust, he returned fire. Three shots in rapid succession.

The first drilled through Tomahawk's right clavicle, exiting behind him with a scarlet streamer, knocking him backward. He collapsed, losing his grip on the tomahawk. The metal handle cracked the glass over the framed English countryside painting before thunking to the floor.

The second and third shots painted dark red holes on Taurus's neck and forehead and matching starbursts on the honeycomb wallpaper behind him. He fell to the floor as if he'd been turned to stone.

The reports—thunder in these confines— reduced Fisk's hearing to a whine, beneath which he heard a Mexican-accented, "Drop your gun and come the fuck out now!"

Graybeard stood beside a petrified Mrs. Cooper, his sound suppressor wedged into her temple.

Fisk fired at him.

At such close range, a bullet would incapacitate Graybeard before he'd processed that he'd been fired upon—if the bullet were on target.

A purple cavity appeared on the man's denim shirtfront, about an inch below the collar. He crumpled to the carpet, spraying a dark red stripe onto the wall behind him.

Mrs. Cooper's eyes went white, and she teetered.

Fisk launched himself toward her, circumnavigating the three prostrate figures, and catching her cleanly, save for her cumbersome evening bag, the contents of which crunched and clanked together on hitting the floor.

"You okay?" he asked.

"I . . ." She looked around, as if struggling to find focus. "I guess so."

Motion drew his eyes to the mirror across the hall from the elevator: Tomahawk rolling on the carpet, snatching up Graybeard's SIG.

Fisk allowed his momentum to carry him and Mrs. Cooper around the corner. She retained enough consciousness to snatch her bag by the leather straps.

Three coughs from the Taurus produced three holes in the wall—right where her head had been a second before.

Fisk set her onto the bench beside the elevator. Flattening himself against the wall, he reached his Glock around the corner and blindly fired. Four shots.

The mirror showed him the results, bullet holes in a row on the wall fronting his apartment, each spewing a ribbon of plaster dust.

Tomahawk, meanwhile, ducked into the emergency stairwell.

So now it was a standoff. Which was an improvement. Reinforcements would eventually arrive. Problem was, Fisk had ten bullets left and Tomahawk had at least twice that many just in the Beretta and the SIG.

"Do you have your apartment key?" he whispered to Mrs. Cooper, who was pressing the elevator call button over and over.

She began rummaging through her evening bag. "I was trying to get out my Taser when they came at me out on the sidewalk, and I think I dropped my key in here—"

The brass elevator door popped open, surprising them both, but offering a potential escape route. It could take them to the lobby faster than Tomahawk could get down seventeen flights of stairs.

The elevator was a better option, Fisk thought, than taking their chances with Tomahawk here until help arrived.

If help arrived.

Fisk fired around the corner to keep Tomahawk at bay, then spun toward Mrs. Cooper. "Come on," he said, taking her by the arm, helping her into the small car and hammering the button for the lobby.

The door rumbled shut. No bullets rang it. No hint of Tomahawk at all, though he had to be wise to their escape plan.

With an electrical grunt, the motor set to spinning the pulley, known as a sheave. (Fisk had learned this as a rookie while busting Alphabet City "shaft hackers," thrill seekers who forced their way into elevator shafts and "surfed" up and down while balancing on the cars' roofs.) The hoist ropes—steel cables that looped around the sheave—groaned as they lowered the car. Fisk sat against the thick brass handrail, deriving a measure of contentment from its solidity. The buzzing ventilation cooled the perspiration coating his forehead.

Mrs. Cooper gripped the handrail as if staying afoot depended on it, the veins and bones in her left hand all in plain sight through skin that was pale to the point of translucent, like an anatomical model. With her free hand, she rifled through her bag.

"Still looking for your key?" Fisk asked. He wondered if she was in shock.

"Oh, no, for this." She fished out a clamshell phone and snapped it open. "To call the police."

Fisk suspected that the shooting had already spurred several 911 calls, but another one couldn't hurt. He started to say as much when the elevator car came to an abrupt and bumpy stop. He suspected that Tomahawk had run up to the machine room on the nineteenth floor, directly above the elevator shaft.

The ceiling light blinked out and the ventilation fan slowed to nothing. The handset icon on the elevator's emergency phone flashed on, turning Mrs. Cooper's bulging eyes pink. "What's happening?" she asked, staggering to the center of the car as if the walls were closing in.

"Please, Mrs. Cooper, try to stay calm," Fisk said.

They didn't need a case of claustrophobia-induced hyperventilation now. "He's just trying to stop us from getting downstairs."

In fact, Fisk suspected that the hit man was trying to accelerate their descent. A clank of metal against metal confirmed it. The guy was trying to tomahawk apart the braided steel cables suspending the elevator, to send the car into free fall.

"What if he cuts the cords?" asked Mrs. Cooper.

"The big pulley has an emergency braking system. When it spins too fast, centrifugal force raises a pair of weighted metal arms that clamp onto ratchets mounted inside the pulley, stopping its rotation."

"What if he whacks apart those things too?"

"We're still okay, because the elevator also has a backup system, electromagnetic brakes that engage when the power fails—"

As if Tomahawk had just taken the power into consideration, the car's ceiling light came back on and the fan whirred to life. So much for an assist from the electromagnetic brakes.

The clanking resumed, sharp blows that resounded through the shaft. Fisk felt them in his teeth. "Maybe we should get out of here," he said, thumbing the "open door" button.

Nothing happened.

The chopping from the top of the shaftway increased in pace and intensity.

Fisk dug his fingers into the narrow gap between the slab door and the frame, then threw his weight backward. To his surprise, the door came with him, revealing a stretch of sheer cinderblock wall be-

tween the fourteenth and fifteenth floors. Whether
or not Tomahawk intended it, he'd stopped the car
in perfect position to preclude their escape.

"Now what?" Mrs. Cooper asked, panic eroding
her newfound poise.

"There are emergency brakes, plus a big piston at
the bottom of the shaft that's like a shock absorber,
to cushion the impact."

Her brow knitted.

With good reason. If this thing were to fall for
three seconds, impact velocity would be near fifty
miles an hour. "I might have a better idea," he said.
Though he didn't. Not yet.

Standing on his toes, he reached up and slid aside
one of the four opaque plastic panels that diffused
the light of a fluorescent ring mounted at the ceiling's center. To one side of the ring was the service
hatch, used primarily to accommodate items like
furniture that were too tall to fit in the elevator otherwise. He tugged at its lever.

Mrs. Cooper gasped. "But he'll shoot you!"

Fisk released the hatch. "His view into the shaft is
blocked by the machine room floor," he said, hoping
he was right.

He slid the service hatch to the side and looked
up fifty feet of dimly lit vertical tunnel with guide
rails to either side of the car. Without the hatch, the
volume of the clanks increased. With each, the vibrations rippled the four steel cables hanging down
the center of the shaftway to the crossbar bolted to
the roof of the elevator.

An odd idea struck him. "Hey, Mrs. Cooper, did
you say you have a Taser?"

"Yes, my daughter gave it—"

"Can I borrow it?"

She searched her shoulder bag, producing a fire-engine-red Taser C2, a state-of-the-art personal protection model the size of a banana. "What are you going to do?"

The car canted, and she fell into him. As his spine hit the wall, one of the four-inch-thick cables hit the roof with a metallic whipcrack before jangling down the shaft.

He reached for the Taser, and she handed it to him.

"Hang on now," he said.

Grasping the light-panel grid, he pulled himself through the safety hatch and into the cold yet musty shaftway.

A clank resounded through the shaft.

Rising so that he stood parallel to the cables, Fisk snapped open the Taser's trigger compartment, automatically activating the system's laser pointer. Steadying the pointer's green dot on the closest of the three remaining braided steel cables, he pressed the trigger. With a hiss of nitrogen propellant and a *sproing*, out jumped two fifteen-foot-long wires, each tipped by a barbed probe. The first barb bit into the braided steel wire, right where the laser dot was. The second flew past and burrowed into the wall. Fifty thousand volts' worth crackled through the wires—forming a circuit including the concrete (a surprisingly efficient electrical conductor), the steel cable, a sheave perched on a rubber vibration damper, and a metal tomahawk.

A bestial scream cascaded down the shaft, along with what sounded like the metal tomahawk dropping to the concrete machine room floor, followed by a body.

Fisk could be gratified later. New York's average 911 response time was eight minutes and twenty-five seconds, so he was still on his own here. He needed to pry open the door to the fifteenth floor, hoist Mrs. Cooper through the service hatch, and get her to safety. And then he needed to alert other intelligence officers whose home addresses were now public along with the contact information for their secret sources—secret until a couple of hours ago, that is.

When his phone rang, Brad Willoughby was walking past *Alma Mater*, the bronze sculpture of Athena that surveys much of the Columbia University campus from a marble throne. The caller was Douglas Moret, the zillionaire hedge-fund manager known to Willoughby's eleven-year-old son, Gates, as Coach Doug. Something had to be very wrong to take Moret's attention from work during trading hours.

Willoughby hit answer and blurted into the mouthpiece, "Hey, everything okay?"

"Good news and bad news, doc," came Moret's rapid-fire rasp.

"What happened?" Willoughby braced.

"The good news is, all of the coaches met last night, and Gates made the Greenwich all-star team."

Relief flooded Willoughby, followed by a bubbly pride. The six hours between now and when he would be able to share the news with Gates would pass like weeks. He stopped next to *Alma Mater*, followed her gaze onto the emerald quad, and breathed in the fresh-mown grass, savoring the moment. Until he remembered: "What's the bad news?"

"That Gates made the all-star team." Moret guffawed. "The Little League World Series regionals tournament is next week. Pretty much all of next week."

"Where?"

"Remember how you said a week in New Hampshire was in the 'category of desirable problems'?"

Willoughby sat down on the pedestal and leaned back into the shade cast by Athena's robe. "When I said that, back in April, I didn't have to make a presentation that's going to take every minute of next week to get ready."

"Well, bud, who knows better than a professor how to get an extension? Gatesy on the mound gives us our best chance at Williamsport in sixty-however-many years. But, you know better than anybody, he's got to be in the right frame of mind."

Gates believed that their ritual father-and-son long tosses before his starts were indispensable, and that Willoughby himself was good luck. Willoughby hadn't missed a single one of his son's games going back to his tee-ball debut eight years ago. He wanted to be in New Hampshire next week for Gates. He wanted to be there for himself too: fatherhood didn't get much better than that. If only it were as simple as getting an extension. The presentation a week from Monday was in Washington at the Department of Commerce. On the line was a $20 million check to Columbia to develop a new firewall for the proprietary data network shared by the Bureau of Industry and Security and the two other major economic intelligence services, the Office of Intelligence and Analysis and the State Department's Bureau of Intelligence.

"I'll try and work something out," Willoughby told Moret before ringing off.

He wasted no time texting his two best assistants

and inviting them to lunch at the Faculty Club, the private four-star restaurant that was second only to being located in Manhattan among Columbia perks. It would help the sales pitch, he thought. He hoped to convince at least one of them to stay on campus and work in his place through next week's July Fourth break.

Two hours later, after they'd given the waiter their lunch orders, he put the question to Mary Ann Hunter. A blonde in the Dietrich mold, Mary Ann might have been a starlet herself if not for her obsession with computer science. She neglected her health, social life, and most everything other than work. In asking her to work through the holiday, he felt as if he were letting an alcoholic stay at the bar past closing time.

"I would totally love to," she said. "The thing is, my brother's wedding is next week, in Anchorage. I'll try, but I don't think I'll be able to get out of it."

"First let's try Plan Ji." Willoughby turned to Ji-Hsuan Lin, a titanic intellect concealed in the form of a demure twenty-five-year-old who could pass for twelve. He'd won a full ride here from a town in western China that had no electricity or running water, let alone computers.

Holding his fork and knife in the wrong hands now, Ji appeared to be puzzling over how to attack the still-steaming Yorkshire pudding on his bread plate. "For the Independence Day, I schedule to go to fish in Maine with friends," he apologized.

"That sounds great," Willoughby said with all sincerity. It was good to know that the kid had friends. But it didn't solve the immediate problem.

"I don't suppose there's any way you could reschedule your fishing trip, with the department reimbursing you for any cancellation fees?"

Ji stared at his Coke. "Possibility," he said.

He probably meant possibility in a strictly mathematical sense, Willoughby thought, for instance a 1-in-100,000 chance. "If it helps, we can pick up your car rental or hotel—or anything, really—if you wanted to choose another week."

"I will see." Ji flashed a toothy smile, although it wasn't warranted.

"And if you can stay here, I'll make it worth your while. I have really good Philharmonic tickets Tuesday night that I wouldn't be using, and I'll throw in dinner at the restaurant of your choice. Any restaurant, really."

Ji bit his lip. Willoughby knew the look: reluctant to let down the esteemed professor and mentor.

It was an act.

"How many tickets to Philharmonic?" he asked Willoughby, intentionally dropping the article, as usual.

The professor sat up, as if electrified. "Two, but if you need more . . ." An IQ of 160, yet a fool.

"No, two good. Thank you, sir!"

Fisk hurried from his latest temporary residence, the Hampton Inn on Pearl Street in downtown Manhattan, late for court. He'd been detained by the desk clerk, who told him that if he wished to remain in his room beyond this morning's eleven o'clock checkout time, he needed a new method of payment: The Diner's Club card he'd given when checking in the other day had just been suspended on account of suspicious charges. Which was par for the course lately. Along with his home address, his date of birth and his Social Security number were in the documents posted by WikiLeaks. About once per day since then, he received a call from a credit-card company about a suspicious charge.

These calls came to an end only when AT&T canceled his account.

And now the suspicious credit-card charges would cease as well, because the Diner's Club was the last of his active cards. To pay the Hampton Inn, he'd gone to an ATM to withdraw the $290 for another night (a pretty good deal by Manhattan standards), only to discover that his checking account balance, which had been $1,104.45 the day before, somehow dipped to $4.12. Later he would need to transfer funds from his pension account (why not, while there were still funds in the pension account?). No telling how late he would be if he hadn't simply returned to his hotel room, stuffed all of his things into his duffel bag, and checked out.

By the time he reached Foley Square, he was twenty minutes late for today's episode of *United States v. Verlyn*, the trial of thirty-two-year-old systems analyst and self-proclaimed NSA whistleblower Merritt Verlyn for violations of the Espionage Act of 1917. Fisk bounded up the massive granite steps leading to the United States Courthouse. The sharp morning light brought the stunning white granite landmark building to a glow. A collector of Manhattan trivia, Fisk knew that the building had been renamed the Thurgood Marshall United States Courthouse in 2001—Marshall had worked here as a Second Circuit Court of Appeals judge before being bumped up to the United States Supreme Court (whose Washington digs were designed by the same architect, Cass Gilbert).

As he shot between two of the giant Corinthian columns and into the portico, the contrast between sunlight and shade was so extreme that Fisk needed to remove his Oakleys in order to see. In the process, he nearly ran into a woman hurrying out of the courthouse. If she were aware that her pink UCLA tennis bag grazed him, she didn't show it.

He kept going, until hit with the realization that his tardiness made no difference. The witness he'd come to see testify wouldn't be testifying today. She was leaving the courthouse. The UCLA tennis bag was probably part of a disguise that included a tracksuit, a Yankees cap, and wraparound shades: so that she could get past the media swarm in the lobby. All good disguise choices, Fisk thought. The baseball cap hid her lustrous chute of black hair, with the bill of the cap draping her sharp features in shadows. The big sunglasses eliminated the pronounced contour of her cheekbones. The loose-fitting tracksuit, ironically, veiled her track athlete's physique. In his professional opinion, the hot-pink UCLA tennis racquet bag was the pièce de résistance. When people see such a unique item on a person, they fixate on that item rather than on the person. In fact, the woman had neither gone to UCLA nor played tennis—if Fisk's memory served, she'd run the 100 at Georgetown, nearly earning a spot on the 2004 U.S. Olympic team.

She passed the last of the journalists, an ABC reporter leaning against a banister halfway down the courthouse steps. The guy didn't look up from his phone.

Fisk followed her the rest of the way down the steps, then called out, "Chay?"—pronounced "Shea," like the former New York Mets baseball stadium (named for William Shea, the Manhattan lawyer who softened the blow of the Brooklyn Dodgers' traitorous flight to Los Angeles by convincing the National League to give the city an expansion team, the Mets).

She kept going, as if she hadn't heard him or were someone else. But, almost imperceptibly, she stiffened.

He tried again. "Chay Maryland, of the *New York Times*?"

She glanced over a shoulder.

He manufactured a smile. "One of your stories changed my life."

A blink and she made him. "Jeremy Fisk. Detective, Intel." She looked past him, no doubt worried about drawing a news crew. Wary, but not nervous or scared. "What do you want?"

"Just to ask you a question, for a change."

She stepped onto the Worth Street sidewalk. The pedestrian traffic was light, by Manhattan standards, yet enough of a crowd that she was lost to the courthouse reporters. "I'm in a rush . . ."

Fisk caught up to her. "Aren't you going to testify?" he asked. Despite an offer of a significantly mitigated sentence, Merritt Verlyn sat in his cell at the Marshals Service detention facility and refused to say a word. No fewer than 122,627 documents remained outstanding from the files Verlyn had stolen, and it was well within the realm of possibility that Chay had the cache on a flash drive bouncing around inside her tennis bag.

"Why would I testify?" She accelerated slightly, her stride widening.

"Chiefly because prison isn't pleasant," he said. "I fear your tennis game might suffer."

"Oh, I don't know," she said. "I wouldn't have to waste time deciding what to wear in the morning. There would be no guys to deal with, no bills to worry about, I wouldn't miss days at the gym. I could catch up on my rest and my reading, maybe write a book."

"That's what vacations are for."

"I take about as many vacations as you do, I'll bet. In any case, Detective, I can't divulge confidential sources on a story, not in court, not anywhere."

"But your source is already on trial."

"Nice try. Merritt Verlyn may or may not be my source . . . but either way, prospective whistle-blowers need to know that journalists are going to protect them, even if it means we go to prison. The bigger-picture issue is that a free press is essential to democracy—you're a great fan of democracy, aren't you?"

"I am. I'm also a fan of national security. Hypothetically, would it ever bother you if your reporting put American lives in danger?"

"I think you mean your American life."

"Okay, maybe it's not so hypothetical. Did you see the stolen document listing our informants on the Kkangpae mob in Koreatown?"

Chay glanced away. "There were more than one hundred thousand documents, I could not read each one."

"The second that Kkangpae file goes up on Wiki-Leaks, the whole op is blown. The mobsters don't exactly take kindly to people who help the police. Real lives are at stake."

"I'd hope you've taken steps to protect your in-formants."

"And that's just one instance. These people have family members who also may be in harm's way." Fisk tried to hold back, but his anger was showing.

Chay said, "Bringing the ops reports to light may also help innocent New Yorkers who are already in the cross fire, placed there by Intel without regard for their constitutional rights."

"Except that in every single case, a judge signed off."

"So it's a case of legal authority versus moral authority." She slowed down now, eager to win this argument. "Then why not let New Yorkers decide which they're willing to allow?"

"They've already done that through the election of representatives who approved Intel's programs. Also there are numerous built-in safeguards: intelligence service personnel have set procedures that allow them to blow the whistle about a classified program without putting agents at risk."

A red palm flashed onto the sign on the far side of Broadway. Stopping at the curb, Chay turned to Fisk and asked, "Is it modesty or some sort of crazy amnesia that kept you from mentioning the attempted Cartel hit at your apartment building?"

"It's part of an ongoing investigation, so I can't talk about it. Except to say that it certainly proves my point. Posting law enforcement agents' private information on the Internet puts us at drastically increased risk of visits from assassins."

"I'm not sure these so-called assassins needed any help from me, informational, motivational, or otherwise. I do hope that the experience of having the informational grid turned on you gives you and your colleagues a taste of your own medicine. In the abstract, that is. You wield an enormous amount of power, and these checks and balances you rattle off are little impediment. Whatever you want to see, you see. Whoever you want to watch, you watch. You've been harassing me and everyone I know in pursuit of the Verlyn document cache, which is what we're really talking about now, isn't it? You're not interested in whether or not I testify. The question you want answered is 'Where are the documents?' Right?"

"I shouldn't need to ask that. I should have faith that if you did know, you would have warned the agents who, along with their spouses and children, are in danger."

She scoffed. "That's just a variation on the old saw that it's the responsibility of the media to join the government in the war on terror. I'm sorry; it's not. It's the media's responsibility to cover the government, not to cover the government's ass."

Fisk remained in place when the sign on the far corner clicked to the man-walking icon and pedestrians shot across Broadway. Did she really believe this? "I feel like you are making the decision that some people's lives are more sacred than others."

"And I feel like you do the same thing, day in and day out. Let me ask you a question. Did you murder Magnus Jenssen?"

Fisk's face showed nothing. "When did you switch gears from an investigative reporter to critic?"

"I'm not sure I did."

"Fun to go thumbs-up or thumbs-down on food you don't have to prepare or pay for."

Fisk started across while the walk signal counted down, leaving Chay at the curb, uncharacteristically without a rejoinder.

Never seen you out of your uniform before, Harry," said Wally from the driver's seat of his hansom cab. "You've got a really nice ass, man!"

Harun weighed a comeback as he jogged past, on Central Park's lower loop. He and Wally had become friends over the years, since an afternoon even hotter than this one. From his post at the door of the luxury apartment building, 122 Central Park South, Harun had been looking out on the horses standing in a row on the park side of the street, tethered to carriages, awaiting fares despite the broiling sun.

He felt especially sorry for Wally's bony old horse, Buckmeister. After enduring an earful from Mrs. Billingham in apartment 19F for using one of the building's pails, Harun brought Buckmeister some cold water.

Harun thought now of a retort involving his ass and Wally's lips. He kept it to himself, rather than risk obliterating whatever tip his friend still stood to collect from the prim, clearly unamused elderly couple in the back of his cab.

Harun also needed to conserve his breath in order to make it up to the reservoir, let alone back to work. Each stride was heavy lifting, his lungs ached, and the air wasn't just searing, it was foul. Although he couldn't see the Central Park Zoo from here, he could sure smell the monkey cages.

He and Durriyah had taken Rudy and the twins

to the zoo to see the new snow-leopard cubs on his
last day off. Not easy getting in from Ozone Park
with the "new" (to them—really, thirdhand) double
stroller on the crowded A train, plus Rudy's stroller.
And, surprise, now that Rudy was three, the price
of his zoo admission ticket had gone from free to
thirteen bucks. Plus another eighteen dollars apiece
for Harun and Durriyah. Plus half his salary for
snacks and drinks and balloons while waiting on
line (almost an hour) for the cat house.

But from the moment they got in, it was worth it:
the looks on the boys' faces, all three of them smil-
ing and laughing.

The image pushed away the pain of running now.
Man, did he love those guys. He'd do anything for
them. Running four miles during his lunch break
was nothing. All for them. You'd've thought pushing a stroller for hours on end to get the babies
to fall asleep counted as exercise, but since he and
Durriyah had gotten into the baby business, as they
called it, he'd somehow put on forty pounds. Now
he ran for the boys, so that they'd have an old man
who could play football with them, instead of just
an old man.

Before he knew it, twenty-five blocks were behind
him and he was on the path through the woods,
toward the gatehouse at the bottom of the Jackie
O. Reservoir. No other runners around. Which figured. It was 2:15, maybe 2:30. The lunch-hour reg-
ulars, the yuppie fitness-nut types, were showered
and back at their desks by now, polishing off expensive salads. Good. He liked the solitude, a commodity in this town.

A dark shadow passed overhead. His first thought was: a bird. One of those falcons the news loves to show nesting at the tops of the buildings surrounding the park. Swooping for someone's late lunch, maybe.

He kept on. The shadow appeared again, out of the corner of his eye. Unnaturally round. Seemed to stay on him as he ran. He looked up, through the gap between the tops of two big trees, squinting into a blaze of sunlight. Using a hand as a visor and squinting against the glare, he made out a dark form above the treetops. Christ, a buzzard? Find someone else, vulture. Harun was running to add years to his life.

It made no noise, or at least nothing he could hear over the din of the city, which, even here, in the depths of the park—

A boom, as from a cannon. That's what it sounded like. Shaking him, turning the leaves all around into a shower of green confetti falling behind him.

Something pinged the path to his side, raising a spark and spraying dirt and gravel into his shins. He glanced down, seeing a few spots of blood.

What the hell?

Spooked, he sped up.

Another blast. This time, it felt like a firebomb went off in his throat. His legs gave out and he went down hard on his side, coming to rest on his back on the path.

He was cold all over, except for a newly formed pit between his collarbones. Hot blood welled there, trickling down his shirt, into his left armpit. None of which made any sense.

No real pain, fortunately. He struggled to get up—and made it as far as his elbows when a dark sheet of blood flooded down his shirtfront. His consciousness flickered.

Three boys in the cat house, balloons in hand, smiles on faces.

A rooster's crow woke Fisk, who didn't immediately know where he was. So what else was new? Lately he'd become Manhattan's answer to George Washington, sleeping in one place after another on account of a digital trail that he couldn't turn off.

He was growing unhealthily paranoid, and he knew it. The usual cop eyes he brought to the street were becoming prey's eyes as he watched each face and clocked each passing car. He was becoming squirrelly. In his least healthy moments, he wondered if it was penance for his own misdeeds: a Sartrean punishment for having exacted his revenge upon Magnus Jenssen.

Flecks of dawn skirting the steel window gates outlined tall bare brick walls against the darkness. The fishy smell of old glue was the tip-off: the building was a onetime book bindery in an old printing house just off Tenth Avenue, two blocks west of Madison Square Garden. The fact that the building was zoned for commercial and not residential use didn't stop the owner from renting out spaces fitted with crude showers and hot plates. For cash, of course. Which aligned with Fisk's interests. The Department had wanted him to get out of town and lie low until there was some closure in the leak case, meaning he was out of harm's way from the Cartel. Fisk maintained that there was no better place for him than Manhattan, with its multitudes—on each block. Also he wanted to be here in order to work the leak case.

Because he needed a name to rent this place, he'd chosen Reynolds. Common enough. The choice was also an homage to Scottie Reynolds, the leading scorer in Villanova basketball history. Fisk figured there was little risk that anyone would make the association: he himself had sunk a pair of free throws in the first varsity game he played at Villanova, the eighteenth game of the season during his sophomore year. At last check, his two points placed him in a twenty-three-way tie for 533rd place on the school's all-time scoring list. Because he'd topped out at five-eleven and, mostly, because he was short on talent, he never made it into a second varsity game. Two points in a Division I game gave him celeb status in his rec league, though.

He snapped on his trusty Pelican 7060—the compact, rechargeable mega-lumen tactical flashlights, popular in law enforcement. Pelicans retailed for about $150 apiece, which, if you asked cops, was a bargain. The 7060 featured a control switch on the barrel and a second one on the butt end so an officer could switch from low beam to high while tracking a perp, holding the light under his weapon or above his head. Fisk's Pelican had become perhaps the most important home-furnishing element.

The rooster's crow was the default ring tone, evidently, on his latest prepaid cell phone, which sat on the pitted hardwood floor beside his new inflatable bed. Goddamn. With three rows of three giant app icons, the phone looked like a toy. Recognizing the number as an NYPD exchange, he hit answer and said, "Walker." Kenny "Sky" Walker had been his favorite Knick as a kid.

"Good morning, Detective Fisk," came a familiar, grandmotherly voice. "It's Sally in Chief Dubin's office."

So much, thought Fisk, for his Walker alias, and the phone, notwithstanding the voiceprint and GPS scrambling apps on which he'd spent $29.98 and forty minutes of download time. He knew of four different electronic signal intelligence collection and analysis networks on which her mention of his name might raise the digital equivalent of a red flag, if so desired by one of five hundred thousand people with the requisite clearance at seventeen U.S. intelligence agencies. Or by a single person at one of those agencies that the Cartel had gotten to. With that information, tracking him could be as simple for a hit man as using GPS.

Here was the source of his paranoia: he knew too much about finding people like himself who did not want to be found. Fisk had never been a fan of karma.

Fisk set the concern aside because a call of any sort from the Department at this hour almost certainly meant urgent business. "What's up?" he asked.

"The chief wants you to go to a meeting at eight thirty."

"Okay," said Fisk.

"At the *New York Times*."

Fisk wondered if Sally had called him in error. "A meeting at the *Times*?"

"On West Fortieth."

*Times*men referred to NYPD Intel as the NYKGB,

and Fisk as Jeremy Badenov. Was Dubin, conscious of public image to a fault, offering him as a sacrificial lamb?

"Any idea what this is about?" he asked Sally.

"A homicide."

Fisk liked the printing house's broad selection of exits—front, service/delivery, basement, and courtyard. Someone waiting outside in ambush had his chance of success reduced by 75 percent right off the bat. This morning, he chose the courtyard exit door, throwing a hip into the crash bar and drawing his Glock as he backed out.

"Courtyard" was a euphemism for a two-hundred-square-foot patch of crumbling cement patio surrounded by a high iron rail fence. Empty now. Weeds coated the fence, depriving someone in the surrounding brownstones of a view of the door to the courtyard, for instance through a rifle scope.

Stepping onto the patio, Fisk was hit by the blare of engine noises and horns and people trying to talk over them—a typical A.M. rush hour, unless you were feeling like a fugitive.

He proceeded down a narrow back alley, at the end of which he peered onto Thirty-Fifth Street, spotting several doorways and other choke points ideal for an ambush. A hit man might also be lying back so that his head was beneath the window line in any of fifty parked cars. And there were hundreds of dark windows behind which a sniper might be readying a rifle.

If so, Fisk thought, holstering the Glock, then they had him.

Starting up the sidewalk, he had the discomfiting

sense, whichever way he looked, of someone sneaking up behind him.

The heat slowed the stream of professionals on their way to work, making it that much easier for him to pick up a tail. Tails are easier to spot than most people think. Sometimes they have no good reason to be where they are. Sometimes they even use hand signals to communicate with teammates. The key is the other times, when they're imperceptible.

Feel them, Fisk exhorted himself, heading up Tenth.

When choosing the printing house, he had composed a mental list of the pros and cons of the Hell's Kitchen neighborhood.

Pros: Proximity to Madison Square Garden, which is to say, Knicks games.

Cons: Everything else.

In taking inventory of his surroundings now, he began to reassess that stance. Hell's Kitchen's gritty reputation was rooted in a preponderance of soot-blackened industrial buildings, the Westies gang, and Damon Runyan stories.

Yet this part of the city had exploded into a district of upscale and exotic restaurants. In and around them were brownstones that had recently been restored to their full nineteenth-century Greek Revival luster. The warehouses had yielded to glossy television studios and extensions of Silicon Alley. Vacant lots had morphed into community gardens and playgrounds. And directly ahead, emblematic of this urban revival, stood the city's fourth tallest building, a stunning metallic cruciform completed in 2007 and known to locals as the Times Tower.

It was Fisk's first time inside the tower, and he was surprised by the relative blandness of the interior, especially within the paper's office. The open newsroom looked like a call center or an insurance agency within a generic suburban office park, its sea of repetitive office-drab gray workstations and cabinets lit by too-sharp fluorescents. On the far end of the newsroom was a conference room that wouldn't have looked out of place in a frequent traveler's lounge at a minor-league airport.

He made out eight-by-ten crime-scene photos scattered atop the conference room table. Like most law enforcement agents, he never liked murders, but he brightened at the prospect of working one now. In the two years prior to his promotion to Intel, at the rank of NYPD detective investigator, he'd worked primarily on homicides, but he hadn't gotten his fill of the one-of-a-kind puzzles. Intelligence work consisted of preventing crimes, a process that lacked the game-winning-home-run rush that came with solving them. In Intel, if you do your job, no one notices; you're more like a good umpire.

The old-school crime-scene glossies, as opposed to digital images, told him that at least one of the ten people around the conference table was a fed. Expect to see time travel before a paperless Bureau, agents there often grumbled. Their presence here signified that the crime involved spies, terrorists, hackers, pedophiles, mobsters, gangs, or serial killers.

On entering the room, Fisk recognized the man seated at the head of the table, FBI special agent Burt Weir, a balding, middle-aged remnant of a high school jock. Weir was assigned to the Bureau's Joint Terrorism Task Force, an organization of agents, investigators, analysts, and various specialists from other law enforcement and intelligence agencies who, alongside FBI agents in field offices all over the country, combated terrorism. Weir wore a dark suit and tie—the G's all did—but looked out of place in anything but sweats.

Waving Fisk into the vacant chair at the foot of the table, he said, "Glad you could join us."

Fisk took this as grudging inclusion; the Bureau wanted something from Intel, probably the contents of a secret dossier or the use of an informant. In any other city, the police would already have provided Weir whatever he wanted. New York was different, not just because of its eight million residents or the stock exchange or 9/11, but because of its singular Intelligence Division, created by a CIA deputy director of operations—David Cohen—and backed by the most potent police department in the world. Intel's resulting autonomy often created a competition with the Bureau, bruising more than its share of FBI egos and sometimes even impeding investigations.

More often, the relationship was like a strained marriage. Federal law prohibited FBI agents from constitutionally protected arenas like religion and political speech. Forget sending plainclothes agents into mosques to gather intelligence, they weren't even permitted to grab a bite at a place like New Persia Diner in Astoria. New Persia served a devout clientele, including two men currently suspected of administering the Jihad Joe website whose content included exhortations to join al-Qaeda in its fight against "infidels" in none other than Queens. Intel knew this because one of the rakers had secured a gig redesigning the New Persia Diner takeout menu and parleyed it into a job administering the Jihad Joe site. Two days later, at a nearby mosque, a Staten Island resident named Abdel Hameed Shehadeh told a friend about his plan to wage violent jihad and die a martyr. Fortunately the friend was an informant, recruited by another NYPD Intel raker.

Weir rattled off introductions. To Fisk's left and right were an FBI computer forensics guy Fisk didn't know, and FBI special agent Dan Evans, whom he did. Evans had earned quite the badass reputation while serving in the Bureau's Las Vegas field office, cemented after successfully going toe-to-toe with a heavyweight-boxer-turned-goon. You wouldn't guess it to look at him, though: slight of frame, clean-cut white-blond hair, the innocent face of a Mormon missionary. Together, Evans and the boxy Weir were a sight gag. They were a natural good-cop-bad-cop team, though in Fisk's experience, they amounted to two bad cops. In fairness, their intentions were good; they just suffered from overexposure to red tape.

Also at the table were the editor of the *Times*'s online edition, the paper's director of security, four representatives of the legal team, and, in the seat across from Fisk's, Chay Maryland, who wore a no-nonsense black business suit that somehow accentuated her steely good looks. Unlike the others, who greeted him with a nod born of the exigency of getting down to business, she smiled.

It wasn't a particularly welcoming or friendly

smile, Fisk noted. More of an I'm-going-to-enjoy-this-more-than-you-are smile.

"Thanks to all for coming," said Evans. "This is an unusual situation, so listen up. This is Harun Ahmed, thirty-three years old, who was shot and killed while he was jogging yesterday in Central Park, on a path through the woods approximately two hundred feet south of the reservoir gatehouse."

He held up a photograph of the bloodied victim lying between trees beside the heavily wooded path.

"Our ballistic tests suggest that two shots were fired from a high-powered rifle. We haven't determined the shooter's location yet, but it was at a point of considerable elevation—one of the low-caliber rounds entered the victim's left parietal, at the top of his skull, and drilled almost straight through the left hemisphere of the brain, starting with the parietal lobe, then the occipital lobe—"

Impatiently, Weir cut in, "The point is, it was a sniper that got him. The question is: Why this guy, Harun Ahmed, a doorman at a fancy white-glove building on Central Park South, with nothing in the way of a record or anything close? One possible answer is that his wife Durriyah's first cousin is Mahmoud Amr, who, as of two weeks ago, is a resident of the Federal Correctional Institution in Fort Dix."

Fisk remembered reading about the Mahmoud Amr case. Amr bought a fifteen-year-old Chevy Trailblazer SUV listed on craigslist in New Jersey. At $2,000, he probably overpaid, given that the Trailblazer had more than 300,000 miles on it. He hollowed out the SUV's running boards, stuffed them with $800,000 in hundreds, then resold it for $525 to a car exporter who shipped it, along with fifty-odd vehicles in similar condition, to Lebanon. There, each vehicle sold at auction for around two million Lebanese pounds, or $1,500. Amr's thinking had been that, even if an extreme bidding war were to ensue over the Trailblazer, if it sold for a record $5,000, his al-Shabaab confederate in Tripoli would still come out $795,000 ahead.

"Other than Muslim heritage, is there reason to believe that the victim had ties to al-Shabaab?" Fisk asked Weir.

Chay grinned. "Doesn't Muslim heritage automatically place someone under NYPD Intel suspicion?"

"Actually, Muslim heritage can get you hired by NYPD Intel—my mother was Lebanese, so I learned Arabic. Wish I could've told you that before your story about our racial-profiling practices."

Weir broke it up. "Our theory is that the victim objected to al-Shabaab, but because of something he'd learned, posed a threat to an al-Shabaab operation."

"So is that what I'm doing here?" Fisk asked. "You want our Shabaab dossier?"

"It would sure help if we could get a read on his sympathies," Evans said.

"Then I guess the question is what I'm doing here." Fisk indicated the newsroom with a sweeping gesture. "At the *New York Times*."

Weir nodded to Ed Norman, the *Times*'s director of security. Even with close-cropped black hair, a

gray business suit and silk tie, the stocky Norman
had the windblown look of an old-time sea captain. Fisk recalled that Norman had retired from
the FBI after twenty-six years, which was unusual.
Most agents who'd been at the Bureau for more than
twenty years hung on until thirty, for the obvious
pension benefits. After that, they commonly left to
cash in, as director-of-security positions like Norman's paid two or three times the GS-15 pay grade
of $99,000, starting salary, not including the annual
bonus. Rumor was that Norman's wife's affinity for
the country-club lifestyle had won out. Norman
wore a suit now that looked decent enough; Fisk had
the sartorial equivalent of a tin ear, but he recognized Norman's shoes. The distinctive boat-shaped
Bettanin & Venturi loafers, handmade in Italy and
fetching in the neighborhood of a thousand dollars
a pair for a reason Fisk couldn't even guess at. He'd
seen them before on investment bankers, at their
trials. So either Norman had materialistic inclina-
tions of his own, or the shoes had been a gift from
his wife.

"This is the reason you're here, Detective Fisk,"
said Norman, aiming his cell phone at the whiteboard on the front wall. The whiteboard filled with
an all-type version of NYTimes.com—devoid of
photographs or graphics. Norman scrolled to a
brief Metro section story entitled "Jogger Shot and
Killed in Central Park."

"You guys are seeing our internal version of the
paper, what we call the backstage. Reporters file here,
editorial goes over copy here, and, after the piece
goes live, moderators come here to choose which

reader comments to post." He lowered the cursor to the comments box, where, beneath each incoming reader comment, there were two buttons, a green one labeled APPROVE and red, DISAPPROVE. Settling on a comment awaiting moderation, he read aloud:

> *Greetings, so-called authorities. I am Yodeler. I have been watching you, watching your campaigns of propaganda and disinformation, watching your suppression of dissent. You have used deception to gain the trust of our citizenry. I have decided to dismantle that trust, starting with the two Hornady 9mm Makarov bullets fired from an AR-15 at the runner at 2:18 yesterday afternoon. For the greater good of the citizens of America, each and every day I shall sacrifice one person in New York City chosen completely at random.*

Evans shook his head, bewildered. "See, here's the thing. None of the articles or news coverage anywhere said a word about the bullets."

"Except that the victim was shot," added Weir.

"Do we have any idea where the comment originated?" asked Fisk.

"Every comment comes with communications metadata, which our system records," said Norman. "We have this Yodeler guy's IP address, and we have the data center his comment was passed through. Apparently he used a Verizon cell phone in midtown Manhattan."

So they had next to nothing, Fisk thought. From time to time, a perp kept a disposable phone on him, or in his car, mistakenly believing that if the device were powered off, it couldn't be tracked. If Yodeler were at all clued in, he would have dedicated a burner phone to his single *New York Times* comment, then flung the thing into the Hudson.

"So is Yodeler right about the bullets?" Fisk asked. Makarov 9x18mm pistol and submachine-gun cartridges had long been a standard Russian and Eastern Bloc counterpart to the Western 9x19mm Parabellum, and they were widely available everywhere in the world. They were designed to kill at relatively short range, fifty yards or so, but a sniper firing from a longer distance in an urban setting might prefer such a low-caliber round for noise reduction. "Could be difficult to trace. Dozens of manufacturers produced 9mm Makarovs."

"The slug recovered largely intact from the dirt near the victim weighs ninety-five grains, or .217 ounces." Evans looked up from the ballistics report. "Usually Makarovs are ninety-four grains, but Hornady's are ninety-five."

"What about rifling marks?" Fisk asked. Rifling is the process of cutting helical grooves in the barrel that impart a spin to the bullet to increase its accuracy. Rifling marks left on a slug—the bullet minus the casing—permit the identification of the gun manufacturer and model.

Evans read, "Clockwise twist of one to twelve." One to twelve meant the bullet needed to travel twelve inches to complete a rotation.

"So we're talking AR-15?" Fisk asked. AR-15s are assault rifles so common that popular belief has it that AR stands for assault rifle, but in fact AR derives from ArmaLite, the corporation that originated the weapon.

"Yes, sir," said Evans. "Colt AR-15 Sporter, a civilian model."

Turning to Fisk, Chay asked, "Can't you search the NYPD's database of recorded signal traffic and map where Yodeler was before and after he submitted the comment?"

A complete fishing expedition on her part, Fisk suspected, which possibly explained her presence here. "The Electronic Communications Privacy Act applies to us the same as it does to any government agency. Unfortunately, we need to serve a warrant to Verizon before we can get that sort of data."

Chay uncapped a pen and put it to the legal pad on the table in front of her. "Why 'unfortunately'?"

Fisk smiled at her gesture—as though a paper and pen could intimidate him. "It's an ordeal to get the data. The Department or the Bureau needs to draft a National Security Letter, and then have it printed out and served to Verizon's legal department. Which is the easy part. The providers send back CDs loaded with 'toll records'—lists of calls to a phone, calls from it, texts, and Internet usage."

Weir chuckled. "We call the CDs 'haystacks.'"

"If we could mine the data now," Fisk continued, "it could mean the difference between life and death if Yodeler intends to make good on his threat. If he had that phone on him or in his car while he was near the victim's place of work or the crime scene, we'd be halfway home."

"How can this help unless he used the phone during that time?" Chay asked.

"Fortunately we do have the Domain Awareness system surveillance cameras. On Central Park South, even within a block of the victim's building, we can reasonably expect to see footage of five hundred people snapping a photo in the past week, it being Tourist Central and summertime. If the phone Yodeler used for his message to us were to have also transmitted from Central Park South, we would know which of the five hundred people to talk to, because taking photos is classic pre-operational reconnaissance activity."

Chay looked at her pad and jotted something down. The fact that she said nothing suggested that Fisk had made his point.

"We'll NSL Verizon," Weir said.

"What about F6?" Fisk asked, on the off chance that the Bureau had some in with the service that the Department didn't. F6 was the code name for the Special Collection Service jointly run by the CIA and NSA. In the way the CIA or MI6 intrigued ordinary citizens, F6 appealed to those in law enforcement—those who knew about the service. The Special Collection Service's sole responsibility was getting information no one else could. In the field, its operators bugged places that had been deemed impossible to access by other agencies. And in cyberspace, the F6 techs were on a level of their own in STG—SIGINT Terminal Guidance, SIGINT in turn short for "signals intelligence"— monitoring, intercepting, and interpreting electronic communications. They ran a battery of proprietary surveillance applications like XKEY-SCORE, CADENCE/GAMUT, HIGHTIDE/

SKYWRITER, and WIRESHARK that allowed them to search—without FISA authorization—through vast databases containing e-mails, online chats, and the browsing histories of millions of individuals, often in real time.

"Does F6 even officially exist?" Chay asked.

"It officially exists," said Fisk with a grin and a glance at her legal pad. "But its existence is classified."

Evans flashed Fisk a look of rebuke. "What would be beneficial, at this point, is for us to work up a background on the victim."

"Any reason to think he wasn't chosen at random?" Fisk asked. "Investigating victims' backgrounds is standard operating procedure. We never take a killer's word that his victims have been selected at random. Some make that claim simply because it terrifies more people than if they were to say they had a specific target, like world leaders. Some make the claim purely as a diversionary tactic. And often the common denominator among victims makes no sense to a rational thinker, but yields a method to the killer's madness."

"We're not buying his ideologue act," Weir said. "If that's what you mean."

Checking his notes, Evans explained, "When Yodeler writes, 'I shall sacrifice one person in New York City chosen completely at random,' there's reason to think the 'chosen completely at random' is a compensatory construct. Also we suspect that 'citizens of America' is a clue that he isn't American, or at least he's not from here, since we always say 'U.S. citizens.'"

Weir cut in, "No one here calls New York 'New York City.'"

Evans went on. "Also we have reason to suspect Yodeler is a reference to the Austrian yodeler who was imprisoned a couple years back for a mocking version of the Muslim call to prayer. He's come to represent Western intolerance. You'd think Yodeler would be the last screen name he'd use if he were a member of, say, al-Shabaab, and he was trying to deflect blame for a hit."

"Sure," said Fisk. "Unless he wants to send the so-called authorities on a wild Muslim chase."

"What's that mean?" asked Weir.

"Harakat al-Shabaab al-Mujahideen—Arabic for 'Mujahedeen Youth Movement'—originated ten years ago as a Somali cell of al-Qaeda before growing into a full-fledged terrorist organization in its own right. More recently al-Shabaab has initiated recruitment and fund-raising within the United States, but the group had never engaged in terrorism here. And al-Shabaab never use snipers, favoring less subtle methods of execution."

"Such as?" asked Chay, as Fisk knew she would.

"Literally tearing victims limb from limb."

Weir didn't like Fisk's answer. "Nothing gets crossed off the list until it gets crossed off the list."

Fisk suspected al-Shabaab had nothing to do with this case, which meant that the FBI had brought him in for no reason.

Didn't matter now. He was in.

"Why don't we ask Yodeler what he wants?" he said. He took in the roomful of blank looks. A start, he thought. "He wants something."

Chay said, "But he's already killed someone without any provocation."

"That's why we want to catch him. To do that, we first need to buy some time."

Evans nodded. "It would be good to be able to bring in the NCAVC." He meant Quantico's National Center for the Analysis of Violent Crime, part of CIRG, the Critical Incident Response Group. CIRG provided support for investigations on serial crimes by deploying specialized analysts.

"They could be useful," said Fisk. But on cases like this, it wasn't a matter of gaining time for reflection. He wanted impetus—to get Yodeler reacting to his moves, if possible surprising the killer. From his reactions, Fisk could glean information, whether it was that the guy was proficient in the use of burner phones or that he was a communist. The more back-and-forth they had, the more Fisk would learn about him. The challenge was to get into Yodeler's mind and to adopt his thinking process.

"What do you have in mind?" Weir asked in the same tone he probably used when the neighbors' kids rang his door to sell him magazine subscriptions he didn't want or need. A decade of turf battles had made him averse to even yielding the floor.

"For that, I need to take this off the record," said Fisk, turning to Chay.

Chay looked to her editor, who nodded emphatically.

Fisk said, "We handle Yodeler the same way we do a hostage taker. The value of the press covering these cases is inestimable, if the press and law enforcement cooperate. There was a case in Guatemala recently where kidnappers were publicly shamed into releasing a hostage, who was a doctor who devoted her practice to the poor. Actually she wasn't, but that's how the media played it. A misplaced story can anger the bad guys. So, in the interest of keeping the body count down . . ." Fisk turned to Norman. "Can you publish an edited version of Yodeler's comment?"

"Edited how?" asked the security man.

Eyeing the comment on the screen, Fisk said, "Cut everything except how the jogger story is yet another part of the campaign of propaganda and disinformation, designed to suppress dissent and gain the trust of our citizenry. Leave in that he's decided to dismantle that trust for the greater good of the citizens of America."

Weir grumbled, "Makes him sound like a loony tune."

"He sounded like that to begin with," Fisk said. "But if we do it this way, in his mind he'll have gotten some of his message out. We'll have acquiesced, which is the old hostage negotiation secret: fool him into thinking that he's imposing his will on us, that he's holding all the aces. Then we post a comment to his comment, from, say, 'Yodelerfan1.' We ask him what else he wants. He can tell us via the comments box or—so he gets the sense he's making progress—a dedicated e-mail address. Or we let him choose the venue. Because we're just trying to do the best we can under enormous difficulties to give him exactly what he wants."

Evans considered this. "Then what?" he asked.

"We wait by the smartphone for him to respond.

If he does, great, it's a negotiation, a protracted negotiation in which we achieve the position where he's reacting to our moves rather than vice versa, meaning he's not shooting people in New York chosen at random or otherwise. Meanwhile we're sneaking up on him."

Evans looked to Weir. With the exception of Chay, everyone looked to the senior case agent, with what Fisk hoped he correctly perceived as an air of solicitation.

"I can't authorize this myself," Weir said. "I gotta run it past the ASAC and the SAC." This meant submitting a written request for approval to the assistant special agent in charge as well as the special agent in charge—which, in Fisk's experience, was as close as it came to getting a yes from the Bureau.

Worst-case scenario, Fisk thought, he could read Evans and Weir's report later; cumbersome FBI reports were near the top of the list of certainties headed by death or taxes. Exiting the Times Tower now, headed for the crime scene, gave him the feel of stepping into fresh air—someplace other than New York that, in fact, had fresh air.

He was always surprised how much came to light at the scene, like eyewitnesses who come forward well after the scene has been processed, sometimes ashamed at not having come forth sooner, always with useful information. And if the scene didn't teach him something about the killer, it would be a first. Getting a fix on the perp was usually the most difficult part of the early chapters of an investigation.

A block later, he'd bought himself a new cell phone replete with five hundred minutes, activated the line, and used it to get himself out of reporting to the office for a couple of hours. Alternating between checking for surveillance and avoiding oncoming pedestrians while glancing at bits of the initial NYPD detective's report on his phone, he made his way up Seventh Avenue to its intersection with Central Park South.

Passing the row of hansom cabs on the park side, he caught a mix of the sales pitches by drivers to passing tourists. He also spotted three separate groups posing by horses for photos. He suspected he'd grossly underestimated the number of amateur photographers the CCTV cams would record in a week here.

Entering Central Park, he turned right onto the lower loop, presumably the same route Harun Ahmed had taken. It was closed now to vehicular traffic, as it had been at the time of the shooting. The city's chalky air, heavy with concrete and exhaust just moments ago, grew redolent of flowers and trees. The clamor of thousands of vehicles and millions of rushing Manhattanites dissolved into the more leisurely chatter of parkgoers accompanied by the buzz of their bike chains and Rollerblade wheels and the trill of countless birds, all of it seemingly in sync with the waltz rising from the carousel's Wurlitzer. Thus it seemed to Fisk as if it took no time at all to walk to the crime scene.

The scene itself had already been processed and released and thus reverted to an unremarkable stretch of gravel and dirt through the woods. If he were sure of anything, it was that the crime-scene investigation unit had literally left no stone unturned here. In 2006, when he was working a homicide case in Alphabet City's East River Park, a trace of anomalous soil the crime-scene team bagged turned out to be from the nearby baseball diamond and led to a conviction of a spectator at a softball league game there. In this case, however, he had a strong sense that the minutiae were obstructing the investigation, distracting from a critical piece of the puzzle.

But what?

As he'd been trained, he cast a mental grid over the death scene, then he walked each of the lines, occasionally stepping aside to let a jogger pass.

He saw no trace of blood, no body outline, nothing to suggest that Harun Ahmed had been gunned down here. He focused on the shadows speckled by light in the few spots where the sun managed to breach the canopy of trees. The crime-scene photos hadn't given him a sufficient appreciation of the extent of these trees. These oaks and elms, at the height of leafiness, posed too much of an impediment for a sniper.

Unless the guy had made his nest in one of them. It was hard to believe, though, that no one in Central Park saw or thought anything of a man with an assault rifle climbing into a tree.

Staring up the trunk of the nearest elm, Fisk speculated that if a sniper had wanted to conceal himself in one of the branches, he could have climbed up at night, when this area of the park was empty. On the plus side for the hypothetical sniper, the area wasn't covered by a CCTV camera. Climbing the tree would be tricky, though. Those in the vicinity offered sheer trunks—no branches or other footholds—for a good twenty feet from the ground. Still they could be climbed, but Fisk saw no evidence that they had been, at least no unnatural indentations or scuff marks in the bark.

In any case, Yodeler would have needed to know Harun Ahmed's jogging route to take him out here, and unless the killer planned to spend several days in the sniper's nest, he needed advance knowledge of when Ahmed ran. As Fisk had gathered in his quick read of the detective's report, the super at 122 Central Park South said Ahmed only ran on days that both the weather and his willpower permitted. So Yodeler could have made an educated guess, especially if he'd conducted pre-op recon. Or he might have gambled. But either way, if Yodeler had good enough intel to predict Harun Ahmed would run along this tiny path, he had to know that the doorman opened the door to the lobby hundreds of times a day at 122 Central Park South, offering a clear shot at him from the park directly across the street, or a car parked parallel to the park. You could make an argument that few New Yorkers presented as easy a target as Ahmed. So why here?

The answer could be that Yodeler had indeed been gunning for anyone. Although rare, it would hardly be the first act of random violence in New York City. But why in this problematic location? And how was it that no one saw him?

For most people, finding a single dollar bill can turn a lousy day around. For Walter Doyle, the magic number was fifty.

In the two years since retiring as the head of Stuyvesant High School's mathematics department, the sixty-nine-year-old had been supplementing his pension by searching for lost change. Tourists in the United States handled cash more often than they were accustomed to when at home, and in the process they each lost an average of eighteen cents per day.

And nowhere on earth, by Doyle's reckoning, did tourists lose as much change as here at Battery Park, Manhattan's twenty-five southernmost acres that included the gamut of outdoor park activities as well as a full restaurant, dozens of other food vendors, several famous sculptures, and the Castle Clinton, the two-hundred-year-old sandstone fort that had originally been a cannon battery. But the main attraction was the ferry across New York Harbor to Liberty Island—the ride coming only after tourists had waited for an hour plus in the hot sun and paid cash for drinks and snacks and items like foam Statue of Liberty crowns. In the vicinity of the ferry dock, Doyle had found a hundred dollars or more here on forty-seven different days. (Three times, he'd even found hundred-dollar bills—experiences that were bittersweet because he pitied the people who'd lost them.)

It was ten o'clock now, and shaping into the sort of day that made it worthwhile for Doyle to come to Battery Park even when he found no money. It was warm, but not too warm, with the sun transforming the Hudson into a mosaic of blues and greens, the trees and lawns at peak verdure, and Castle Clinton shining like a castle out of a fairy tale. Better still, hundreds of enchanted tourists stood on line for the ferry.

He also saw two of his "colleagues," Archie and Roberta, sweeping their Fisher Gold Bug Pro metal detectors over the lawn where a yoga class had just wrapped up. Good, thought Doyle. That left him exclusive access around the Battery Place benches, where, between seven and nine, Wall Streeters nursed coffees from the carts, savoring nature before having to trudge off to windowless trading floors.

Now, shoving off, the last of the coffee and pastry cart vendors waved to Doyle. It was prime hunting time.

As Doyle started toward Battery Place, a strong gust off the Hudson raised the breakfast debris from beneath the benches—the usual spent napkins, disposable cup lids, wax-paper wrappers. Much of the litter lodged in the row of arborvitae shrubs along the back wall of the castle. Doyle thought he spied the corner of a bill protruding from the leaves. That unique stiffness of the blend of linen and cotton was unmistakable even through his declining trifocaled vision. He fought the urge to run to it, reluctant to draw attention to his find.

Fortunately, no one else was even in the vicinity. When Doyle was thirty feet from the bill, a bit of breeze swayed the shrub, causing the ink on the uppermost corner to glint from black to green, in turn giving him an exhilarating jolt. The most remarkable of the security features on the recently redesigned hundred-dollar note was the Treasury Department's proprietary color-shifting ink, black when viewed from some angles, green when seen from others, the result of multifaceted metallic flakes mixed into the ink.

As he knelt to collect his prize, he felt a stinging blow to his left shoulder blade. A sharp, stabbing pain, as though he'd been speared. He pitched forward into the shrubbery, which should have felt sharp and scratchy. He should have felt the branches scraping into his flesh—but he did not.

And then the shrubbery seemingly engulfed him, and after a moment everything went still and silent and black.

Ji-Hsuan Lin wasn't really a student. Nor was he actually named Ji-Hsuan Lin.

He was an intelligence officer who had been sent on a mission to New York twenty-one months ago. Attaining the key to the American economic intelligence services network firewall could provide his service access to everything worth having in the Department of Commerce's 1.8-million-square-foot headquarters in Washington, which would be the greatest intel "get" since the Enigma machine.

In the short term, having the run of Willoughby's lab would allow Lin to penetrate the *New York Times* firewall, which Willoughby had designed. Within twenty-four hours of the paper's report of leaked NYPD Intel documents last month, the FBI captured the leaker, Manhattan-based NSA systems analyst Merritt Verlyn. However, the Bureau failed to locate the thousands of valuable classified documents Verlyn had stolen and had yet to upload to WikiLeaks. Lin would not fail. National security reporter Chay Maryland, who had reported only on the first batch of NYPD documents, had the document cache, probably just sitting on her hard drive.

Citing freedoms guaranteed to the press by the U.S. Constitution, she refused to cooperate with the FBI or the U.S. attorney prosecuting Verlyn. Lin was unsure who the bigger fools were, Maryland or the framers of the Constitution. In any case, if he had his way, she would turn over the documents to his people without ever realizing it.

Ji-Hsuan Lin—or the young man who went by the name Ji-Hsuan Lin—believed that he would be awarded an intelligence medal—along with financial security for the rest of his life—if he succeeded in penetrating the *New York Times* firewall. Although the notion of assaulting a firewall existed only in Hollywood productions. In reality, firewalls function like a ticket taker. To get the requisite material for his ticket, Lin needed an hour to himself in Willoughby's secure lab.

First he needed to gain admission to Columbia University's Interdisciplinary Science Building at Broadway and West 120th Street, an austere blue-gray steel tower that housed science lecture halls as well as laboratories and offices dedicated to as many as twenty classified military and intelligence research projects at a given time. Usually getting in was a simple matter of pushing through a revolving door and into the lobby, the most notable feature of which was an absence of security guards—not even the half-asleep senior citizen checking IDs whom the university posted at the entrances to dorms or the campus grocery store.

Tonight the lobby was utterly deserted. On his way to the elevators across the skating rink of a white marble floor, Lin reflected that with just a few helpers here, he could take down the entire U.S. economy overnight.

For now, the fourth floor, the location of Willoughby's lab and offices, presented his first obstacle. Stationed at the entrance to the main corridor, 24/7/365, there was a security guard. The guards, employed by the Pentagon, were glorified rent-a-cops. The exception was nights, when retired army colonel "Hawk" Griffin, manned the position. Sure enough, when the elevator doors hissed open, Lin found himself the recipient of Hawk's laser stare and half expected to see red dots on his body. The guard stood, as usual, despite the table and chair in the elevator landing, his gun hand hovering atop his belted holster. He'd added just two pounds to his sinewy frame in the forty years since he played tight end at West Point.

Lin knew that Hawk wouldn't hesitate to unload his Beretta M9 on a foreign spy. If anything, the guard lived for that opportunity.

In a gravelly baritone, he said, "Ji, howya doin'?"

"Very good, Hawk. How you?"

"Better than I deserve, buddy." Hawk flashed a Texas-size smile. "Don't tell me you're thinking of working tonight instead of watching the Mets game."

Lin had no taste for baseball, but he'd studied it—he'd even endured a game in person at Citi Field—so that he and Hawk might bond over the New York Mets. "I feel bad. Matt Harvey pitch for us. I hope to finish in time to see final innings."

"You best hustle, then, partner." Hawk waved him in.

Lin made a show of hurrying down the hall until rounding the corner to the western corridor. The lab area was still and silent other than the occasional keyboard click from behind one of the closed doors. Light from the overhead panels caused the gray walls to shimmer purple.

Stopping at the lab known as DC²—Distributed Computing and Communications—he unlocked the door to the antechamber using a common cut key like that to the front door of a typical house. This was another example still, he thought, of the seeming disinterest in security on the part of the Interdisciplinary Science Building planners, even though the building had opened in 2010, when retina and iris scanners had long since become security standards in comparable private facilities in other countries.

Americans were far too trusting.

Stepping inside, he swatted on the lights, revealing a generic comp-sci room with a pair of swivel chairs and flat panel monitors on three long tables, everything facing the whiteboard on the front wall. Unlike most labs, however, there were no windows. Odder still, on close inspection, you would see that the cottage-cheese ceiling tiles were suspended from a sheet of Plexiglas. The Plexiglas continued down the wall, disappearing behind the wall paneling, then continuing under the floor, forming a case around the room.

The result was a sensitive compartmented information facility, or SCIF, essentially a vault designed to keep electronic signals from escaping. Even the electrical current was filtered. The six computers were networked to one another, but there was no Internet. Data could exit the lab only on disks or drives. Stealing the key to the *New York Times* would be a matter of copying a TCP—Transmission Control Protocol—packet onto a flash drive. The problem was that in doing so, Lin's every action would be recorded. Every keystroke was logged here, and it was a fair assumption that everything else was recorded by concealed security cameras.

While logging in, he had an edgy sense that accessing the *Times* TCP pack would bring a tactical team crashing into the lab. Could Willoughby have set him up? Getting to this point had almost been too easy. He fought the urge to take a deep breath. A display of nerves might be caught by a camera system running a Behavioral Recog application, in which case a duty officer at the Fort—the NSA in Fort Meade, Maryland—would receive notification and monitor Lin in real time.

Lin operated under the assumption that they were already monitoring him in real time. A little over two hours later, in the course of his regular work on the Department of Commerce project, he opened—purportedly for reference purposes—the Structured Query Language injection tool Willoughby had created for the *Times*. With the injection tool, Lin could go elsewhere, connect with the paper, and then access the trove of classified documents that Merritt Verlyn had given Chay Maryland.

Of paramount value was what NYPD Intel, the FBI, and the NSA knew about the businesses fronting Lin. The hitch was that the SQL comprised more code than he could memorize—more than he and the entire population of China, working in concert, could take out of this lab in their heads. Copy it, take a cell-phone photo of it, even write a line down, and he risked setting off alarm bells at the Fort. He had a plan, though.

Sitting back, he rubbed at his temples, as he had done several times already this session, and as he often did when fatigued. This time, he pressed the spring hinge on the left side of his eyeglass frames. This activated a subminiature video camera concealed by the nosepiece. He began scrolling through the SQL.

When he was nearly finished, a bell sounded—like a typical home door chime, though it had the effect on him of an air-raid siren.

Trying to appear merely curious, he punched up the controls for the special SCIF intercom, which transmitted on a push-to-speak basis, like an old-fashioned walkie-talkie. "Who there?"

"Hey, Ji." It sounded like Hawk was calling from deep space, a function of a specialized local amplifier that prevented the receiver from serving as a microphone.

"Everything okay?" Lin saw that he had the equivalent of two pages remaining to scroll through and record.

"You gotta come out here."

"Why?"

"Take a couple seconds off, willya, buddy?"

Without the final two pages of the SQL file, the first hundred would be useless. "Hang on," Lin said. Video the rest of the file first, then deal with Hawk, he told himself.

"Come on, I'm telling you!" Hawk sounded feverish.

"Okay, okay."

Lin captured the last page, then rose, preparing to take out the guard, who, alerted to malfeasance, would be waiting in the hall with his Beretta drawn.

In his wallet, Lin carried an ultrathin blade made of surgical steel. It unfolded from a polypropylene fake Visa card that served as knife handle. He'd had ample training in defending himself with the weapon. Hawk would only pose a threat if he were expecting a knife, for which reason Lin didn't dare reach for it, not now, while the action might be broadcast live.

He pulled the door open and stuck out his head. No sign of anyone in the corridor, or on the floor for that matter, other than Hawk, who held a computer tablet so that the red light cast from the screen turned his wrinkly face into a road map.

Lin did not let himself relax. "What's up?" he asked, going for nonchalance.

"Check this out." Hawk beckoned him with an exaggerated motion.

"Hawk, I'm in middle of something."

"No, no, no." Hawk reached for him. Startled, Lin tried to dodge the thick hand, then felt himself lose balance. As he attempted to regain it and go for his knife, Hawk thrust the bright green tablet monitor toward his face. On a baseball diamond, shown from a camera in center field, the batter swung and missed, the catcher squeezed the ball into his mitt, and leaped up.

Along with one of the broadcast announcers, Hawk shouted, "Harvey just pitched a perfect game!"

Early the next morning, Lin purchased a can of Coca-Cola from a vending machine and found a seat at a back corner table of the food court at a New Jersey Turnpike rest stop he'd selected for its crowds, free Wi-Fi, and lack of surveillance cameras.

Powering on a virgin, seven-inch Nextbook computer tablet that had run him sixty-nine dollars in cash, he inserted a flash drive loaded with the injection tool. His video capture had been digitized overnight at headquarters and then transmitted back to him along with a depressing electronicom from his boss: the Interdisciplinary Science Building penetration had been ill-conceived, the North American Division chief complained, also requesting eyeglasses matching Lin's, custom-fitted with a video camera (they'd cost the equivalent of $10,000 U.S.). Far worse, HQ's search of the *Times* system had yielded little intel that they couldn't have accessed with the basic ninety-nine-cent introductory special subscription. If Chay Maryland or another reporter indeed had the Verlyn cache, they hadn't been foolish enough to upload it to the *Times*.

Lin would reply that the reporters' discretion was understandable. But as anyone who'd operated in the United States knew (the North American Division chief had never once set foot in the field), such discretion was an anomaly. First he needed to go online and see for himself. With Willoughby's Structured Query Language, he was able to waltz into the *New York Times* system and then go to the backstage area, where reporters read internal memos, posted stories, and stored large files.

To her additional credit, Chay Maryland, the reporter on the Verlyn story, filed stories she composed on a secure personal computer. Secure, that is, until Lin accessed it.

If he could get Maryland's home address, he could break in and copy the entire contents of her hard drive, or he could simply steal her computer. Her address was listed nowhere, however, not on voting or tax records, not in the aggregators and databases private investigators pay fifty dollars a month for. She was a cipher, either naturally or as a function of her experience.

Thankfully, the *New York Times* Human Resources Department's complete staff directory was wide open to him now. It listed each employee's date of birth, salary, Social Security number, and, yes, home address.

FBI special agent Evans could have said, in about ten seconds, "Walter Doyle was found shot to death in Battery Park yesterday in a manner similar to Harun Ahmed."

Including extraneous information like the courses the victim had taught at Stuyvesant High School prior to his retirement, Evans took twenty minutes to impart the same information while briefing a small group that included Fisk. They sat in the smaller of the two conference rooms at the FBI office on Ninth Avenue, above Chelsea Market. Fisk might have arrived via the footbridge connecting the FBI to the NYPD Intel offices, which were directly across Ninth Avenue, but the footbridge was always locked on both ends. Symbolic of the relationship between the two services, he thought.

At the head of the table, Evans went on, reading directly from the medical examiner's report: "Entrance wound one inch to the right of the left scapula. The projectile perforated the heart through the right atrium, .5 inches above the right ventricle, exiting the left pectorals major three inches below the clavicle, leaving a wound of 1.6 centimeters by 0.9, with no abrasions, soot, or stippling."

It seemed like he would read the bulk of the report—ten single-spaced pages was a medical examiner's norm—before getting to the most critical piece of information.

Fisk cut in. "Quick question: Was the projectile recovered?"

Weir looked up, annoyed. He reached onto the conference table for the ceramic mug imprinted with COFFEE FIRST, THEN MAYBE YOUR TEDIOUS BULLSH*T WON'T SEEM SO BAD and took a swallow. "Answer's yes, same Makarov nine-mil, same gun. So we told Norman at the *Times* to go ahead and roll the dice with the comment thing. We just all need to be able to access that Hotmail account you opened."

Fisk's inclination was to take point. With hearts and minds affected by a killer on the loose, tactics were deliberated for too long (the FBI's industrial-strength brand of red tape aside). At this juncture, however, the committee managing to field an e-mail from Yodeler would be progress.

"Sure thing," Fisk said.

"Good," Weir said. "Not to waste any more time, I want to turn things over to Supervisory Special Agents Flynn and Morgan, who are up here from the NCAVC." Weir indicated the middle-aged white professorial types across the table, National Center for the Analysis of Violent Crime agents who performed the task known in common parlance as "profiling." Unlike Hollywood profilers, they didn't do so by walking around crime scenes and picking up vibes. Instead theirs was a world of criminal behavioral data and statistical likelihood.

The focus of the meeting shifted to the application of NCAVC intel to Yodeler. "The tactical choice, sniping, is rooted in fastidiousness," said the bespectacled Special Advisory Agent Flynn. "Now, here's a nifty stat for you all. In Vietnam, the United States expended fifty thousand rounds of ammunition for each enemy killed. Snipers expend less than two rounds per kill."

Fisk had never thought about it that way. But, yes, the snipers he'd known shared that trait. Interesting . . .

"There are a number of characteristics shared by criminal snipers that can help us whittle down the list of suspects," said the other Quantico man, Morgan. He spun his laptop so that the others around the conference table could see its monitor, then he clicked open a PowerPoint slide show and began to read the captions aloud. "Ritualistic behavior, compulsivity—often at obsessive levels, suicidal tendencies, history of serious assaults, hypersexuality, history of drug and/or alcohol abuse, parental history of drug and/or alcohol abuse, arsonist tendencies . . ."

Fisk was unsure how these symptoms differentiated the criminal sniper from the garden-variety serial killer.

Morgan continued, "Many also suffer from chronic depression, feelings of powerlessness or inadequacy, and feelings of interrupted bliss during childhood—in fact, many have stated that they were the result of an unwanted pregnancy."

Fisk's attention drifted toward the special advisory agents' shoes, shiny black wing tips, laces tied in near-perfect symmetry, no blemishes. The case would be better served, he thought, if the special advisory agents walked around crime scenes.

Shortly thereafter, after making an excuse about an important phone call and five minutes on the 1 train, Fisk climbed out of the Bowling Green subway station and took in a busy Battery Park on a sunny day suitable for a Visitors and Convention Bureau commercial.

Behind the Castle Clinton, the two policemen guarding the crime scene were lost in the crowd, or at least their presence had no ill effect on the passersby. Fisk doubted that the couple dozen yoga practitioners on the adjacent lawn would continue their meditative recline if they had any inkling of the nature of the crime.

Entering the park, he had the sensation of eyes on him, or rather a single eye, through a spotting scope from one of the tall buildings uptown. As in Central Park, however, the wall of trees between the buildings and the crime scene would pose a substantial impediment to a sniper shooting from a high floor.

Despite its proximity to the water, the park was essentially windless. As Fisk walked down the paved path to the castle, an unnaturally elliptical shadow caught up to him and then slowed to a stop, as if it had hit the brakes.

He looked up. He might as well have been staring directly into the sun. Popping on his Oakleys and then squinting, he managed to distinguish from the blaze the silhouette of a round object hovering overhead, a blimp-shaped balloon no bigger than a bolster pillow.

It appeared, in the glare, to be made of chrome, but really it was nylon. Fisk had seen refillable helium balloons like it before; you controlled them using a key-chain-size infrared remote. They also came in the form of a shark and as Nemo, the clownfish from the animated movie. Vendors by the ferry sold them for fifty dollars apiece, meaning you could probably find them in toy stores for ten.

Piloting the little blimp was an Asian boy, seven or eight years old, with an oversize foam Statue of Liberty crown falling into his eyes. His mother watched his display of piloting with an open mouth. Dad snapped pictures with a phone.

Fisk tracked down a vendor and paid his fifty, asking if he could have the Nemo model the guy was using to demonstrate the device, rather than taking the time to open a new one. Fisk piloted the nylon dirigible over an unoccupied patch of greenery. He sent it out, slowed it to a hover, and then brought it back around over his head, settling it in place to blot out the sun.

With such a device, Fisk thought, trees would provide very little if any impediment—

"Nice day for flying clownfish in the park," came a woman's voice.

Fisk turned to find Chay Maryland, in an outfit that enabled her to blend into the crowd here or perhaps help her get answers from the crime-scene cops: An I ♥ NY T-shirt and cutoff jeans that directed attention to long legs—and spoke to her sprinting career more capably than a Georgetown track-team uniform would have.

Fisk brought his flying fish in for a landing. "You didn't follow me," he said.

"No need, I thought I knew you'd wind up here." She looked at the remote control in his hand. "So this is what you do to blow off steam?"

"Yeah," he said, playing her game. "Calms me down."

Her smile faded. "I wonder if you could deploy a rifle with one of those?"

To stonewall her further here would only send the reporter, with a vengeance, to another source. Countless unmanned aerial vehicle experts would be happy to regale her—and effectively millions of New Yorkers—with details of the lethal capability of microdrones. Better to stay in front of the story in order to control it, and, ideally, prevent it. "No, I don't think you could use a balloon. Not one that small, anyway. It's barely strong enough to transport a water pistol. But other systems could carry a rifle, absolutely."

"Which ones?"

"That's the question I'll be trying to answer as soon as I get back to my office, if not sooner. I can tell you now, though, that five years ago, the Department tested the Shadowhawk UAV."

"The remotely piloted helicopter, right?"

"Miniature helicopter. It weighs only about forty-five pounds. But it's able to fly seventy miles an hour and fire stun baton rounds, shotgun shells and grenades, not to mention nine-millimeter bullets." Fisk hoped that tossing her some background information might satisfy her investigative nature. "You can't publish that, of course. The Department has managed to keep the Shadowhawk tests under wraps. A news story now would only compromise our methods if the city purchases the system, as Miami, Houston, and London have."

"And nobody knows this?"

"Best if they don't, at this point. The drones could do anything a police helicopter could do, at a fraction of the cost."

"A system with that capability seems wide open for abuse," she said. "Any chance that's what Yodeler used here?" Chay aimed a thumb at Castle Clinton.

Fisk shook his head. "Shadowhawks run a couple hundred thousand bucks apiece. Yodeler's going to use something more commonplace, assuming he wants to avoid getting caught."

"For the same reason he used an AR-15 and commonplace bullets?"

"I don't know a whole lot about drones, but I'd guess that the same relatively simple and inexpensive systems that can deliver packages from Amazon could be modified to carry an AR-15."

Chay looked toward the sky, not in trepidation, but with wonder.

"The good news is that those drones are a lot fewer and farther between than AR-15s," Fisk continued. "If we can get surveillance cam imagery of the drone in flight here or in Central Park, we can trace the drone to Yodeler. We also might be able to trace the radio signal he used to control it."

"If he was careful enough to use an untraceable gun and bullets, what would be the odds he used his Amex if and when he bought a drone?"

"The odds aren't great. But they're a little bit better that he would use a prepaid Visa card to buy a drone online and have it delivered to, say, an out-of-the-way UPS store he'd chosen for his PO box because the place had no security cameras and the employees didn't ask questions."

"Then he would have picked up his drone and left without a trace."

"As far as he knows. This is one of the reasons we're not keen on publishing the locations of the cameras—or publishing any of our methods."

Chay crossed her arms, looking around the park again. She said, "If he is using a drone, even if you find surveillance camera footage of him, it may not be in time to stop him. He's killed two people in the last two days. If people are forewarned, they can stay inside today. At the least, if there were a drone overhead, they would know not to stand on the sidewalk and gawk at it."

"Forewarned isn't forearmed if there's no way of seeing or hearing the thing coming," he said. "Anyway, a drone can target people who are inside buildings. So by warning them, you'd be doing little more than telling Yodeler that we're onto him, in which case he covers his tracks and we're back to square one."

"Detective Fisk, how would you feel if by the end of the day, you've found no further clues to Yodeler's identity, and, meanwhile, he's killed a child who was on a playground because his parents didn't know to keep them indoors?"

"I'd feel terrible. But you understand why we can't evacuate the city every time we have a killer on the loose. And in this case, it'd be based on a hypothesis developed on the basis of a kid flying a remote-control blimp."

"Actually, a detective from Intel flying a remote-control blimp. But—point taken." Fisk didn't quite believe her. She plucked a spiral-bound reporter's notebook from her back pocket and clicked a mechanical pencil to readiness, walking away.

The sun slid from behind a cloud and through the corner windows, setting aglow NYPD Intel chief Barry Dubin's eggshell head and all but igniting his golden Ermenegildo Zegna Venticinque silk tie, the sort more commonly seen on hedge fund bosses than on public servants. "I've gotta tell you, this reminds me of the time Salinger met with your dad in '61," Dubin said from Wallace McElhaney's couch.

"About the Air Force crewmen?" asked McElhaney from a wing chair across the big cherrywood coffee table.

"Exactly. Their lives were at stake."

McElhaney was two years old in 1961, when his father, then the editor in chief of the *New York Herald Tribune*, received a surprise visit over the weekend from White House press secretary Pierre Salinger at their house in Princeton. One of the *Trib*'s Washington correspondents had gotten wind of President Kennedy's plans to negotiate the release of the two surviving members of the Air Force RB-47 spy plane shot down by the Soviets over the Barents Sea. Salinger hoped McElhaney's father would hold the report of the negotiation for fear of antagonizing Soviet premier Nikita Khrushchev and poisoning the deal. McElhaney, who went on to follow in his father's footsteps—he was now the national news editor here at the *New York Times*—

had learned that there is a presumption that news-papers publish whatever they get, in the hope that it will sell papers. In truth, editors and publishers routinely listen to and take into account concerns of government officials. When the government has a clear case that a story places a life in danger, it's an easy call: you don't publish.

Unfortunately it's seldom a clear case. Often officials seek to stop publication for reasons of policy, partisanship, or to avoid embarrassment. In the RB-47 case, the Air Force crewmen's lives were demonstrably at risk, so the *New York Herald Tribune* held the story.

"Dad liked to say that dozens of journalists got Pulitzers, but not many got handwritten thank-you notes from President Kennedy," McElhaney told Dubin.

Dubin laughed, a laugh that was both pitted by cigar smoke and, in McElhaney's estimation, longer in duration than the preceding remark merited. This meeting was beginning to have the feel of a sales call. Almost certainly the ex-spy's spontaneous recollection of Salinger's visit was anything but spontaneous. Likely he had first heard of the 1961 case on the limo ride up here, while being prepped for this meeting by a member of the slick publicity team brought in by the commissioner. The same initiative, to buff the Department's image, probably explained Dubin's recent embrace of $300 silk ties and distinctive Campagna suits that dipped below $1,500 only at annual clearance sales, and were wasted on him. Dubin was the sort who would look rumpled even in a gleaming suit of armor.

No, Dubin's was not a finesse game. Never had been. Before joining the NYPD, when serving as deputy director for operations at the CIA, Dubin notoriously treated the media to just two words: "no" and "comment." In New York, where the media had more leverage, he'd successfully kept reporters from publishing his secrets by guilting them into helping their government in the war on terror. But that line was losing traction in the face of a growing recognition by journalists that carrying the ball for the government was not their job; the job was to report on the government. The Constitution had abolished governmental power to censor the press precisely so the press could censure the government. The press did so by baring the government's secrets and informing the public. McElhaney viewed it as his responsibility now to find out if NYPD Intel's secret programs deserved a place, as Chay Maryland believed, in the same conversation as waterboarding and warrantless wiretapping.

"Why isn't the Bureau looking at drones?" McElhaney asked him.

Dubin tugged at the sharp tip of his black goatee—dyed, McElhaney suspected. "Wally, I don't want to criticize the FBI."

"Now *that* is news," McElhaney said.

The Intel chief chortled. A beat too long again. "Let's just say that Ms. Maryland's role in developing the drone hypothesis speaks to the merits of expending shoe leather at the crime scene instead of pontificating in the conference room. I understand why she thinks it's her job to inform the public. What she doesn't get is that Detective Fisk is playing a long game. This Yodeler didn't mind revealing the model of his rifle, his ammo, and his plan of action to the whole World Wide Web, but he didn't say boo about a drone."

"If there even is a drone."

"A lead's a lead. Now, if we can figure out what kind . . ."

"You'll follow the trail from the factory to Yodeler's lair?"

Dubin leaned back and sighed. "I'm not going to lie to you. It's a long shot—but when isn't it a long shot? There are some three hundred thousand drones owned by civilians in this country. But a lot of the time, our only clue is that a perp is driving a black Ford SUV, and there's, what, ten times as many Ford SUVs as drones? We open a lead on every one, then whittle away at the list, and sometimes it works. In this case we'll knock on every drone manufacturer's door, every hobby shop, check out the drone groups' pages on Facebook or whatnot."

"You have children, right, Barry?"

"Yeah, a daughter—just had her first child, little girl named Madison."

"Congratulations," McElhaney exclaimed.

Dubin grunted. "Save it. I only mentioned her so you could use her by name in any hypothetical designed to play on my guilt."

McElhaney smiled. "Okay, what if your daughter were pushing your granddaughter in her stroller this afternoon and saw a drone zipping around the corner ahead of them. Would you have her point it out to the little girl and say, 'Look, Madison, that's the future of aviation,' or would you want them to take cover?"

The Intel chief shrugged. "Coventry."

"Are you talking World War Two or the town upstate?"

"The first one."

This came from Dubin, McElhaney thought, not a publicist. In 1940, Allied code breakers who had cracked the Enigma rotor cipher machine learned of the Luftwaffe's plan to bomb Coventry, one of England's largest cities. If Churchill were either to have ordered Coventry evacuated or to have sent forces to defend it, he would have risked revealing to the Germans that their Enigma system had been compromised, in turn costing the Allies their means of decoding enemy communiqués in critical battles to come. So he let the Luftwaffe bomb Coventry.

McElhaney nodded. "I get it. If Yodeler realizes we know about his drone, and if there is any sort of paper trail to it, he would just change tactics. At the same time, there is almost zero chance that the same criminal who used a disposable cell phone only to comment on the *Times* site would be foolish enough to leave a paper trail to a drone."

McElhaney wondered if Dubin was seeking to protect something else altogether, like a heretofore secret camera network capable of yielding footage of the drone. Or maybe NYPD Intel had drones of its own; maybe they'd merely pretended to pass on the Skyhawk system five years ago.

McElhaney set his qualms aside to play a long game of his own. "We'll withhold Chay's story," he said, "on one condition."

The shine from Dubin's power tie preceded him into his office, casting a lightning bolt onto the windows overlooking Ninth Avenue. Fisk watched from a minimalist modern armchair that looked like a squatting gingerbread man, yet another part of the chief's efforts to gussy up. Flushed, Dubin peeled off his suit coat, dropped it over the back of a matching gingerbread man, and plopped heavily down. By way of greeting, he groaned.

"I take it they're running the story," Fisk said.

Dubin dabbed perspiration on his forehead with his tie. "That's up to you, junior."

So there was a catch. "Great. I say no."

Dubin tossed his wing tips onto the coffee table, a wad of chrome that could pass as modern art. "Deal is, the *Times* holds the story if you let Chay Maryland shadow you on the investigation."

Fisk hoped he'd missed something. "Shadow me?" He shook his head firmly. "If Chay Maryland had been shadowing Seal Team Six, she would have live-blogged the mission to capture bin Laden."

Dubin said, "We can ask them to run topics past us before she writes anything."

"We sure can. Would any newspaper ever agree to that?"

"Probably not." Dubin cracked a smile. "Alternatively, you can utilize your talents as an agent handler." His smile disintegrated. "Don't know if you've noticed this, kid, but the Department's been working to get the press to help our cause, for a change. I know you don't like it, and I can't say I'm thrilled with it either, but for better or for worse you're the face of the NYKGB. It might help if the lady who's been our single harshest critic sees the way you really go about business. This is the kind of public relations opportunity we've been trying like hell to buy."

BOOK TWO

Blackwell almost didn't hear the trill of his cell phone over the pulverizer, a thousand-dollar version of a food processor.

Normally they're used in labs to turn carbon into carbon dust. Knowing Miami would be a tough place to dispose of a body, Blackwell had stopped at an academic wholesaler in Nashville on his drive down here, paying cash for one of the machines. Toggling off the grinding-chamber motor, he dropped the DEA mole's left forearm back into the bathtub, atop what was left of the guy's torso, softening in a cocktail that included hydrofluoric acid and lye.

Blackwell answered the phone. "Freeman." Which signified he could talk freely.

"Marvelous evening to you, Mr. Freeman," came Segui's voice. So blithe that Blackwell knew that the Cartel fixer was in hot water, again. But no one was holding a gun to Segui's head—the use of "marvelous" was intended to communicate that.

"How are things?" asked Blackwell, covering the mouthpiece in order to mask the plop when the mole's left hand, now grainy pink sludge, slid from the pulverizer's spout and into the hole where the toilet had been—removing the toilet allowed direct access to the largest sewer pipe leaving the Motel 6 room.

"My sales team had some bad luck in Appleton,"

Segui said. "Appleton" was code for New York City. "Bad luck" meant Segui's hit team had failed altogether. That part wasn't code. Segui was just inclined to positive spin, which served him well, given the temperaments of his masters, the Zetas. In the course of Blackwell's two-year working relationship with Segui, which had consisted only of brief phone calls or clandestine electronic communications, the fixer had also shown an extraordinary capacity for denial, which served him well given what he had to work with: cokeheads who tended to shoot first and think later, if they thought at all. The good news was their screw-ups meant business for Blackwell.

"Well, shit happens," Blackwell said, pouring a pint or so of chlorine bleach into the pipe to mitigate the stench of the sludge. "But like I always say, buddy, 'Weakness isn't about falling down, it's about not getting up.'"

"That is exactly right," Segui chirped. "All this account needs is someone with a bit more experience. So, as you may have guessed, the company is hoping you could go make a sales presentation in person, work a little of your magic."

"I'd be happy to." Blackwell meant he'd be happy to do the job if he thought he could get away with it, and if the price was right. "What's the who, the what, the where, and the when?" He keyed the phone to speaker so that he could keep working. In order to hear Segui, he switched to a bow saw in lieu of the power tools.

"You have a copy of the brochure handy, my friend?"

"Sure, hang on just a sec." With minimal effort

on Blackwell's part, the saw blade parted the DEA kid's left biceps, turned gummy by the tubful of water, more chlorine bleach, and sodium hydroxide. Then he drew a burner computer tablet from his gear bag, powered it on, and clicked open the website belonging to a junkyard in Tucson that sold used auto parts via the Internet. "Okay, hit me."

"F-dash-F-dash-24029-dash-1," Segui said.

The first *F* and the 1 were essentially camouflage. The middle six characters, F-24029, however, were the actual part number for a 1997 BMW Z3 1.9 radiator in moderate to good condition, on sale for $89.95 plus shipping. The photograph of the grimy radiator, sitting in the donor car, comprised several thousand pixels. Activating an app that was essentially a microscope, Blackwell zoomed in on pixel number 4,029—the last four digits of the part number communicated the location of the digital dead drop.

Sure enough, Segui had placed a dossier there. Blackwell decoded it, a matter of activating another app.

He thus was able to see the details and photographs of the target, Detective Jeremy Fisk of the NYPD Intelligence Division. Blackwell knew of Fisk. He remembered wondering if the Mexicans were Segui's boys when he read about the botched hit in New York last month.

"The only issue is I'm in the middle of a big job in Kansas City right now," Blackwell said. This phone, which had cost him two grand, transmitted bogus metadata that would lead any eavesdropper this side of the NSA to conclude that he in fact was in Kansas City, Missouri—a priceless safety measure.

"When's the soonest you could make it to Wisconsin?" Segui asked.

"How about early next week?" Blackwell said. This was an attempt on his part to bag overtime. The Zetas were notoriously impatient.

"Hold on, let me look at the calendar," Segui said, then put the line on hold, probably to confer with the boss.

While waiting, Blackwell returned his attention to the current job. The mole's now-brittle left humerus snapped in two in Blackwell's gloved hand. He removed the lower half of the bone, along with the attached tissue, and slid the chunk down into the grinding chamber.

Segui returned to the line. "If we pay you time and a half, could you do the job by the end of the week?"

Time and a half meant $125,000 on top of Blackwell's standard $250,000 fee on these jobs. Which, after it was laundered through Blackwell's mistress Franciscka's statuary in Chicago, would net him a good couple hundred thou. Plus the down payment on the new Porsche he wanted, the RFF 28 powerboat.

He separated the remainder of the mole's upper arm from its socket, easy as picking a flower.

"Consider it done," he said.

Dawn turned the Upper West Side silver. Ji-Hsuan Lin was casing the Montana, on Broadway between Eighty-Seventh and Eighty-Eighth Streets, a high-rise home for seven hundred or so busy young professionals.

As was often the case in luxury buildings, the Montana furnished tenants with a legion of employees to prevent the sort of things that go wrong in a home from disrupting the workday. When a cable or telephone repairman gave a resident an eight-to-noon window for a service call and then showed up at four, it was no problem. Not in the slightest. The doorman would let the repairman into the building, and one of the valets would show him up to the apartment and then watch him intently every minute he was at work, usually under the guise of talking baseball or similar banter—Montana staffers were all collegial. If a tenant had bigger problems, a plumbing issue for instance, the building deployed its own skilled—and free—technicians who were on premises all day, every day. If you were worried about burglars, you could forget about it. The place had competent security guards on duty 24/7 and more cameras than a cruise ship at capacity. NYPD patrolmen were all but fixtures in the lobby, lured perhaps by the urns of fresh, free coffee.

Valets often doubled as elevator men, and when the valets were off late at night, tenants were required to swipe key cards through a magnetic reader atop the elevator button panel in order to access their floors. The same key cards operated state-of-the-art locks on each apartment door. And, key card or not, if the door ever opened without prior verbal communication between the tenant and either the concierge in the lobby or in the rooftop health club, an alarm sounded.

Still, it would be no big deal to get into Chay Maryland's apartment, Lin thought. He'd accessed similar buildings by taking the place of an actual messenger. That's what he planned to do here, once Chay left for work. Runners from midtown or from Wall Street streamed in and out of places like this all day long, mostly bringing documents in need of old-fashioned signatures. There were few things these messengers wouldn't do for five hundred dollars in cash. And for a tenth of that, they would happily stand around doing nothing while Lin delivered one of their packages to its legitimate intended recipient. After the delivery, Lin would stop by Chay's apartment.

He could defeat most any traditional pin and tumbler lock using a bump key—one on which all of the pin positions have been cut down so that if you tapped it with a hammer while applying turning force, it would "bump" open the lock.

The newer key-card locks were even easier. Every key card had a DC power socket at its base. This socket was used to charge the battery inside the device, as well as program the lock with the building's site code, a thirty-two-bit key that identified the specific building. You simply plugged a micro-controller into the socket, allowing you to read the key from the lock's stored memory. Then all you needed to do was play back the thirty-two-bit key and, just like that, the apartment door opened. At most it took two hundred milliseconds from plugging the device in to opening the door.

As for an alarm? No problem. You just activated a few others beforehand—a swift roundhouse kick to the door handle when no one was looking did the trick—and the concierge assumes the problem is systemic and passes the buck to the alarm company. And all of that was in a pinch. Time permitting, Lin's agency's Special Collection Service hacked into the building's security system, remotely disarmed the alarms, and supplied him with a working key card.

But this job brought an additional challenge: he needed to know ahead of time where Chay kept the item he wanted, the Merritt Verlyn document cache. Also time was of the essence, because other services would try to get it—they might be trying already.

It was amazing that the American authorities hadn't forced the reporter to turn the documents over. Amazing unless you knew the Americans, Lin mused.

He walked past the building's façade, which accounted for the lower third of the east side of Broadway. The sidewalk was still dark, the air still cool and still—stagnant, as if holding its breath in anticipation of a scorcher of a day. Other than a team of sanitation workers collecting trash, only a few of the earliest birds were out, traders who concentrated on the Nikkei or Europe, Lin guessed. Now in a khaki suit, with his hair slicked back, he would be taken for one of them. He had his regulation messenger's uniform, including the black spandex bicycle shorts, in his computer case.

At the corner, he turned left onto a tree-lined stretch of West Eighty-Seventh, both brighter and warmer on account of the sun climbing over the rooftops on the East Side. He unpocketed a crawler, a remotely controlled video camera about the size of a cockroach. Thanks to a pair of miniature tank tracks that provided suction, the crawler could move up and down walls or buildings.

Lin checked to see that no one was looking. Vehicular traffic, a trickle to begin with, was nil. The sidewalk was now populated only by a jogger absorbed in whatever was pulsing through her headphones. Lin placed the crawler onto the wall three stories below Chay's apartment, in the shadow cast by a utility pipe. The device adhered to the bricks. Thanks to a realistic plastic skin, from more than a few inches away, it looked like any other bug. From more than three feet away, it wouldn't be noticed at all.

Lin walked to the Starbucks at the far end of the block, entered, and purchased a ridiculously expensive iced coffee drink. All but one of the ten tables were empty.

He chose a two-top in the back corner. While nursing the iced coffee, he used the control app on his phone to send the crawler scurrying up the wall. A tap at the phone and the controls shifted to the live feed from the camera on the bug's belly, giving Lin a view of red bricks, graying mortar, then, finally, glass—a window into Chay Maryland's apartment. One of her three windows, he hoped, would be open a crack—this was the preferred method of temperature control in so many New York City apartments.

The crawler crept the length of the ledge running beneath the three windows, all of which, it turned out, were sealed tight. Lin would not be able to get the robot into the apartment this morning.

So he shifted tactics, parking the device and activating the wide-angle lens in its head. He aimed it through the glass, giving him a close-up of a beige venetian-blind slat. He sent the bug crawling until it found a gap between a slat and the window frame.

Through it, he could see only darkness. No surprise there: like everyone else on the planet, the reporter slept with the lights off.

Fortunately the crawler was equipped with forward-looking infrared. Another tap at the controls activated the FLIR, affording Lin a view of the entire apartment, which wasn't saying much. The studio was four hundred square feet, if that. The reporter paid $3,500 a month in rent, Lin had read in the dossier compiled by the station. A studio apartment on a high floor in this building ran north of $4,000. More insanity.

She lay asleep now, or at least unmoving. Eyes shut, breathing softly. Her full-size bed unfolded from the wall, taking up nearly one-fourth of the available floor space. Another fourth of the room was taken up with moving boxes in stacks, which was odd, Lin thought, because she'd moved into this apartment almost a year ago. Why hadn't she unpacked by now?

The answer came to him as he took in the apartment: No artwork, no plants, not a single tchotchke. It was the apartment of a workaholic who was in New York to work, using a home merely as a place to sleep, shower quickly, and store her belongings.

He shifted his focus to the small granite-topped kitchen counter, which also served as dining table and desk, as evidenced by the stacks of books and clippings wedged between the open MacBook and the coffeemaker. Once he broke in, Lin would use a five-terabyte pen drive to clone the MacBook's hard drive. Or, if time were an issue, he would just steal the MacBook.

Ideally, though, no one would know he'd been there—no American, that is.

The problem lay in the likelihood that she had stored the documents somewhere else more secure than a PC, in a hiding place. He suspected that the NSA man had given the cache to her on a flash drive. It would have been laborious as well as foolhardy to transmit thousands of classified documents over the Web, and nearly impossible to produce and traffic hard copies. In the course of writing about national security, Chay had no doubt learned of dozens of clever and effective dead drops and other hiding places. If she'd hidden the flash drive—and why wouldn't she have?—it might require hours for Lin to find it.

He texted the station (although if anyone intercepted the message, it would appear to be sent from Dick's Sporting Goods in Monmouth, New Jersey, to an Adidas sales rep):

PLEASE SHIP 60 UNITS MODEL 731-1

The key was the first digit, 6. This instructed Ops Support to go ahead and activate the Montana's fire alarm—they'd already hacked into the building's system last night.

He sat back, sipped at his coffee drink, which wasn't bad, meanwhile wandering to the Major League Baseball site and clicking open last night's New York Mets box score. Force of habit.

The klaxon startled him.

It emanated from the Montana. Perfect.

He clicked back to the crawler controls and reactivated the forward camera to see Chay Maryland up, hurrying into a tracksuit and a pair of cross-trainers that had been within arm's reach of her bed, her fluidity suggesting she'd woken up and dressed in a flash before. Without turning on a light, she snatched the MacBook from the kitchen counter, stuffed it into a neoprene case, and hurried toward the door.

Just shy of the door, however, she stopped and knelt, putting her weight into one of the stacks of moving boxes and sliding it a few inches, revealing a wall outlet about a foot and a half from the floor. She dug her fingernails beneath the edge of the plate, which turned out to be hinged; it opened outward like a laundry chute door.

From the miniature safe the wall plate concealed, she withdrew a necklace and—Lin zoomed in—a flash drive.

He zoomed in further. HOYAS, it said in big letters. He had no idea what that meant, but he would find out. Unless HOYAS was of significance or immediate national security importance, his people would either procure a flash drive just like it within an hour, or produce a duplicate themselves.

Two taps at the control panel and he photographed the Hoyas drive and sent the image (a proprietary steganography app automatically concealed the image within the pixels comprising a comma) to the team.

After Chay left her apartment, he counted ten seconds and texted again, *MAKE THAT 72 UNITS*, the key this time being the 7.

Within half a minute of his sending the message, the klaxon faded to a faint echo and then to nothing, the alarm company evidently having received the diagnostic message that purportedly had been generated by the Montana's system.

The Montana staff would now inform the residents that it had just been a false alarm. Like most of them, Lin supposed, Chay would go back to bed—as soon as she returned the flash drive to its hiding place.

He was wrong, he realized, when the door to Starbucks opened, and one of the baristas, a plump Hispanic woman, called out, "Chay, how're you doing, sweetie?"

Lin cursed himself for coming here rather than his standby, Burger King. None of his targets went near the place.

"Rude awakening," said Chay, entering the café with a look of resolve, as if she were bent on capitalizing on the klaxon's early wake-up. "But I'm up. How are you?"

A flood of morning light through the big front windows brought her necklace to a glow. She surveyed the tables, flashing a smile Lin's way. He responded in kind, watched her advance to the counter, then resumed reading MLB, losing himself in the statistical league leaders while she ordered her caffeinated drink.

She soon returned to her apartment and replaced the flash drive, along with the necklace, then got dressed for work and hurried off.

Lin had no trouble finding a courier, a Wall Street runner who was elated at the prospect of being paid to have his job done for him. Lin passed muster at the Montana front desk and delivered an envelope to a yuppie lawyer in 20C, who tipped him ten dollars.

Everything was going freakishly well, he thought. Maybe too well. The inevitable hitch came at Chay's door.

The door was protected by a biometric lock requiring a fingerprint scan as well as a five-digit code in order to turn the handle. It was the only such lock Lin had seen in the building. In fact it was the first time he had ever seen a biometric lock in an American residence; first time he'd ever heard of it. Rare and expensive. The flecks of sawdust atop the door-handle plate and on the carpet by the door suggested to him that the new biometric lock had been installed recently—perhaps as an additional security measure Chay had undertaken to protect something. Good, he thought.

He had a contingency plan in his back pocket: a small crowbar. However, there were workmen from AT&T working on an apartment near the elevator, and a valet was watching them. Certainly the valet would hear him prying open Chay's door. If the valet even saw Lin in the hall, it wouldn't be long before a cop was up here.

Lin left the building empty-handed. Two hours later, a truck labeled MANHATTAN TREE TRIMMING turned off Broadway, double-parked on West Eighty-Seventh, and set to work on a spruce tree that reached just past the target's window. The leaves, which indeed needed a trim, provided cover for one of the men wearing white coveralls and a Manhattan Tree Trimming helmet to climb into Chay's apartment.

Published: June 30, 2015 *2 Comments*

NEW YORK—Police are conducting an investigation following the discovery of the body of Walter Doyle in Battery Park late Tuesday night.

Doyle, 69, a retired schoolteacher, was found under bushes behind Castle Clinton by sanitation workers at about midnight, according to the NYPD. He appeared to have suffered a gunshot wound. He was pronounced dead at the scene.

The police have released no other information about the case.

Fisk read the story in his office—actually, the office belonging to Detective Dan Werner, who was on medical leave. Fisk's regular office had a window that overlooked Ninth Avenue, or rather offered a decent shot to a gunman who might have been on Ninth Avenue, or in an office or on a rooftop across the street. So Fisk had relocated temporarily. Story of his life lately.

"I liked your piece in today's paper," he told Chay when she arrived.

"I'm glad to hear it." She took the seat facing his desk—glided into it, actually, her every movement fluid. Her gray business suit was matronly, he thought, the boxy skirt dipping well below her knees. But it worked, particularly now, as she crossed her legs, giving prominence to a calf muscle that looked to have been sculpted from amber—

He reminded himself that she was an obstacle; his objective was to get rid of her.

From her bag, she produced a Krispy Kreme box. "I don't mean to be cliché, arriving at a police station with doughnuts," she said, "but would you like one?"

Fisk's culinary leanings generally extended only so far as trying to mix a dinner other than a slice of pizza into his diet. On occasion, though, he found himself going out of his way to patronize the twenty-four-hour Krispy Kreme store on West Thirty-Second Street. He decided to decline, until she opened the box. Warm air rose from it, carrying the enticing aroma of chocolate frosting and reminding him that he was starving.

"It is cliché, and terribly offensive," said Fisk, helping himself to one of the chocolate glazed doughnuts.

"You're welcome," she said.

"So what do you have in mind for shadowing?" he asked.

She sat back. "I'll follow the story, ideally, until the case is closed."

"The Zodiac case in San Francisco has been open since 1969."

"If this case lasts that long, then I suppose I'll get to write a book after all."

"What about your other work? Or has your desk been cleared for this exclusive?"

She looked across the desk, as if reading his mind,

eyes like lasers. "My job is to follow the story. I followed it right here."

"I'm not the story," Fisk said.

"You're part of it."

Fisk frowned, showing her his displeasure. "Do you know how few NYPD officers fire a gun in the line of duty in a given week?"

"No, but let me guess. The Department has, what, about thirty-five thousand four hundred officers?"

"Give or take." She was off by all of twelve officers, he thought. Or, more likely, she'd read a more recent Department personnel profile than he had. "And they discharge their weapons an average of six hundred times per year . . ."

What didn't she know? "Where did you get that figure?" he asked.

"I've seen the totals posted at the police range in Astoria."

He'd seen them too, the annual printouts, taped to the front door at the range. They listed the number of rounds expended in the line of duty by the NYPD along with misses—seldom were New York's Finest accurate with more than a third of their shots.

"Are you a shooter?" he asked.

"Only to be better acquainted with my subject matter, and my subjects."

Wow, he thought. The reporters he knew liked to go to Upper East Side cocktail parties to get better acquainted with their subjects. She was the first he'd heard of to opt for a loud, poorly ventilated pistol range.

"How about updating me on the investigation?" she asked.

Oddly, he felt inclined to respond with the truth, which was that he had nothing new to report, and that he would happily sacrifice a year of his life if the computer would ping right now with an incoming e-mail bringing news of any development whatsoever in the case. He also wanted to say that if that didn't happen soon, the suspense would cost him five years of his life.

"Nothing to report," he said.

"You and this 'Yodeler' haven't become pen pals yet?"

"Silence sometimes is a tactic."

"In which case—you feel you've learned something about him?"

Charitable of her, he thought. "Could be."

"What about the surveillance-camera footage?"

What he wouldn't give for a call bringing news of a cold hit from the tech room, four members of which were currently scouring the video database for so much as a frame of drone footage in either Central Park or Battery Park at or around the estimated times of the killings.

"We're following a number of leads at this time," Fisk said. A law enforcement brush-off line as old as the profession.

"That's not going to fly this time. What leads specifically?" Chay asked.

"Nothing worth wasting your time on. But how about this? Since your office is so close, how about I just text you if anything happens?"

She looked him over. "If there's so little going on, why were you here all night?"

Damn. Did she have a source within Intel? He'd

had no choice but to stay here overnight. Because being on cases like this one was like being at a crucial hockey game that's gone into sudden death. The big cases usually did feel that way. The next call or e-mail or seemingly innocuous document that dropped into his mailbox could provide a crucial puzzle piece. Or *the* crucial piece. So it was hard to leave the office. He hadn't, not even to grab a slice of pizza last night or breakfast this morning. Afraid of missing another call, he hadn't wanted to get on the phone to the diner a block away. And so that Chay wouldn't suspect that he'd been here all night, he'd changed into a fresh white oxford shirt—he always had one or two spares in his lower desk drawer, still in the plastic packaging they came in from the dry cleaners.

"How did you know that?" he asked her.

"I didn't." She curbed a smile.

He started to roll his eyes when his computer pinged with the arrival of an e-mail. He spun his chair toward the monitor, clicking open the mailbox.

He found one new item in his in-box, headed TO THE SO-CALLED AUTHORITIES.

Taking in the subject line of Yodeler's e-mail, Fisk experienced the same jolt he did when he was fishing and felt a big one strike his line. He tried to hide it.

"What is it?" asked Chay.

"An e-mail," he said. Technically, it was a Hushmail, a message from an e-mail service that encrypted all traffic and routed it in such a way that it couldn't be traced, thus making Hushmail the Hotmail of spooks. This message, "TO THE SO-CALLED AUTHORITIES," was from USER435982768.

"I know it's an e-mail," she said. "Let's see it." She waved at the monitor.

Why not? He thought. He double-clicked to open the message. In order for the text to be decrypted, he cued a prompt that informed him that he needed to supply the correct response: A PATRIOT WHO USED MARKAROV 9MMS? Grudgingly he entered YODELER, which worked, allowing him to read:

One way or the other, I shall bring to light your violations of the public trust. One way is the continuation of the daily sacrifices. The other way is the immediate release from captivity of the patriot, Mr. Merritt Verlyn, so that he may in turn release the truth.

—YODELER

P.S. Perhaps the alternate ammunition has
thrown your confederates. This morning's
victim, whose blood is on your hands, has
Remington 9mms in her.

Chay might be of use to the investigation after
all, Fisk thought. If she saw blood on her own hands,
she might give up the Verlyn documents.

"I'm not the only one who might be part of the
story," said Fisk.

He pivoted his monitor toward her side of the
desk so that she could see Yodeler's e-mail, then
he watched while she read. He hoped to catch her
reaction to the Verlyn bombshell. She blinked, but
no differently than people did ten or fifteen times
during a given minute, to keep their eyes clean.
She played her cards close to the vest. A compelling quality, he thought, except if you're trying to
read her.

He asked, "Do you think he's a fan of Verlyn's or
he's just after the release of the documents?"

"Maybe both."

He watched her. "Does that make you more inclined to cooperate?"

She glared. "Why would it?"

"The Department's objective on this case—the
FBI's objective too—is to bring the killer to justice
at the lowest possible cost, with cost measured in
bodies. If releasing the documents prevents killings,
we'd release the documents. We would just need to
get a look at them beforehand."

"So that you could redact the incriminating stuff?"

"I was thinking more along the lines of looking at

the documents ahead of time to make sure releasing them wouldn't put a different set of lives in danger, like men and women who are working on behalf of our national security."

She raised her shoulders. "I don't have anything to say that I didn't already say in court."

"All you said in court, if I'm not mistaken, was that you weren't going to testify."

She said, "Exactly."

"Super." Her philosophy aggravated him; her gumption impressed him.

"What about the Remington nine-millimeter bullet part?" she asked.

"I was just going to ask the computer that," he said, pivoting the monitor back to its original position and typing his way into the Department database.

New York City averaged north of four hundred homicides per year, so it was quite possible that one—or five—hadn't made it onto his radar.

In fact, there had been two in the past twenty-four hours. Both were news to him. The first was at one in the morning, a bodega owner pumping a wannabe thief full of buckshot. The second was reported two hours later. Hoping that the details might nudge Chay to a philosophical middle ground where he could get a look at the Verlyn cache, he said, "The victim was a young African American woman, Tameka Ann Crowley. Tameka spent the vast majority of her waking hours at St. Vincent's Hospital in the West Village, where she was an oncology resident. She lived alone—and died—in number 435 West Seventeenth Street, apartment

9E. She was found here by police who broke down her door after neighbors heard gunshots and called 911. The crime-scene unit found a small-caliber bullet in her inner wall. It could be a Remington nine-millimeter. The other slug is still in her head."

Chay's brow knitted. "But she was inside her apartment when she was shot?"

Fisk nodded. "A minimally furnished five-hundred-square-foot studio."

"So if Yodeler did it, wouldn't he have had to be in the apartment with her?"

"Unless . . ." Fisk let his thoughts settle, reminding himself he was in the presence of a reporter.

"Unless what?"

Fisk said, "If whoever killed Tameka Ann Crowley had been inside her apartment, the responders shouldn't have needed to break down the door."

"Meaning . . ."

She knew full well what it meant. But in true reporting fashion, she wanted him to say it.

"Unless he used a drone."

Fisk snapped up his sport coat from its usual position, in a ball on the nearest free surface, in this case the top of a stack of moving boxes. "I'll be right back."

She stepped into his path to the door. "No, you don't. You're not going to the crime scene without me."

In his rush to get to Tameka Ann Crowley's apartment, Fisk realized, he'd neglected to formulate an exit strategy. Maybe for the best. Because all of a sudden he had some leverage: Chay wanted to go to the crime scene. When told by police that they could not enter a crime scene, reporters and photographers bleated that news gathering was protected by the First Amendment; otherwise freedom of the press would be eviscerated. But in fact the courts had never spelled out the privileges that news gathering entailed, meaning that keeping reporters out of a crime scene violated no constitutional rights.

"If you want to shadow me to the crime scene, you have to agree that any information you gather there is off the record."

"No problem," she said with zero hesitation, making him wonder if there was in fact a problem that he'd overlooked.

"That includes anything you hear."

She shrugged. "Every syllable is off the record and for my background use only, of course. I wouldn't want my presence to impede your investigation."

Surprisingly reasonable, he thought. And highly suspect.

He led her out the basement exit, which he'd been using for two weeks. It took them into an air shaft. Its cement floor was caked in droppings from the pigeons that roosted in and around the window air conditioners on the adjacent ten-story apartment building.

Chay either wrinkled her nose in mystification, or held it against the stench. "Is this a shortcut?"

He didn't feel the need to share his paranoia about Cartel hit teams.

He used his key to the neighboring apartment building—best she didn't know how he'd obtained it—and ushered her into the labyrinthine basement, which gave him three different ways out: the service entrance, the main lobby, and the laundry room. He opted for the last, an expanse of rusty washers and dryers and cracked linoleum whose fire-door alarm was broken. The door led up a few steps to an alley, which in turn led to West Sixteenth Street, which was clear. Or it appeared to be.

They walked the block and a half to West Seventeenth Street between Ninth and Tenth. At ten on an overcast morning, traffic consisted of a trickle of pedestrians.

They looked up at Tameka Ann Crowley's building, a slender prewar construction that, a few architectural flourishes notwithstanding, amounted to a fourteen-story stack of limestone blocks. It was similar to several other tenements on the block, grayed to further uniformity by weather and soot. A narrow alley separated the eastern side of the building from its neighbor, a ten-story warehouse. The entirety of the warehouse's brick sidewall was covered by the peeling remains of an ad for Horn & Hardart's Forty-Second Street and Broadway Automat, a Rockwell-type painting of a young woman happily placing a coin in a sandwich vending machine, the slogan LESS WORK FOR MOTHER.

Fisk counted nine picture windows up the eastern side of Crowley's building—she had lived in 9E. There were two windows on the ninth floor, a sliver of a frosted-glass casement, probably belonging to the bathroom, was closed—painted shut, if it was anything like the majority of bathroom windows in older New York buildings. The larger of the two main windows was open halfway. The combined bedroom and living room of Tameka Ann Crowley's studio, Fisk figured. Possibly the young oncologist relied on the narrow alley for ventilation. According to the detective's report, she had paid $2,500 a month in rent. Which was cheap for Manhattan; this was as low-rent as buildings got around here. Even if she had been able to afford an air conditioner, old buildings like this one couldn't handle the power requirements. The residents often hoisted up their windows on summer nights, only closing them, for security purposes, when they left for work the next morning.

"So can we go up there now?" asked Chay.

"No," Fisk said. "We've already seen all we need to."

Upon entering the Joint Terrorism Task Force's lobby, Fisk checked his cell phone with the security officer—cell phones were prohibited in the Sensitive Compartmented Information Facility where he was headed. Chay was required to stay in the lobby as well, her status as his shadow having failed to impress Weir.

"Hey," she said, calling after Fisk as though they had been partners forever.

Fisk shrugged. "Maybe next time," he said.

At the entrance to the SCIF, he entered the code on what appeared to be a digital version of a telephone keypad. The difference between it and other such keypads was that the keys themselves couldn't be seen from any angle but yours. Also, as you input the code, the numbers on the keys rearranged themselves, at random, to prevent anyone who was sneaking a look from learning anything based upon your hand positions.

Gaining admission, Fisk stepped into a work space that was cavernous not just in size but in its subterranean feel, a result of the absence of windows. Windows were prohibited in SCIFs, as were wall hangings or anything else that required putting a hole in the wall. Although everyone in the Chelsea FBI office had passed thorough background checks and polygraph exams, they didn't need to know what was being said in the SCIF. For the same reason, the walls of the SCIF contained three times the requisite number of Sheetrock layers, each layer surrounded by cotton-fiber acoustical batting and coated with latex sound-dampening sealant.

The heating and air-conditioning ductwork was soundproofed too, and access to the ducts required a key to the steel sleeves around them, essentially cylindrical cages, comprising half-inch-thick bars welded horizontally and vertically at six-inch intervals. The FBI guarded against off-site eavesdroppers as well: all of the plumbing in the SCIF and in the vicinity was wrapped in special padding to prevent it from carrying electrical signals. For the same reason, utility lines weren't permitted within ten feet of the room, save for the single cable dedicated to the SCIF that threaded through a secure aperture less than an inch in diameter. Everything was swept by security each morning and evening, seven days a week.

Fisk passed agents working at terminals in fifteen clusters of four workstations—the SCIF's computers, containing classified information, had their own network. He entered a compact conference room where Weir and Evans sat at a table with three other men—two Field Intelligence Group analysts, or FIG, and a psychologist from the FBI Behavioral Analysis Unit—and a woman, a CIA Middle East analyst who was assigned to the JTTF.

By way of greeting, Weir said, "Fisk, I was just getting into how we ought to respond to our e-mail."

Sitting down, Fisk smiled to himself. "Our e-mail?" he asked. There was a lot of truth to the old saying that the FBI is a company of ten thousand agents all struggling to stay at the bottom so they could keep fighting crime. But Weir hadn't made it to the head of this table on selflessness alone.

"Here's the reply that we propose," Evans said. Then he read from a legal pad: "'We do not, as a matter of policy, negotiate with terrorists.'"

Which was the opposite of the approach the case merited, Fisk thought. He asked the table, "What if instead we were to suggest to Yodeler that the 'so-called authorities' see that there is no choice but to bow to his leverage?"

"What's the upside in that?" asked the young woman from the CIA. Intelligence shone through cat-eye glasses that better suited a woman fifty years her senior.

Fisk liked her instantly. "During the early stages of an investigation, I'm always asking myself, 'Who's out there?' From the e-mail, we've learned that Yodeler is a Merritt Verlyn fan. Verlyn, of course, is an NSA analyst. And Yodeler is familiar with Hush-mail. So probably he's been around the law enforcement or intelligence community block, or at least he knows enough about it that he probably won't be affected by the usual law enforcement strategy of breaking his resolve by dissing him."

The CIA woman nodded. The two FIG agents reacted in similar fashion. Weir cleared his throat. "So, what, Fisk, you want to give him Verlyn?"

"Of course not," said Fisk, trying not to tip his aggravation. "The trick is to convince Yodeler that he's making progress."

"What do you have in mind?" asked Evans. His interest, unlike his partner's, seemed sincere.

Fisk said, "We write him back and say something like 'Thank you for your response, Mr. Yodeler. Of course our wish is that there be no further slaughter of innocents. So I will, at once, investigate obtaining a conditional release of Mr. Verlyn. The thing is, this is an area in which law enforcement has very limited powers. We can influence decisions, but it may take time. How's that, Yodeler?'"

"It might be beneficial for Yodeler to have one person here to talk to," offered the psychologist, a thirty-something man with immaculate skin named Pole. "Otherwise he's getting a memo from the nameless, faceless authorities whom he holds in contempt."

Decent point, Fisk thought. "Most of the homicidal maniacs in town already know where I live," he said. "We can give Yodeler my phone number while we're at it, on the off chance that he slips up and calls in a way that gives us something."

"Yes, dialogue's now the key," Weir said, as if he'd advocated the tactic from the get-go. "Fisk, give me your message in writing, and I'll run it up the flagpole."

Ideally Fisk would have already e-mailed his response to Yodeler. The Bureau's multiple layers of approval would only slow things down. But he needed the FBI in order to effectively play his lead. J. Edgar Hoover's genius had been in amassing manpower; he capitalized on superior numbers as well as any tactician in history. Now, with people at more than four hundred field offices and resident agencies in the United States, the Bureau was better equipped than any service on the planet—

probably better equipped than any five services put together—to work this case the old-fashioned way, doggedly pursuing leads one at a time. Which is what was in order. A lead would have to be opened on every single one of the hundreds of thousands of people who owned a drone, or even the parts, then they would have to investigate one person at a time.

The FBI might also claim jurisdiction to task the NSA and National Reconnaissance Office resources, the politics of which would be problematic if the NYPD were at the helm of the case. Although the hourly operational cost of a satellite exceeded that of a 747, a single frame of imagery, even a blurry one, could be almost as helpful as videotape of the killer at the drone's controls; no more than three or four drones took flight on a given day in New York City without FAA clearance.

Weir ceded the floor to Pole, the psychologist, who was from the FBI's Behavioral Analysis Unit. He had scruffy-chic hair and a shiny olive-green suit—anything but close-cropped and drab stood out as quirky in the staid Bureau. He began with "The suspect is now wanted for murdering three New Yorkers, and in his choices of victims, he is slowly revealing how he thinks, which can help us hone in on his true identity. What I'd like us to do first is take a look at his 'hunting zone.' As you all know, killers are usually reluctant to venture too far away from their homes because they like having the ability to get back to safety as expeditiously as possible. We should also spend time on behavioral clues, like who the victims are and where the killer has chosen to murder them. That way we can get an idea of what he's like in the rest of his life, which will help us find him."

This sounded to Fisk like the introduction to a two-hour tangent. He asked Pole, "What if we just consider for a moment the possibility that the guy is simply choosing victims at random?"

Stroking an invisible beard, the psychologist said, "Random actions are by definition chosen without method or conscious decision. The decision to take victims purely at random is in and of itself a methodology, and from it, we can get a glimpse at his thinking, and perhaps derive evidence that can help narrow down Yodeler's true identity—for example that he's intelligent, orderly, quantitative."

Taking in the nods around the table, Fisk wondered: Were these people just being polite? "What if he's flying a drone around and using it to shoot whoever he happens to see?"

"A drone?" said one of the FIG agents as if the word were foreign to him. Or maybe, Fisk thought, he was among the many in intel and law enforcement who abhorred the term "drone."

"A UAV," Fisk said, again exercising maximum patience. The term they preferred—unmanned aerial vehicle—encompassed the entirety of the unit, the vehicle itself as well as the ground-based controller and the communications connecting them. A drone, they maintained, was just a mindless weapon.

"Is this just a hypothetical?" asked Weir, reaching for his coffee cup.

"Have you been to the Tameka Ann Crowley crime scene?" Fisk asked.

Weir picked up his coffee mug, the vapor blurring his features. "No, why?"

"Her living room window was open."

Weir slurped. "So Yodeler shot her from outside?"

"The window faces a brick wall. To get a line on her, either he would have had to use a remotely controlled weapon. Or be Spider-Man."

No one said anything right away. Processing, Fisk hoped.

Weir asked, "Why couldn't the shooter have used an elevator or the stairs to get to a roof on one of the buildings across the street?" He turned to Evans. "Isn't that what happened?"

Evans opened a folder and ran his index finger down a report. "That's what it looks like, yes. Of course air resistance, gravity, wind, et cetera, make it easy to incorrectly analyze the flight path of a bullet . . ."

"A UAV explains how he could shoot around all the trees in the parks," Fisk tried, resulting only in the sound of keyboards clicking, from the cubicles outside the conference room, the SCIF equivalent of crickets.

"Maybe." Evans sounded like an encouraging parent of a slow child.

"If the shooter had used a remotely piloted system, wouldn't we be able to see video of it?" asked the CIA woman.

"Unfortunately the cameras in these areas are all angled downward, because all the action we're usually interested in is on the ground," Fisk said. "Yodeler could have sent in a remotely piloted jumbo jet and the cameras would have missed it."

"Except a jumbo jet would've cast a shadow," said Weir, turning to Pole as if in search of a lifeline.

A decent point, Fisk thought. "Certainly the tech group looked for shadows on the ground. Maybe the angle of the sun was such that the drone cast a shadow on a tree. Or a cloud might have precluded a shadow altogether?"

"This is really excellent stuff, Detective Fisk," said Pole with too much gratitude. "If the suspect were in fact using such a device, that would be considerable 'leakage'—insight into his psychology that we can glean from his methodology. Sketching a profile of such a killer really does require a complex blend of art, science, and psychology, and it can be especially useful in cases like this where the evidence is lacking."

The shrink was right about one thing, Fisk thought: the evidence was lacking.

He left at the first possible opportunity.

He found Chay in the lobby, studying the FBI's Ten Most Wanted board. Quietly fuming.

Fisk decided he preferred her doggedness to the dissembling he had experienced upstairs.

"Let's go get some evidence," he said.

There's never been a better time to be a sniper," said the onetime Army sharpshooter Pete Peavy as he ushered Fisk and Chay out of his company's reception area and toward his office. "Take this one job I did back in 2000, when we were in Sierra Leone. I had to lie in full camo in cold, rank muck for the better part of three days, sometimes having to stay so still that the leeches had the run of me—and took full advantage of it. Today I could do the same job from my house in East Hampton, thanks to these guys." He tapped the cartoon painted on the wall above the receptionist's desk, a trio of badass anthropomorphic warplanes. It was the logo of his UAV start-up, Flying Robots, LLC.

"What exactly can they do for a sniper?" Chay said.

It was for this information, Fisk thought, that they had come to Tribeca.

"I'll try and show you," Peavy said, leading them down a long corridor that, like the reception area, was lined with bamboo rods. In rows on the walls were framed action photos of surfers, all autographed—Duke Kahanamoku, Kelly Slater, Laird Hamilton.

The beach theme matched Peavy's laid-back appearance, which was purely cosmetic, Fisk thought. On the inside, his friend was filled to capacity with a desire to compete, or, specifically, to win. Fisk hadn't been surprised when Peavy went, in just two years, from a lowly instructor at a little Krav Maga studio on the Lower East Side to the proprietor of eighteen state-of-the-art self-defense training centers in New York, New Jersey, and Tel Aviv. It was just a matter of time, Fisk thought, until Peavy laced a tie through the collar of one of his signature Hawaiian shirts and rang the bell at the New York Stock Exchange to open trading on the day of the Flying Robots initial public offering.

"People think what we do here is on the cutting edge." Peavy ran his hand along a glossy white polyurethane surfboard, mounted on the wall. "But the truth—between you, me, and any NSA folks listening—is that there's nothing being done here, or in the whole commercial UAV industry for that matter, that wasn't already done forty years ago." He stopped before the lone still photo, a black-and-white seated portrait of a relatively somber man in a suit, his dark hair slicked back in the midcentury business fashion. "Now this here is the man!"

It was a blowup, Fisk guessed, of a faculty photograph from a midcentury university course catalog. There was no autograph, just a printed label on the base of the frame: DR. FOSTER.

"The inventor of parasailing?" Fisk guessed.

"Way bigger, bro. Dr. John S. Foster was the physicist who ran the Livermore National Lab, the federally funded nuke research place. At home, in his spare time, he dabbled in remote-control airplanes, for fun. Until one day in 1971, he said to himself, 'Hey, this little hobby of mine could be turned into shit that's more effective against the enemy than the nukes I work on at my day job.'"

"Is that a direct quote?" Chay asked blithely.

"Yeah, verbatim," said Peavy.

She smiled, apparently taken with him, which should have pleased Fisk. For some reason, it rankled him.

Peavy went on: "So what Doc Foster did was he stuck a lawn-mower engine into the fuselage of a radio-controlled fixed-wing plane that had a little push propeller in back—the kind that looks like a desk fan. A little trial and error and he had himself a system that could stay in the air for two hours, with a payload of twenty-eight pounds."

"Can a sniper operate a UAV?" Chay asked.

"That depends on the sniper." Peavy pushed open a door to a spacious office that continued the seaside theme, patio furniture substituting for the traditional appointments, but with a two-story ceiling. "Have yourselves a deck chair."

Fisk and Chay each sat, and Peavy dropped into a seat behind the slatted table that served as his desk. From its lone drawer, he produced what appeared to be a pair of mirrored Wayfarers and slid them on. Sheepishly, he said, "The specs are a little gimmicky, sorry, but the model I'm going to show you is the one we use for sales presentations—as our marketing guy likes to say: 'Whistles and bells sells.'"

He clicked a button on his desk, and with a hiss, a panel rolled up into the far wall like a garage door. Peavy cocked his head and out rolled a miniature version of a familiar-looking stick figure of an aircraft, with fixed wings spanning about five feet. "This here is basically a one-tenth-the-size version of General Atomics' MQ-1, which you know as the Predator, which is the Elvis of UAVs. The Predator was developed in the nineties for recon. Then, one day, a U.S. Air Force general said, 'Dudes, this is amazing, I can see the enemy's tank trying to sneak up on us. Any way I can use the drone to blow the tank up?' So the Air Force stuck on a couple of AGM-114 Hellfire missiles. And that worked great, so they built a bigger version, the Reaper, which has about seventeen Hellfires and a pair of five-hundred-pound laser-guided bombs. Now it's just a matter of time until we have stealth fighter drones and bombers that can deliver nukes."

Peavy tilted his head. As if in response, the miniature Predator whirred toward him on the floor.

"This is our current bestseller, Yona, which is the Hebrew word for dove. Yona can cure what ails you with a couple dozen rocket-propelled grenades or, if you're into bullets, a modified M230 chain gun."

Fisk hoped Yodeler had nothing like Yona. "How do you launch it?" he asked, thinking that the launch might require considerable open space, which would significantly limit Yodeler in a city like New York.

Peavy sat against the edge of the table. In sync, the drone bucked. "I've used my driveway out on Long Island for a runway. It's a hundred feet and change. Ideally you'd need a couple hundred feet. Yona's designed to take off from an offshore oil-rig deck—we're going for the petro-security market."

"What if a sniper wanted to deploy it in an urban theater?" Chay asked.

"Say, this urban theater?" Peavy indicated the window behind him and its view of rooftops rising toward midtown.

Chay looked to Fisk, who said to Peavy, "Sure."

"It would be easy enough to launch here; any old sidewalk or street will do as a runway."

"And what about operating Yona?" Chay asked.

"What used to be known as the 'ground station' now fits into a book bag," Peavy said. "You connect it wirelessly to the glasses or a phone, so you can see what your UAV sees, and it moves the way you do. To fire, you push a button." He pointed to one of the buttons on the eyeglass frame by his right temple. "With a twenty-mile radius, Yona effectively makes all five boroughs your sniper's nest. And because target acquisition is so much easier when you're using a flying robot, a sniper mission that used to take five, six days in the field is now something you could do while you eat lunch at your desk."

"And what if you wanted your whole op to be black?" Fisk asked.

"That makes it harder, because Yona, just like the Predator and all the rest, is controlled by radio or, for shorter range missions, Wi-Fi. So figuring out where someone has launched from and landed and everything in between is like playing connect the dots with his signals after the fact. If you don't want anyone to be able to do that, you could disguise your radio signals. Or you could get a UAV that's small and slow enough that, in a crowded city, its signals would make it look like just another cell phone."

"How would you get a UAV like that?" Chay asked.

"Go to any shopping mall. Here . . ." Peavy took off his glasses, set them on his desktop, then crossed the room to a file cabinet. From it, he removed an aircraft with a black plastic fuselage the size and shape of a papaya mounted on a crossbeam, the four ends of which held a rotor. "This here is a quadrocopter—also known as a quadcopter. It's basically a multirotor helicopter that is lifted and propelled by four rotors; they're also available as hexacopters and octocopters—six rotors, eight rotors. You can get a quad in any hobby shop. Spend more than two hundred bucks, you've been had. It has vertical takeoff and landing, so you don't need any runway at all."

"And what if you wanted to weaponize it?" Fisk asked.

"This baby could deliver a lightweight grenade or a small gun." Peavy flicked one of the black plastic rotor blades, which was about five inches long.

"How do you fly it?" asked Chay.

"I'll let you try it for yourself." Peavy fished a cell phone from his board-shorts pocket. "What video-game apps do you play?"

Chay shrugged. "Text messaging."

Peavy turned to Fisk, who shook his head. "Nothing since Coleco stopped updating their handheld basketball game."

Peavy laughed. "I'd heard there were a couple of you out there."

He set the quadrocopter on the floor and flipped a tiny switch on the fuselage. Light beamed from the base of each rotor, casting bright red circles on the slate-gray carpet.

"The quad's using lasers to get her bearings," he said. One by one, the lights turned from red to green. "So, older pilots, other folks who aren't into apps, it can take those people a week to get the feel for fly-by-phone. But my five-year-old niece, because she plays an app called Doodlebug, like most of her friends from kindergarten, she just took one look at this . . ."

He showed Fisk and Chay the face of his phone, which displayed the drone's view of the carpet with the now-green dots. To the side of the footage were sliders for UP/DOWN and LEFT/RIGHT and a steering-wheel icon.

". . . And she could fly this quadrocopter without a hitch."

He tapped the wheel, setting the rotors into motion accompanied by shrieks like that of a hand vac, then dragged the up/down slider upward with his thumb, causing the drone to take flight. He released the slider, halfway up, leaving the quadrocopter in a hover seven feet from the floor.

"The quad's got an accelerometer, so it does what my body does." Peavy raised his voice to compete with the blenderlike rotors. He spun around, turned the phone end over end, and then stood still. Like Yona, this quadrocopter moved in sync with him, rotating and then somersaulting before returning to a hover. "It can literally turn on a dime, unlike a fixed-wing craft. And there's no worries about going too slow and stalling. This system would be perfect for the sniper in your urban theater." He tapped again at the controls and the drone floated to the carpet, landing smoothly, the rotors slowing to nothing. "The thing is, if it's going to carry anything more than a popgun, you're going to need a model with more oomph."

"Where do you get oomph?" asked Chay, her playfulness gone.

Fisk saw that she too was now immersed in the hunt.

"That kind of UAV is more of a specialty item, but nothing you can't order on the Web and have at your house the next day—with free shipping— for six, seven hundred bucks," Peavy said. "There's a model called the Specter that Domino's has been using to deliver pizzas. A pizza weighs about three and a half pounds including the pizza box. So let's say the Specter's max payload is four pounds. I've never heard of anyone weaponizing a quad, but if you did, low recoil would be the key if you want to be able to get off a second shot, let alone stay in the air. As long as your range is sub–three hundred yards, you could start with, say, a basic low-end Bushmaster—the Superlight Carbon weighs five and a half pounds. If you take off the Bushmaster's furniture—the grip, the stock, the rail system—and then replace its barrel with a ten-and-a-half-inch pencil barrel, you could get it down to three and a half pounds. Hell, a little custom work and you could just as easily send up an AR."

Chay swallowed a gasp. "An AR-15?" she asked as if merely curious.

"Sure. Or something that shoots a five-point-seven-mil cartridge would still have enough bite. Heckler & Koch's MP7 would do it for you."

Fisk said, "If you're on the ground, how would you get the AR-15 to fire?"

"That's nothing," Peavy said. "There are a dozen apps, like Ultimate Sniper, that sync the ballistics calculator on your gunsight to any cell phone. The app lets you correct for prevailing wind direction and speed, temperature, humidity, air pressure, all that. You could get a kit from any RadioShack or hobby store to build a little actuator to adjust the barrel and to pull the trigger."

Fisk was unnerved by the ease with which Yodeler—or anyone—could acquire such a system. This was what he had come here to find out, though. Rising to go, he said, "Now we know what to look for."

Chay remained seated. "I have one more question." She turned to Peavy. "If a sniper were using a quadrocopter with an AR-15, what sort of countermeasures could you employ?" She always asked open-ended questions, Fisk had noticed, the sort that netted insights and additional information, and she had a chess player's talent for thinking several moves ahead.

Peavy thought for a few seconds before answering. "You'd best take him out first."

Evans spent several minutes getting his laptop computer connected properly, projecting Yodeler's new e-mail on the screen in the smallest of the three NYPD Intel conference rooms. Never mind, Fisk thought, that the message could be read just fine on the phones of everyone present—Evans, himself, Weir, Dubin, and Chay. Or that they all had already read it.

"Okay, here goes nothing," Evans said. With a flourish, he double-clicked the track pad, projecting the decrypted Hushmail.

HELLO DETECTIVE FISK:
DO YOU TAKE ME FOR AN IMBECILE, WITH
THE ENTRY-LEVEL STALL TACTICS? EACH
DAY MR. VERLYN REMAINS IN CAPTIVITY
SHALL MEAN ANOTHER SACRIFICE.
YODELER

Weir said, "Good thing we haven't pissed him off."

Which was a version of *I told you so*, thought Fisk. "It's fine. He's engaged. It's not like he was good-natured before."

Only Dubin laughed, the way chagrined parents convey to a guest that their child had been trying to be amusing.

"So why are we here?" Fisk asked.

Dubin had convened the meeting, hoping to, as he put it, "help."

"Primarily, we want to discuss our response to Yodeler," said Evans.

"Naturally," Dubin said.

Fisk could have easily written Yodeler back from the sidewalk outside Flying Robots, LLC, where he'd first read the e-mail. But he was obligated to first get input from Weir and Evans. And he still needed them. He admitted, "The dialogue with Yodeler isn't working—"

Weir cut in. "You think?"

Fisk ignored the barb, continuing, "Isn't working if you presumed his response was going to be surrender and a plea for forgiveness. Maybe Yodeler breached his tradecraft to write while full of piss and vinegar, using all caps. If not, the goal is still to buy time. So what we might do is tell him that the U.S. attorney may be amenable to adjusting Verlyn's terms of custody, say, to house arrest—or maybe, 'home confinement with travel restrictions,' because that sounds better."

Weir looked to Dubin. "Have you been in contact with the U.S. attorney?" By which he meant, *What the hell are you doing talking to the U.S. attorney behind our backs?*

Dubin smiled Fisk's way. Not really an expression of pleasure or amusement, Fisk knew. "No, wouldn't talk to him without you."

Fisk said to Weir, "But he may be amenable. Worst case, it takes Yodeler an hour to get a new burner phone and go to Penn Station or wherever he goes to read the message, and it takes him the same amount of time or more to compose and send a response. That's time he's not working on sacrifices."

He was surprised to see Chay nodding her accord. One of the things he'd learned at the Farm—the CIA-run field-officer training base just outside of Williamsburg, Virginia—was that a mere nod of corroboration by a second party almost always causes the target's trust-governing synapse to fire. And approval from a woman is almost twice as effective on the Weirs and Evanses of the world, which is to say: men.

Indeed Evans appeared impressed. He looked to Weir. "Flagpole?"

"As long as we red-team it," Weir said, in turn looking to Dubin, probably because he sensed that Fisk would try to spike the red team. In which case Weir was right. In red-team sessions, the Bureau brought together an assortment of agents and analysts and specialists and tried to see things from the adversary's perspective. While that could be valuable, Fisk thought, in this context, "red team" was a euphemism for more sitting around pontificating.

"Can't hurt," Dubin said. Which was more politics. Or maybe too many years out of the field had softened him.

"Great," Fisk said. He meant it too. The red team would convene in the SCIF at the JTTF, meaning Chay would be excluded. He would claim something came up, precluding his attendance. And something would definitely come up. Unencumbered by meetings and his shadow, he might just get some work done tonight.

The Cartel ought to make a donation to the Online Foundation to Support Whistle-Blowers, thought Blackwell.

Last week, he'd been able to find the Drug Enforcement Agency's mole hiding in a safe house in Miami thanks to a leaked law-enforcement-expenditure form listing the dummy corporation the DEA had used on a previous sting operation in Key Biscayne, a cigarette-boat dealership. The same dummy corporation paid the utilities bill at the safe house.

Locating Fisk was even easier, thanks to the leaks of his Social Security number, date of birth, and mother's maiden name. There wasn't much about the detective that wasn't available online now. While still in Miami, Blackwell was able to hack Fisk's Diner's Club credit-card account, and found the purchase of a prepaid cell phone prior to the card's suspension following a suspicious purchase of a $2,200 Les Paul electric guitar. He then tracked the prepaid phone to Hell's Kitchen thanks to one of the myriad mobile locator services available online (you have to pay $4.95 per locate with the purchase of a $19.95 monthly plan—and you have to check the box promising that you weren't using the service in conjunction with any illegal activities). Last night, during a couple of McDonald's stops on the drive up from Miami, he determined that Fisk had been crashing in an industrial building in Hell's Kitchen, the Manhattan epicenter of hostels, illegal residences in commercially zoned buildings, and other cheap crash pads. A quick bit of Internet digging said that the developer who owned Fisk's building owned nine others in Hell's Kitchen.

It was a sound investment strategy, Blackwell thought. You buy a run-down factory or warehouse cheap and with zero down payment thanks to various urban economic development programs, then you spend next to nothing running it thanks to Con Ed's Project Appleseed. Meanwhile you collect 100K in rent each month under the table. And five, ten years down the road, when you have to make good on your urban development commitment and renovate the building, you've got the cash several times over. And after you renovate, you sell the place for millions, all of which is profit. His mistress's statuary benefited from a similar deal from the city of Chicago. Decaying buildings are fine for casting plaster statues and lawn art, desirable even, because a place where you do that sort of work is going to get trashed no matter what. Blackwell hadn't thought of it as an investment initially, but rather a place to launder money. But now he was making a handsome profit there because other than cheap labor and even cheaper plaster, the business had virtually no expenses. Plus he'd gotten Franciszka out of the deal—although that was in jeopardy on account of the broken jaw, the second time it had happened. She'd been in his face again the night before he left for Miami. Of course he couldn't give her any details about his trip, for her own good, but she wouldn't shut up. The weird thing was, he'd barely hit her this time.

He parallel-parked his rented Toyota Something-or-Other, a piece of shit. In real life, he alternated between a Porsche Cayman and a 1955 Mercedes-Benz CLS, the one with the gull-wing doors. On the job, though, the goal always was to blend in. It was also a goal of his to surveil the hell out of his marks before striking, for a week or more, to learn their schedules, their routes, their susceptibilities. Like so many other guys, the DEA mole had had a weakness for the fairer sex. All it had taken to get him out of the safe house and to the kill room was a scrawny chick from a low-rent escort service willing to pose as a tourist staying nearby. Plus Blackwell had given her an extra fifty bucks.

Fisk would be cagier. Of that Blackwell was sure. With thirty-five dollars sent via PayPal to a Park Avenue messenger service, Blackwell had already learned that Fisk hadn't stayed at the Sutton Place apartment since the bungled hit. The Diner's Club statement showed that the detective had spent a night at a private club in midtown that provided hotel rooms to members and guests, then a couple of nights at a Hampton Inn. And after that, he went black, no doubt worried that someone like Blackwell would show up to finish what the Mexicans had started at Sutton Place. Procuring a burner phone using a traceable method of payment had been Fisk's one mistake. Pros like him make mistakes, but not often. If he were to realize this one, he would move again, in which case it might be weeks before Blackwell tracked him down again, so success tonight was critical.

It was almost midnight. There were still enough people wandering the streets that Blackwell wouldn't stand out in any way—he was fairly average in appearance, and forgettable by design. He had time for a quick scout of the place Fisk was staying in, a dilapidated World War I–era building, originally a factory of some sort, like so many of the buildings around here.

Getting into this one through the front door required a sturdy numeric lock. Windows were a possibility, though he could count on window alarms on the first three floors, probably the roof too. Blackwell might also talk his way in, or, if that failed, let Smith & Wesson do the talking for him. The problem with any of these entries was that once he was inside, he would know nothing of the layout, other than, thanks to the mobile location service, that Fisk was on the third floor, facing east, near the uptown corner. Fisk would then have a hell of a home field advantage. But the location was also Fisk's susceptibility. The guy was a pro, but he was on the run, which means off balance, easier to take down.

The industrial building had massive windows, ten feet high, lots of them, dating to a time when the sun was the best means of lighting a room. Anyone staying in a place like this would want curtains or blinds, even if they weren't worried about someone popping them through the window. Otherwise they were guaranteed to be woken at sunup each and every day. Looking up now, Blackwell ascertained that Fisk hadn't installed blinds yet, though he'd improvised, affixing a sleeping bag to the steel window gate.

If ever a job called for popping a scope on your rifle and taking a shot, Blackwell thought, this was it.

He returned to the shit Toyota, opened the trunk, and took out a racquet bag, which contained a Mark 14 Mod 0 rifle with a collapsible stock that he'd brought on the trip for this sort of contingency. He proceeded to the building one down from Fisk's, a forgettable, pollution-browned, yellow-brick tenement. Residential, fortunately. Getting in required hitting enough buttons on the front intercom panel—three—until a resident bent on sleeping decided anything was better than hearing more of that damned buzzer.

Blackwell entered a worn lobby consisting of a narrow corridor leading to the stairs. On one side was a row of mailboxes, all of them locked except for 3W's, which was missing its hatch—but not the sticker advising the mailman of the previous resident's forwarding address.

The assassin climbed the stairs and rang 3W's bell just in case. No answer. He slipped on a pair of cotton gloves and quietly went to work on the lock with a torsion wrench and a feeler prong. Sometimes this took five minutes. Sometimes it didn't work at all. This time he heard the faint snap of the bolt leaving the doorframe in about forty-five seconds.

The apartment was hot and smelled of dust. He waited for his eyes to adjust to the dark. Nowhere better for that than Manhattan, with all the street light. It took five seconds. As expected, the place was vacant but for a few chairs and a bookcase that must not have been worth the effort of transporting anywhere.

The lone bedroom had a chair missing one arm and a radiator. This was all Blackwell would need. He approached the window from the side, peering out, and, through an alley full of misty street light, found Fisk's crash pad. The light inside formed a halo around the sleeping bag.

Blackwell popped the rifle together and set it onto his bipod, positioned on the radiator cover. The shot ought to be a lay-up, he thought. No obstructions save the sleeping bag. Through the ample, exposed windowpane to either side of the sleeping bag, he could see his target, sitting alone in a beanbag chair, watching TV and picking at a guitar.

Blackwell cracked the window in the borrowed apartment. Then, dropping to a knee in front of the radiator, he positioned the barrel. Shooting at a downward angle complicated matters far more than people thought: gravity could severely mess with a shot traveling three thousand feet per second. But not from this distance. The hardest part would be pulling the trigger. He leaned into the stock's cheek piece and squinted against the scope, still warm from the trunk, giving off a slight whiff of exhaust. He found the back of Fisk's head centered almost exactly within the crosshairs.

Rather than draw attention with the laser range finder, Blackwell used the mil dot reticle in the scope to find the range—a mere sixty-one feet. He zeroed the scope, took a deep breath, and let the air out in small increments, the idea being to hold his lungs empty at the moment of the shot.

Finally he focused on Fisk, whose minimal motion took him in and out of the crosshairs. Anticipating the target's behavior is integral to a precise shot, Blackwell knew, and took it into account.

He readied his index finger by the trigger—he would squeeze straight back with the ball of the finger to avoid jerking the gun sideways. To minimize barrel motion, he would fire between his heartbeats.

As usual, a calm enveloped him. It's a one-of-a-kind rush, to have this power over another person's life, he thought, when he noted that Fisk's hair was shaggier and darker than it had been in the photos. A disguise element? Also Fisk didn't look quite as sturdy as usual. And his sharp features were softer, beyond the powers of a disguise kit.

Because Fisk hadn't made a mistake. Wouldn't have, in hindsight. Blackwell cursed himself for failing to figure it out from the moment he saw the guitar. This guy at the other end of the scope had purchased the guitar using the Diner's Club card he'd lifted from Fisk—yeah, a shiny electric Les Paul. *Shit*.

That same night Lin slept in the safe house in Chinatown. Or, rather, he tried to sleep.

His service rented the little apartment in the name of Han Zhijun, a young woman who three years ago had been hit by a bus around the corner, on Canal Street, permanently disabling her. She was subsequently institutionalized in upstate New York. If you're going to appropriate an identity, you can't do much better than hers, particularly for use in smuggling female agents in or out of the United States: Han Zhijun wasn't going anywhere. She wouldn't notice.

Lin decided to spend the night here because Chinatown was one of the best places in the world to detect surveillance, and come dawn, he would need to run the SDR—surveillance detection route—of his life. He also loved this place. Not because it was comfortable or luxurious. The furnishings were sparse and old, the carpets threadbare. Typical safe house, in other words. And it smelled strongly of the salted fish drying in the sun on the neighboring rooftops—typical Chinatown. What's more, the bed in the single bedroom was large, but worn to concavity, probably before Lin's service acquired it, probably left out for trash collection.

Nevertheless Lin jumped at opportunities to stay here because of the respite from his cover. Although he had his own spacious apartment near the university, on 118th and Riverside—and it was quite well-appointed thanks to a fellowship his cover story had won him—he was on guard there. Eternally, it seemed. He had to play the role of Ji-Hsuan Lee, the country-bumpkin-turned-computer-prodigy, always, even when he slept—wearing earplugs because the din of the city kept the "country boy" awake. Even when there was no conceivable reason that anyone could be watching him, he had to operate as if they were. With its external cameras and myriad other countersurveillance measures, the safe house allowed him to breathe freely.

But not tonight.

Lin couldn't sleep in spite of a deep well of self-relaxation techniques. No matter which way he lay or turned, he soon felt an urge to roll over.

The North American Division chief was unhappy; that was putting it mildly. Chay Maryland's personal computer had proven worthless from an intelligence standpoint, and the Hoyas flash drive worse than worthless: in a rush to get another one to swap for it, the agency had decided on a course of action beginning with sending a diplomat from the embassy in Washington to Georgetown University's bookstore to buy a drive, then getting the woman on a plane—a private plane—to Teterboro Airport in New Jersey to deliver it. Once swapped, Chay's drive had yielded documents that Lin's people initially suspected were from Verlyn, disguised using sophisticated steganographic techniques: the drive purported to contain only a personal diary that the reporter had kept since she was a girl, begun using a now-defunct software known as MacWrite. After the cryptologists and computers at HQs were flummoxed, the service reached the conclusion that the drive was what it appeared to be, Chay's means of safekeeping her diary. And although an exhaustive chronicle, nowhere did it mention the Verlyn documents.

The window for obtaining the documents was now closing, said Lin's division chief, who didn't trust the usual electronic commo for planning the next step. Or maybe that was just cover, Lin thought now, lest he run for fear they would erase him tomorrow.

No wonder he kept finding himself staring at the water stains on the ceiling, so dark that they were obvious even with the lights out. Of course the lights from the neon-happy Mott Street could get past any blind, let alone this tattered one. He drew the drapes, plunging the room into blackness. Then got back into bed.

And still didn't sleep.

A while later, he struck upon the idea of the bottle of antianxialitics he kept on hand, in the medicine cabinet, to quell the occasional agent's panic. The recommended dose was one tablet. He took three.

He awoke in the morning, as usual, just seconds before the alarm sounded, and astonishingly refreshed. He showered, got into his business suit, and sprayed the same stuff into his hair as did the other Asian yuppies who lived on this stretch of Mott, along with whom he would commute to work, or so it would appear.

All of its one-way streets, pedestrian alleys, and subway stations made Chinatown the foremost SDR zone in the city. Your surveillant has little choice but to fall in step behind you here, Lin reminded himself as he slid on a pair of eyeglasses with "rear-view mirrors"—strips of mirrored film adhered to the inside of the lenses in order to give him a look at who or what was behind him. And if your tail is white, he's that much easier to see among all the Chinese.

Shoving open the heavy steel-cage-encased lobby door, Lin stepped out of the onetime tenement house. A sharp dawn highlighted the hundreds of pieces of litter, another category in which China-town had no rivals in the city. Everything was still, as quiet as it got downtown, just the whir of fans and the rumble of early traffic coming in from Long Island and New Jersey.

Mott Street remained asleep save for a couple of taxis and one of the city sanitation trucks that never seemed to make more than a dent in the mounds of black bags on the sidewalks here. A watcher would have stood out against the contiguous garish-colored façades. Lin didn't put it past the FBI to use surveillance UAVs, though, like the $200,000 Black Hornet Micro, essentially a high-performance stealth helicopter reduced to the size of a moth. The slats on the decorative safe-house window shutters concealed sensors that could detect radio trans-mission in the range such electronic surveillance systems would conceivably use—900 MHz to 2.52 GHz. Lin's phone (a five-thousand-dollar knock-off of the CIA Birdbook devices that couldn't be tracked) remained silent, meaning the sensors had detected no threats.

As he turned west onto Canal, he saw nothing out

of the ordinary. The McDonald's was busy. Always was. The salty aroma of the hash browns enveloped him, and made his mouth water. He proceeded to the 1 train. In search of a tail he hoped he would fail to find, he would take several subway rides, and walk at least a mile in the train tunnels, and several miles on the sidewalks. Along the way he planned to shop for clothing—he would go into a tourist boutique in Penn Station and leave in a new outfit, through the back exit.

Like a commuter, he hurried down the stairwell, then into the subway station via a humid tunnel with smog-grayed white-tile walls that amplified the sound of his steps, his breaths, and, it seemed, his accelerated heartbeat.

He was alone other than the sanitation worker using a mop to move the filth around the turnstiles, an old man with gaps in his teeth that defied the abilities of the FBI's Costume Department. Even so, Lin might have maintained his circumspection, but he'd seen the guy here before often enough to establish his authenticity.

Two more men entered the tunnel at its midpoint and followed him toward the platform, both Asian American yuppies, both of them glancing at their phones while they walked.

FBI agents? Why chance it?

At the end of the tunnel, Lin turned onto a near-empty platform just as an uptown-bound 1 train shrieked into the station. No one got off. Using the rearview mirrors, he watched the two yuppies diverge, boarding cars of their own and, seemingly, entering worlds of their own.

Lin darted into the lead car, boarding just before the doors banged shut, meaning anyone following him would be obvious. He saw no one. The lights flickered as the train launched into a tunnel lit red by traffic signals that the conductor disregarded. Among the dozen other passengers were suits—bankers and lawyers who would take the 7 or the Times Square Shuttle over to Park Avenue.

Lin etched each one into his memory. If he were to see one of them again this morning, he would abort the meeting. The exigency sharpened his senses.

A few minutes later, the subway pulled into the Times Square station and the doors snapped open. He hesitated as long as he could before making his move. Finally stepping onto the platform, he regarded the mirrored film to find no one following him, no one muttering into a lapel mic, no one doing much of anything.

He climbed up to the street, walking against traffic on Seventh Avenue, coming to a standstill suddenly midway up the crowded sidewalk between Forty-Second and Forty-Third Street and waving, as if to hail a cab. This was a timing stop, to see if anyone behind him halted or shifted behavior abruptly.

Again, all clear.

It was a ten-minute walk across Forty-Sixth Street to the tunnel through the MetLife Building that allowed for commuters to get to and from Grand Central. Zigzagging the midtown grid, turning randomly and making sure no one else was turning, Lin spent two and a half hours getting to the MetLife Building, changing along the way into a T-shirt with a New York Mets logo.

At last he entered the MetLife skyscraper, which had gained iconic status on account of the hawks who nested in the letters spelling out the company's name just below the roof. He timed his entrance so that he would cross paths with the commuters arriving on the 8:04 express train from Stamford, Connecticut.

Anyone else plunging into that tide would have to be a tail.

There was no one else.

At the passageway's midpoint, he ducked into a Citibank, joining a moderate line—a dozen or so people—waiting for the ATMs. A portly man waddled into line behind him, reading a *Wall Street Journal* folded into thirds the way the practiced train commuters did.

He said to Lin, "How ya doing, fellow Mets fan?"

"Happy because of last night's game against the Orioles," Lin said. The Baltimore Orioles played in a different league; the Mets weren't facing them this season.

The guy groused, "I missed the seven nineteen from Stamford, had to take the seven thirty-seven." This told Lin that the North American division chief would be in the Grand Hyatt in room 1937.

"Then you're due for some good luck," Lin said in acknowledgment.

The Grand Hyatt was three blocks away, two if you cut through Grand Central station. It took Lin forty-five minutes to get through the station, and another ten minutes at Modell's Sporting Goods, just across Vanderbilt Avenue, to buy and change into a Nike tracksuit.

He exited Modell's, turned east onto Forty-Second Street, and walked a block, passing the entrance to the Grand Hyatt before doubling back, satisfied that he hadn't been tailed, and pushing through the door to the hotel. In the palatial, contemporary lobby, he took a tour of the men's room for good measure, then rode the elevator to the nineteenth floor.

Meeting Dr. Jun was surprisingly anticlimactic. After Lin knocked on the door to room 1937 four times (people almost always knock three times), he found himself face-to-face with a woman who reminded him of his grandmother, licking at lips likely dehydrated from the long plane ride. Her eyes were puffy, as if from sleep (so much for the rumors that she never rested). She appeared uncomfortable in the Western business suit; at home she always wore an army uniform. She offered nothing in the way of small talk or even a greeting, telling him, "Sit." She waved at the bench meant for suitcases by the foot of the bed.

He followed her instruction while she dropped onto the bed, her back against the headboard, oblivious to the fact she was displaying the entirety of her bony thighs—unless she was doing it intentionally, to unsettle him. In which case she was succeeding. He tried to focus on her gray eyes.

"What made you think the flash drive had the documents?" she asked.

"It was a mistake," he said, with remorse, which, rumor had it, she liked. "In hindsight."

She cackled. "Is it a matter of hindsight? How is it that you failed to consider that a flash drive the reporter bought when she was a student at Georgetown University, back when such drives had storage capacity for only a hundred such documents, would not be used to store the hundreds of thousands of NSA documents?"

Don't dig yourself in deeper, he told himself. "I'm sorry, ma'am. Hoyas was a clue I overlooked."

"After all of your spook games, you really aren't any closer to knowing where she has them, other than not on her computer or tiny flash drive, correct?"

It dawned on him that the scolding was a good sign. She wouldn't waste the time to do it if she planned to have him zapped.

He said, "I am afraid that, yes, that is an accurate assessment, ma'am."

"What other intelligence service, including the one from whom the documents were stolen, would not want them?"

Play her game, he exhorted himself. "I can't think of any, ma'am."

"We've picked up chatter suggesting that at least six other services have covert operations under way targeting the Verlyn cache. Fortunately no one has succeeded yet—or at least the Pakistanis have done a good job pretending to have blundered as badly as you have. The Israelis sent a columnist from a tabloid we know to be a Mossad front. She offered the *New York Times* director of security, Ed Norman, one million dollars for the files, a hundred thousand up front, another nine hundred if and when he came through. Norman didn't collect the nine hundred. Why the Israelis didn't just ask Ms. Chay Maryland, I have no idea. Do you?"

"She seems to have no interest in material things. She's willing to go to prison for a year and a half to keep the secret."

"I didn't say make her an offer. I said *ask*."

Was this a test? If so, she liked to be smarter than anyone else. "I wish I could follow you, ma'am," he said.

"This is what you will do. This is what you should have done from the beginning. You will bring her to the safe house on Mott Street and ask—interrogate her if you must. Do whatever is required in order to ascertain the whereabouts of the documents. Once you have the documents—I should say, when we have verified that you have them, and when you are given the go-ahead—you will put her in a taxi that will have an unfortunate accident. Do you understand?"

It was a good plan, Lin admitted. He nodded and stood to depart.

Fisk had spent most of the night looking for leads and striking out, which, he thought, described the vast majority of his time at work. And in his personal life too, since his eventual return to the playing field after Krina's death—but that was another story. Sure, every second on the case was fraught with tension, but Fisk wasn't complaining. If anything, the strike-outs made the hits that much more rewarding. What he should have done from the start, he realized, was call the National Geospatial-Intelligence Agency.

The NGA was based in Springfield, Virginia, in a 2.3-million-square-foot building that resembled a sleek modern ocean liner, the atrium alone big enough to fit the Statue of Liberty. The agency's sixteen thousand employees put a $5 billion annual budget toward the production of stunningly sophisticated logistical data in support of national security. Perhaps the best example of its product came in 2011's Operation Neptune Spear, the U.S. raid of Osama bin Laden's secret compound in Abbottabad, Pakistan. The agency used satellite imagery to generate three-dimensional renderings of the compound, and to create freakishly accurate empirical and algorithmic-prediction-based schedules of the local pedestrian and vehicular traffic in the vicinity. The reconnaissance systems also determined the gender, height, and weight of each of bin Laden's housemates.

In New York, the agency occupied a twenty-eighth-floor office in the World Financial Center, a suite so small and unassuming that other tenants probably concluded that the NGA on the frosted-glass door stood for the names of the principals of a boutique accounting or actuarial firm. If that weren't enough, the lone professional at the NGA's New York office, Roy Plummer, more closely resembled an accountant than he did a spy. He wore thick-lensed glasses, his stoop belonged to a man of twice his thirty-one years, and he had a pallor attributable to too much time spent beneath the office's fluorescent lights. He came off as quiet too, shy to the point of diffident, and withdrawn. But that was only because he had a lot on his mind, as Fisk had come to appreciate.

"Other than a coffee machine, all an intel agency really needs these days is one decent computer," Plummer explained, tapping the tinted glass top of the square conference table around which he, Chay, and Fisk now sat. Fisk knew from previous visits that the tabletop doubled as a computer monitor. "This system represents the digitization of what ten years ago was the combined product of seven different National Geospatial-Intelligence Agency divisions working together. Each division had its own large-format printer. Each would generate a huge printout and then run it into one central room and pushpin it to the bulletin board. The bulletin board would be the agency's product. Now, this"—he tapped the glass—"has taken the place of the bulletin board."

The room lights dimmed, revealing a luminous touch-sensitive keyboard on the glass in front of him. From tiny nozzles at each of the table's four corners rose a whitish vapor, which blended with vapor emitted by a parallel quartet of nozzles on the ceiling. The result was a pale green glowing box the size of a cube refrigerator. On its base, the surface of the table, appeared a two-dimensional map of the section of Central Park where Harun Ahmed had been killed, Fisk figured.

"A Greek named Anaximander invented this in the sixth century BC," Plummer said to Chay.

Her eyes widened with incredulity. "The vapor screen?"

"I don't know what you mean by 'vapor screen,'" the NGA man said with a vaudevillian display of confusion. "Jeremy, you know what she's talking about?"

Fisk made a mental note to buy Plummer a steak dinner. He turned to Chay and said, "If we're going to make any progress here, you need to assure us that if the topic of three-dimension vapor projection technology comes up after you leave here today, you won't disclose your knowledge of its existence."

She hesitated. "Okay?"

"Good," said Plummer. "Actually, I meant that Anaximander invented the sort of two-dimensional map that you currently see on the tabletop. This one represents the two-thousand-square-foot area of Central Park where the first victim was killed sometime between two and two thirty in the afternoon." He tapped at his touch-sensitive keyboard. "Now we'll add a dimension with the help of a proprietary Innovision aeronautical app called PHAERO that aggregates available data from that time period cap-

tured by eyes in the sky—satellites and other reconnaissance platforms, including unmanned aerial
vehicles, like the RQ-4 Global Hawk drone, and
manned systems, like the U-2 spy plane, which has
been in service since 1955." The map transformed
from a drawing to a color photograph, springing
into three dimensions, with 3-D images including
a female jogger, a blue sky with wispy clouds, and,
hovering above one of the trees, a disk-shaped white
blur.

"The bulk of this imagery was snapped by the
IKONOS satellite while it was on a routine overpass
of the city at 2:09:20 P.M.," Plummer said.

Fisk pointed to the round blur. Chay beat him to
asking, "What is that?"

Plummer aimed a stylus at it. The beam of red
light cast by the stylus's tip transformed into a
cursor arrow inside the vapor cube. With it, Plummer drew a circle around the blur, enlarging the
white disk. As it expanded, its edges grew rounder
and the color sharpened to a Day-Glo yellow.

"A Frisbee," Chay realized aloud.

"We're hoping to find a weaponized drone," Fisk
said.

"Not to worry, folks, we're barely into the first
inning," said the NGA man. "Next, one by one, I'll
add any available imagery from the GeoEye satellite, which was also in the neighborhood at the time,
along with any data we can get from the seventy-
two satellites in Motorola's Iridium consortium.
Also I'll mix in a couple of our own satellites."

He hit a few keys and the three-dimensional
imagery grew better defined, with richer hues. A

three-dimensional image of a man's body materialized, lying still on the running path. In contrast,
two female joggers running around the reservoir
were actually moving. The trees too came to life,
with branches swaying in the wind. A horse lum-
bered around the loop, towing a hansom cab containing the driver and what appeared to be a family
of four tourists, three of them apparently using
their phones to record the ride.

"What you're looking at now is a photograph that
was taken by one of the Iridium birds at 2:30:44,"
Plummer said. "The animation is generated by
EQUIS, our Enhanced Quality Image Search.
They might in reality be Olympic marathoners, but
EQUIS is just rendering their motions based on av-
erages of female joggers of their sizes."

Chay pointed at the man lying still on the running path. "That's the victim, isn't it?"

"Yes." Plummer brought up a window full of
numbers. "His thermal metrics are the same as the
other people in the vicinity. He may have been dead
a matter of seconds before the satellite passed over,
or he may still be alive here—it's impossible to know
from this data alone. As for a UAV, it could have
come into this part of the park during the twenty-
one-minute gap between the satellite pics we have."

"What about other kinds of images?" Fisk asked.

With a nod, Plummer returned to the keyboard.
"That brings us to the second inning, incorporat-
ing data from surface cameras." The picture sharpened again, but only slightly. "As you can see, there's
almost no surface data from that time frame."

Fisk had expected as much. "So far the drone—or

whoever or whatever it is—has been no-hitting the Department's cameras."

Plummer asked, "Were your camera locations part of the Verlyn leak?"

By way of reply, Fisk turned to Chay. With less conviction than usual, she said, "Not that I know of."

"It's spilled milk now," Fisk said. He turned to Plummer. "What about radar?"

"Radar is in our toolbox." Plummer went into a pianist act on his keyboard. "For Central Park, we have an amazing array of radar systems on account of the proximity of JFK and LaGuardia as well as Newark—Terminal Radar captures every plane within fifty nautical miles of a control tower."

The upper levels of the vapor cube began to fill with objects. Fisk recognized the form of a commercial passenger jet. "Any micro UAVs by any chance?"

"The Coast Guard's radar can give us a flying object as small as a baseball within a hundred miles of any coastline, and of course Central Park is less than a mile." Plummer keyed in smaller objects, rendered in all of the primary colors, which proliferated in the projected sky.

"What are these?" Chay said.

"Could be birds, or kites, or baseballs, or tossed bridal bouquets, drones," Plummer said. "Resolution and classification of small objects is extremely difficult, particularly if they're flying at low speeds. Micro UAVs, like a quadrocopter, average about eleven miles per hour—Little League pitchers throw a ball five times that fast. Add in the clutter of trees and buildings, it's almost impossible to tell anything about smaller objects. What I can do, though, is eliminate anything with a radar cross section bigger than an ultralight airplane and ask EQUIS to use empirical-data-based algorithms to fill in the blanks for us." Two clicks and most of the sky clutter vanished. "As you can see distinctly, now there are birds. There's a kite. Looks like some poor kid lost a balloon over here."

"But no drone?" Chay asked.

"Not yet," said Plummer. "We can enhance the photo by using even more tools. Here's some radio signal data recorded by the FAA, here's NORAD, here's J-STAR, and good old AWACS. Now EQUIS will attach icons based on its best guess as to which system provided the data . . ."

Icons of cell phones popped up above each of the pedestrians. Above one of the treetops, a small black airplane icon materialized. Fisk sat bolt upright, as did Chay. Plummer followed their stares, using his stylus to outline and enlarge the icon.

"It's just a little radio-controlled plane," he said. "A toy. Probably too small to haul a ballpoint pen, let alone any kind of gun. But it's possible that an algorithm-based system like this wouldn't differentiate a weaponized UAV from an RC plane because we haven't written UAV parameters for it yet. Frankly, this is the first time I've heard of anyone wanting imagery of a UAV outside of war theaters, and most of the military UAVs are way bigger than an ultralight airplane. If LaGuardia's ground control or the Coast Guard or Homeland were concerned about a blip like that on their screens, they would basically zoom in and find out what it was in real time—or they would send up an F-16 to investigate. Probably the NGA system needs a tweak."

"What about this tourist family here?" Chay pointed to the hansom cab on the loop. "It looks like they're taking pictures or videos. Is there any way to access what they captured?"

Plummer gestured to Fisk to take the floor. "Once we get warrants, figure out who their carriers are, send the carriers NSLs and get the data back," Fisk said, "it's possible. In the meantime, our options are down to what Anaximander had: we need to find a human eyewitness."

"We can still build imagery from the other crime scenes," Plummer said.

Fisk had hoped so. Hoping now to increase Chay's appreciation for the surveillance technology, he said, "Your choice, need to choose between canvassing the city on foot and sitting here in the a/c watching more videos."

She flashed a smile, revealing a well of mirth beneath her hardened exterior.

Plummer went back into his pianist act, fading the Central Park scene to the vapor's chalky-white default, then refilling it with a two-dimensional map of 435 West Seventeenth Street, victim Tameka Ann Crowley's apartment building.

The image rose into three dimensions, morphing from drawing to photograph, then became animated, with pedestrians wandering along the sidewalks, a few trees swaying in a light breeze, and a trio of yellow cabs and a UPS delivery truck rumbling westward between Ninth Avenue and Tenth.

Again, all manner of flying objects filled the sky,

until Plummer filtered out small birds and large aircraft, leaving just one object over West Seventeenth Street.

Seen from above, the object had the general shape of two rows of conjoined circles. Drawing a red loop around it, Plummer said, "EQUIS must be confused. It's saying that this is a McDonnell Douglas MD-88, but that's a commercial jet with a hundred-and-three-foot wingspan."

"Could it be as simple as that it looks like the number eighty-eight?" Fisk asked.

"It's a quadrocopter," Chay exclaimed.

"That's it," Fisk said. If it weren't just the three of them in a small, quiet room, he would have cheered.

Plummer opened an Internet Explorer window on the tabletop and scrolled through images of UAVs. "Evidently the eighty-eight shape is a foam safety hull that protects the fuselage and extends into a ring around each of the four rotors," he said. "Without it, if the rotor blades were to brush against a streetlamp or some other hard object, the quadrocopter could experience catastrophic failure."

"What about radio frequency?" Fisk asked. "Can we use the radio signals to track the thing?"

"Yes and no. It looks like it used multiple frequencies, hopping randomly from one frequency to another every nanosecond, probably implemented for the express purpose of thwarting someone who would go hunting for the transmitter."

"What's the 'yes' part of yes and no?" Fisk asked.

"The data we have is sufficient to see if the quadrocopter turned up anywhere else." Plummer banged away at the keyboard. The area in the projection expanded to include, in three-dimensions, the lower half of the island, with thousands of objects above the buildings, like a hailstorm of cannonballs.

A keypunch—and they disappeared, all but three, in its original position at the 88 on West Seventeenth Street and in two other positions depicted by 88s close together on the surface of the Hudson River, just off Pier 52. "I don't know where it came from, but given that it spent enough time in positions two and three to be photographed by two satellites, I have a pretty good idea of where it is right now." He pointed to the floor. "At the bottom of the Hudson River."

In Fisk's collection of Manhattan trivia was the little-known fact that the city has a Thirteenth Avenue—most New Yorkers would tell you that their island runs into the Hudson at Twelfth. In the nineteenth century, Thirteenth Avenue ran parallel to the Hudson River, reaching from West Eleventh Street up to West Twenty-Ninth. At the beginning of the twentieth century, the city needed to fit the newer and bigger breed of foreign ships, like the RMS *Titanic* and the RMS *Lusitania*, into its ports on the Hudson. The planners lopped off all but one block of Thirteenth Avenue. The remaining block became the Gansevoort Peninsula, also known as Pier 52.

Now the pier consisted of a square block of asphalt parking lot serving a couple of NYC Sanitation Department buildings that matched the industrial scheme of the meatpacking district across the West Side Highway.

Fisk stood on the pier's southwestern corner now, with Chay. They'd been here for more than an hour. On the bright side, it was a picture-perfect July morning, with seemingly every water molecule in the Hudson sparkling beneath myriad boats and a colorful array of sails and spinnakers. Waves rhythmically slapped the pier's wooden fenders.

Chay focused on a brownish, sour-smelling patch of water fifty yards west of the pier. There, four divers from the FBI's Underwater Search and Evidence Response Team looked for the downed drone. Two more divers from the NYPD Scuba Team assisted. Nearby, a thirty-foot FBI cruiser dragged a sonar unit along the river bottom. Four cables sprang from the deck of a slightly smaller boat before disappearing below the surface, connected to four search robots known as ROVs—remotely operated vehicles—that might remind you of canister vacuum cleaners, until you knew that each cost $120,000.

Likely as not, the divers and the ROVs would happen upon other weapons before finding the drone. New York's criminals treated the local waterways as an evidence dump.

"What's it like down there?" Chay asked.

"Even on a hot day in the middle of the summer like today, it's pretty cold thirty-two feet down. The water moves fast, and hard. Everything's pitch-black; you literally can't make out your hand right in front of your face. You're basically just feeling around, meanwhile trying to avoid getting stuck in muck or snared by rocks, fishing line, bodies—you name it. All of which makes it pretty fun, actually."

"Sounds it," she said matter-of-factly.

"Have you ever been scuba diving?"

"No. Can't you use infrared to see underwater?"

"You would just illuminate all the dirt and the pollution. It's only very recently that we've begun to use anything other than feel; the Department's experimenting with handheld sonar guns. The display is inside the diver's face mask."

She nodded. "What will happen if they find the drone?"

"They'll put it in a PVC container along with Hudson River water, to preserve the evidence."

"How long can the drone retain fingerprints?"

"A drone? Tough to say. On a gun, it's four days, maybe five."

"And what if you're able to lift prints, but they're not in the national fingerprint and criminal history database?"

"That's a seventy-five percent likelihood. Sort of makes you wish we had everyone's prints in the database, doesn't it?"

She smiled, but dismissively.

He tried again. "When I was a rookie, we found a .357 Magnum on the bottom of the East River that had been there for three years. Prints were long gone, but it still yielded a ballistics report, which was part of the evidence that brought down Vincent Gigante, the 'Oddfather.'"

"The head of the Genovese crime family?"

"He used to wander the streets here in the Village, wearing just his bathrobe and slippers, muttering incoherently. He eventually admitted that he was just faking insanity so that he could avoid prosecution."

"Didn't Vincent Gigante die behind bars?"

"In Missouri."

"Good." Chay continued to fixate on the area beneath which the divers had disappeared, a mosaic of browns, blacks, and grays.

A minute ticked by. She asked no more questions, said nothing.

"So where are you from?" Fisk asked.

She stared ahead. "Why?"

"Just curious."

"Don't you already have that information?"

"Do you always answer a question with another question?"

"I'll answer your question if you answer one of mine. Magnus Jenssen died of a fast-moving cancer, the symptoms of which were almost identical to previous cases of poisoning by polonium-210."

Hell, he thought.

She went on. "Three days later, at Memorial Sloan Kettering Cancer Center, you received an injection of a protein called 'granulocyte colony-stimulating factor' as a treatment for radiation sickness. Do you expect anyone to believe that that's a coincidence?"

She wasn't just fishing this time. Obviously, she'd learned of his admission to the cancer treatment center. He needed to make sure she didn't learn the full truth. Jenssen had plotted to kill former president George W. Bush and hundreds of spectators at the Ground Zero ceremony, and he came within a fraction of an eyelash of succeeding. He did succeed in killing Fisk's girlfriend, Krina, in the process essentially snuffing Fisk's life as well. Or so it had seemed at the time, when Fisk used the oven in his kitchen—for the first time in the two years that he'd lived in the Sutton Place apartment—to bake a cupcake for Jenssen.

Along with flour, baking powder, butter, sugar, and frosting, Fisk added a microgram of the polonium-210 that had been confiscated—fittingly, he thought—from Jenssen's Swedish Muslim terrorist brethren. The thick foil wrapper was supposed to shield Fisk from radiation exposure when he brought the cupcake to Jenssen at the Metropolitan Correctional Center. Like his plan for retribution, it seemed to work at first. Jenssen ate the cupcake and died. Almost immediately, Fisk regretted his plan—and that was before the bleeding and the unrelenting fever kicked in. Then he considered that it would have been wrong to let Jenssen live. So he'd been neither right nor wrong. It was a gray area. Unfortunately, a jury wouldn't see it that way.

"I was kind of hoping you'd ask me a sports question," he said.

"He gets cancer, you get radiation sickness. That's just a coincidence?"

He felt an urge to tell her. Cathartic? Maybe. Stupid? Definitely.

The signal saved him from having to lie: with a pop, a bright red Styrofoam orb, like a kickball, flew up from the area of the river where the divers had submerged. A matching nylon streamer tailed it. Both settled to a bob on the surface.

This signified that the drone had been found.

The UAV was "rendered safe"—declared free of booby traps and other hazards—by scuba divers from the FBI's Hazardous Devices Operations Section, then placed in a special transparent polycarbonate case with the dimensions of a steamer trunk. Fisk and Chay had their first glimpse of the drone—a quadrocopter similar to Peavy's—when the NYPD Harbor Patrol officers winched the evidence case onto the stern of one of their cruisers. A member of the Bureau's Evidence Response Team videotaped every step for the chain-of-custody log.

When the Harbor Patrol boat docked at the pier, three crewmen were required to dolly the heavy evidence case up the steep gangway. One of the divers opened the door and the other two hoisted the evidence case into the cargo bay of the black late-model Chevy Suburban—unmarked, but unmistakably a "G-Ride"—that would take the quadrocopter 250 miles to the FBI laboratory at the Marine Corps base in Quantico, Virginia.

Locally the Bureau could log all of the serial numbers from the quadrocopter and the rifle, assigning them as leads for agents to follow. Locally the Bureau could also check for fingerprints and blood, but that was basically the extent of it; as far as forensics went, field offices didn't have a fraction of the equipment seen in the evidence lab on a typical *CSI* show. In Quantico, specialists on a TEU—Trace

Evidence Unit—would search microscopically for trace materials like human hair, textile fibers, fabric, soil, and building materials.

The divers huddled with three other men: the FBI evidence unit's supervisory agent, the forensics operations director, and the logistical management specialist, all with clipboards thick with FD-192s, the Bureau's evidence data-loading forms. They also packed FD-1004s, the evidence chain-of-custody forms, among other documents, one of which yielded carbon copies using actual carbon paper. Outside of the FBI, Fisk had seen carbon paper only one other time: to duplicate the parent signature on his first elementary school report card.

With a wave at all of the paperwork, he asked Chay, "Ever wonder if the word 'bureaucracy' originated at the Bureau?"

She smiled. Only politely, he thought. From behind the smile, he suspected, she viewed him as a criminal.

He wandered over to the Suburban, where the drone sat in the evidence case between two duffel bags, like just another piece of luggage.

Chay followed him in true shadow fashion. "What are you looking for?"

"Ideally, the killer's name," he said. "Short of that, any clue that will get us to his name."

She read aloud from the fuselage: "Specter." The sporty red logo of the drone's manufacturer featured an *S* drawn in the shape of a ghost.

The Specter's fuselage was shaped like an X, with sleek and sturdy black rotors atop each of its four arms. A polypropylene protective hull fit over the fuselage, branching into four loops, all of them six inches in diameter, each surrounding a rotor. Parallel staple-shaped brackets hung five or six inches from the base of the fuselage, supporting a block of black foam that had been hollowed to accommodate the rifle. Waterlogged now, the foam drooped, enabling Fisk to glimpse the stripped-down barrel, its magazine, and a Band-Aid tin wedged beside it.

From the tin sprang three thin rubber-coated wires. He couldn't see where they went, but he figured that one wire terminated at the scope's eyepiece. The second wire would lead to an actuator in the form of a tiny robotic arm that adjusted the barrel. The last wire probably fed a similar contraption that either pushed the trigger toward the stock or bypassed the trigger and directly released the hammer.

One of the rotor blades was bent at its midpoint, while the other three lay flat. The Styrofoam loop surrounding the bent rotor looked to have been split or sliced in two. A jagged hairline fissure separated the two pieces. Probably an accident had caused the quadrocopter to go swimming, or damaged it to the point that Yodeler was unable to get the thing home, causing him to ditch it.

"How long will it take Quantico to return the results?" Chay asked.

"Could be a day, could be weeks. Depends on caseloads, and, mostly, Weir and Evans. Even to walk the four blocks here from their office, they need to fill out an 'electronic communication' stating their plan, and get written approval."

Chay sighed. "At least Yodeler doesn't have his drone anymore."

Fisk was about to challenge her supposition, but instead held his tongue.

The job is fun, and it's easy," Mrs. Herzog, the head of Upper West Side Daycare, told Mary Rose Chaney. "You just have to escort small groups of four- and five-year-olds either to the playground in Central Park or to the Museum of Natural History, all of four blocks round trip."

Mary Rose, a nineteen-year-old Cornell University student home for the summer, loved children. She worried, though, about the responsibility of safeguarding them in the streets of New York. It didn't ease her mind any during the subsequent classroom visit when Alice, the grouchy senior teacher she stood to assist, said, "The hard part is protecting other humans from these monsters. If Mrs. Herzog told job candidates the truth, which is that we should get combat pay for the outings, you think anybody would ever sign on here?"

Mary Rose was in her sixth week without finding work—or, as her father had put it that morning, she was in her "thirty-seventh day of unemployment." So she accepted the job at the day-care center.

Today was her second day on the job. She was still frazzled from the first. Fortunately this morning's outing, to the Hall of Ocean Life at the Museum of Natural History, had been uneventful. Not a single mad potty dash in the whole hour! Alice led the group out of the museum now, towing the Walkodile, a green vinyl leash with two rows of four harnesses, one row to either side of the leash, accommodating eight children. ("Don't call it a leash," Mrs. Herzog had insisted. "It's a walking rope.") Mary Rose brought up the rear—the caboose, Ethan called her. The train-obsessed four-year-old had memorized the entire Metro North New Haven–to–Grand Central schedule (his grandmother lived in a New Haven suburb). He walked just ahead of Mary Rose. It was an idyllic sunny afternoon, the air mild with a hint of dogwood blossoms. Not that Mary Rose could enjoy any of it. She walked on the balls of her feet, her knees tensed, ready to spring forward to the aid of a child who stumbled. The Walkodile was designed so that if one child fell, he or she couldn't pull down the others, meaning that the child who fell could be dragged along. It had happened twice on Central Park West yesterday. That was why Mary Rose wore her New Balances today instead of her usual clogs.

Descending the steep granite staircase, she realized that she'd never previously considered just how sharp the edge of a step could be. Each one looked capable of severing a small limb, if, say, a child lost balance and were dragged by the seven others to whom he was tethered.

"Thirty-three, thirty-four, thirty-five," said Ethan, his glance preceding them down the stairs. "Is that the world's record for stairs?"

"I don't think so," said Mary Rose.

"Careful now, people," Alice barked as she took the first step.

The group followed—like it or not, Mary Rose thought. The Walkodile meant that while the four

kids on the left side could now grip the banister, the
four on the right had nothing to hold. The group
was jerking Olivia—third kid back on the right,
the tiniest of the bunch—so that her tiny pink left
Nike came down onto air where she was expecting
a step. The little girl gasped, then dangled, arms
flailing, before her sneaker landed on the next stair
down. She regained her balance and continued on
as if nothing had happened. Still Mary Rose's heart
beat at twice its normal rate. Although it couldn't be
much more than seventy-five out, hot perspiration
sprang from her scalp and spilled down her forehead.

The steps were dotted with a lunch-hour crowd,
professionals who worked nearby joining tourists
in a picnic catered by an array of food carts parked
below, on the Central Park West sidewalk. Obsta-
cles, Mary Rose thought of the picnickers. Fortunately, many got up to clear a path for the children.
Many more glared at Mary Rose. Yesterday, some
crazy old bat hissed at her, "They're children, not
dogs." As if a nineteen-year-old assistant teacher
made the day-care center rules. Today she ignored
the people. Had to. She focused on the little feet,
feeling their way down, her stomach clenching
anew with each step.

The group successfully navigated the first flight,
passing the giant bronze statue of Teddy Roosevelt
on horseback, when Mary Rose noticed the drone.
It rose slowly from the stairwell leading to the underground Eighty-First Street subway station. Nate,
her boyfriend, had one like it: the kind with four
propellers. Nate's older brother had one too. The
two of them played some sort of game with them,

firing virtual missiles at each other in their parents' backyard in Westchester.

This one must be some kind of publicity stunt, she thought, maybe a promo for a *Terminator*-type movie. This area was Publicity Stunt Central. She had heard that last week a hot-air balloon had landed in the park advertising some new real estate site. Also, not one but two people dressed in Chuck E. Cheese suits had shown up at the playground, fifteen minutes apart, to hand out discount coupons for the arcade or something like that. The kids had leaped off the jungle gym and then sprinted to see Chuck—both times.

Mary Rose hoped they wouldn't notice the drone. It was hard to discern its high-pitched buzz from the jackhammers and car horns. Once they saw it, it would be tough to contain them. Other grown-ups began to notice it. Suddenly heads in the crowd turned in unison, like stalks in a wheat field swept by a single gust. They took in the drone, now floating toward the museum. Most people quickly returned to what they'd been doing, to their sandwiches or to whatever was adhering them to their phones.

"Look!" squealed Madison A., a future cheerleader for sure, second kid down on the right, her arm like a fixed bayonet pointing at the drone.

"Wow!" said Ethan. "A flying robot."

Only Olivia kept silent, standing on her toes but still unable to see over the boy in front of her, Derek, who was a head taller than any of the others. Mary Rose remembered his name because today, just like yesterday—and, according to Alice, every day—he wore a New York Yankees shirt.

Madison B. jumped to get a better look, without thinking where on the staircase she might land, or how. In a flash, Mary Rose shot forward and wrapped her arms around the girl, catching her.

Mary Rose then felt the tug of all of the other kids at once, launching themselves and their combined three hundred pounds toward the "flying toy." All of them except Ethan, who remained in place to declare, "It's not a toy, it's a quadrocopter." Or rather he tried to remain in place. The Walkodile pulled him into the air like a kite.

Mary Rose lunged, coming up with a fistful of his gym shorts. She set him down and tried to rein in the rest. Combined, they were too powerful. It was let go or be dragged face first down the stairs.

"Halt!" Alice screamed, her brows dropping and her chin jutting into her fiercest "teacher face."

The kids put on the brakes. All, incredibly, remained afoot.

Alice inhaled, apparently fixing to deliver a stern rebuke. Her attention was diverted by a collective megawatt smile from the children. The drone was heading right for them, with an increase in altitude of a few inches as it passed over each step.

The kids called to it, as if it were a puppy.

Mary Rose looked to Alice, who, like her, grabbed on to one end of the Walkodile. "I guess it can't hurt to look at it," the teacher said. Turning to her charges, she added gruffly, "If you can stay still, monsters. Those propeller blades can chop off your fingers."

"They're rotor blades," said Ethan.

Alice asked, "What's the difference?"

"Propellers propel, rotors lift."

"Can rotor blades hurt you?"

"Yes."

"Okay, then. Be still, all of you!"

The tide of people going up and down stepped aside to let the drone pass. Pointing at the black block of foam the drone carried, a middle-aged man said to the woman accompanying him, "That looks like a rifle."

The woman with him stopped and stared at the metallic cylinder—like a gun barrel—that protruded from the foam. "Can't be . . ." she said, more hopeful than certain.

"Better safe than sorry." Grabbing her elbow, he led her away.

What if he's right? Mary Rose wondered. This sure wasn't like any publicity stunt or promotional gimmick she'd ever seen. The drone carried no ad or signage, save SPECTER, whatever that was, in fairly small letters that she had been unable to make out until right now, as the thing came to within ten feet.

"Maybe we should go," she said to Alice, having to raise her voice over the buzz of the rotors.

"No," the kids pleaded at once. "Please!"

Alice looked over their heads to Mary Rose, with entreaty of her own. "Why not stay one minute?" she said, waving at the kids, standing still in two rows. Mary Rose interpreted Alice's question as, "I get so few of these moments when the rug rats' attention is fully occupied, where I can relax. Why not just let me enjoy it?"

Mary Rose relented in spite of the fear clawing her intestines.

The drone descended so that the barrel sat at

her eye level, allowing her to see into the gaps in the foam to either side of it. The barrel—gunmetal gray—had a worn authenticity. It lacked the usual sleek shell of a rifle barrel, but its various bolts and pins and vents seemed designed for specific and genuine functions, as opposed to the relatively random placement on toy guns or the arcade versions. And the telescope atop it had no frills whatsoever, the way the good toys do.

"Alice, I think it has a *G-U-N*," Mary Rose said, cupping her hands on the nearest shoulders, aiming to steer the kids away.

"A gun?" Ethan asked.

"I so want to get a gun!" exclaimed Derek.

An illuminated red dot appeared at his hairline and slid down his forehead. The barrel traced its path.

Goose bumps jumped up all over Mary Rose's body. She knew—or at least she felt that she did—that things were about to get very bad. She stepped between Derek and the drone. The red dot reappeared on her shirtfront.

"Let's go. Now!" she barked, tugging her end of the leash.

The kids didn't heed her order, yet, somehow, as though she'd come into superstrength, the whole Walkodile came with her. It took a beat for Alice to help; it appeared that she first had to process the situation and then shake off her shock. Soon they were moving down the stairs, their twenty feet moving in sync and at a good pace. Unfortunately, the drone stayed with them, the red dot fluttering about Mary Rose's shirtfront, seemingly trying to fasten itself to the area of her heart.

Gathering the two nearest children toward her, the younger of the two day-care teachers turned her back to the quadrocopter and attempted to inch down the Museum of Natural History steps.

Two views of the scene, one recorded by the Department's Domain Awareness cam at Eighty-First Street and Central Park West, the other from the museum's security camera, were projected onto giant screens at the front of the secure auditorium at the NYO, the FBI's New York headquarters at 26 Federal Plaza.

Like the Strategic Information and Operations Center in Washington, this windowless SCIF accommodated more than a hundred people, each in a comfortable leather desk chair at a workstation with a landline telephone, a pair of power outlets, a legal pad with the Department of Justice logo, a cup holder, and an adjustable desk lamp. The sort of place where you stayed awhile. This was where the 9/11 Commission had been entrenched.

Fisk sat at the farthest of five concentric half-circular table rows from the screens, watching the laser marker run up the young day-care worker's sternum and the back of her neck. The red dot settled on the base of the skull, above the medulla oblongata, the part of the brain stem that controls the heart and lungs. Fisk felt the collective cringe of the hundred law enforcement people in attendance. Snipers, this crowd surely knew, aim for the center of the medulla oblongata, the "apricot." From this proximity, even if the Ultimate Sniper app made colossal errors in calculating the effects of wind direction or velocity, the AR-15 aboard the drone would have zero difficulty in killing the woman. The only question was whether the round would bore through her and then into the head of the tall boy in the Yankees jersey.

The quadrocopter pivoted toward the museum entrance, the laser dot falling on the face of the bronze Teddy Roosevelt, allowing the two teachers to hurry off, towing their charges with one of those giant multikid leashes that had become increasingly popular in the city. The device then drifted up the steps, where people hurried out of the way. Although the NYPD Domain Awareness cam provided audio, their dialogue was lost beneath the high-pitched whirring of the rotors. But it was clear from their faces that they had grown quite aware that this was no kid's toy or publicity stunt.

"Here comes our hero," said Weir, who stood at the lectern at the head of the room.

Both screens shifted to the Domain Awareness cam's view of the middle-aged African American man bursting out of the museum lobby and onto the steps. He wore a Museum of Natural History security guard's uniform, which resembled the NYPD's summer class-B uni, the one with the light blue short-sleeve shirt. He drew a "26"—a twenty-six-inch black polycarbonate straight baton—as he charged the drone, meanwhile shouting to the people standing around watching—instructions to get to safety, based on their rapid departures.

The guard circled the Teddy Roosevelt statue, meanwhile winding the baton back, apparently trying to sneak up on the quadrocopter and swat it from behind. As he stepped in front of Roosevelt's horse, the drone spun around, as if it had sensed his presence. Its gun barrel flashed twice. Explosive reports drowned out all other sounds.

The guard staggered backward, bloodstains blooming on his shirtfront, and crashed into the pedestal. More blood splashed the horse's forelegs. He appeared to be unconscious by the time he'd slid to the base of the granite pedestal. Around him, people ran screaming in horror or dropped to the ground themselves, in order to present the smallest target to the drone.

"Security guard Earl Johnson was pronounced dead in the ER at Mount Sinai at one twenty-three P.M.," Weir said.

Fisk cursed himself for not doing more to get Yodeler.

"And this is the last anyone saw of the shooter." Weir waved at the screen nearest him, which, like the others, played a low camera angle of the drone descending the stairs to the subway, like just another hurried commuter. People trying to flee into the stations flung themselves out of the way, into the walls of the stairwell. Those exiting the station quickly got the picture one way or the other and did likewise. Another camera showed the drone sailing over the turnstile at head level, again parting the commuters before descending to a train platform and disappearing into the dark tunnel.

"The end," said Weir. "The thing headed into the D and F train tunnel uptown, where the MTA's got no more cameras, and it hasn't turned up on any others."

The screens reverted to a map of the United States and the FBI shield with the scales of justice and the motto *Fidelity, Bravery, Loyalty*.

"Now let's turn to putting this SOB in the Box." Weir's reference to the Metropolitan Correctional Center's SHU—the infamous special housing unit—drew a smattering of applause. Like Fisk himself, most of the audience seemed to be waiting to hear the FBI agent's plan before cheering it.

"Detective Fisk of NYPD Intel has been leading an initiative to draw Yodeler into negotiations over the release of Merritt Verlyn, to at least put the shootings on hold, but . . ." Weir cocked his head at the giant video screens, frozen on the image of people screaming in horror on the steps in front of the Museum of Natural History.

Fisk tasted bile. Had the agent meant to imply that the guard's death had been a consequence of the lack of progress in the negotiation?

"Here's the latest from Yodeler," Weir said as the image shifted from the e-mail Fisk had received from makarov228 on the way here:

Jeremy:
Another day, another death. Tomorrow too is another day, and tomorrow too there shall be another victim, needlessly, unless . . .
Yodeler

Before sending his response, Fisk had shared a draft of it with Weir and Evans. He sat with them in a borrowed office down the hall, watching their brows furrow and their lips purse as they each read over the draft, which had been printed out and carried in to them by a secretary. Fisk, who had e-mailed it to them ahead of time, had no idea why they couldn't have just read the thing on their phones.

Dear Yodeler:
Be reasonable. Democracy entails due process. Even if the president himself decided to pardon Verlyn, the process would realistically take several days. Hold off for, say, 48 hours, until I give you a detailed progress report? You seem somewhat intelligent. Is that asking too much?
Det. Jeremy Fisk

Weir sighed. "This is just gonna honk him off."

"Part of him believes we're going to release Verlyn because of what he's doing."

"But that's crazy."

"I think so too, but if he agreed with us, he wouldn't be doing this."

Evans weighed in with a click of his tongue, his version of raising a hand. Thus getting Fisk and Weir's attention, he said, "Why not ask him to please be reasonable?"

"If any of the digs works, if he gets hot enough under the collar to fire off a response, mission accomplished," Fisk said. "The hope is he'll slip up and we'll find out where he sent his angry response from."

Weir and Evans shared a look known to any child who has just told his parents of a wild plan involving the family car. Weir then shook his head. "You tell him."

"His last e-mail was from Diego Garcia," Evans said. "Do you know what that is?"

Fisk did. "Tropical island in the Indian Ocean."

"Do you know about the U.S. Navy base there?"

"Yes."

"Do you know about the CIA black site down the beach from it?"

"I've heard the rumors, sure."

"The rumors are accurate. Diego Garcia is British territory, the facility was used for interrogation techniques prohibited on U.S. soil. The facility was closed over a year ago. Completely razed."

Fisk knew most of this. The rest, he guessed, he could have learned on any of a thousand spook fanboy websites.

"Ain't no one there now but the crabs," added Weir.

Evans sighed. "Yet it's where Yodeler's e-mail originated."

"Good," Fisk said. "We've learned that he knows his black sites, and that he's got mad tech skills if he can make it seem like he and his ten-buck burner phone are transmitting from there."

Now, in the NYO secure auditorium, as their e-mailed response to Yodeler was projected, Weir gave a brief summation of Fisk's rationale, adding with, "We're rooting for Detective Fisk to be on the money."

In other words, Fisk thought, if things went

wrong, the FBI had distanced itself from the communication. And if things went right, the Bureau had supported it. Standard CYA procedure—Cover Your Ass.

"So here's what we've got on tap," Weir went on. "The op name was chosen at random, in case you're wondering." With a nod, he cued Evans, who hurried into action with his laptop. Both of the big screens launched a PowerPoint slide show, commencing with, in bold white letters on black that reminded Fisk of an action movie title, OPERATION QUIZ SHOW.

"First up is ATF," said Weir, trading nods with someone seated in the front row of tables, the screens dissolved to the official shield of the Bureau of Alcohol, Tobacco, Firearms and Explosives, which also featured the scales of justice. "They're sending up two of their mobile crime labs. Technicians will be able to analyze bullets and shell casings at the scene, rather than waiting on Quantico. Now, casings and bullets can be cross-checked instantly against the ballistic evidence database at ATF's national lab down in Rockville. They're also deploying eighty-five of their special agents."

Good, thought Fisk. Boots on the ground. Finally. And top-quality boots. The ATF agents were a breed apart in terms of their ability to canvas neighborhoods and ferret out weapons.

The screens shifted to the Secret Service's star insignia superimposed over a photograph of four Secret Service agents guarding President Obama during an outdoor speech. Weir said, "Secret Service will also be assisting local police. They have units dedicated to protecting against the sort of scenario we're facing."

The next slide up, a photograph of a blonde wearing a blue jacket the back of which was nearly filled with FBI EVIDENCE RESPONSE TEAM. She was snapping a photograph of a midnineties SUV at a gas pump—a Beltway sniper crime scene, Fisk guessed.

"Also the Bureau has some four hundred agents around the country working the case, following leads on the gun we recovered earlier today, talking to people at every UAV manufacturer, every hobby shop, checking out social media. We've issued a carefully crafted note telling the public that we have reason to believe there's a sniper and requesting their help. Plus we've set up a toll-free number and a reward and a Web presence to collect tips from the public, with teams of our agents-in-training working the phones."

Fisk got the familiar sense that something was wrong, that the operation was missing something. He couldn't put a finger on what.

Weir had the bases covered, including—and this perhaps was an historic first—working in concert with the NYPD: the Department's Emergency Service Unit was deploying to rooftops and other appropriate vantage points along with the countersniper division, just to look for drones. Also, to intercept drones, Intel chief Dubin had brought in a team from NYPD's office in Tel Aviv, Israel, which had been established to gather intelligence on Middle Eastern threats at the source. The team would deploy in New York City a version of Israel's vaunted Iron Dome, the mobile all-weather air system that uses state-of-the-art APG-70 radar to detect short-range rockets and artillery shells fired from distances of four to seventy kilometers away, and, lately, Hamas unmanned aerial vehicles. APG-70 saw everything bigger than a baseball, through rain or even thick fog.

In addition, the Air Force would deploy a trio of Boeing E-3 AWACs Sentries, the aircraft that carried the distinctive thirty-foot-in-diameter rotating radar domes, capable of detecting and tracking hostile aircraft operating at low altitudes over any terrain. Commissioner Bratton had assigned one of the Department's Hercules teams—elite, heavily armed, Special Forces–type police units—along with the NYPD aviation unit, 24/7, based on a pattern analysis of killings.

The Aviation Division had fifty-seven cops in four Agusta A119 Koalas and three Bell 412s, each of which were equipped with 360-degree cameras and sophisticated sensors far more sensitive than those normally used by police. If that gang didn't know already how to intercept a drone, Fisk would bet they were at their Floyd Bennett Field base in Brooklyn being briefed right now.

What's more, Weir went on, the JTTF was bringing in the intelligence community and its satellites. If that weren't enough, the JSS—the Joint Surveillance System of the U.S. Air Force and the FAA for the atmospheric air defense of North America—was in on the act. Weir had sent in everyone but the Marines.

The sum total was that Weir had managed to galvanize his fellow law enforcement officers into action; the room practically buzzed with their electricity.

Fisk wondered what was eating at him.

The crowd applauded and banged approval onto the table rows when Evans reprised the Operation Quiz Show slide, this time with the insignias of two dozen agencies beneath it, the way corporate benefactors are listed on the backs of the T-shirts given out at benefit 5Ks.

And it hit Fisk: for all of its might and sophistication and number of boots, the joint operation had overlooked the simplest and fastest way to determine Yodeler's identity: ask Merritt Verlyn.

Fisk found Chay in the FBI cafeteria, at the table where he'd left her prior to the meeting in the SCIF—her cup of coffee still full, her sandwich still in its plastic wrap. She was typing furiously on a tablet computer.

"How about a fresh cup of coffee?" he asked her.

"Um . . ." She kept typing. "No, thanks."

"Anything?"

Eyes on her screen, she raised her index finger, for an instant, then returned it to typing.

Fisk waited. Ten seconds, fifteen.

Finally she looked up.

He was only mildly curious about what she was working on, but primarily because interest seemed appropriate, he asked, "Are you writing about the incident at the Museum of Natural History?"

"There's not much I could write about that that hasn't already been on every major news outlet, and every minor outlet. I've been trying to come up with a response to the blogger."

"Which blogger?"

She grumbled. "The *Mighty Pen*."

"Should I know the *Mighty Pen*?"

"No, definitely not, but, unfortunately, a lot of people do. The *Pen* thinks of itself as New York's answer to the *Drudge Report*, and just about every day they get on the *New York Times* for being a tool of the liberal elite. Check out their 'reporting' on the Museum of Natural History . . ."

Holding up the tablet, she tapped a headline.

Times Reporter in Bed with NYPD Intel
on Drone Killer Story

She said, "The story devotes maybe a column inch to the arrangement the paper made with Dubin so that I would withhold the story that the killer was using a drone, his demand that Merritt Verlyn be released, et cetera."

"Any idea how they found out about it?" Fisk asked.

"Leaked by an insider." Her face tightened, as though she'd swallowed something bitter. "Presumably at the paper."

A teachable moment, Fisk thought. But that would rub salt in her wound.

Returning her focus to the tablet, she said, "This is basically a feature-length insinuation that the *Times* is now a wholly owned subsidiary of the NYPD, aiding and abetting the department in its cover-ups. And of course that the blood of the Museum of Natural History security guard, Earl Johnson, is on my hands." She resumed typing. "I'm trying to set the record straight."

She had her work cut out for her, he thought. She had lost a major exclusive, and deserving or not, she might well wind up on the metro beat until she could mend her credibility—if she could mend it. Yesterday he would have seen a net gain in this turn of events: he was rid of her on this case, and rooting for her removal from the intel beat, especially the Jenssen story. Today, though, he needed her. And his leverage was depleted. Almost. Taking the chair across the table from her, he played his one remaining card. "The *Mighty Pen* doesn't mention Yodeler?"

She shook her head.

He asked, "Would you like the exclusive on him, all the way to his capture?"

She typed another forty or fifty characters, so fast that her fingers were a blur. "That's awfully nice of you," she said sardonically.

"I'll need one thing in return."

"I never would have guessed."

"I want to go talk to Verlyn at the U.S. marshals' office."

She stiffened. "Why?"

"If you ask him if he knows Yodeler, there's a chance he might answer."

Her gaze dropped to her monitor. She typed a few words, then looked up. "I can try, but one thing I need first."

Surprise, surprise. "What?"

"Just a bit of info, on the record, for the story I'm writing."

"What do you want to know?"

"What does the public need to know?"

"The Department now has reason to believe that a killer has used a miniature unmanned aerial vehicle armed with a rifle in four different killings. We're requesting the public's help in bringing Yodeler to justice. I don't know yet, but I suspect there will be a substantial reward offered for any information leading to his apprehension."

Chay returned her attention to her tablet and began typing again. Without looking up, she asked, "Why didn't you tell the public about this before?"

"We weren't certain he was using the UAV until this morning."

"Oh, please." Hitting the return key with much more force than was necessary, she glared across the table. "You suspected it was a drone two murders ago. Otherwise I wouldn't be here right now."

Fisk exhorted himself to remain calm. Without her, Verlyn would only meet if U.S. marshals dragged him to the meeting. "You already agreed that the drone theory was on background only. That's why you're here right now."

She folded her arms. "Off the record and for my background use only, has this case informed the way you would approach a future case, if you suspected that a serial killer were using a drone?"

Fisk readied the stock answer, that in a case where the full information was explosive enough to create public panic, it was in everyone's best interest to withhold information, especially if disseminating the information jeopardized an investigation. But that answer didn't sit well with him, for some reason. He replied, in all sincerity, "You were right before about giving the public a heads-up."

She regarded him with disbelief.

"Really," he said. "I wouldn't have speculated for public consumption that there was a madman with a weaponized drone. But I would have floated a cover story to inform the public of a drone presence, something that implied a risk so that people would be observant, and so that those who did see the drone would keep their distance. The cover story might have been something innocuous enough on the surface, but still have had the effect of keeping them safe. For instance, the device is malfunctioning and could suddenly discharge rapidly spinning and dangerous rotor blades, or crash. So definitely avoid contact, maintain considerable distance from the device, and immediately report any sighting and location to the police."

Chay looked him over, as if reappraising him. "I'm impressed," she said. "Not that many people are willing to admit to their mistakes."

Fisk suspected she was talking about something else. "What else do you want?"

"What else would you ask if you were me?"

A smart question, he thought, particularly if he were withholding something. "Information on the victim?"

"Got it already. While you were sitting around upstairs, all of the details that a reporter could ever want came across my Twitter news feed alone— did you know that the victim, Earl Johnson, briefly played second base in the San Diego Padres organization?

"Already the public demand for Verlyn's release is so intense, the biggest question I had was whether the discussion would shut the Internet down."

"So do you have what you need to write your piece now?" he asked.

She stood up, in the same motion dropping the tablet into her shoulder bag. "I already filed the story. Let's go."

While walking with Chay from the FBI to the Metropolitan Correctional Center on Park Row, Fisk wondered if they were witnessing the early stages of a public panic.

The two-block walk would have ordinarily taken them four or five minutes, but this afternoon, it would be half that time: The Wall Street rush-hour crowd was noticeably thinner than usual. He guessed that many people had left work early. And those out now were literally in a rush, all oddly quiet too—as if no one wanted to be slowed down by chatting. The air seemed to buzz with their tension.

Foley Square, typically a hive at this hour on summer days with government agency staffers celebrating the end of the workday, was deserted save for stragglers hurrying across it. The hot-dog vendor and Italian-ice vendor huddled in conversation; no customers waited at either of their carts— whatever the hot-dog man said prompted the other man to hurriedly collapse his cart's sun umbrella.

As Fisk and Chay rounded the corner onto Park Row, they heard a screech of tires and a deep and resounding metal-on-metal crash. At the far end of Park Row was a taxi, the hood of which had practically become one with the side of a parked UPS delivery truck. Standing on the street with the UPS man, the cabdriver pointed to the sky, as if in explanation. An NYPD patrolman tried to reach them on foot but was besieged by passersby asking questions, looking over their shoulders and up, or both.

Chay asked Fisk, "What can we do to keep people from panicking?"

"One thing." He pointed to the Metropolitan Correctional Center at the far end of the block and said, "Let them know when we've put the killer in there."

At first glance, the federal administrative detention facility looked like a modern high-rise. A closer look said something was amiss, or even sinister. Most of the windows were slits, like the rectangular peepholes on the doors to the cells themselves. Other windows were entirely blacked out. The facility's reputation as a squalid hellhole explained the wide berth it was given by pedestrians. New Yorkers all knew it contained the worst of the worst among its population of eight hundred, crammed into a space for half that many. They'd seen the news clips of Junior Gotti, Bernie Madoff, Ramzi Yousef, and Magnus Jenssen hop-marched through its dark subterranean tunnels, shackled at the ankles, chained at the waist, wrists cuffed.

Inside, Fisk saw on Chay's face the same surprise he always saw on first-time visitors: the facility was far from the dungeon they imagined. The common area Fisk and Chay were led past, by a Metropolitan Correctional Center's escorting officer, resembled those at a modern university student center: airy, done in cheery colors, contemporary IKEA-type tables and chairs, arcade-quality Foosball and air-hockey tables, and a stunning amount of elbow room by Manhattan standards.

The cells weren't much larger than the bunk beds inside them, but rather than cramped or constricting, they appeared cozy, like sleeping berths on European trains, everything white, the mattresses surprisingly thick and inviting. Other than security-risk cases, who were limited to tele-visits, inmates here met friends and family members in a common institutional visiting area that accommodated a hundred people at a time. Inmates working with lawyers could qualify for small private meeting spaces within the institutional visiting area.

A guard took Fisk and Chay to the sixth floor in Private Visitation Room E, "private visitation" serving as a euphemism for interrogation; these rooms essentially belonged to law enforcement officers and prosecutors. Like all of the facility's private visitation rooms, this one had a two-way mirror fronting an adjacent observation room, and it was wired with concealed video cameras and microphones. Otherwise it was forgettable, a drab twelve-by-twelve-foot space.

Fisk and Chay took chairs on one side of a sturdy metal table that was bolted to the floor. Soon thereafter, the guard returned with Verlyn, who lit up at the sight of them.

"Ms. Maryland, Detective Fisk, I hope I haven't kept you waiting," he said breathlessly. His lilting voice was at odds with his sturdy, angular Teutonic features. As was so often the case, the dossier, even with its plethora of videotaped interviews, hadn't captured the subject's character.

Fisk had learned that Verlyn was a bright guy from New Canaan, Connecticut, who'd compensated for a lack of social skills with raw intelligence, earning a scholarship to the Massachusetts Institute of Technology. Despite completing just two semesters at the school, he went on to work in a series of high-profile government systems positions. Now he reminded Fisk of an overly busy party host trying his damnedest to please everyone.

Striding up to the table, Verlyn extended his right hand until his escorting officer, a big man with tired eyes, cleared his throat. Verlyn's hand dropped to his side almost immediately. Fisk guessed Verlyn had been excessively sociable more than once before. Physical contact in these rooms was prohibited.

"Hi, Merritt," Chay said, but without the familiarity Fisk had expected, or the congeniality he'd hoped for.

"We're good," Fisk told the escorting officer.

With a nod, the man withdrew, the door thudding shut behind him.

"Thank you," Verlyn said.

"You're welcome," said Fisk, although his request for the escorting officer to wait outside hadn't been made out of consideration for Verlyn, but to allow the inmate to talk more freely. For that same reason, Fisk had also requested an interrogation room without the metal mesh divider between interrogator and inmate. In general, however, Fisk wanted his interrogation subjects to be uncomfortable. For that reason, by design, the chair reserved for Verlyn wobbled, the metal tip on one of the front legs clattering against the tile floor.

Earlier, per Fisk's request, a U.S. marshal had removed the leg's rubber tip. The ideal seating for the subject of an interrogation was a wobbly swivel rocking chair on wheels, with loose armrests, because it amplified the movements of the parts of his body that anchored him, his feet and his elbow and his ass, known as "anchor parts." People discharge anxiety through their anchor parts, which gives the interrogator an indicator of nonverbal deceptive behavior.

Verlyn might talk a blue streak. More than anything, Fisk needed to know what was true.

"So, how are we doing today?" Verlyn asked as he dropped into the chair, his air of enthusiasm unaffected by the wobble. Like this was happy hour at his favorite tavern.

"Can't complain," Fisk said, before starting the interview with a textbook rapport builder: "How are the accommodations here?" He might have instead let fly with *Merritt, who the hell is Yodeler?* But casual conversation created a nonthreatening atmosphere. Get Verlyn going on neutral topics about which he had no reason to lie, like the weather or what they served here for breakfast, and it would be easier to tell when and if he began to lie.

"How do I like it here?" Verlyn said, essentially repeating Fisk's question, which was troublesome. To buy time to think, a person bent on deception often repeats a question or takes an inordinate amount of time before answering. Verlyn had no reason to lie about the accommodations, but he might be attempting to throw a wrench into Fisk's efforts at establishing a baseline for honesty so that later on, when the small talk was in the rearview, he could pause to buy time with impunity.

"It's funny that you should ask that, Detective," Verlyn went on, his big gray eyes sparkling. "When I first started at the NSA in 2004, I was typically at work by eight thirty in the morning and stayed until after midnight, then spent another forty-five minutes to an hour driving to and from Georgetown, where I'd managed to buy low on a condo. Because that was my routine six days a week, sometimes all seven, there was little time for anything else, on top of which the job itself was quite stressful. Consequently I began to have a recurring dream, the only one that I've ever had, in which I was arrested on some odd technicality—like the character Josef K. in Kafka's *The Trial*—and then taken to a Spartan penal facility where my cell resembled the room I'd had in the dorms my freshman year at MIT: a single bed, a tiny desk, whitewashed cinder blocks, and that was it. And in the dream, I loved being imprisoned, because I was able to catch up on sleep and reading and thinking; in a way, it was the ultimate intellectual's vacation. And this place"—he indicated the surroundings with a wave—"has actually been better than the one in my dream, by a fair margin. They have e-book readers, and the food is pretty good . . ."

This overly specific answer—the question had been simply how were his accommodations, and "fine" would have sufficed in response—put Fisk on guard. He'd seen this before, with subjects bent on deception: they inundate you with unrelated facts intended to enhance your perception of them. In maybe half a minute, Verlyn had dropped MIT (never mind that he'd been expelled after his freshman year for poor grades), his work ethic, a knowledge of modern European literature, that he was an intellectual, and the Georgetown condo he managed to buy at the bottom of the market—what a modest guy. When the interview shifted gears, he could now get away with obscuring what he knew of Yodeler by piling superfluous detail upon superfluous detail. Alternately, he was simply insecure and hungry for attention, hence his self-aggrandizing essay-length response, not to mention his star turn as a whistle-blower.

As Verlyn detailed the Metropolitan Correctional Center food and its surprisingly creative ambience, Fisk looked for other signs of deception. At the Farm, he'd learned to detect dozens. Contrary to popular belief, liars had no difficulty looking you in the eyes. Fisk searched for relative subtleties. For instance, newly incarcerated prisoners typically cleared their throats when lying because they didn't adequately hydrate behind bars, and anxiety manifests itself as dryness in the throat. Verlyn wasn't doing that, nor was he shifting uncomfortably in his seat, or grooming himself—smoothing hair, flicking away dust particles, and scratching were also classic means of shedding the anxiety that accompanies lies.

Of course, Verlyn could know most or all of this. The same CIA polygraph examiner who'd taught Fisk's three-week interrogation course at the Farm had lectured at Verlyn's NSA orientation. Then again, professionals with knowledge of lie-spotting techniques often make the worst liars because they have too much to think about while lying.

"Glad to hear you're having a good time here," Fisk said.

Chay added, "Yes, that's nice," but only after Fisk had looked her way, wondering why she was being so quiet. She'd said that journalistic principle precluded her from engaging in police work. But her overriding journalistic objective in this instance coincided with that of the police: find out what the hell Verlyn knows.

Also odd, Fisk thought, was that Verlyn continued to focus on him rather than on her. It wasn't as simple as shyness or intimidation. Could they be engaged in some form of subterfuge?

"I should note that the unexpectedly pleasant accommodations are considerably offset by the knowledge that high-ranking members of the United States government would like to murder me," said Verlyn. He gripped either side of his seat to precisely push himself into an upright position, at the same time centering himself. Fisk knew such tidying to be another classic means of discharging anxiety.

"Have you received threats?" Chay asked.

"Hundreds if you include anonymous Internet trolls." Verlyn sighed. "Of greater concern to me is the member of the National Security Council who said, according to your newspaper, that he would like to take me out into the desert and put a bullet in my head. Incidentally, there is a drill sergeant at Fort Hood who is already doing that, almost literally. He posted my photograph on targets at the pistol range there. Also one of the Marines who guarded me after I was apprehended, while jabbing me in the kidney, so as not to leave a mark, told me, 'I'm gonna volunteer' "—here Verlyn pantomimed punching someone, speaking a word with each punch—" 'to be on the firing squad after they convict you of treason.' There was no heed to due process, from any of these individuals, not even an iota of consideration that I'd done the right thing."

Petulance often went hand in hand with deception. Fisk judged Verlyn's indignation to be genuine, though. His naïveté too. He reminded Fisk of the kid who snuck into the zoo after-hours to free the animals, opened the lion's cage, then was surprised when the lion attacked him.

Time for the change of pace, Fisk thought. "Maybe there's something we can do about that," he said. "First, I need to ask you one question: How much do you know about Yodeler?"

The question presumed Verlyn knew something about Yodeler, although the pseudonym had been made public in the past hour, while Verlyn was alone in his cell without access to media. If Verlyn knew nothing, he would say as much—I don't know him. When lying, people take pains to avoid direct answers.

Verlyn hesitated before answering, "Is Yodeler a website?"

Fisk couldn't tell whether the man's confusion was genuine. "No, I'm talking about the person responsible for the drone killings at the Museum of Natural History, Chelsea, and Central Park and Battery Park."

"Of course that's all anyone here was talking about today," Verlyn said. "I hadn't heard anything other than conjecture about the killer. The person's name is Yodeler?"

Truthful, Fisk thought. Or demonstrative of a talent for deception. Or a sociopath—Verlyn had offered plenty of substantiation for that diagnosis this evening.

"Is there any reason that you would have been in communication with this person recently?" Fisk asked him. This was an interrogation technique known as "baiting"—you tried to hit the subject with new concerns, in this case that there existed, some- where, some record of his being in contact with Yo- deler. If he hadn't been in contact, he wouldn't take the bait; he would simply say no or shake his head.

Verlyn pivoted in his chair, angling away from Fisk, then uncrossed his legs. "Are you asking me this because he's rumored to be seeking my re- lease?" He looked to Chay, as if in search of a clue. She remained oddly silent.

Fisk lamented that a coin toss stood as good a chance as he did of determining whether Verlyn was being honest. Verlyn could still be of help, however. Fisk looked to Chay, imploring her to speak. Verlyn would be more likely, he'd thought, to cooperate with her than him, the NYKGB agent.

She said, "Merritt, we're here because this Yo- deler is murdering innocent people."

"Ah!" He brightened. "I think I can be of help. As much as I like it here, I will leave."

"It's possible," Fisk said. Anything was possible. "In the meantime, how about releasing a statement via the *New York Times* asking Yodeler to stand down?"

Verlyn edged forward in his chair, locking his eyes on Fisk's. "This is because you don't want innocent people to die?"

"That's why I'm here."

"Is it really?" Verlyn sat taller. "So the Police State has a new game plan, then?"

Fisk needed this nut to utter just a few words—as simple as *Yodeler, man, please hit the pause button.* "I can't really speak for the 'Police State,' but the mission of the New York Police Department is—"

"Oh, please!" Verlyn swatted the air, as though dispelling a bad odor. "One of the documents I saved from the NSA X Keyscore burn bag was the nondisclosure agreement Commissioner Bratton forced your public relations firm to sign. I know that, as a result of the publicist's coaching, the members of your department are quite adept at spin and doublespeak. What I want is for everyone to see that nondisclosure agreement."

Fisk inhaled, so as not to groan. "Here's a bit of perspective. A lot of our officers, especially in the Intelligence Division, could have earned more money in the private sector their first year out of school than they will if, late in their careers, they reach GS-18, the highest government pay grade. They went into public service because they legitimately care. And there's nothing they care more about than human lives."

"I don't doubt that was true when they signed on, still young and idealistic!" Verlyn sprayed saliva. "The Police State plays on that—it uses the dogooders as cutouts, in essence. They believe they're serving the public good, but in reality, their efforts line the wallets of an altogether different master, at a cost that is measurable in human lives—as of my incarceration, the figures were nine hundred and ninety American nonmilitary contractors lost in the nebulous name of national security since 2007, plus another one hundred and seventy-four foreign nationals killed doing our bidding. And those figures don't include the casualties that conventional records don't account for, like the cancer patients who lost their chance to live when ten million dollars was diverted from Columbia Presbyterian's research clinic to bribe a Ministry of Health official in Azerbaijan who had influence on assigning offshore oil-well rights in the Caspian Sea." He added, as if it were an afterthought, "Or my brother's death."

Fisk sensed that Verlyn had inadvertently revealed one of his cards. "What happened to your brother?"

Verlyn stared at the floor.

"Boyden Verlyn was a chemist at Princeton," Chay said.

Verlyn shook his head. "No. Boyden's salary was paid by Princeton—he was on the books as an assistant professor, and he taught a class. But his research was funded by the Department of Defense—although he would have paid for it himself if he'd been able to; he was a patriot through and through. When things went wrong on the project, even though it was no fault of Boyden's, the generals acted as if they'd never known him. As he saw it, tragically, he had no option but to take his life."

"I'm sorry," Chay said, and Fisk followed suit,

meanwhile wondering how Boyden Verlyn might factor into the case.

Verlyn went on. "If this Yodeler takes a life a day, that will be tragic, of course. However, there are at least twice as many deaths per day as a consequence of U.S. covert actions in sub-Saharan Africa. If Yodeler's activities bring about my freedom, if the one thing I'm able to accomplish as a result is to bring the sub-Saharan operations to light, perhaps we will come to view Yodeler's victims as—to use the Gulf War Coalition's phrase—'acceptable collateral damage.' The result will be fewer casualties on the balance, because the generals and their corporate masters will be incarcerated." Verlyn dabbed at his brow with his sleeve. "The citizens have a right to know what the government is doing in their name, with their tax dollars. That's what's right."

This had dissolved into a waste of valuable investigation time, Fisk thought.

For some reason, Chay appeared to hang on Verlyn's every word. She said, "Merritt, it would seem then that you have the opportunity to be a hero to the citizens twice over."

Verlyn perked up. "How?"

She inched closer to the table. "What if the authorities were to make an arrangement where if you reveal what you know about Yodeler, you are released so that you can upload the remainder of the documents?"

A hell of a question, Fisk thought.

Verlyn said matter-of-factly, "I'm surprised a journalist of your repute would pose a hypothetical, Chay."

She turned to Fisk. "Would the Department go along with that?"

"At this point, hell yes," Fisk said to Verlyn. "You give up Yodeler, we'd let you walk away. Absolutely."

Sitting up straight, Verlyn said, "What guarantee could you give me that I wouldn't walk away, as you put it, and a block or two later, an NSAC or CIA goon puts a bullet in my head?"

Fisk tried to wave off his concern. "I'm sure we could work out some sort of plan for your approval, some sort of Checkpoint Charlie–type exchange, information for freedom."

"And then what if it turns out that I'm wrong about Yodeler?" Verlyn asked.

A good question, Fisk thought—that is, a good question to ask if you realized you'd said too much and now were trying to minimize the damage. The damage had come thanks to Chay's question, *What if the authorities were to make an arrangement where you reveal what you know about Yodeler?* In all likelihood, if Verlyn hadn't known Yodeler's identity, he would have simply answered, *I don't know who Yodeler is.*

Fisk wrestled the wind for control of the Metropolitan Correction Center door, pulling it open just enough for Chay to slip out sideways onto a rainy and prematurely dark Park Row. Traffic, like activity in general, was minimal for six o'clock, a function less of the downpour, he thought, than of plans canceled for fear of the drone.

Chay started to thank him for holding the door when a sheet of rain hit her with a force seldom seen outside of a tsunami—or during routine rainfall within one of downtown Manhattan's many wind tunnels. Looking back at him, she arched a brow. "You saw that coming, didn't you?"

"Don't tell anybody this," he said, stepping onto a section of sidewalk sheltered by an overhang. "Intel controls the weather."

He'd hoped for a smile, but instead she looked down to avoid the rain, which reflected the glow of a bright, neon-green sign. Before he could get a better look at her, his focus was captured by illuminated medallion numbers on the rooftop sign of a cab, meaning the cab was free—a commodity on a night like this. He started toward it, then watched helplessly as the medallion number stayed lit for only the few seconds it took for its passenger to exit, her place taken by the two businessmen who'd been waiting beneath a newspaper kiosk. The nearest subway, the 4 train at the City Hall station, was a

four-block walk, or, effectively, a four-block swim.
Up and down Park Row, people huddled in doorways and beneath overhangs, angling themselves
so as to keep their phones dry. Another option presented itself to Fisk via the green neon.

The light was in the shape of a four-leaf clover, part of a sign that protruded from a pub up
the block. Fisk was reminded that, other than the
Krispy Kreme doughnuts Chay brought to his office, he hadn't eaten in a day and a half. Pointing
that way, he asked her, "Want to shadow me there
for a quick bite?"

She nodded. "I was beginning to think you didn't
do food."

They ran. She sprinted and he did his damnedest
not to fall too far behind. His coat and dress shirt
were almost immediately soaked through, leaving
his chest and arms stinging from the chill. Spinning tires raised puddles, soaking the rest of him.
He looked up to find her holding the door.

He tried not to pant. "Thanks."

Entering the dark tavern, he was enveloped by
warm air. On the blank order form taped above the
frosted-glass panel in the door, someone had handwritten *sorry folks, no a/c* in ink that bled down the
glass. Still, the warmth felt good. The hint of stale
spilled beer was oddly comforting too.

He'd never been here, although, in a way, he had.
They were a dying breed, these pocket pubs, always
called something that included the word "blarney"
or "clover" or just the possessive form of an Irish last
name, with tables and chairs and walls coated with
worn, dark wood, and lit primarily by the brewery

promotions. When Fisk first came to New York, pocket pubs were as prevalent as Starbucks. In his opinion, the burgers in these places were the best in the city. Or maybe it was the pints of Guinness that invariably accompanied the burgers.

"Table or bar?" Chay asked.

"Up to you," he said.

As she led the way, he tried to ignore the way the rain made her skirt conform to her body. She weaved in and out of the light crowd, the government happy-hour celebrants having given way to Wall Streeters whose happy hour began later. Some ate dinner at the copper-plated bar. Most drank in silence, listening to the tinny Sinatra drifting from the jukebox that played 45s. She passed the bar, and the tables too, stopping at the farthest of the four booths, the only one that was free. Fisk peeled off his sport coat and hung it from the thick brass eagle head extending from the high back of the booth. Once he sat down, sinking into the red leather bench, the bar chatter seemed to fade. He had the sense of being transported somewhere else.

"So did you think he knows who Yodeler is?" Chay asked.

"I do. Thanks to your question. Until that point, I thought he didn't, but I was wrong."

She looked him over. "I've got to hand it to you. You have a rare capacity for admitting when you've been wrong."

He shrugged. "I've had a lot of practice."

She sat back, getting comfortable, it seemed. "So do you have ways of making him talk?"

"I was hoping you might."

"MICE?" The acronym, which stood for Money, Ideology, Coercion, and Ego, was well known in espionage circles as a summation of individual motives.

"Maybe." Fisk had read the FBI dossier, but perhaps not closely enough. "Boyden Verlyn would have been Merritt's last living relative, right?"

"As far as I know."

"Could Merritt be interested in clearing his brother's name?"

"Possibly."

"What exactly did happen to his brother?"

"Boyden Verlyn's nerve-agent experiments resulted in the death of one of his students, a college junior named Ella Barr, and landed a second student, Darren Draco, in an institution, permanently brain-damaged. Boyden may have been left to twist in the wind by the Defense Department. 'The generals,' as Merritt referred to them, asserted that Boyden was grossly negligent. In any case, Boyden faced a civil lawsuit from both the Barr and the Draco families, plus a prison sentence. His solution was to row a boat out into the Atlantic in the winter of 2010. The boat washed ashore three days later, with his suicide note taped to one of the seats."

Fisk didn't immediately see a Yodeler connection. "The answer might be in his past," he said. "The Bureau is opening leads on anyone who's bought a Specter drone or as little as a new Specter rotor blade—evidently they require constant replacement. Can you cross-reference that list with everyone Merritt's been in contact with?"

"As soon as we have his toll records."

"The so-called haystack?"

"Yes." Recalling her hostility toward Intel's data-mining practices, Fisk braced himself for her response.

She leaned forward, into the plum-orange glow of the fake candle mounted on the wall, and said, "Let's drink to finding the needle."

She'd certainly come around, Fisk thought. It felt like an unexpected victory. He looked to the bar. The waiter, who looked as though he'd been here since the place opened—without taking a day off—stood fixated on a horse race on the chunky TV bracketed to the wall above the liquor bottles. For the first time in an awfully long time, Fisk looked forward to a drink for a reason other than escapism. He wanted to sate his curiosity about Chay. "So where did you say you were from?" he asked.

"I didn't."

There was only one person Fisk could think of who had a greater aversion to answering personal questions than she did: himself. "I'm wrong again," he said.

"You need to ask the right questions."

"Please enlighten me."

"Okay." She flicked a wet tendril of hair out of the way of her eyes. "You need to think of this as an interrogation."

"Are you a proponent of that sort of thing?" he said, willing to bet against it.

"Absolutely. But I mean interrogation, in the original sense of the word. The root of the word is *rogare*, Latin for ask, and *inter*, of course, is between. It's a back-and-forth. If done right, both parties get something."

"More tit for tat?"

"Exactly."

Interesting, he thought. He indicated the menu board, a medieval-style scroll cast in plaster and hand-painted with a list of the entrées: hamburger, shepherd's pie, liver and onions, corned beef, bangers and mash, and the chop of the day. He doubted she would want any one of them. He said, "If you answer my question, dinner's on me."

A glance at the scroll and she said, "As a matter of principle, I would never pass up a burger in a pub like this, so I'd like one of those."

Yet another point added to her score, he thought. "Okay."

"Along with a couple answers from you."

Not more Jenssen. "Great. What?"

"Where are you from?"

"Why would I answer now?"

"Because you want me to tell you where I'm from. While you're at it, tell me how you got into law enforcement."

"You want my origin story?"

"Please." She gestured for him to proceed.

"It's not much of a story."

"Then you can pick up my bar tab too."

"I would have done that anyway." Fisk scanned the bar, hoping for a pint of Guinness sooner rather than later, and a Jack Daniel's Old No. 7 while he was waiting for the Guinness. The waiter, holding open a copy of the *Daily Racing Form*, was on the phone.

"The other condition is you need to answer me today," Chay said.

He laughed, then found himself saying, "Actually,

I grew up all over the world. We lived in seven countries in eleven years: France, Belgium, Abu Dhabi, Germany, places like that. So how about you?"

She didn't blink. "I don't see how globe-trotting whetted your appetite for police work in New York."

"More like American school after American school, full of overprivileged kids who believe the world is theirs by divine right."

"So, what, you chose a profession where you do something about them?"

"If that's what I wanted to do, I would have become an IRS agent." He couldn't pinpoint what about being a cop had appealed to him, or if, in fact, there was any one or two or three specific reasons. Her questions demanded more introspection than he would have liked.

"Then why a cop?" she asked.

"I don't know."

"Do you remember when you first thought about becoming a policeman? Was it while you were at one of the American schools?"

"I think so, yes."

"Maybe you saw a world that wasn't just, and you gravitated toward one where justice is more clearly delineated?"

Her insightfulness impressed him. "Sounds about right."

"Good to know, but since I answered the question, you may still owe me one."

"So do I get your secret now?"

She plucked a cardboard coaster from a stack of them between the ketchup and mustard dispensers against the wall. *Rheingold Extra Dry*, it said.

Rheingold Beer was a Brooklyn company that had gone out of business around the time he was born. In its day, though, it was legendary, its annual Miss Rheingold contests garnering as much attention as games between the Yankees and the then Brooklyn Dodgers.

"This is the secret right here," said Chay.

"Rheingold?"

"Any kind of beer, in my experience."

"Is this a variation on *in vino veritas*?" He hoped he hadn't botched the Latin maxim, which translated to something along the lines of "in wine, there is truth."

"Coming up, I used to hear this old journalist maxim that there's a tendency among a class of sources to withhold information from a reporter until the reporter has ordered the Second Beer. The Second Beer is a trust threshold; I can't tell you how many times I've been sitting in a booth in a place like this with a hardcase source who seems like he'd rather die than reveal even his favorite color, but as soon as the waiter takes the order for the second round and walks off, the hardcase opens up like a canyon."

"It's that simple?" Fisk looked toward the waiter, who was crumpling what looked like an offtrack betting-parlor receipt.

"A lot of the time, it *is* that simple, yes," said Chay, "to the extent that it feels like cheating."

He caught the waiter's eye, and the man began lumbering toward the booth. "You like Guinness?" Fisk asked Chay.

"The way you like Krispy Kreme," she said.

Pulling up, the waiter mumbled something that Fisk took for "What do you want, folks?"

Fisk said, "Two pints of Guinness, please."

"I'd also like two pints," said Chay, delighting Fisk but confusing the waiter. She added, "One for each of us now, one more when you bring our cheeseburgers."

After the waiter walked off with their order, Fisk asked Chay, "How did you know I wanted a burger?"

"Use your deductive reasoning, Detective. At worst, it's a one-in-four shot, one-in-five if you included the liver and onions. But if you're a liver-and-onions guy, I would prefer to be wrong."

Fisk smiled, mostly at the thought of a context in which his having eaten liver and onions would trouble her.

She stiffened suddenly, before producing her phone from her bag; Fisk hadn't heard it ring over the Sinatra—*"I've got you under my skin,"* Frank was singing.

"Maryland," she said, clamping a palm over her free ear. "No, call anytime . . . Okay, I'll be right there." She dropped the phone back into the bag and, in the same motion, slid out of the booth. "I need a rain check on those two beers," she said to Fisk.

Fisk caught her arm. "Hold up. You're shadowing me, I think that gives me the right to shadow you too."

She thought about that for a moment before coming clean. "Ed Norman has a tipster claiming to know who Yodeler is. I'll keep you in the loop. Promise."

On the face of it, *New York Times* director of security Ed Norman had a simple task: get Chay Maryland into a car.

He was standing outside in the doorway of the Tech and Design School on the middle of West Thirty-Seventh between Seventh and Eighth Avenues, puffing intermittently on a Pall Mall cigarette. For whatever reason, Pall Mall had been the cheapest brand at the kiosk he passed on the five-block walk from the Times Tower. Most were $13 a box. At $12, he knew, Pall Mall was still three times the average price in many other states. Albany imposed a tax of about $4.50 per pack, and the city added another couple bucks on top of that. It had never bothered Norman until today, because he didn't smoke, hadn't in twenty-odd years. But the cigarette gave him license to loiter outside the Tech and Design School, along with students and faculty members on their nicotine breaks. Otherwise his presence might have seemed suspicious.

In the five minutes he'd been here, both of the other smokers had gone back into the building, leaving him alone to look up and down the rain-slicked block. Any moment Chay would round a corner, probably on foot; the weather would have made it difficult for her to get a cab downtown. As soon as he spotted her, he would click the Weather

Channel app on his phone, reconfigured to covertly notify Lin of her arrival.

Once Norman verified that she was alone and that no one was tailing her, he would click the Weather Channel app a second time to close it, providing the go-ahead for the yellow taxi in which Lin waited now.

The cab was a good choice of venue for the sort of discussion Lin had planned. A ten-buck gadget powered by the car's cigarette lighter could jam the signal to a cell phone or any RFID device on a person, precluding electronic eavesdropping and leaving a trail. A two-hundred-buck device could make it appear to eavesdroppers that the conversation was taking place fifty blocks away, or fifty states away. The cab, as opposed to the use of a private car, was also designed to minimize Norman's exposure. According to Lin, the Ministry of State Security, the agency of the People's Republic of China responsible for foreign intelligence, had further use for the ex-FBI agent.

If Chay were to link Norman to the Chinese, however, he would be an accessory to kidnapping, for starters. No reason at all she would make the connection now, he thought. Yet something troubled him about the arrangement.

He couldn't put his finger on it, but he'd learned to pay attention to such instincts. So what the hell was it? He'd orchestrated exponentially more complex operations before, including the exfiltration of a Pakistani national from Pakistan's consulate on East Sixty-Fifth Street here in New York. When Pakistani ISI officers first began to suspect that the woman was cooperating with the FBI, in their typical fashion, they decided they would pack her off to a dark cell in Islamabad and ask questions there. Norman's team planned to rescue her the night before she was to leave. Entering the New York consulate along with a legitimate local party-supply company working an event at the consulate, he and two other agents concealed the woman in what appeared to be one of the band's speakers. They dollied her out in the speaker, right past the ISI officers, and handed her over to U.S. marshals, who spirited her into WitSec. He hadn't heard of her since, meaning she was okay, probably in a sweet three-bedroom house in Scottsdale or some such perma-vacation town favored by defectors, with a new Cadillac Escalade in the carport—defectors were crazy for Escalades.

He had to admit to himself now that he was concerned for Chay's welfare. Yes, Lin had assured him that it would be a simple Q&A. But Lin lied for a living. On the other hand, to Lin's credit, each of the previous three times Norman had worked for the MSS, $45,500 appeared in his Bank of Reykjavik account before the op, and another $49,500 twenty-four hours after mission accomplished, like clockwork. And even in the deception business, reputation mattered. But what if, once Lin had gotten the location of the Verlyn cache from Chay, his people decided to cover their tracks by killing her on the spot and putting her body in one of their notorious "golf cases" (the Chinese solved the problem of urban-theater body disposal with mobile liquefaction chambers that, on the outside, looked like the hard plastic cases used by wealthy executives and PGA players to bring their golf bags on flights)? It was more likely that the Chinese would be averse to killing an American on U.S. soil, especially someone of Chay's prominence.

Right?

Yes, yes, of course, Norman told himself. Probably Lin would put a hook into Chay, give her no choice but to cooperate. She had an older brother who paid for his heroin habit importing alpaca sweaters from Bolivia, selling them for twenty times what he paid for them. Lin's people would fix things so that Chay's brother was picked up on a narcotics charge and sentenced to twenty years without hope of parole in a filthy Bolivian hole—unless she gave up the goods. If she still refused, her brother's life would be brought into play.

Norman asked himself for the thousandth time whether he was giving Lin too much this time. No, for God's sake. It was just a bunch of documents that had already been stolen and would surface one way or another. Someone was going to profit; might as well be the Norman family. And he desperately needed the money now to clean up their latest messes. His son the gambling addict was in serious debt to "heavy guys," on top of the usual alimony and support for his other two children, his grandsons, and granddaughter. Then there was Norman's wife, with an addiction of her own to expensive purchases—like a pair of Italian shoes she "picked up" for him at $1,100. He tried to return them to the fop shoe store, but was unable to because $1,100 had been a clearance price. Craziness.

Chay rounded the northwest corner from Seventh Avenue, walking east across Thirty-Seventh Street. Her face was veiled by her umbrella, but he recognized the long legs and proportionate gait. Still he wasn't certain it was her until he caught her reflection in a storefront window across the street. Anxiety began to press at Norman's chest. Locking the cigarette between his lips, he drew his phone from his suit pants pocket and clicked the Weather Channel to life. He glanced at the results—sixty-three and raining—only for the sake of appearance. Really he was searching the street for surveillants.

No one followed her around the corner. Pedestrian traffic was negligible to begin with due to the rain and, perhaps, the drone. Ordinarily New Yorkers moved as swiftly as anyone, but the rain not only slowed them but caused greater variation in their paces than usual, making it easier to pick out a tail. Norman saw nothing suspicious on the sidewalks. And unless the Bureau had commandeered an M7 bus and its twenty-some passengers, there was nothing doing on the street. He clicked out of the Weather Channel app and repocketed his phone. Time to go to work.

When Chay was halfway to him, a yellow Crown Victoria cab turned right from Seventh Avenue and onto Thirty-Seventh Street, the "off-duty" sign illuminated. The taxi rolled past Chay and then Norman, pulling up at the curb on his side of the block, its "off-duty" sign dimming and the medallion number flashing on, signifying its availability.

Chay stopped a few feet from Norman and said, "I'm afraid this is a setup."

Shocking him.

How had she figured it out?

"No, no," he tried to assure her. "The source is just afraid that the drone will get him, so he wants to talk to you in a taxi."

"You're in on it, aren't you?" she asked.

Norman wondered how the hell she could have known. Or was this just one of her trick questions? She was known for that. Relax, he exhorted himself. "In on what?"

"The cab pulled up to the curb when I was on Seventh. The driver told me to keep on going, and to stay on the uptown side of the street. He wanted to make sure I wasn't being followed."

"Maybe it's just a case of reasonable paranoia?"

"Maybe."

The choice of the uptown side of the street made no sense to Norman. It also troubled him that Lin would have made contact with Chay already. Hot and prickly perspiration rose from his scalp. This wasn't just a change of plans, he thought. This was the Chinese trying to tie up all loose ends, including their agent at the *New York Times*.

The taxi stood at the curb, engine still idling, the fog of exhaust fumes rent by the rain but still blurring the figure climbing out of the backseat, leaving the door open as he mounted the sidewalk. It was Lin, gripping something the size and shape of a pen, but something about the way it glowed red in the reflection of the taillights told Norman it wasn't a pen, and put him on guard. Reflexively, he reached for his shoulder holster. Which wasn't there. It had been two years since he'd worn it. The best course of action, he knew, was to retreat. Turn and run as fast as he could into the Tech and Design School.

Lin's hand jumped back, the pen appearing to recoil. Norman felt a stab in his chest, just left of his sternum, like a bee sting. It shook him.

Chay, standing with her back to Lin, asked Norman, "Are you okay?"

"Yeah, I'm fine," he said.

But he wasn't fine. It felt like his brain was turning to soup. He looked to his lapel expecting to see some sort of entry wound. A few tiny crystals shimmered there. He'd heard of darts made of ice that completely disintegrated upon entering the target—the CIA had used them in the seventies. They left nothing but a tiny red dot on the skin, but released a poison that rapidly entered the bloodstream, fatally, denaturing quickly so that an autopsy wouldn't detect anything out of the ordinary about the heart attack.

He fell to the sidewalk, shoulders hitting first, head bouncing off the cement. But he didn't feel anything. He lay flat on his back.

"Ed!" Chay dropped to his side.

He tried to shout to her to run. Run came out as a feeble "Rrr."

"Is he okay?" asked Lin, jogging up.

Chay pressed a finger against the side of Norman's neck. He could see her do it, but he couldn't feel a thing. "His pulse is awfully low," she said.

Lin looked him over. "Is his skin always that pale?"

Taking in Norman's face, Chay's eyes widened in alarm. "Looks like cyanosis."

"What's that?"

"I think he's having a heart attack!" She quickly looked around. "We need an ambulance or—"

"We could take him to hospital." Lin aimed a thumb at the cab.

"Yes, good idea," she said to Lin.

The driver, a heavyset Hispanic man, bounded out of the taxi to help them. If it occurred to Chay that he'd sized up the situation and acted a beat too quickly, she didn't show it. "You're going to be okay, Ed," she said to Norman as she took his ankles. The two men each gripped a shoulder and hurried him toward the cab.

Norman attempted to scream, to tell her to run, to at least draw attention from passersby. Nothing happened. He couldn't move. Not a muscle. Not a thing, including his lungs. He figured he had two minutes left.

Together, the taxi driver, the passenger, and Chay carried Ed Norman into the backseat. Then the three got in, closed the doors, and the cab darted off.

Fisk watched on his phone while riding uptown on a 1 train going slower than he would have liked, but, fortunately, a beneficiary of the $200 million Transit Wireless program. The Wi-Fi allowed him to get into the Department system, which included a direct link to 911, the crime information database, the warrant system, readings from the city's radiation and chemical detectors, and the feed from the Domain Awareness cameras. Several of the cameras were making use of the beta version of a system enhancement that intelligence and law enforcement insiders had taken to calling God's Eye, due to its capabilities as well as the rumor that the Dayton, Ohio–based computer scientist who invented it had once attended divinity school with the intent of becoming a Catholic priest.

In her reporting on the NYPD's data network and electronic surveillance capabilities, Chay hadn't mentioned God's Eye, probably because she hadn't known about it. Fisk thought of the application as a live version of Google Earth, only with TiVo capabilities: it allowed you to rewind, zoom in, and automatically follow certain targets. In many stretches of the coverage, the target no longer disappeared off the screen to the right or left. The system blended the feed with that of a high-resolution camera aboard either an airplane or a helicopter—soon to be replaced by far cheaper unmanned blimps—that captured a twenty-five-square-mile segment of the city, for six hours at a time. It was a tool as potent, he thought, as anything in the vaunted F6 arsenal.

He began with DOM-CAM 37-E8, Thirty-Seventh Street east of Eighth Avenue, finding the block quiet, as usual for this time of night. If you were going to set up a *New York Times* reporter for a drive-by abduction, Fisk thought, this was a prime location. You had a minimum of witnesses and on-lookers who might interfere, plus you were close enough to the Times Tower that it seemed like a plausible meeting place for a source who was skit-tish about showing his face at the paper. It hadn't aroused Chay's suspicion. It aroused Fisk's, but not until she'd left the pub. He had no idea why, though, until he was on the subway heading uptown to the office and his thoughts turned to Norman's distinc-tive boat-shaped Bettanin & Venturi loafers at a cost of five hundred dollars—each. Then his inter-nal alarm went off.

The bad guys, whoever they were, were trying to kill two birds with one stone. They were getting rid of Norman and, at the same time, using him to rob Chay of time to think, and to get her into the car. Fisk watched the cab zip across Eighth Avenue, unimpeded by traffic. If the driver were heading uptown, he would have turned right on Eighth—the avenue goes one way, uptown. So the cab was either continuing west or going downtown.

Fisk clicked his way to an operator at the EOC—

Emergency Operations Center, the same place that fielded 911 calls—and he reported the 10-33 (kidnapping in process). Meanwhile he clicked into the feed from DOM-CAM 37-E9 in time to see the taxi sail along Thirty-Seventh Street between Eighth and Ninth. At the midpoint of the block, the cab's left-turn signal began to flash, and then the brake lights glowed as it slowed to turn downtown on Ninth.

Fisk relayed these details, along with the cab's license-plate number, KBY-2092—thank you, Microsoft numeric recognition software. "And, of course, it's a Crown Victoria," he added of the taxi—for what that was worth. If you're going to snatch someone off the streets of New York, Crown Victoria was the model for you. Crown Vics comprised more than half of the New York taxi fleet, with Ford Escape hybrids and Nissan minivans a distant second and third.

The 1 train shrieked to a stop at Penn Station. As soon as the doors opened, Fisk flew out. He jogged in and around the passengers waiting to board, ran up the stairs, and surfaced at the intersection of West Thirty-Third Street and Seventh Avenue, two blocks west of Ninth Avenue, where he hoped to intercept the Crown Vic cab.

He could probably run the two crosstown blocks in a minute. But once at Ninth Avenue, he would have to pick the Crown Vic out of a sea of essentially identical cars—at this time of night, two-thirds of the vehicles on the streets of Manhattan were yellow taxis. Assuming he could pick out the right Crown Vic, then what? Wade into traffic and flag the cab down, waving his Glock for incentive? Shoot at its tires? To brandish his gun carried a willingness to use it, and any shot in that environment risked a fatality. As little as stepping off the curb and waving a Glock might frighten a passing driver into sending his vehicle into another or onto the sidewalk. And all of this was assuming Fisk got to the intersection of Thirty-Third and Ninth in time, hardly a given.

His eye fell on a guy about his own age, in a lemon blazer and the sort of cowboy boots that could only be for show, much like the copper-gold Jaguar XJ sedan he was lowering himself into. The car was overpriced, in Fisk's opinion, but quick.

He pulled up to the driver's door as the Don Johnson wannabe turned over the engine. Rapping the driver's window, Fisk got the guy's attention. "Police business," he said, flashing his shield. "I need to commandeer your vehicle."

The guy didn't budge. "Why *my* car?" he asked indignantly.

Fisk might have explained to him that if you're an adult and a law enforcement officer with proper identification requests your help in catching or arresting a suspect, recapturing an escaped arrestee or prisoner, or preventing a crime, you are required by law to oblige; otherwise you face a fine ranging from fifty to a thousand dollars.

Pressed for time, he ripped the door open and made for the safety-belt release button. The guy hadn't buckled. Fisk seized him by the shoulders, hauled him onto the street, and jumped into the bucket seat, landing with his foot on the accelerator and his hand on the shifter. An automatic. Figured. He rammed it into D, the engine growled, and Thirty-Third Street began to jet past.

He heard a wail, the electronic version of the old air siren. It switched to a yelp, signifying that the operator of the emergency vehicle was approaching an intersection. Could be an NYPD cruiser closing in on Chay's cab. Could be another squad car responding to another disturbance. Sirens were part of New York's sound track.

A station wagon shot out of a parallel spot to the left and onto the single-lane street, two car lengths ahead of him. If the driver had seen the Jaguar at all, she grossly underestimated its speed. The city, in Fisk's mind, compacted to only the wheel and hood of the Jaguar, the passenger side of the station wagon, and the Jaguar-width gap between the station wagon and the van parked on the opposite side of the block, a gap that was now narrowing.

He sped up, shooting the car into the gap, threading the needle, sending him hurtling into the four lanes' worth of brisk crosstown traffic at the intersection of Eighth. Wary of hydroplaning on the rain-slicked street, he pumped the brake. The Jaguar slid nevertheless, the tires howling, edging the hood across the stop line, inches from broadsiding a speeding cab, before Fisk brought the car to a halt.

The cab, whose driver honked angrily, was a Crown Victoria. Not the right driver, though. The vast majority of the vehicles on Eighth were yellow, with as many as twenty of them, to Fisk's glance, Crown Vics.

One outpaced the rest, shifting lanes and weaving recklessly around cars and trucks. The driver was crazy, Fisk thought, even by the high standard of crazy set by New York cabbies.

He couldn't see the driver. But the woman in the backseat was white, and corpulent, with short blond hair. Essentially Chay's opposite. Which didn't preclude Chay from being in the taxi, along with the young Asian, the two of them perhaps keeping their heads below the window line, the blonde serving as a decoy.

Yelps emanated from a Ford Taurus NYPD cruiser five cars behind the taxi in question, the cruiser's light bar alternating between red and blue. The new Taurus cruiser didn't intimidate anyone on appearance or muscle, but it was "smart," equipped with an infrared monitor capable of scanning license-plate numbers, and 360-degree surveillance cameras that transmitted live video to NYPD headquarters, where it was analyzed by powerful computers.

Fisk followed the Taurus driver's line of sight to another taxi, three cabs ahead, also a Crown Vic. Chay was in plain view in the backseat, across from the Asian. Along with traffic, the cab was heading downtown at about thirty miles per hour.

Fisk jumped the red light at Thirty-Seventh, turning left onto Ninth. His Jaguar fell in two lanes to the left of the Ford Taurus cruiser. The two taxis ahead of the Taurus peeled off in deference to the lights and the yelp, looks of profound relief from both drivers upon realizing that the police car was after someone else.

Paying no heed to the police car, the Crown Vic taxi shot ahead, slaloming around a sanitation truck.

Traffic began to part in deference to the police, al lowing the cruiser to get within a few car lengths o the taxi.

Fisk had no such luck, blocked by the cars slow ing and stopping to let the police car past. Still the policemen's options weren't much better than his own, a function of departmental pursuit policies designed to protect bystanders. In this instance the police were prohibited from discharging their weapons. Shooting at the driver of a moving vehi cle is a low-percentage play at best. Shooting ou his tires carried too many risks to bystanders. The Department's recommended Pursuit Intervention Technique, using the car to strike the fleeing ve hicle behind one of its rear wheels and put it into a spin, was even riskier. So the cops' objective now was probably just to keep tabs on the Crown Vic and report its progress to headquarters so that other units could lay spike strips and roadblocks and bring the pursuit to a safe conclusion.

Finding a gap between two other taxis, Fisk ac celerated the Jaguar, rounding a sanitation truck and yet another taxi, trying to get closer, but not too close. No reason to reveal himself, or even bring the Jaguar close and provoke Chay's captors, who might have few compunctions about taking a risky shot. He figured they had an escape route planned. All of the cameras notwithstanding, a city of eight million was a great place to get lost. But would they have planned on a helicopter? Surely they heard it now, and felt the chops, as Fisk did, all over. The Jaguar's sideview mirror showed him its skids. A Bell 412, about two hundred feet up.

Motion ahead snapped Fisk's attention back to the street; he needed to brake to avoid rear-ending the taxi in front of him, a—what else?—Crown Vic.

Traffic congealed where Ninth Avenue met Twenty-Fifth Street. To continue, Chay's Crown Vic taxi would have to drive over the four vehicles ahead of it. All traffic was now stopped for the light. Cars to either side penned the taxi in place. It was as though the chase had been put on pause. Red lights in Manhattan lasted from forty-five to a hundred and twenty seconds, based on traffic patterns at the time.

In waiting it out, Chay's captors risked falling into the crosshairs of a shot that would qualify as relatively low risk. A cop or tactical-team member could advance on them and threaten to fire point-blank if they didn't release Chay and then get out of the car, hands in the air. That was what the police had in mind, Fisk suspected, on spotting two more police vehicles, a GMC Yukon cruiser and a tiny Smart car used by traffic enforcement. They both parked on Twenty-Fifth Street, one vehicle on either side of Ninth Avenue. An officer hustled out of each, toward the Crown Vic.

The taxi's rear passenger-side door snapped open, and out slid the Asian, having put on a navy-blue armor-plated vest and a high-ballistic face shield—a black mask made of Kevlar. He cradled a TAR-21, a black, fully automatic assault rifle that looked more like a weapon from the *Terminator* movies than anything from present day. It included a 40mm grenade launcher and an optical scope that provided target images in 3-D via a holographic weapons sight.

The Jaguar was no longer of use. Fisk pulled it in front of a fire hydrant on the right side of Ninth. Before he could get out, while he jerked the shifter into park and readied up his Glock, the Asian leveled the TAR-21 at the cop approaching on Twenty-Fifth Street from the east, a big guy, who, at the sight of the rifle, ducked behind a parked van.

The Asian pressed the trigger, issuing three booming shots in rapid succession. The rounds tore into the steel siding of the van, exiting on the far side with enough force to lift the cop and hurl him backward, onto the street, where he didn't move, and, from the looks of it, wouldn't again.

Pivoting 180 degrees, the gunman sprayed a series of rounds, so close together that the staccato blasts blended into a continuous blare, felling the traffic cop, a young woman coming down Twenty-Fifth from the west. As the reverberations from the reports faded, the air filled with panicked screams of people running for cover or diving to the pavement. Vehicles near the intersection tore off, or tried to—several crashed.

Fisk dropped out of the driver's door of the Jaguar and into a crouch below the roofline of the SUV parked between him and the gunman. He plotted a route in and around parked cars and a bus shelter that would permit him to advance the twenty or thirty yards, as quickly as possible, in order to get a shot at the Asian.

As if reading his mind, the Asian pivoted, aiming the gun up Ninth Avenue, on a line toward Fisk, and pulled the trigger.

Diving for the pavement, Fisk heard a *sproing* like

that of a spud gun firing. The assault rifle's grenade launcher, he realized, in the same instant that the grenade clanked into the hood of the Ford Taurus cruiser. Both policemen knelt in firing position on the street, shielded by their engine block. The explosion transformed the hood into a burst of fire, shrapnel, and glass that laid out both men and spat the rest of the car backward, into the grille of a *Daily News* delivery truck.

Most glass in the vicinity—cars and store windows—shattered. Shards that had been the Jaguar's driver's window cascaded down the driver's door and onto Fisk.

He crossed his forearms over the back of his head to protect himself, meanwhile turning his head away, allowing him to see the gunman raise the rifle and launch a second projectile.

It buzzed upward until exploding and ripping through the tail boom of the helicopter, sending the craft into a downward spiral from which it couldn't recover. It crashed into a wooden water tower on the roof of the corner apartment building.

Fisk braced for the explosion and fireball. Neither happened, but water gushed over the cornice, falling like a chute down the red brick façade, turning the roofs of cars parked below into a set of steel drums and knocking pedestrians to the sidewalk.

Fisk jumped up, found the Asian in his gun sight, standing on the street, on the passenger side of the taxi. Chay sat on the driver's side. Far enough away for Fisk to take a shot.

He squeezed off two rounds. Meanwhile the Asian ducked back into the Crown Vic cab. One of

Fisk's bullets dinged the rear passenger-side door-frame, the other hammered the roof, and the cab took off, knocking aside the lone vehicle left in its path, a Civic, and banging a right onto a tree-lined, almost entirely residential block of Twenty-Fifth Street, between Ninth and Tenth Avenues.

Fisk hurried back to the Jaguar and into the driver's seat, turning over the engine. Too many stopped vehicles stood on the street between the Jaguar and Twenty-Fifth Street. He sent the car up the curb, raking the undercarriage. Dodging a parking meter and circumventing the bus shelter on the sidewalk meant clanking against one of the city's new eighty-five-pound steel trash cans.

It might be telling, he thought, that the cab turned onto single-lane Twenty-Fifth Street rather than continue down four-lane Ninth Avenue, a relative speedway. If her captors intended to take Chay downtown, there was just one route left before they ran out of island, Eleventh Avenue, two blocks over. After Eleventh, Twenty-Fifth Street terminated at Chelsea Piers.

The Jaguar thumped onto Twenty-Fifth Street, affording Fisk an unimpeded view all the way to Chelsea Piers, overlooking the Hudson River. The Crown Vic, the only other moving vehicle on the block directly ahead, came to a red light at the intersection of Tenth.

It stopped, its new relaxed pace perhaps signifying the captors' belief that they'd gone black. Fisk fought the impulse to accelerate and catch up to them. Instead he called in the update to the EOC, meanwhile rolling ahead at fifteen miles an hour. He slowed here and there, as though he were searching for a parking spot.

When the light at the end of the block turned green, the taxi drove across Tenth Avenue and onto a onetime industrial stretch of Twenty-Fifth Street that was now an odd mix of auto-body shops, trendy art galleries, and a combination of the two, the Tesla Motors showroom. Midway down the block, the cab stopped suddenly.

Driving onto the block, Fisk sensed that the driver was executing a timing stop. If he were to hit the brakes too, he might reveal himself as a tail. So he continued to within five car lengths, at which point the taxi turned left into a parking garage.

Fisk continued past, catching the cab halt just inside the dimly lit garage, the brake lights turning the parking attendants' stand red.

Fisk pulled the Jaguar into a loading-zone space in front of a giant green Perrier delivery truck—which figured in an art-gallery district. He got out, trying to appear unhurried, and wandered back toward the parking garage. He passed an art gallery fronted by a wall of tinted glass, through which he saw a dressy and well-heeled crowd sipping champagne. One couple, venturing out and onto the sidewalk, looked with consternation at the rain. Clearly no one had a clue about the melee two blocks away or the kidnappers next door.

Fisk called into EOC with the address of the parking garage before ambling past the entrance, a concrete chute about the height and width of a van. He saw Chay and the two men at its base, boarding a car lift and then descending.

He kept walking for fear that a sudden stop on his part might alert the captors. He monitored their descent in the angled glass mirror on the upper corner of the entrance. When their heads dipped below ground level, he hurried back into the garage.

On the main level, which included about fifty cars improbably packed into space for half that many, he found the Crown Vic cab parked by the unmanned attendants' stand. The entire level seemed deserted, save for Norman, who lay in the backseat of the taxi, his face drawn in, skin a bluish-gray, eyes bulging, open and unblinking. He'd died a horrible death.

Fisk peered down the open elevator shaft. The car—which consisted only of a platform, with no walls or roof—sat one level below, empty but for a pair of legs, in navy uniform pants cuffed over work boots. It was the body of the garage attendant, lain across the elevator threshold, Fisk guessed, for the dual purposes of preventing the elevator from returning to the main level as well as preventing him from revealing where Chay and her captors went. If they'd intended to flee the garage in a different car—a sensible tactic—why hadn't they done so already?

Fisk looked around before finding the door to the stairs leading down a level. A glossy black late-model Bentley sat directly in front of it, in the New York parking-garage tradition of showing off the fanciest car without letting an inch of space go to waste. It was easier for the captors to take the elevator down, Fisk thought, than wait while the attendant went to the lockbox, got the key for the Bentley, got it running, and then moved it out of the way.

He checked his phone. No cell reception. Should he take the time to go back outside to call in an update? Backup would be here soon enough regardless, he decided.

He sat down on the edge of the shaft, dropped his legs in first, lowered the rest of himself as far as he could reach, then jumped the remaining five feet. Concerned not so much for his knees or ankles as landing face-to-face with one of the captors, he hit the oily metal floor in a roll and sprang up, leading with his gun, to find . . . only the garage attendant. He lay splayed on his back, his head at a preposterous angle, neck broken. A metallic winged letter *B* dangled from his pocket. The Bentley key fob.

Fisk stepped out of the elevator. Sputtering fluorescent tubes on the ceiling revealed a subterranean level packed with a hundred more cars, and no people. At least no sign of people. On the far side was a dark alcove. Leading with his gun, Fisk wormed his way through the parked cars and proceeded into the alcove. At the end was a rusty fire door, closed but unlocked—it had to be bolted from within.

He pulled it open half an inch. The cool air that seeped out reeked of mold and rats. On the other side of the threshold was a dark space. Here and there light trickled in, not enough that he could see anything, but the vibrations from the traffic and the power grid overhead and to either side gave him an immediate sense that it was spacious. Creeping in, he heard no one, no whispers, no breaths, no telltale weight shifts—and this was the sort of place that magnified sounds. The door groaned shut behind him, plunging him into blackness. He was reluctant to use his Pelican flashlight, even on low, for fear of giving away his position.

Although the floor was dirt—or something else completely covered in dirt—his footfalls, even in stealth mode, were thuds. His eyes acclimated just enough to make out the form directly ahead. A cage of some sort. Horizontal bars a foot apart, from the floor to his head level. The whole thing as big as his office. Which gave him an idea of where he was.

In the nineteenth century, he knew, New Jersey cattle were transported by barge across the Hudson River to the docks on the west side of Manhattan, then walked through the streets to the meatpacking-district slaughterhouses. When the advent of automobiles made that walk problematic, the city dug a network of cow tunnels. Fisk figured he was in dirt-caked remains of the main cow thoroughfare, looking at a cattle pen. He was running his hand along a cold, rust-encrusted bar when a blast shook the tunnel. Out of the corner of his eye, he saw a burst of yellow light. Muzzle flash, he knew on some level.

By the time he'd fully processed it, the bullet whacked the tunnel floor a few feet in front of him, dirt and gravel leaping up at him, sharp edges biting into his face and hands. He dropped to the dirt, flattening himself behind the base of the cattle pen, trying to present the smallest target.

Another percussive blast and a round sparked the crossbar—the one on which he'd placed his hand a moment ago—before ricocheting away. The spark revealed a small, open-topped boxcar on a pair of railroad tracks about twenty feet away. The car, which was the size of a station wagon, might have been for cattle. Or maybe it was a transport installed by the rumrunners who frequented these tunnels during the Prohibition. Or the Army in World War II.

Now it was a stroke of luck. The ancient wood-slatted railcar couldn't protect Fisk against a bullet traveling a couple thousand feet per second, but it could conceal him.

He took four running steps and dove for it. With three more flashes and booming shots, one after the next, three bullets traced his route, spraying dirt. He landed face first in muck.

Through the swirls of kicked-up dirt, the waning flashes showed him the shooter. The thickset taxi driver, fifty yards down the rails. The Asian was a few feet farther down the tunnel, with Chay in tow. The two men apparently wore goggles—night vision, almost certainly. Hell of an escape route they'd chosen, Fisk had to give them credit for that.

He fired his Glock, aiming for the ground near their feet, but not close enough to endanger Chay. His hope was to keep the taxi driver at bay. The shot, which bored into the dirt between railroad crossties, caused both men to drop back, the Asian simultaneously tamping the goggles as though they'd caught fire. The Glock's muzzle flash, as seen through his infrared lenses, must have been exceedingly bright. So long as they kept their goggles on, Fisk thought, he might be able to blind them using the six-hundred-lumen beam of the Pelican flashlight, giving him the advantage in a shootout, though only a momentary one. Another problem was that the distance between him and them was too great for him to fire with any real degree of accuracy. And if he were to attempt to advance, he would relinquish the cover of the car.

His best chance was to retreat, to return to the parking garage and connect with backup there. But then Chay would be lost. If these guys got out of here—and they'd certainly thought that part out—they wouldn't permit her to walk away, not even after they'd gotten what they wanted.

He felt his way to the steering-wheel-like brake release, which was atop a knee-high spindle at the front of the car, still slick with grease after all the years. Yet the wheel wouldn't budge, not until he put his full weight into it. With a whine, the swinging hook at the bottom of the spindle pulled free of the axle, and the car began to roll, but in the wrong direction, it seemed.

It was difficult to say for sure due to the darkness and because the car was moving so slowly. Fisk cursed himself for failing to think of this ahead of time. The rails were level. Gravity wouldn't move the car one way or the other. Hell, this was why trains had engines.

With another ringing shot, a bullet pounded through a slat at the head of the car, slicing apart the air to his left before drilling into the rear wall. A barb ripped into his forehead, loosing hot blood. Something to worry about if and when he made it out of this.

He wondered whether he could move the rail-car himself. Circus strongmen traditionally pulled train cars four times the size, right?

With both hands, he gripped the top of the side-wall facing away from the taxi driver, and hurdled it. The guy fired, twice, one bullet and then another buzzing over Fisk's head and striking the far wall of the tunnel. Landing, with a crunch, in the mound of gravel in and around the tracks, he took a quick inventory of himself.

Everything where it was supposed to be, except the blood that slid down his forehead and seeped into his eyes. Blinking against it only spread the stinging.

The railcar now stood between him and the taxi driver. Another shot hit the far wall, popped free a wooden slat, then pierced a slat on the near wall, inches to Fisk's left, at eye level. The muzzle flash, which he viewed through the newly created apertures, appeared bigger than before. Under cover of darkness, the shooter was coming to get him.

Fisk crawled through the gravel, gingerly, so as not to telegraph his movements, reaching the back of the car. He rose until he could get his full weight against the platform, then he drove with his legs, trying to heave the car ahead as though it were a football sled. Except it was unyielding. His knees were at the point of snapping, it seemed, when the car finally fell away and rolled forward.

A shot cracked through a slat by his left shoulder. A chunk of wood flew up, knifing his shoulder before clinking against the rail. Another bullet sparked the metal lip of the car inches to his right and ricocheted to God-knew-where. The taxi driver had managed to find his range, that was for sure. The good news was that Fisk now had a pretty good idea where the guy was: twenty-five yards up the tracks, to the right, in the open. He resumed firing, the reports thunderous at close range, the rounds pounding and splintering the slats, through which Fisk's thermal signature clearly revealed too much. The air swirled with dirt and pungent gunpowder.

He kept pushing the railcar ahead, its increasing momentum easing his task. Quickly he was jogging to keep up with it. Then he let go and sprinted along the left side of the car, opposite the taxi driver, stopping ten yards down the rails and readying both his Pelican flashlight and his Glock. As soon as the car passed, he clicked the single button on the base of the Pelican, igniting its harsh high beam, finding the wide face of the taxi driver, and bringing his goggle lenses to a glow, which sent him reeling. Fisk followed with gunshots to the chest, dropping the taxi driver to the tracks—and he would not, it appeared, be getting up.

Fisk then had to contend with Chay's other captor, the Asian. Having flanked Fisk, he was firing at his back. All Fisk saw was the flash, and by the time he'd registered that much, the bullet had knocked him onto his side and, it felt to him, set a fire inside his hip, the pain maddening and so intense that it caused his consciousness to flicker. He rolled to tamp the pain with the dirt, meanwhile swinging his flashlight beam to delineate the guy from the darkness. He stood fifteen feet away, his pistol pointing down at Fisk's face.

And he started to press the trigger, just as Chay slung a brick at him. He turned toward her motion, causing the brick to merely graze the back of his skull rather than smack it full-on.

The shot sailed high.

Loosened dirt from the ceiling fell on Fisk. He swung the flashlight toward the Asian, catching him in the eyes, causing him to whirl away without looking. His wrist caught one of the cattle-pen crossbars, hard—Fisk heard bone snap. The guy lost his hold on his pistol. He ran in retreat, toward the far end of the tunnel. Keeping the beam on him, Fisk fired twice, the first round raising a cloud of dirt in the guy's wake. The second round and he grabbed at his thigh and collapsed.

"This way," Fisk shouted, beckoning Chay toward the railcar.

She ran to him, no words, arms and legs pumping hard. She let out a gasp once she was safely behind the car.

He took in the shaft of light at the far end of the tunnel, a doorway opening. Through the doorway ran three men, their pistols unmistakable even in silhouette a block away. Could they be backup?

The Asian struggled to his feet and limped to them, screaming something Fisk couldn't understand, except for the unmistakable urgency. The guy flung a hand toward the railcar and the three men started that way, toward Fisk.

They were backup, all right.

For the wrong side.

By Fisk's count, his Glock had just five left of the eighteen rounds he'd started with, one for each of the men now hurrying down the cow tunnel after him and Chay—one for each of them, that is, if he were to shoot with freakishly good luck.

"This way," he said to Chay, flicking the light toward the door through which he'd entered the tunnel.

As she started toward it, he fired a shot to keep their pursuers at bay. She was uncommonly quick and nimble, outrunning him to the door, making it through unscathed. Fisk fired one more round for cover. It had the effect of a clothesline on one of the attackers. Fisk had expended, he knew, his good luck.

He hastened through the door and locked it behind him, then dead-bolted it too, possibly buying them a few seconds. He found Chay waiting at the far end of the alcove.

"Elevator," he said, starting that way.

Chay hesitated by the stairwell door. "How about this?"

"The exit door upstairs is blocked by a car." Which, the more he thought about it, might work to their advantage.

He ran as far as the dead attendant, his position atop the elevator threshold unchanged. Stepping onto the elevator, Chay gave the corpse a wide berth. Fisk knelt and snatched up the Bentley key fob dangling from the guy's pants pocket, then hauled his body along the floor, out of the way. Hurrying aboard the elevator, he hammered the button, releasing the lift with a hydraulic hiss.

Chay gaped at his hip. "Oh God."

Blood swamped his light blue dress shirt, turning the tail that protruded to purple. More blood dripped onto the floor. "Looks worse than it is," he said. He had no idea if that was true.

A gunshot rose from below, the report playing over and over again off the damp concrete walls and ceiling. Over it, Chay asked, "Are they trying to shoot the lock out—" She was preempted by an earsplitting metallic clank.

"Succeeding, sounds like," Fisk said.

As the main level dropped into view, they heard the door to the tunnel swing inward, whacking the wall. Kicked in, Fisk guessed. He gestured Chay toward the sidewall, reaching the Glock into the garage.

He squinted against the glare of the streetlights outside. He got the sense that they were alone in the garage. Across the street, though, walked three men in dark suits, typical Wall Streeters in appearance. Which was odd in Chelsea.

"See them?" Chay said under her breath.

"Give me to three-Mississippi and then come get in the car, but look like you're in no hurry," he said, starting toward the Bentley.

Each time his left foot touched down, his hip had the sensation of being shot again. He aimed the keyless remote, unlocked the Bentley, and lowered himself into the driver's seat, drawing no looks from the suits across Twenty-Fifth Street.

The cabin was clammy, the leather sticky with heat, and it would stay that way; Fisk could locate and turn on the air-conditioning later. For now, he slotted the key into the ignition, twisting it and bringing the throaty engine to life. The passenger door opened and Chay dropped in.

Her good looks were to her detriment in this instance: all three heads snapped toward her, gazes lingering. The trio flew at the parking garage, drawing guns from within suit coats and pant waists.

"Get down," Fisk said, shifting into drive and mashing the gas pedal.

Chay heaved herself into the passenger footwell as the car lurched forward, the squeals of the tires boosted to howls by all the concrete. The men leaped from the street, landing on the near curb, stopping at nine, twelve, and three o'clock of the garage entrance, and assumed standing firing positions, with a precision and fluidity suggesting they'd done this hundreds of times. The Bentley, a heavy car, was made with twice as much metal as an ordinary sedan, Fisk thought. Probably weighed north of five thousand pounds. Still it would be no more effective than butter against bullets.

A bullet smashed through the windshield to his left, exiting through the rear window. Another spanked his window frame before raising a haze of foam particles from the backseat. A third gonged the hood and ricocheted into the garage's ceiling, where it ruptured the fluorescent tube, killing the light and sending glass flakes clattering onto the windshield.

As the car continued ahead, Fisk stuck the barrel of his Glock out the newly created aperture in the windshield, firing at the suit at nine o'clock, missing, the bullet disappearing into a van parked across the street. He fired again, the bullet finding the man's stomach, knocking him to the street.

Fisk aimed the Bentley's hood at the guy at twelve o'clock. The gunman turned away, too late. The grille rammed him, taking his feet out from under him and sending him thumping onto the hood. He remained in possession of his gun, though, and his faculties.

Fisk swung the Bentley left across the sidewalk and onto Twenty-Fifth Street. Fighting centrifugal force, the guy clung to the hood and pressed his muzzle against the glass, giving Fisk a view up the barrel. Fisk expended his last bullet. It appeared to paint a third eye between the guy's original two before he rolled off the hood and onto the street.

The third suit, who'd originally positioned himself at three o'clock, now stood directly behind the Bentley, firing.

Bullets blasted cavities into the rear window before boring into the dashboard, instrument panel, and center console stereo, raising sparks and smoke.

Keep going, Fisk told himself. He floored the accelerator.

"Shit," Chay said, looking over his left shoulder.

He turned to see the Perrier truck backing up, toward him, its green back fender filling his side window. Then the vehicles crunched together, the driver's side of the Bentley swelling and bulging at Fisk, the windows exploding.

He propelled himself out of its way, in Chay's direction. Meanwhile the truck driver clomped his brakes, halting the Perrier truck, but not before its back fender lifted the Bentley onto its passenger side wheels.

When it came to rest, at a forty-five-degree angle from the ground, Fisk and Chay's egress was blocked by the truck's fender to his side and by concrete to hers.

He squatted on the passenger seat, his gun hand pressed against the windshield, the other against the headrest to keep from falling against her. She looked okay. She said nothing, maybe at a loss for words. He followed her wide eyes to the suit who was still standing. He circled the hood, cautiously, apparently trying to line up his best shot at Fisk. Twenty-Fifth Street was oddly still.

Although the Glock was empty, Fisk stuck the barrel through one of the apertures in the windshield. "Drop your weapon," he shouted.

The guy bent over and placed his gun on the pavement. But as he rose, a smile twisted his lips. The rearview showed Fisk why: the reinforcements from the tunnel were now exiting the stairwell through the doorway the Bentley had blocked.

Regarding the rearview mirror, Chay sighed. "Fuck." Echoing Fisk's sentiment.

He reached back to the driver's side, into the footwell, pressing the accelerator by hand. He hoped that the weight shift in combination with the friction from the two tires still on the ground might be enough to right the car. The tires shrieked. The rest of the car vibrated, but didn't move forward, not an inch.

Oddly, the reinforcements from the tunnel didn't advance either. And the reason for that came to Fisk in blue and red flashes on the garage's façade, from the light bars atop the police cars at either end of the block, and more joining them.

"We timed that well," Fisk said.

"You did a really good job of getting shot," Fisk was told by Larry Driessen, a thirty-something Emergency Service Unit paramedic with the look and mannerisms of a Borscht Belt comic. "The bullet drilled through your hip, yes, but it came and went without messing with the hipbone or any blood vessels, and without leaving anything behind that shouldn't be there."

"So you're trying to tell me I'm lucky?" Fisk lay on his side on a gurney inside one of the two ESU ambulance trucks—essentially mobile hospital rooms—that sat outside the parking garage entrance on the now sealed-off West Twenty-Fifth Street block. Inside the garage, much of which was now a crime scene, Chay was being interviewed by homicide detectives. "I don't feel lucky."

Driessen packed the hole in Fisk's hip with Celox, a fine yellow powdered hemostat, intended to stem the bleeding. It offered none of the burning or stinging threatened by its danger-nuclear-radiation-yellow tint, but the pressure felt like being kicked by a horse.

Stretching a field dressing over the wound, the paramedic said, "This is cliché, I know, but—you should see the other guy." He patted the dressing into place. "Now we just need to give the Celox five minutes to clot the blood, then get it back out, put a couple skin staples in you, and you'll be battle-ready again."

"Back up a sec," Fisk said. "Which other guy?" Police had quickly rounded up the survivors, then gone into the cow tunnel in pursuit of the Asian who'd abducted Chay.

"The Chinese kid."

"Any idea who he is?" One of the advantages of the ESU responding to these scenes was a battery of facial recognition, fingerprint, and DNA analysis to aid in identifying perps and victims on the spot.

"A Columbia graduate student named Ji-Hsuan Lin." Driessen chuckled. "At least as far as we know."

"Shot in the leg?"

"His right leg, yeah, but in the femoral artery, which is the Mississippi River of the circulatory system."

"So what are the odds of him ever making it back to school?"

"One in three," the paramedic said matter-of-factly.

"Tell me something: How do you treat that sort of wound?"

"By ligation—you close off the artery with a ligature. For now, though, pretty much the same as with yours, you try and clot the blood—Warthog's on it in the other meat wagon." Driessen used the departmental nickname for the notoriously belligerent Eunice Wortheimer, a longtime ESU veteran and, prior to that, an Army triage nurse.

Fisk pointed to his field dressing. "This comes off in five minutes?"

"Give or take."

Fisk sat up and slid off the gurney. Though he landed gently on the floor, the hip felt like it had been speared. Which was an improvement.

The paramedic stammered. "What are you doing?"

"I'll be back in five minutes, give or take," he said.

The young man who went by Ji-Hsuan Lin lay on a surprisingly comfortable gurney. I am Ji-Hsuan Lin, he told himself once more. It was important not just to play the role, but to be Ji-Hsuan Lin, now more than ever, with the painkillers putting him at risk of babbling. His training had pushed him as close as possible to the edge, but of course, in the back of his mind, he was always aware it was training.

The issue was, you couldn't train away susceptibility to narcosis. It was physiological roulette. Twenty-five percent of agents unwittingly blabbed under the influence of one drug or another. The moment when the painkiller kicked in had felt like the best moment of his life, although he knew better.

Certainly the moment they'd found him on the tracks was better. He'd lost so much blood. The average man has five liters in him.

Think like a Westerner, he exhorted himself. The average man has 1.5 gallons of blood in him. Lin weighed 140, so he had closer to 1.25 gallons. It looked like half that much had soaked into the pant leg the jowly nurse had scissored off.

She now packed the wound with a bright yellow hemostat. "If the police had gotten there half a minute later, you'd be on your way to the medical examiner now," she said. Her gruff voice matched her demeanor.

"It's just a flesh wound," Lin said, mustering a chuckle.

"It's a good thing you're brave, because—" She was interrupted by the creak of one of the rear doors swinging outward. "What the hell?"

Lin thought he recognized the man, who appeared to fight back a wince as he hoisted himself into the van.

The nurse growled. "Fisk, you can't be in here. You know that!"

"Didn't you get my text?" he asked.

"I don't like texts, especially not when I'm treating a damned patient."

"I need to ask your damned patient a quick question."

"No chance in hell." She folded her arms over her broad chest. "Get out now."

Fisk appeared to soften—changing tack, Lin guessed. The cop said, "Nurse Wortheimer, I shouldn't be telling you this." He paused, as if having thought better of it.

"What?" she asked, taking the bait. *Fool.*

"The charming Ivy Leaguer on the gurney here has already killed four New Yorkers, and preprogrammed one of his weaponized drones to assassinate Liang Huan Ding at the United Nations today. That's the leader of the China Democratic League, the party in China that opposes the Communists. We want to stop that."

Lin knew the name Liang Huan Ding. Yes, an

opposition party leader in China. But he'd die
years ago!

The nurse stabbed a thumb at Lin. "This is th
drone killer?" she asked Fisk.

"No, no, I have nothing to do with that," Li
protested. "He is either trying to frame me, or h
is crazy."

Fisk scoffed. "*Admit nothing, deny everything, mak
counteraccusations* . . . Your team must have gotte
ahold of our spooks' playbook."

Topping off the Celox, the nurse said to Lin
"Relax, I get it. Fisk is clever. He was just tryin
to play on my anti-Communist sympathies. But h
wasn't clever enough tonight. So now he has to th
count of five to get the hell out of here or he's goin
to be an ex-cop." She stretched a large pressure pa
over the wound. "One . . ."

Taking a flying step across the truck, Fisk yanke
open a metal-faced drawer beneath the supply cabinets and rifled through its contents, flinging aside
syringes and medication in some sort of search.

The nurse charged him. "Asshole," she exclaimed,
clamping her stovepipe arms around his back and
trying to pull him away.

He spun away from her, meanwhile winding his
right arm back as if to throw a baseball, revealing
the preloaded syringe in his hand.

At the sight of it, she gasped. "You are crazy!"

He lunged at her, apparently sticking the needle
into her shoulder and hammering the plunger, at
the same time pressing a palm over her mouth to
muffle her screams. She kicked, and squirmed, but
he was too strong. In seconds, her body went limp,

and he shook her onto the floor to the foot of the gurney, out of Lin's sight.

"Ketamine," Fisk said to Lin, casting aside the spent syringe. "She'll be out for at least five minutes." He rose, looming over the gurney. "If you want to last that long, tell me who you are."

Lin was stunned, and he suspected that it had nothing to do with his general drug-induced stupor. This Fisk deserved his hard-core reputation. But he was hardly the equal of the interrogators Lin had defied in the past. Lin had taken his country's version of the American military and intelligence officers' SERE—Survive, Evade, Resist, and Escape—course, which would have driven the Westerners to look instead for work as schoolteachers. Eight or nine days he spent in the dark pen, maybe ten—it was hard to keep track of the exact passage of time. Broiling hot, no food, no water, he couldn't see his hand in front of his face. Other than the stench, his only sensation was the click of tiny insects' feet against the cement floor, walls, and the four-foot-high ceiling. And that was before the sixteen-hour interrogation, during which they'd broken the same leg Fisk clawed at now. Lin knew that all he had to do was hold out for five minutes—Fisk had made a mistake in telling him that.

"Okay, I am a member of the Chinese diplomatic mission to the United—"

"Bullshit," Fisk cut in, at the same time firing a fist, and before Lin could react, sluggish as he was, knuckles smashed his upper lip into his front teeth, loosening one of them and filling his face with searing pain. Which was nothing compared to pain

from the gunshot wound—the savage ripped away
the compress. The pain traveled up and down Lin's
body like an electrical current.

Finally blood bubbled up from the hemostat, now
a reddish-purple putty. "Looks like the Celox isn't
going to work."

Lin bit the side of his mouth to counter the pain,
then lowered his head as if defeated. "MSS," he said.
Ministry of State Security.

"More bullshit!" Fisk thumped the wound.

Blood jetted out of it. Every last cell in Lin's body
ached. A hot, acidic vomit flew up his esophagus and
out of his mouth, spilling down his chin.

"Our MSS person told one of our guys they've
never heard of you," Fisk said. "There are a
thousand-something Ji-Hsuan Lins in China, but
you're not one of them."

Lin felt his body temperature dropping. Plummeting. His vision began to blur. His systems were
failing. Death had entered the room, and it fright-
ened him more than anything ever had, more than
he'd imagined anything ever could. He doubted that
he would be able to stall much longer. But he tried.
"Of course they said that," he said, each syllable
sending a flare of pain into his skull. "I'm an NOC.
Means you rot if you're caught."

"I know what nonoperational cover means."
Glancing at his reflection on one of the mirrored
supply-cabinet doors, Fisk rubbed the blood off the
tip of his nose, then ran his fingers through his hair.

Was he leaving now?

Yes, the interrogators fractured Lin's right fibula
in a training session. They break one of everybody's

bones. You know that going in. For which reason, Lin realized now, no training course could adequately simulate a life-or-death proposition. This was a real life-or-death proposition. He had believed he would die for the cause. He'd been wrong.

Lin, whose real name was Ryang Yong, found himself saying, "Ryang Yong, DPRK," and then admitting that he was an officer of the State Security Department—the North Korean spy agency.

Flying a false flag as China?

Yes, in order to get the Verlyn material.

Why?

It had not been his place to ask. But he speculated now: "Knowledge is power."

Then blackness devoured his consciousness.

No sooner had the North Korean spy lapsed into unconsciousness than Fisk became aware of Nurse Wortheimer stirring on the floor behind him. As he turned around, she reached for the open cabinet door, evidently to support her weight as she tried to get up.

Fisk bounded over. "Hell of an acting job, Eunice," he said, helping her to her feet. "I thought I'd actually knocked you out."

Wortheimer laughed. "In your dreams, ace."

Manhattan Plastix on Canal Street sold a variety of plastic products—sheet rubber, foam, stair treads, hoses, tubing, and floor tiles—and did a side trade in random items including cell phones, televisions, laptop computers, textbooks, and infant formula.

The single common denominator of these products, Blackwell suspected, was their provenance: they'd "fallen off the back of a truck." As far as computers went, for him, stolen was the best kind because the user was that much harder to trace. Outside the store, while rummaging through a carton of high-grade Ray-Ban knockoffs among the quick cash sale items, he discussed a new Hewlett-Packard laptop with one of the proprietors' nephews.

Two minutes later, three hundred-dollar bills lighter and wearing a new pair of sunglasses in spite of the rain—they'd been a gift from the nephew—Blackwell walked away from the store with the new computer tucked under his arm. He turned uptown at a stretch of Sixth Avenue that he knew had a plethora of drugstores.

In the smallest, oldest, and dingiest drugstore—chosen because it appeared the least likely to have any sort of cameras, he paid another hundred, in small bills this time, for a prepaid American Express card. Which would put him back in the business of tracking Fisk.

A few blocks further up Sixth Avenue, he took his new purchases into the Jefferson Market Library, a nineteenth-century red-brick assembly of steeply sloped roofs, gables, and other Gothic bells and whistles; Blackwell liked it for the free wireless. Lucking into a carrel in the crowded reading room, he bought himself—or rather, Cameron Milner, whom he concocted on the spot—an eighty-nine-dollar-per-month membership to DataBanq, a private investigators' resource that leveraged some thirty billion public data sources, including millions that were difficult to obtain otherwise, like voting records, bankruptcies, liens, and judgments. DataBanq also had thousands of proprietary databases, an aggregation of supposedly private social network information. But DataBanq's special sauce was the data it shouldn't have had.

Log onto DataBanq and you'll get the impression that it is a respectable organization, along the lines of the Legal Aid Society, dedicated to helping investigators solve cases. In fact, Blackwell knew, the company was a one-man shop, the one man being a forty-something ne'er-do-well who, practically overnight, turned his computer skill and the basement of his father's Milwaukee office-supply store into a multimillion-dollar business. He paid top dollar for the data equivalent of items that had fallen off trucks—motor-vehicle records, personnel files, medical records, drug prescriptions, utility bills, credit-card statements, airline reservations. No ten sites put together were as useful. Blackwell would have happily paid $890. Or, in this case, tonight, ten grand.

But—shit—DataBanq turned up nothing recent on Fisk, no record of recent financial transactions connected to his Social Security number, no expenditures, no withdrawals, no digital contact with friends or family members.

Fugitives left more of a trail than this guy.

Which left Blackwell back at square one, an old-school stakeout. Square zero, really. He knew Fisk was going to work; getting the proprietary address of NYPD Intel had been child's play and he'd staked it out, not in person but with Koolcams—camcorders concealed in what appeared to be empty, discarded packs of cigarettes—placed early in the morning in braided steel city-street trash barrels so that they captured twelve hours of activity. Fisk hadn't shown up in the footage. Probably he had a covert way in and out. For all intents and purposes, the guy was working in Fort Knox.

In desperation, Blackwell entered *Jeremy Fisk* as a search term on Google, and a recent news article turned up, straightaway:

WHY THE *NEW YORK TIMES* HELD THE DRONE KILLER STORY
By Chay Maryland

Published: July 1, 2015 *16 Comments*

NEW YORK—Following the shooting death of retired schoolteacher Walter Doyle in Battery Park late Tuesday night, the *New York Times* came into evidence that the killer, going by the pseudonym Yodeler online, had employed a remotely piloted unmanned aerial vehicle. The paper made an editorial decision to hold back the story so as not to compromise NYPD Intelligence leads on the case. As a measure of checks and balances, this reporter has since accompanied Detective Jeremy Fisk on the investigation.

Blackwell stopped reading, sat back, and allowed himself to exhale. Finding Fisk, he thought, would now be as easy as finding the reporter.

While Wall Street teetered, another New York City investment was rolling—literally, Blackwell reflected. Taxi medallions, the licenses that owners were required to fasten to the hoods of yellow cabs operating in the city, were now going for $800,000, an increase of 150 percent over ten years. Blackwell had been playing the stock market over the same period of time. New York taxi medallions had outperformed his portfolio by . . .

Best not to do the math, he thought.

With a booth to himself on the upper level of a two-story McDonald's in midtown—enjoying a Big Mac, a chocolate shake, and free wireless—the hit man returned his attention to the website of the New York City Taxi and Limousine Commission, the municipal organization that sold the medallions. He input the user name and password of a cabdriver he'd met. The guy had been more than happy to trade Blackwell his log-in information for a pair of hundred-dollar bills.

That $200 quickly started to look like one of Blackwell's better investments of late: he accessed the Taxi and Limousine Commission's proprietary traffic tracker, where medallion owners could keep tabs on their $800,000 cars in real time. Not only was each cab equipped with a transponder; each time a driver picked up a new fare and keyed in the destination, you could access that information on the traffic tracker.

Accordingly Blackwell was 98 percent sure that Chay Maryland had just gotten into a cab at the corner of West Twenty-Fifth Street and Tenth Avenue, about thirty blocks south of the McDonald's. He was 100 percent sure that her iPad, whose IP address he'd scored using Twitter Tracker, was in the cab—a Toyota Prius, according to the traffic tracker. Earlier this evening, via her iPad signals, Blackwell had been able to track Chay to a parking garage on West Twenty-Fifth, which was also a crime scene right now, according to his police scanner app, and not just any crime scene: an army of emergency responders was present. Fisk's latest case, Blackwell figured. To find Fisk now, Blackwell hoped to learn where Chay was going next.

With a tap at the Prius taxi icon on the traffic tracker, the destination input by the cabbie appeared in a pop-up window: *121 East 74th Street New York, NY 10021*. Blackwell clicked the address. Another window opened, offering a satellite view of a tree-lined stretch of East Seventy-Fourth Street. Building number 121 was one of several brownstones. Blackwell hurried out, leaving his empty Big Mac container and half-finished shake on the table. His rental car was parked at a meter on East Fifty-Ninth Street, a block away. He would drive to East Seventy-Fourth to meet Chay. If Fisk was along for the ride, great. That would save Blackwell a lot of time. If Chay were by herself, not bad either. He would use her to bait Fisk.

Madison Avenue glowed red and white as rain-slicked asphalt reflected the brake lights and headlamps. Most of them, thought Fisk, belonged to cabs returning residents home from evenings of theater or opera or similar tedium. From across the backseat of the Toyota Prius taxi, he took in Chay's lithe form silhouetted against the blur of neon bar and restaurant signs. He was pleased that she'd asked him to escort her to the FBI safe house. He wanted to be with her for reasons that had nothing to do with her security. For now, though, her security was paramount.

"And what about your phone?" he asked, part of a checklist of potential vulnerabilities.

"I pried the battery connector from the socket on the logic board," she said. "I have a Mossad source in Brooklyn who insists I do this every time I meet with him. It's getting to the point that I don't have to pry the battery so much as flick at it."

"Very good. How about that computer tablet you were using at the Bureau—is it Wi-Fi enabled?"

"The iPad? Yes, it has Wi-Fi, but it's not mine. It's one of the loaners from the bullpen at the *Times*."

"Have you checked your e-mail or anything on it?"

"Yes, but unless Twitter has also been infiltrated by the North Korean State Security Department . . ."

"Better safe than the other thing, right?"

She withdrew the tablet from her bag. "Do you know how to disable the signal?"

"It's a piece of cake," he said. When she handed it to him, he added, "After you spend an hour and a half learning how to do it from one of our tech guys."

Her laughter made him feel as though he'd sunk a three-pointer.

He began the complex procedure of neutralizing the iPad by inserting one of his apartment keys between the top edge of the display assembly and the rear panel assembly. Then he used the key to pry the two pieces apart.

Forty blocks later, as the taxi slowed on approach to Seventy-Fourth Street, he had succeeded in derouting the Wi-Fi antenna through its channel in the speaker assembly. He asked the driver to continue past Seventy-Fourth Street, go to Seventy-Sixth. His plan was to have the driver turn back downtown via Park Avenue before dropping them off on that side of Seventy-Fourth. The address he'd given the driver when they first got in—121 East Seventy-Fourth Street—was chosen at random. He didn't know what was there. Probably a brownstone. He had seen no reason to let the TLC log the real address of an FBI safe house. The purpose of going past Seventy-Fifth, the actual location of the safe house, was reconnaissance.

The taxi slowed for a red light at the intersection of Madison and Seventy-Fifth, permitting Fisk an extended look at the safe-house block, to his right. To his eye, the block was a still life. He also used God's Eye. DOM-CAM 75EMAD, the nearest NYPD cam, showed nothing out of the ordinary on the block.

After directing the taxi driver back downtown, Fisk was given one more angle onto Seventy-Fifth. Again, okay.

Finally he and Chay were dropped at the dummy

address on the equally quiet and mostly dark Seventy-Fourth Street. Taking inventory, he saw no one in the cars in the vicinity.

Starting onto the sidewalk, heading back toward Madison, he heard someone get out of a car parked behind them. Odd. The gentle way the person closed the door, as if trying to make as little noise as possible, set off Fisk's internal alarms.

He spun around, meanwhile drawing his reloaded Glock, coming to a stop so that his back was against Chay's, so that his body shielded hers from the man seventy-five feet away on the sidewalk—a sturdy middle-aged Caucasian with thick-framed glasses, a baseball cap pulled awfully far down his forehead, and a .22 tipped with a sound suppressor in hand. Burned into Fisk's mind, if not his muscle memory, were the five most common outcomes in this situation:

1. You die.
2. You spend a long time in the hospital.
3. You try to run away.
4. You shoot, prompting the other guy to retreat.
5. You shoot, injuring or killing him.

Fisk fired three times.

The first shot flew past the guy, the report scaring unseen pigeons into flight from between the curb and a parked car and resounding off the wet street, cars, and buildings.

The second shot appeared to shear the button off

the top of the guy's baseball cap, raising a puff of fibers into the cone of light cast by a streetlamp, but no more.

The third round stung his gun, sparking the suppressor as he aimed it and pressed the trigger, costing him his grip on the weapon. The report sounded like a dry cough.

His bullet tore into a few leaves on the bough over Fisk's head, sending particles drifting to the sidewalk. He took a step backward, positioning himself between Chay and the gunman to give her much more protection against the next shot.

But there was no next shot. The guy lost his hold on the silenced pistol altogether, and it clattered to the sidewalk before bouncing into the dark gap between the curb and the front tire of a parked Jeep. If he tried to recover it, he'd be a sitting duck. Not surprisingly, he turned and sprinted in the opposite direction.

Fisk started after him. One step into the pursuit, he knew that it was over. It felt as though his hipbone had exploded in the vicinity of his earlier wound. He tried to ignore it, but his body simply wouldn't permit him to proceed, and he fell forward, face first. Still he got off another shot at the shooter, but missed by a wide margin, taking out more leaves and a side mirror on a parked car. He hit the concrete, his free hand breaking some of the fall, his jaw absorbing the brunt of it.

Chay scrambled to him. "Are you okay?"

"Fine," he said, trying to appear that way as he struggled to his feet.

"Do you think he tracked me by the bloody

iPad?" Although the temperature was close to seventy, she was trembling.

"Maybe at first. But the only way he could have gotten this address was from the taxi driver, after the driver logged the dummy destination into his system." It was well known in the Department that with thirty thousand active drivers able to access the Taxi and Limousine Commission's traffic tracker, and even more ex-drivers still in possession of the log-in info, the site was practically open to the public. Because the man had been shooting to kill, as opposed to trying to snatch Chay, Fisk couldn't dismiss the possibility that he had been the target. "He might have been a representative of my friends at the Cartel."

She looked around, bracing, it seemed, for another attack. "I don't see how it's safe anywhere on the grid."

Actually, he thought, she would be okay in almost any hotel. Just check in under an alias. Either the Department or the Bureau would deploy watchdogs.

He said, "I know of a place that's off the grid."

Chay said, "Does it have beer?"

Fisk ushered Chay into darkness. At night, especially this late, with only a smattering of lights still on in the surrounding buildings, stepping into the new apartment had the feel of embarking on a spacewalk.

"Where are the lights?" she asked.

"Here." He pulled the Pelican flashlight from his pocket and clicked on its low beam, which he aimed at the cube fridge. "There's also a light in there."

She knelt and opened the door, the bright light snapping on and forming a halo around the six-pack of Brooklyn Lager, of which five bottles remained. She drew out two of them. "Don't suppose you have a bottle opener?"

"Right here." He tapped the adjacent counter.

"I don't see anything."

He took one of the bottles and laid it on the countertop so that the edge crimped the underside of the bottle cap. He gave the bottle itself a sharp tap. With nowhere to go but off, the cap flew into the darkness, landing with a jangle that echoed in the vast, empty room, of which Fisk said, "Sorry, the interior decorator and I haven't been able to find a time to sit down yet."

He led her to the small round table and its pair of folding chairs, the only furniture save for the TV and the inflatable bed—that there was just the one bed, he knew, would be an issue for later.

With the Pelican balanced on its base, serving as a candle, they sat at the table and recapped the events of the day. Quickly they finished their Brooklyn Lagers. Chay found her way to the kitchen and returned with two more bottles.

"The opener," Fisk reminded her.

"It's okay," she said, retaking her seat and crossing her legs. "I've got this one." She took up one of the bottles and wedged the bottle cap into the underside of her chiseled calf muscle, giving her a hold on the cap's teeth. She applied pressure, meanwhile twisting the bottle, bringing three tiers of sinew in her forearm into play. And off popped the cap.

Fisk had thought this method of opening a bottle the stuff of urban myth. Amazing. It made him hard.

After she uncapped the second Brooklyn Lager, in the same fashion, he raised his bottle to toast. "Here's to your origin story."

She held her bottle back. "Because this is the Second Beer?"

"Will you tell me where you're from now?"

"I'm going to need one more thing from you first."

"Now what?"

"This . . ." She leaned closer to him and kissed him on the mouth. And didn't back away. Her breath tasted like Brooklyn Lager, and her scent—a fragrance of flowers with a trace of peppermint in combination with a long summer day's worth of salty perspiration and New York City emissions—was intoxicating. To keep it coming, Fisk laced his arms around her back and drew her closer. She slid from her chair and onto his lap. She was firm in the right places, and soft in the right places, and he set about exploring them all. Ever the investigator, so did she, with caresses and kisses. His hip flared with pain. Small price to pay, he thought. They proceeded slowly and gently. But inevitably, fueled by the release of pent-up feelings and desires, the intensity ratcheted up, forcing them beyond the limits of the folding chair.

"Do you want to see the bedroom?" he asked.

"There's a bedroom?"

"Actually, we're already in it, but if you want to see it . . ." He took up the Pelican and swept the beam along the floorboards, toward the bed.

They raced that way, unbuttoning, unbuckling, unsnapping each other, and leaving a wake of tossed clothing before plunging onto the mattress. They made love at a sprint, both of them ravenous, and it seemed concerned that, at any moment, another attack or drone strike would forestall them.

The next morning, that's exactly what happened.

Still in bed, Fisk and Chay turned on the TV to watch one of the rebroadcasts of the *Today* show. They saw the beginning of the attack the way millions of other Americans had. The hosts—Al Roker, Matt Lauer, and Savannah Guthrie, seated in a row at their elevated news desk—turned around and stared in mystification through their window onto Rockefeller Center, where the crowd of spectators was bolting en masse, many of the people shouting, one of them casting aside her hand-painted "Al for President" placard.

The bulk of the news reports of the incident featured cell-phone videos taken by tourists who had been eating breakfast around the corner at the Rock Center Café, in the same sunken plaza that served as the ice-skating rink during winter months. What appeared to Fisk to be a black Specter quadrocopter descended like a feather into the sunken plaza, coming to a hover at its center stage, in front of the famous gilded statue of Prometheus. The burble of the surrounding fountains masked the whine of the rotors. Still, each of the two hundred heads spun toward the drone.

This time, no one sought a closer look. No one exhibited the slightest curiosity. No, they knew full well whose drone it was and why it was there. It was the reason so many of them had scored Rock Center Café tables this morning—after the Yodeler story broke, tourists who'd made their breakfast reservations months in advance decided they were better safe than sorry.

Now parents seized their children by the wrists, and, in many cases, picked them up out of their seats. All around, chairs toppled and plates and glasses shattered against the granite floor. Everyone charged the stairwell leading out of the sunken plaza, up to street level. There were other ways out, Fisk knew, through the indoor section of the restaurant or the Rockefeller Center subway station or the adjacent underground shopping center. But if you're in a rush—this sort of rush, you don't take time to read signs or venture into the dark recesses of an unfamiliar sunken plaza in hope that one of the bronze-plated doors happens to be an unlocked path to safety. No, you take the sure thing a thousand times out of a thousand: the flight of stairs with an upper landing, Rockefeller Plaza, right there in plain view.

Sure enough, every last one of the two hundred diners swarmed into the base of the narrow stairwell, which was suitable for perhaps ten people—if those ten were proceeding in an orderly and unhurried fashion.

To Fisk's surprise, the crowd did remain orderly, several with cool heads among them hanging back to assist the pair of policemen in funneling the patrons into two single-file lines. Fisk recognized one of the cops, Larry McCone, who was known to fellow officers as "McClone" because of his seeming propensity to be in several places at the same time: on duty as well as a devoted father to four young boys, a leader of the Patrolmen's Benevolent

Association's World Trade Center efforts, and the shortstop for the NYPD Blues, perennial contenders for the Police Softball National Championship. McCone was aided by restaurant staffers, who managed to steer many of the patrons to safety via the subway station. Nobody would be trampled today, it appeared. Fisk and Chay already knew, however, that the death count stood at three, but even if they hadn't known, a tragic end was indicated by the demeanor of the anchorwoman narrating the story, particularly when she warned that the footage was about to get "graphic."

The quadrocopter fired three shots, each hitting Larry McCone in the back, spraying blood onto the patrons assisting him and creating the panic that spurred the stampede. As the anchorwoman related, a young mother from Iowa was trampled to death along with her eighteen-month-old daughter she'd been trying to protect.

Well after the report had ended, Fisk remained in bed, his back against the brick wall. He was feeling more guilty by the minute. Chay lay beside him, her head wedged into the crook of his neck, a gesture of commiseration. Her long hair, hot from the influx of sun, warmed his rib cage. He wondered how long she'd been in that position. Last he'd noticed, she was sitting on the far side of the mattress, watching the telecast in horror.

Turn off your emotions, he exhorted himself, and get to work. He could do that, to a fault, he'd been told many times. *Use it to your advantage now.*

He returned his thoughts to the investigation, going over everything that had happened. He tried to form different perspectives, in search of a clue he might have overlooked—

All of that went out the window with the incoming text from Dubin—who barely knew how to text. Encrypted no less.

SHT/FAN. GROWNUPS WANT US TO IBB RAPUNZEL.

The shit had hit the fan. RAPUNZEL was Merritt Verlyn. The GROWNUPS were some combination of the commissioner, the mayor, the governor, and the president. IBB originated in baseball, where it stood for intentional base on balls, better known as an intentional walk. The brass wanted to let Verlyn walk.

After squaring Chay away in his apartment, Fisk headed down to Intel on foot, which was always the fastest way to go twenty blocks or less in New York. Fury doubled his usual brisk pace and relegated the stabbing pains in his hip to an afterthought.

The city was freakishly quiet, perhaps 10 percent of which was because of the July Fourth holiday—Independence Day was tomorrow. The other 90 percent was attributable to the Yodeler news. Hearing it, commuters on the way into town had turned around. Everyone else who could miss work stayed home. Summer camps were suspended until further notice, leaving wary parents to draw the blinds and explain to children why they couldn't play in the park on this, the most beautiful day of the summer.

When Fisk got to Dubin's office, he found the chief standing by the row of windows looking onto Ninth Avenue, where almost as common as Crown Victoria taxis this morning were boxy olive-green trucks. Deployed by the Army, the trucks comprised the ground-based component of the airborne warning and control system intended as the city's answer to Israel's Iron Dome. The NYPD Hercules teams implementing this system had taken to calling it the Iron Apple.

Evans was standing oddly straight, considering he was holding a laptop computer and typing on it. He read aloud what he and Weir, who sat on the back of the couch, maintained was their lone remaining lead:

FISK:
DID YOU REALLY THINK YOU COULD PUSH
MY BUTTONS? I WILL CONTINUE TO PUSH MY
OWN BUTTON (THE TRIGGER) UNTIL MERRITT
IS FREE.
    DON'T WASTE MY TIME OR YOURS ON
COMMUNICATION (READ: STALL TACTICS)
UNTIL YOU HAVE SECURED HIS RELEASE.
YODELER

"For what it's worth, the e-mail originated in Loch Ness," Evans said. "And that's not just us, that's according to Lackland." Lackland, Fisk knew, was the NSA's Cryptologic Center at Lackland Air Force Base in San Antonio. Lackland had been the best hope of electronically tracing Yodeler.

"In Loch Ness?" Dubin asked. The morning light streaming in added depth to his worry lines.

Evans nodded. "The communication was sent— or at least appears to have been sent—from the exact mathematical middle of the twenty-two-point-seven-square-mile loch, yes, sir."

Dubin sighed. "Clever guy."

"Which he reminds us in every e-mail," Fisk said. "It's a weakness of his."

Both Dubin and Evans reacted as though he'd said something off-color, and Weir grumbled, "Bastard's been a step ahead of you all along, Fisk."

Not ahead of *us*. Ahead of *you*. Anger heated Fisk. A waste of heat, he thought. Similarly, the blame game wouldn't get them any closer to Yodeler. He said, "We just need time until it causes him to make a mistake."

Dubin turned away from the window. "You've had plenty of time, Jeremy."

Again *you* rather than *we*. And *had*, past tense. This meeting wasn't about a game plan, Fisk realized, as much as it was about Monday-morning quarterbacking.

"So you guys hear how Iron Apple detected the drone?" Dubin grinned as if telling a joke.

"How?" Weir didn't ask so much as egg him on.

"The sensor operator in one of the trucks happened to be watching the *Today* show broadcast live. The best detection system on the planet, and it didn't detect shit. Turns out Iron Apple is useless against anything that's launched from within two kilometers, however much that is in nonmetrics."

"One and one-quarter miles," Weir offered.

Dubin ignored him. "The Israelis don't have anyone launching at them from anything close. And

when their Iron Dome does detect a UAV, you know
how they intercept the thing? They scramble F-16s
to shoot it down, or drop flares or fire lasers to fuck
with its sensors. But you can't very well fly F-16s
here—half the streets, the wings wouldn't even
fit. We do have lasers, all six of the laser cannons
available east of the Mississippi, on rooftops. And
the Hercules guys have been given flare guns. The
thing is, they have a tough enough time shooting
accurately with a handgun, a one-in-three proposition. And the flares still don't work half the time."

Which was why the grown-ups, Dubin went on
to relate, were now en route to One St. Andrew's
Plaza, to the U.S. attorney's office. Commissioner
Bratten, Mayor de Blasio, Governor Cuomo, and
the assistant director in charge of the FBI's New
York Field Office, George Venizelos—Evans and
Weir's boss's boss—were meeting with U.S. Attorney Preet Bharara to discuss the possibility of releasing Verlyn, as early as midnight tonight, in order
to satisfy Yodeler before another day had elapsed.

Recognizing that his own outrage was of no use,
Fisk clung to the hope that such a release would be
illegal, or that the U.S. attorney would block the
move on moral grounds. "Forgetting that letting
Verlyn walk would be idiotic from a law enforcement perspective, how can we just let him go from
a legal standpoint? Get the judge to waive the U.S.
Constitution just this one little time?"

"Maybe the judge will knock down his bail out of
the stratosphere," Dubin said.

Fisk hoped logic would prevail. "The bail's in the

stratosphere because Verlyn's a flight risk, not to mention a couple of mouse clicks away from posting the NSA family jewels to the World Wide Web. The Russians would literally kill to exfiltrate him."

"Well, we've got to figure something out." The chief lowered himself into his desk chair as if he were getting into a cold bath. "For now we need to face the facts. It's late in the game, and Yodeler's kicking our ass."

Evans closed his laptop and took one of the chairs in front of the desk with a similar air of defeat. Weir dropped into the adjacent seat.

Still pacing, Fisk said, "If we quit now, it's not just that Yodeler wins, it's encouraging the next guy who wants something to stick a gun on a drone."

Dubin shrugged. "The grown-ups are saying that by the time there's a next guy, Iron Apple will be fully up and running."

Of course they're saying that, Fisk thought. Politicians almost always viewed technology as a cure-all, or at least they knew that they could sell it to the voting public that way. He said, "When Clinton was president, he concluded that intelligence officers could be replaced by satellites. Where would the four of us be now if that had happened? Where would the country be now?"

"You're preaching to the choir, kiddo," said Dubin.

The world's most dispirited choir, Fisk thought. "So let's tell them that Iron Apple isn't the solution now, that we can't give in to the Yodelers of the world no matter what. If and when the Iron Apple is working, the next bad guy will find a way to—I don't know—glue C-4 to cockroaches and remotely detonate them."

Dubin stiffened. " 'The Israelis let terrorists walk all the time'—that's a direct quote from the governor, who I was talking to on the phone right before you got here, and he has a point."

Weir and Evans nodded like bobblehead dolls. In national security circles, Israel was Hogwarts. But the Israelis would never swap out a Hamas prisoner, Fisk thought, if the guy were poised to upload files that would cost Israeli lives. Israel routinely traded prisoners by the truckload for just one of their own men. More than once the Israelis had traded a dozen live prisoners for the body—*only the body*—of one of their men. And often, Israeli intelligence officers turned a prisoner so that, on return to Beirut, he acted on behalf of Jerusalem, whether he was aware of it or not.

It dawned on Fisk that this might be the play here: an intelligence operation. What if Yodeler believed he was winning the game while, in reality, he was scoring points for the NYPD?

Finally taking a seat, Fisk thought aloud: "Maybe it's a good thing that Verlyn's a flight risk. Maybe there's a way to play it so Verlyn leads us to Yodeler."

Weir chuckled. "Can he do windows too?"

Fisk reminded himself that he needed Weir. Between now and midnight, one of the hundred-something FBI staffers working the phones might learn of a delivery of a four-pack of Specter rotor blades to a local post office box belonging to a person who, it turned out, didn't exist—or who used to exist but didn't anymore.

"There's reason to believe Verlyn and Yodeler are confederates," Fisk said.

Weir seemed surprised. "There is?"

When Evans muttered a reminder to his partner about the NYPD record-of-interview PDF he'd forwarded to him, Fisk took the opportunity, for Dubin's benefit as well as Weir's, to recap what he and Chay had gleaned in their interview of Verlyn at the Manhattan Correctional Center. He'd put as much in the record of interview, but the significance of the Verlyn-Yodeler connection wasn't as great then as it was now.

Weir turned to Dubin. "We wish we'd known the NYPD was going to question the suspect. We would have tried a few different things."

Dubin looked to Fisk with eyebrows raised, turning the lines on his forehead into channels. His unasked question, Fisk knew, was, *Have you gone rogue once again?*

Fisk wanted to reply that the FBI had already taken multiple cracks at Verlyn, and that if, prior to last night's interview, the Red Team had produced any useful elicitation tactics, it would have been an historic first. Instead he said, "If we can black out the media when Verlyn walks, our line of communication with Yodeler won't have been for nothing. We'll shoot him an e-mail that says something like, 'You've won, Yodeler. We'll let Verlyn go tonight at such and such time and place.' Without media coverage, Yodeler will want some other verification that his man is out."

Weir chuckled. "So, what, now you want him to send his drone?"

Fisk wanted to thank him. "Exactly. We may not be able to shoot it down, but we can at least follow it back to Yodeler."

"Not bad," Dubin said. "Except what's preventing Yodeler from tipping off the media to the time and place of the release? A single New York One camera would save him from having to send a drone."

"He'll want protection for his man, Verlyn. Rival intel services are after Verlyn. Also a member of the New York One audience could decide to be the next Jack Ruby."

The chief nodded, impressed, then, with a look, put it to the feds.

"I don't know," said Evans.

Weir grumbled. "Hard to say."

They were busy trying to think of objections, Fisk suspected. There were alternative plans of action they could take, maybe even better plans. But they had nothing because they'd been too busy ass-covering.

On the website AirBnB.com, Blackwell booked a "breezy East Village apartment with old-world charm" at $75 per night. Way cheap for anyplace within fifty miles of New York, he thought. But it turned out to be overpriced. "Old-world charm" meant a lack of modern amenities. "Breezy" meant no air-conditioning. The place was secure, however, and had wireless Internet. He would have happily shelled out $750 for that package.

Taking a seat at the ironing board that folded out from the wall beside the refrigerator—a future ad might refer to this as a "contemporary dining room," he thought—he checked in on Chay. The iPad hadn't transmitted since last night, just before the cab dropped her and Fisk at East Seventy-Fourth Street. It was possible that she was onto Blackwell and had disconnected the transmitter. Or maybe she'd spent the night somewhere that interfered with transmission—New York could be one giant signal jammer.

Whichever way it was, she'd certainly been busy today, he thought as he read the *New York Times* front page. Merritt Verlyn's bail had been reduced on appeal to $10 million following his agreement to wear an electronic monitoring device.

Chay had broken the story—for what that was worth to her: within fifteen minutes of its posting, the same story was on every other news site in the country. What it could be worth to Blackwell was a shot at Jeremy Fisk, who would likely be on hand at the Metropolitan Correctional Center when Verlyn walked. Chay did not report when the release would take place. If she even knew, she probably withheld the information intentionally. Blackwell scoured the piece for clues.

The nonprofit First Amendment Society had ponied up a million bucks to a New York bail bondsman who told Chay he planned to have Verlyn bonded out within twenty-four hours, though details of the release were being withheld for the suspect's protection. Of course, Blackwell thought. Otherwise the release would be a circus. He considered that most prisons processed out inmates first thing in the morning in order to allow themselves time to get ready for new arrivals. Just like hotels.

He eyed the clock in the upper right corner of his latest burner laptop. 4:20 P.M. So it stood to reason that Verlyn would be sprung first thing tomorrow. But in Chay's story, according to NYPD Intel's Detective Jeremy Fisk, Yodeler had agreed in an e-mail to cease the drone attacks once Verlyn was safely out. So maybe the release would go down today so that New York could avoid another death from above? Blackwell decided to take his act to the Metropolitan Correctional Center.

He wasn't the only one with that idea. He realized as much while driving through Chinatown, the streets and sidewalks eerily underpopulated for a weekday, a function of Yodeler, not the light drizzle. Two different news vans—NY1 and 1010 WINS— blew past Blackwell's rental car, their drivers clearly not as concerned as he was about getting pulled over. Backing into a parking spot, still two blocks from the Metropolitan Correctional Center, he caught sight of the tall, telescoping antenna of yet another news van.

As he got closer to the center, on foot now, it appeared that about half of the pedestrians in the vicinity were journalists. A hundred of them, easy, many gathered under white temporary sun shelters, four-legged canopies labeled in block letters, TARU, whatever that was. Several men, wearing navy-blue uniforms with TARU emblazoned on the back in bright yellow, had the bench-press-intensive build of military.

TARU?

Blackwell put it to his latest burner smartphone: Technical Assist Response Unit, a division of the NYPD that officially "provided equipment and tactical support." Unofficially, he gathered, they were narcs. The unit had repeatedly come under fire for violating the court-imposed Handschu Guidelines, which restricted the NYPD from building files on innocent citizens. It was doubtful that the TARU was here to install canopies; more likely they were gathering intelligence, perhaps from members of the media trying to trump one another with tidbits obtained from sources on the condition of anonymity, or from WikiLeaks members with loose lips. And there might well be a Verlyn confederate in the crowd. The sun shelters were probably bait.

Unfortunately, between TARU and all of the news cameras, this was quite possibly the worst place in the city to have a go at Fisk. If he was even here. More likely the detective would oversee things from an ops center. And an NYPD ops center would be the second worst place for a go at Fisk.

Blackwell decided he was better off working at his own ops center, aka the "breezy East Village apartment with old-world charm." Dropping his phone into his pants pocket, he turned back to his car. He wasn't dispirited. He never was. He had always found a way, and always would. Someday, he thought, scientists would find a telepathic correlation between positive thinking and positive outcomes. As if on cue, his phone vibrated against his hip, with a texted alert:

CALL ACCOUNTANTS

This was his own code, to be delivered to him as a text message if and when Chay's iPad came back online.

He launched his DataBanq app, selected the file of his saved IP addresses, and selected 001, his code for Chay's iPad. It appeared as a pulsing blue circle on a rudimentary map of Manhattan. She—or at least her iPad—was just a few blocks away, at 240 Centre Street, the copper-domed landmark still known as NYPD headquarters, although the building had long since been converted to condominiums after the police moved to One Police Plaza. But possibly the police maintained a presence there, a safe house or maybe something that was off the books entirely, the sort of place from which Fisk could covertly run TARU agents in knowing violation of the Handschu Guidelines.

Blackwell hurried back to his car to get his rifle.

Mounted on the wall in three rows of three, the nine monitors in the ops-center viewing room played feeds from surveillance cameras within the Manhattan Correctional Center and Domain Awareness cams outside.

On the lower left monitor was the feed from DOM-CAM PRW W-PRL (Park Row west of Pearl Street). Seated at a table in front of the monitors, Fisk and Chay watched a throng of journalists making room under one of the canopies for yet another camera crew.

"If the Department had obtained this without the requisite warrants, would you tell me?" Chay asked.

"Yes," Fisk replied, although he doubted it. Which left him conflicted: He wanted to eliminate barriers between them. He wanted to tell her the truth. Deception was part of his job description, but he took pains to avoid it in his personal relationships. Of course, they were at work now. At work, he wished she could understand that justice was like triage: saving patients came first. Sometimes that meant skipping paperwork. The truth was, if red tape or misguided politics had prevented the Bureau from securing the requisite warrants tonight, he would have bugged the hell out of the Metropolitan Correctional Center anyway, because losing track of Verlyn would be catastrophic.

"So if everything goes as planned, what happens?" she asked.

"If everything goes as planned, that would be an historic first," he said just as motion on the middle right monitor caught his eye.

A Metropolitan Correctional Center escorting officer was leading Verlyn out of his cell.

Game time, Fisk thought. Or, at least, hoped.

The inmate's eyes darted around, as if he were expecting someone to run up with news that his release had been postponed or canceled. In Fisk's experience, inmates were often on edge when being processed out. They had dreamed of their release so often, it was only natural for them now to expect that, at any moment, they would wake up, back in their cells.

The escorting officer directed Verlyn to an elevator, down two floors, through the common area, and finally into the administration room, a cramped space that reminded Fisk of the office in a big high school. Staffers at six small desks—in a space designed for three—looked up from their terminals briefly before resuming work.

Fisk pressed the talk button on the intercom panel. "How about the dust?"

"Coming right up on seven," came the voice of David Rettenmund, the short and stocky tech everyone called R2 after the similarly proportioned droid. Fisk thought of R2 as incredibly resourceful with computer skills and a good nature to match. As ever, the kid was at his station in the control room, two doors down the hall. The feed he directed to the lower left monitor shifted from an empty cellblock to an overhead map of the Metropolitan Correctional Center and the vicinity, with a cluster of flashing green dots superimposed over the facility.

"Are those transponders?" Chay asked.

"They're remotely activated particles of smart dust," Fisk said.

"The same stuff the CIA deploys from Predators?"

He knew that she meant the tiny, undetectable radio-signal transmitters the Agency's MQ-1s dropped by the thousands from altitudes of five thousand to ten thousand feet in hope that two or three would adhere to a human target, enabling intelligence officers halfway around the world to track him. "Pretty much," he said. "It's a hell of a lot more effective if you sprinkle it onto your target's clothing and shoes from six inches away."

The green dots jumped upward, in unison. The motion was explained to Fisk by the monitor with a close-up view of the administrative officer retrieving a brown shopping bag from a cubby. Setting the bag on the countertop between herself and Verlyn, she said, "Inmate Number 61729-013, this is dressout. Once we've gotten back all the items you were given while you were incarcerated, you'll get back the clothes you were arrested in plus any items that you had on your person."

Pulling his orange prison-uniform shirt free of his waistband, Verlyn asked, "So are you going to play some *Flashdance* music for me?"

"Ha," said the officer, a sleepy-eyed Hispanic woman who must have heard similar lines every day for years. She pointed to an accordion-style changing screen that stood in the corner. "Please change behind that, then hand the items to Officer Perez."

Looking into the shopping bag, Verlyn was given pause. "I was supposed to receive a fresh dress-out."

"You got it. It's waiting for you on the chair behind the screen."

Verlyn disappeared behind the screen.

"That would be our first thing gone wrong," Fisk said. "Someone sent him new duds."

"To thwart the smart dust?" asked Chay.

"Could be nothing. Family members send dress-outs to inmates all the time. All mail entering a correctional facility is searched for contraband and scanned." He hit the intercom button. "R2, do we know who sent him the clothes?"

"Checking," the tech said, a half second later adding, "Arrived by messenger just an hour ago from the First Amendment Society's office in United Nations Plaza."

"Too bad their advocacy of transparency doesn't extend to keeping us in the know," Fisk said.

Chay asked, "Before you got into business with the First Amendment Society, how thoroughly did you check them out?"

"They were vetted by Evans and Weir," Fisk said of the FBI agents, who were monitoring the proceedings in a similar setup at 26 Federal Plaza. Fisk had judged the First Amendment Society to be harmless. Nevertheless it wouldn't be the first time that an honorable proponent of American intelligence-agency transparency acted, unwittingly, in the interests of enemy spy services. There was evidence that the Sluzhba Vneshney Razvedki—or SVR,

Russia's external intelligence agency—contributed heavily to WikiLeaks, using a front organization to issue the checks.

Verlyn emerged from behind the changing screen, having replaced his orange uniform with a tight-fitting black tracksuit unadorned by piping or racing stripes or even a logo. Just black.

"Is he planning to disappear?" Chay asked.

Fisk had been wondering the same thing. "If he is, the all-black action's a bit obvious, isn't it?"

Verlyn returned the orange uniform, which he'd folded as neatly as any item on display at a clothing store, to the administrative officer. "Please donate my other things to the Salvation Army," he told her.

"You got it," she said. With the assistance of the escorting officer, she proceeded to fit an all-black device resembling a wristwatch around Verlyn's left ankle. It registered on one of the viewing room monitors as a pulsing red circle labeled *EMD-61729-013*, shorthand for electronic monitoring device, along with Verlyn's inmate number.

Fisk and Chay were left to watch as Verlyn was processed out, a routine as monotonous for everyone else as it was exhilarating for the inmate. Standing at the counter, Verlyn filled in the blanks, checked the appropriate boxes, and signed form after form, including a confirmation that all of his personal items had been returned to him along with a consent to the terms of his release on bond and a separate agreement to reappear in court. Finally the admin officer counted out fifteen dollars, a five and ten ones, and pushed it across the countertop. This was his discharge allowance—because the cost of living was so much higher in New York City, discharged inmates received five dollars more than their counterparts elsewhere in the state.

"You are also entitled to an amount equal to the least expensive means of transportation to your point of sentencing," the administrative officer told Verlyn.

"Thank you, ma'am," he said, "but I have a ride."

Fisk muttered, "He must have covertly corresponded with someone about the details of his release."

"News to you?" asked Chay.

"I'd expected as much. This is the reason we put a surveillance team in place."

He and Chay watched as the monitors shifted to feed from cameras on Verlyn's walk from the administrative offices to the departure area. Idling by the loading bay in the garage was a late-model black Lincoln Navigator with exceedingly dark windows. When Verlyn entered the garage, the driver popped out and hurried around the hood to open the passenger door for him. Verlyn climbed in without a word to the man.

"First Amendment Society booked the Navigator too," came R2's voice.

Fisk felt a cool trickle of adrenaline. "The nonreflective tinting on the windows can't possibly meet the legal requirement of allowing in at least thirty-five percent of outside light."

Chay slid forward in her seat. "What do you think he's up to?"

"Hopefully he's up to no good. We don't get any actionable intel if he just goes home to his apartment and orders a pizza."

The garage-door-style gate rolled open and the Navigator chugged out, across the sidewalk and onto the street to the rear of the facility, Cardinal Hayes Place. It was met by three others just like it.

"Good or no good?" Chay asked.

"Probably just a diversion for the reporters," Fisk said, "though if he thinks we're going to be that easy to lose, God bless him."

"The Navigators were dispatched by Kelly Limo, the same guys the Department uses," came R2's voice. "All four of them."

"How many surveillants do you have?" Chay asked.

"Only about fifty," Fisk said.

She didn't blink, just nodded. As she surely knew, surveillance teams of more than a hundred people were quite common in New York and D.C. Because the streets were so much less crowded than usual, Dubin and Fisk had selected a smaller team of elite NYPD operators. Weir and Evans had ceded the reins without protest, which surprised Fisk—that is, until he considered that the Bureau had little to gain by participating in a successful surveillance op. If the team were to somehow lose Verlyn, Weir could demand Fisk's head.

Night was falling outside the Metropolitan Correctional Center, where the journalists weren't decoyed by the other Lincoln Navigators. All of the reporters who had been staking out Cardinal Hayes Place now swarmed the SUVs. But it quickly became apparent that getting the vehicles to stop would place them at risk of being run down. Just like that, they lost any chance of a sound bite from

Verlyn or a photo of anything more than a tinted window.

The monitors cut from a loading bay to the feed from nine Domain Awareness cameras on the street. Chay noted, "Martin Scorsese could only hope for so many camera angles. Is this the God's Eye system?"

He wondered how she knew about the system. "The what?"

"No need to be coy, it's old news. I reported on Father Phil two years ago."

"Who's Father Phil?" Fisk's curiosity was genuine.

"Philip Borbon, the ordained-priest-turned-computer-scientist in Dayton, Ohio, who created the system. I saw that he donated twenty million dollars to Catholic University recently, so I figured he must have reeled in some customers."

"I wouldn't know anything about it," Fisk said. Which was true. It was news to him.

Digging her phone from her bag, she said, "If the NYPD is using God's Eye, I hope you've solved the glitch that the Metro Police in D.C. discovered last week."

"What's that?"

She held up her phone, showing a broad overhead view of Washington at sundown. He made out the Capitol Dome, bathed in pink light. "Father Phil thinks too well of his fellow man," she said. "His aerial feed has almost no security. Bank robbers hacked in—or, really logged on—and were able to disable the view of the sixteen-square-block section of Adams Morgan that included the bank they robbed—two hundred and fifty thousand dollars in cash."

The breadth of her knowledge and sources left Fisk, once again, flabbergasted. If he ever was going to learn anything about the officially nonexistent Special Collection Service, F6, he thought, his best chance was to ask her about it.

"You hearing this, R2?" he said into the intercom.

"That's not the half of it, sir," said the tech. "Right now anyone can access Domain Awareness feeds on faa.gov from the air-traffic-control page because the God's Eye birds fly out of the Marine Air Terminal at LaGuardia. We're working on that."

Seeing Chay keying away at the notepad on her phone, Fisk wondered if he needed to tell her that what R2 had just said was privileged, when his attention was diverted by the procession of SUVs on the monitors. Within two blocks, they'd outpaced the last of the reporters chasing on foot. After another two blocks, as the convoy rumbled past the ramp to the Brooklyn Bridge, the pulsing green circle representing the electronic monitoring device on Verlyn's ankle was replaced by a red hexagon. The speaker carried the sound of a buzzer from the control room.

"His electronic monitoring device is experiencing technical difficulties," explained R2.

Fisk sat up. "About time!"

"Could the Brooklyn Bridge be disrupting the signal?" asked Chay.

Fisk smiled. "That's what he'd like us to think."

R2 said, "U.S. marshals are on line one, wanting a patrol car to stop Verlyn, for violating his bond agreement by monkeying with his EMD."

Fisk took out his frustration by choking a chair

arm. "Please tell them, again, that we want him to think that he's gone black."

"Yes, sir."

Continuing past the Brooklyn Bridge, Verlyn's Navigator took a left onto Spruce Street, passing Pace University, where traffic thickened. Not unrelated, perhaps, teenagers and twenty-somethings streamed out of an auditorium building toward the Brooklyn Bridge 4, 5, and 6 lines subway stop, at the hurried pace that had become the norm with drones liable to appear at any second. The Navigator turned abruptly into the five-story Pace Plaza parking garage. And was lost to Fisk and Chay.

Hitting the intercom, he asked R2, "Can you get video in there?"

"The Pace Plaza Parking Garage security cams are streaming live on monitors one, two, and three," R2 said.

What? The upper-row monitors were all dark. Wait. No, they weren't. Fisk could make out shades of gray and dark green and the occasional sliver of light.

"I'm trying to boost the light values," the tech added.

Fisk could make out other cars exiting, and waiting to exit. A bad feeling came over him, like a cold coming on. Had he overestimated his team's ability to track Verlyn? If Verlyn now had a confederate at the wheel of a car other than the Lincoln, or even if he had access to another car, he could get away.

No sooner did he think it than Fisk was on the radio with the surveillance team's chief, pleased to hear that she was sending all available units into the parking garage. After that he could only sit and watch as the monitors brought video of a young man in a Pace University T-shirt hurrying away from his table and then out of a Starbucks, slowing as he entered the garage. At the same time, a woman in her early twenties, clad in a Yankees jersey as well as a cap with the interlocked *N* and *Y*, ran toward the parking garage, relaxing her pace on arrival.

Pointing at them, Chay asked, "Won't a sudden influx of people tip off Merritt?"

"Yes," said Fisk. "But only if he sees a lot of them. They're each being deployed to a different sector to search, so there's no reason he would."

"Iron Apple has a fix on a drone," announced R2, going on to detail the Specter quadrocopter hovering at 108 feet above Park Row, blocked from the view of those on the street by a canopy of trees in City Hall Park, by the intersection of Spruce Street.

Fisk gathered as much with the vibrant green thermal imagery on the centermost monitor, replete with data readily accessible to any amateur, like AIR SPEED 0 MPH and SYSTEM'S BEST GUESS: SPECTER QUADROCOPTER MODEL Q4.3. His attention went to ARMAMENT: NOT RECOGNIZED.

"Any idea what it's packing?" Fisk said into the intercom.

"Zooming," said R2. The image of the drone enlarged, filling the monitor. In the craft's payload area, where the assault rifle had been in the past, hung a box about the size of a pint of milk. "Looks like an HDR-AS100VR."

"Please translate to English."

"Action video camera—Sony's smaller, cheaper version of the GoPro."

"So this is a recon mission?"

"Apparently."

So if they couldn't find Verlyn, the drone could give him away soon enough, Fisk thought. Why else would it be here but to confirm that the inmate was free?

But before he could relax, Chay exclaimed, "What in the world is that?"

He followed her stare to monitor 3's image of a bright beam of light rising from a rooftop and enveloping the quadrocopter. Then the drone plummeted, end over end, its descent slowed by a tree limb, but only slightly. It struck the sidewalk, the fuselage popping apart at the seam connecting the upper and lower halves, the camera exploding into too many shiny pieces to count, some of them bouncing as far as half a block. Then there was no movement at all.

Disappointment numbed Fisk. "Let's hope Yodeler has a better backup plan than we do."

"What is your backup plan?" Chay asked.

"Follow Verlyn to Yodeler." Fisk fought an urge to run down the stairs and across three blocks to the parking garage to recover their lone remaining lead. He regarded the monitor. No movement on Spruce except for an NYPD cruiser that appeared to be on routine patrol. It pulled up at the curb opposite the Pace Plaza garage, and two officers hurried into the street and whisked the quadrocopter debris into their trunk—into evidence cases, Fisk hoped.

As the two men went back for the remains of the

camera, a lanky college-age kid—or maybe he was a full-grown but scrawny twenty-something—ran up to them, his exuberance obvious from half a block away and through the grainy infrared security cam feed. As the kid jumped up and down—you'd think he'd just scored the game-winning touchdown—a metallic baton in his hand caught the streetlight glow. The baton had what looked to Fisk to be a folding back sight and foresight, and, between them, a trigger. The kid plunged it into a sheath that hung from his belt.

"Where does this leave us?" asked Chay.

"Ah, this is just another day at the office." Fisk wished it were true. Things usually go wrong. Lots of things go wrong.

Today, everything had.

The six-story apartment building, directly across Centre Street from the old police headquarters, looked to Blackwell to have been built a hundred years ago—and like it ought to have been torn down fifty years ago.

But around that time, he knew, artists and other bohemians in search of cheap loft space started buying up these outmoded commercial buildings in this part of the city and turning them into co-ops. Urban hippie compounds. They'd painted this one maroon for some reason. Probably because they were on acid, he thought, slinging the duffel bag containing his rifle over his shoulder and falling in on the sidewalk behind two couples who looked like members of the newest bohemian generation, on their way toward the maroon building. One of the dudes carried a liquor bottle in a paper bag. The other had a hookah protruding from his knapsack.

The first of the group to reach the building entrance was the girl whose down-to-her-ass hair almost matched the paint on the building. She punched in the door code. Blackwell slowed, trying to time it so that, without drawing their attention, he could grab the door as it fell shut behind them.

Act like you live here, he told himself. Wealthy guy, maybe Silicon Alley money, who dropped $2 million on a dinky two bedroom because . . . Blackwell couldn't think of a reason to live in this dump for any price.

The second girl gave it to him, though. The sight of her inspired him. Her body, emphasized by a miniskirt and halter top that combined used less fabric than a typical hand towel, reminded him of a statue of Venus, the goddess of beauty.

You invested $2 million on a two-bedroom loft here, he told himself, because of the girls. And it's paying off.

His gait slowed to the sort of strut befitting a Silicon Alley prince on the prowl. He reached the entrance to the building just as the last of the four, the guy with the hookah, pushed his way through the door. Blackwell prepared to spring and catch the door, when the hookah guy spun around and said, "Whoa!"

Shit, Blackwell thought.

The guy snared the door, preventing it from falling shut, and held it open.

"Thanks, man," Blackwell said.

"*De nada*, bro."

Blackwell followed the four into the ancient industrial elevator. Venus pressed six. "How about you?" she asked Blackwell.

"Two, please." He was actually going to three, having calculated that Chay's iPad was in a room on the third floor of the old police headquarters building.

"You got it." She pressed the button, the old kind that snapped into place, staying flush with the elevator panel until the car reached the floor. With a series of grunts and groans, the elevator began to rise.

"So is 4A having another party?" Blackwell asked the group.

"The girls in 4G," the hookah guy said, as if anyone in the building would know those girls.

"Oh, the girls, yeah." Blackwell flashed a smile. The elevator ground to a stop, the door chugged open. Stepping out, he said to the hookah guy with a wink, "Don't do anything I wouldn't do."

As soon as the elevator door closed behind him, he turned in to the stairwell. Exiting on the third floor, he found the light-switch panel and snapped the switch down, killing the row of fluorescent tubes on the ceiling, dropping the hallway into darkness. He quickly flicked the lights back on.

"Oops," he said, in case whoever was in 3E had come to the door.

Three-E was the only apartment that was occupied, he'd determined by the light that shone beneath the door when the hall was dark. Three-C's placement in the center of the building was ideal for his purposes.

In twenty-five seconds, his feeler prong and torsion wrench had defeated the lock and he was in. He didn't have to wait long for his eyes to acclimate to the Manhattan take on darkness; he was in a one-bedroom space so Spartan that it had to be a single guy's. The blimp of a black leather couch, matching recliner, glass-topped chrome coffee table, and chrome floor lamps all looked to have been picked up in the same place as the La-Z-Boy. The air was still and warm. Maybe the guy was away on business. Taking no chances, Blackwell bolted the front door. You couldn't open this one from outside. If the guy who lived here came home, Blackwell would hear him, and he would slip out while the guy went back downstairs to ask the super WHAT THE FUCK?

Blackwell set his duffel bag on the coffee table, unzipped it, removed the components, and put the rifle together on the couch. He set the bipod on a windowsill that was so deep you might think it was designed for use by a sniper. Before opening the window, he knelt and peered into the scope, searching for Fisk. Like the majority of the third-floor apartments across the street, in the old police headquarters building, the one Blackwell had identified as containing the iPad was dark. But inside, something flickered.

Blackwell brought the scope into better focus, enabling him to see an iPad sitting on a table beside the window. Two people were visible on a couch, their backs to the window, watching the flickering TV. A man and woman. Oddly still. Extremely still. In fact, Blackwell realized, they weren't moving at all.

Because they were mannequins.

Because—*shit!*—this was a trap. The iPad had been the lure. The cops were probably on the roof of their old headquarters building, on the lookout for a rifle scope—and/or they had their fucking Big Brother cams and sensors trained on the buildings a sniper might use. Meaning they'd probably made him by now. Maybe not, but he couldn't chance it. He had to assume men were on their way up to this apartment right the hell now. And fast.

So, no time to break down the rifle, to get it back into the duffel bag. And carrying it as is would slow him down, not to mention make him a million times

more conspicuous as he tried to get away. He decided to leave behind the rifle, bipod, bag, ammo,
everything. It was for this sort of contingency that
he'd been on Capecitabine, the antimetabolic drug
given to patients for whom chemo had been successful. Cancer cells needed to make and repair DNA in
order to grow and multiply. The drug stopped those
cells from making and repairing DNA, keeping the
cancer from returning. Capecitabine's almost uni-
versal side effect was inflammation of the palms and
the soles of the feet, leading to peeling and blistering
of the skin. It was a small price to pay. The downside
for patients was it also eliminated fingerprints, making identification problematic. But if you were in the
liquidation trade, Capecitabine was a godsend.

He ran for the door. Every fraction of a second
counted, he knew. He unbolted the lock. Flung the
door open. No time for stealth. He launched himself toward the stairwell. Got there just as the elevator ground to a halt ten feet away from him.

Now stealth was a matter of life or death.

He opened the door to the stairwell a crack and
listened. Footfalls rose up the stairs. Two men, he
thought, entering at the ground floor. Planning to
be upstairs before they could see him, he darted
through the door, closing it behind him, but not
before glimpsing the two men emerging from the
elevator. SWAT. As were the two guys now jogging
up the stairs. And the fifth guy he could hear running down from the roof. Damn. The roof would
have been the ideal escape route. Of course it was.
That was why Fisk had sent people there.

Trying to move quick and silently—*Be a cat*—he

took the stairs three at a time. Reaching the fourth floor, he exited the stairwell and gently closed the door behind him. It shut just as the guy from the roof ran onto the landing. And kept running, down to the third floor.

Blackwell had asked the kids in the elevator where the party was as a contingency. The girls in apartment 4G. That information was superfluous now. The loud music left no doubt about the party's location. The door to 4G was open.

He stepped into a clove-intensive cloud of cigarette smoke and made his way down the spacious entry hall, past two girls making out, into the loft space, a huge room lit by digital Lava Lamps that also splashed bright and psychedelic-colored amoeba shapes onto a hundred guests, all of them standing around and drinking and smoking, many swaying to the music. Decent place to hide, he thought.

"Hey, you came!"

He spun around and found himself looking into Venus's alluring eyes. He said, "I decided I didn't want to stay in."

"Awesome."

The entry door swung open. Blackwell made out the silhouettes of two men in the doorway. Big men. Scoping the place out. SWAT, almost certainly.

Blackwell pointed to Venus's beer bottle. "Hey, you need another drink?"

She smiled. "Sure, that'd be great." She cocked her head toward the kitchen, the entrance to which was the epicenter of the party.

"Be right back," he said, regretting that he couldn't be.

He started toward the kitchen, then swung into the corridor leading to the bedrooms, the farthest of which overlooked a trash alley. He entered the dark room, startling the couple going at it beneath the comforter.

"Yo, dude!" one of them protested.

No time to worry about them. Blackwell crossed the room, nearly tripping on their clothes.

"Dude, what the fuck?"

He unlocked and raised the window. Lights from within the surrounding apartments showed the alley to be a weedy, dismal repository for trash, much of which was piled against the walls, possibly because the boxcar-style Dumpster directly below was overflowing with bags that reeked of spoiled food.

In the main part of the loft, the music ceased midsong, allowing Blackwell to hear a booming voice, elevated, as though addressing the whole crowd: "No one here may leave . . ."

Blackwell damned well was going to leave. But would the window work? The onetime commercial building had no window ledges to climb out onto. He hoisted himself onto the deep sill and raised the narrow window. Narrow, but, fortunately, just wide enough for him to fit through.

"Dude, I mean, what the hell, man?"

The couple in the bed. Good-looking twenty-something black guy and an even better-looking blonde. Could have met at a fashion shoot.

Blackwell tapped the pistol grip protruding from his waistband. "Next one of you who says a word, the other gets shot," he said.

They said nothing. Good.

But how to get out of here?

He considered the Dumpster brimming with garbage bags. Three stories was a big jump in a regular building, Blackwell thought. Twenty-seven feet, as much as thirty-three. In a loft building, closer to forty. Into water, that wasn't a big deal, but into a pile of trash bags, even if the contents were mushy, he would hit at twenty miles an hour. Bones could break. But jail would be worse. He leaped out.

The hit man took the bait, but then, improbably, escaped. It was shaping into a banner night, Fisk thought. What were the odds of losing the quadrocopter and the human targets of two different major investigations in the span of five minutes?

At least there was still a chance of finding Verlyn. Texted status reports from the surveillance team in the parking garage began to pepper the monitors.

1E NEGATIVE
2W NEGATIVE
5W NEGATIVE

"A positive would be a sighting of him," Fisk explained to Chay, sitting next to him at the 1PP—One Police Plaza—ops-center viewing room.

"Do any of them have handheld thermal imaging units?"

"You mean, so that they can detect him even if he's hiding behind a car?"

"That's what I was thinking, yeah."

"The Department does have those. They would have come in handy now if we'd thought to bring them . . ." He paused to read two incoming reports.

1W NEGATIVE
2E NEGATIVE

It went against Fisk's nature to just sit here, the texting equivalent of waiting by the phone. He thought about going and getting a cup of coffee from the machine. If only for an excuse to move. What he really could use, he thought, was the opposite of coffee. Whiskey.

Finally, something: a Domain Awareness camera on the street showed a Lincoln Navigator, the one that had taken Verlyn into the garage, rolling toward the cashier by the exit. Through the windshield Fisk saw only the driver in the dark SUV.

The tech, R2, reported, "The cashier's one of our guys, Detective Fisk. He's got the one handheld thermal imaging sensor we had, and it's picking up nobody in the Navigator now except the driver."

"What about him?"

"He's a Kelly Limousine employee, been there eight months. One of our people talked to him, and he didn't seem to have the first clue. Want us to hang on to him?"

Hell yes, Fisk thought. The guy is the closest thing we have to Verlyn now. But because Chay was there, he said, "Make sure his license and registration are in order." That would buy twenty or thirty minutes. A driver who allegedly knew nothing wasn't likely to recall something of use—but stranger things had happened.

More texts appeared:

3W NEGATIVE
4E NEGATIVE
3E NEGATIVE

Each one irked Fisk.

"Detective Fisk, your guest is in the waiting area," said R2.

"Send him in."

One of the officers from the street brought in the kid who had shot down the drone, minus his weapon—he wore a scabbard on a thick black belt that was an amalgam of military and Goth. He was slight and baby-faced, his eyes too big for his head to begin with, and magnified by thick glasses.

"Detective Fisk, meet Shane Poplowski," the policeman said.

Flashing a salesman's smile, Poplowski started toward Fisk, a bony right hand extended.

Fisk remained in his seat. The kid got the message and stopped, his eyes widening as he took in the dark room and the monitors streaming thermal imagery. He stood straighter. The old animal instinct, Fisk figured. To dissuade an attacker, you make yourself appear bigger. Why cats arch their backs.

"Why do you think you're here?" Fisk asked. Such open-ended questions played to the subject's fear that you already knew. Often in defending himself, he filled in the blanks for you.

"At first, I thought you were going to thank me," Poplowski said, his voice high-pitched, the words rushed.

"Why?"

"For defeating the drone, of course."

So that was what the kid was up to, Fisk thought. "How'd you do it?"

"It's a secret weapon, literally."

"A bazooka?"

"It's not a bazooka. It's a modified TALI." The kid said "TALI" as if Fisk ought to know what that was.

Fisk turned to Chay, who raised her shoulders. "Threat assessment laser illuminator?"

"Yeah, that's it," Poplowski said. "We've been calling our version the LightningRod. Essentially it's a laser fitted with focus-adjustable collimating lenses." He appeared to rein in a grin. "I took out the quadrocopter by flooding its sensors."

"With what?" Fisk asked.

Poplowski seemed to enjoy the stage. "In layman's terms, the LightningRod sends a beam that analyzes the target's sensors. My company's proprietary system sends the exact blend of light from the spectrum to confound the system. Tonight the quad was firing its infrared, so all it took was white light."

Fisk was reminded of the trouble his flashlight beam had caused the men wearing infrared night goggles.

"Should we know your company?" Chay said to Poplowski.

"Good question," Fisk said, putting it to the kid with a wave.

"Lightning Factory, LLC," Poplowski said. "We would think nothing of going to the mattresses at our facility in Portland to produce as many LightningRods as New York needs, at a reasonable price."

"How did you know where the quadrocopter was?" Chay asked. Also a good question, Fisk thought.

"I, uh . . ." Poplowski eyed his shoe tops. "I

hacked the Iron Apple system—well, not hacked, technically, because the X-band radar transponder beacons respond to radar using horizontal polarization."

This kid was somebody the city wanted on its side, Fisk thought.

"Looks like we've got our rabbit on monitor four," R2 said over the speaker.

Fisk looked to monitor four, which showed a Domain Awareness cam's view rendered in shades of greens and gray by an infrared filter. On the screen was a man driving a Honda Accord on Spruce Street. A light-skinned guy of medium build, but with a thick mustache, sideburns and a goatee, and dark, curly hair.

To Poplowski, Fisk said, "Thanks for coming. I hope we can do business."

The kid called out Lightning Factory's Web address as the police officer steered him out of the room.

Fisk caught Chay's grin and responded with one of his own. Sharing a thought with her had a unique and exhilarating intimacy. Which he could look forward to experiencing again some other time. For now, his attention shot back to the view on the monitor of the Honda Accord (New York City's most popular car, with Honda's similar-looking Civic a close second). The driver slowed at the end of Spruce and squinted through bulky eyeglasses as he turned left onto Park Row.

"That can't be Merritt, can it?" Chay said.

"It doesn't look like him, but evidently it is."

"What's the evidence?"

Watching the Accord turn left onto Worth, Fisk hit the intercom and put the question to R2, who replied, "The measured distance between the geometric centers of the Accord driver's pupils and Merritt Verlyn's pupils is the same to one one-hundredth of a millimeter. The width of the noses is exactly the same too. Ditto the depth of the eye sockets. The length of the jawline is off by the amount added by the fake sideburns. He did a fine job of fooling humans, but old-school disguise doesn't get you very far against Elastic Bunch Graph measurement-based facial recognition software. And you really need to cake on the makeup to thwart the new dermal analytic apps. I'd input the facial presets for Merritt Verlyn into Domain Awareness essentially as search terms, and the system gave us this guy in this car."

"Whose car is it?" Fisk asked.

"Check monitor two," said R2.

The middle monitor on the top row showed a freeze frame of the license plate. The data crawl at the bottom of the picture streamed New York DMV information. The 2012 Honda Accord was registered to Car-Go!, a local knockoff of Zipcar, the popular car-sharing club.

"Who signed it out?" Fisk said.

R2 apologized. "No additional information."

Which was additional information to Fisk. It meant that Verlyn had capable help from the First Amendment Society or a foreign spy service or, possibly, Yodeler. Could Yodeler be the agent or a construct of an enemy intelligence agency?

Motion drew Fisk's attention to one of the monitors, on which appeared an overhead view of the Accord, the video shot from above by one of the Aviation Division's Bell 412s. Verlyn was turning left onto Ann Street, at the top of the financial district, bringing the total number of vehicles on the narrow commercial block to two. This late at night, the financial district was all but closed. The Accord took another left onto William Street, disappearing from the helicopter's view, but reappearing on the adjacent monitor courtesy of DOM-CAM WM-WGOLD.

Chay's brow knitted. "It looks like he's headed right back to the correctional center."

"It looks like he's running a surveillance detection route," Fisk said. "In Driving Training, you're taught to take a series of consecutive left turns."

"Why?"

"The odds of anyone staying with you for more than two lefts are astronomical."

"But why would he bother to lose the cars tailing him if knows about your surveillance cameras?"

"He's already eluded the cameras once."

Verlyn took two more lefts, onto Beekman Street and then onto Barclay, where, as if satisfied that he wasn't being followed, he continued crosstown. Block after block, God's Eye picked him up. He gripped the wheel with both hands and kept his eyes on the street ahead, and, to Fisk's eye, displayed none of the self-consciousness people usually do when they're aware that they're being filmed.

The Accord finally took a right turn, onto West Street, which a few blocks later became the West Side Highway. The smattering of traffic there allowed him to cruise at sixty miles per hour. Within minutes, with Manhattan in his rearview mirror, he shot onto the Henry Hudson Parkway and zoomed north, the monitors showing the Accord periodically from the vantage point of the Bell 412.

"What's preventing him from disappearing altogether now?" Chay asked.

"The surveillance team has a helicopter and fourteen vehicles, including this truck." Fisk pointed to the overhead view of a lumbering pickup truck piled high with rusty coils of wire and other scrap metal, but still capable of keeping pace with the Accord.

Along with a Ford Taurus, the pickup truck followed Verlyn into Westchester, but it would have been too conspicuous had it also turned with him onto the Hutchinson River Parkway. They soon came to the Connecticut border, where the Hutch became the aptly named Merritt Parkway.

In Connecticut, two cars took the pickup truck's place, a Honda Civic and a white utility van. All-white vans were America's most common, which made them a staple of surveillance and reconnaissance ops (in a distant second place were vans that featured utility-company names or logos). A third car pulled onto the highway ahead of the Accord, from Round Hill Road in Greenwich, Connecticut, a wealthy coastal suburb that Fisk knew well. He was surprised that the median home value was $1,260,200—at least according to U.S. Census data on the crawl beneath the helicopter's infrared display. He would have guessed a lot higher.

The Merritt Parkway was striking, lined by old New England trees, crossed by a series of historic landmark overpasses, and divided by a grassy median so inviting that motorists used to stop for picnics on it. Verlyn pulled over at the first gas station he came to, a Mobil. He parked in front of the minimart, got out of the car, and looked around. Evidently satisfied with what he'd seen, or hadn't, he locked the car and went inside the store.

"Monitor three," R2 said, a moment before grainy high-angle video of Verlyn appeared in the upper right monitor. He was coming through the minimart door.

The only other person in the store was the clerk behind the register, a turbaned graybeard who barely looked up from his magazine when Verlyn walked past.

"Is that the minimart's security camera?" Chay asked.

"One of them."

Verlyn plucked a five-dollar can of Sapporo from a refrigerated case, then carried it back toward the counter, with a bounce in his step that Fisk hadn't seen before. A good sign, he thought.

"But how can you access Mobil's security system?" Chay asked.

Fisk bit back a grin. "Mobil rents the property from the government."

Apparently whistling, Verlyn inspected a personal-size cherry pie in a rack by the register, then added it to his purchase.

"What do you think he's doing?" Chay asked.

"They don't have beer at the Metropolitan Correctional Center. He's probably been dreaming of this. Or maybe he's celebrating."

Verlyn returned to his Accord with his purchases, leaving the beer in its paper bag as he started the Accord and drove back onto the parkway. Fisk bet himself that Verlyn wouldn't pop the Sapporo, unwilling to risk drawing the attention of a Connecticut state trooper. It would be a good sign if he felt relaxed enough to go at the cherry pie, though.

Two tails picked him up, a Toyota SUV and another Civic, this one silver.

The Toyota was equipped with a dashboard-mounted video camera with forward-looking infrared that transmitted to monitor 3. In Fisk's experience, these cameras rarely offered anything that the surveillant himself couldn't see. In this case, however, the dashboard camera showed Verlyn devouring the cherry pie with a ferocity that suggested he had no inkling that he was on camera.

A few miles later, he shifted from the left lane into the right and began to slow the Accord. The next exit, 36, was in New Canaan, Connecticut, another coastal New York bedroom community, with a population of 19,682 people.

"He grew up in New Canaan, didn't he?" Fisk asked.

Out of the corner of an eye, he caught Chay's nod. She too remained rapt on the monitor. He suspected that, as he did, she smelled blood.

The surveillant in the Toyota, who would have been conspicuous dropping to fifty miles per hour along with Verlyn, continued north on the parkway, passing him. The silver Civic, driven by a woman, was now tabbed to tail Verlyn. Women, statistically, are slower drivers—they typically drive five miles per hour over the speed limit versus ten—making her the less likely of the two surveillants to rouse Verlyn's suspicion.

Another car, a black late-model Nissan, sped from a mile back to take the Toyota's place. The driver of the Civic waited until the Nissan was behind her before turning to the right lane.

Verlyn didn't signal to turn off at exit 36. He continued ahead at fifty-five miles per hour, the posted limit. At the last possible moment, however, he sent the Accord onto the off-ramp for New Canaan. A surveillance detection maneuver, Fisk suspected. The Civic had been far enough behind the Accord on the parkway that, two seconds later, in signaling to turn off at exit 36, the driver probably didn't give herself away.

Reaching the end of the off-ramp, the Accord lingered at the stop sign. A beat too long, Fisk thought. Had Verlyn made the woman in the Civic?

Verlyn signaled a right turn onto the drab stretch of the Old Stamford Road, nothing but overgrown grass on either side, the entire area dark save for the occasional pair of passing headlights from the highway overpass. There was no traffic from either side of Old Stamford. Yet Verlyn just sat in the Accord, turn signal blinking away. With no street-level cameras, there was no telling what he was doing. He could be calling or texting someone. Or maybe he'd succumbed to the Sapporo.

The spray of the Accord's brake lights onto the black off-ramp was engulfed by the headlights of the approaching Civic. She too braked, waiting for Verlyn to go. On Old Stamford Road, a quarter of a mile to his left, a dangling signal light popped from red to green, setting in motion the six vehicles that had been stopped for it.

Now Fisk got it. "Damn. He's waiting for traffic."

"Why would he do that?" Chay asked.

"Watch."

Led by a long, rear-loading garbage truck, the half-dozen vehicles accelerated on Old Stamford Road, heading toward the parkway off-ramp.

As Fisk had anticipated, Verlyn waited at the stop sign as long as he could before gunning the Accord, sending it leaping into traffic less than a car length ahead of the garbage truck. Clearly his plan was to force the driver of the Civic to remain on the off-ramp until all of the cross traffic had passed. That would put six vehicles—and as much as a mile—between her and him.

It was an Escape and Evasion 101 method way of losing a tail. But Verlyn didn't execute it properly: he hadn't given himself ample time to get ahead of the garbage truck.

The truck driver now slammed his brakes, sending the gargantuan vehicle into an abrupt deceleration—too abrupt. Without audio, Fisk was left to imagine the bellow of his horn and the howl of tires, drowning out all other sounds on the bucolic road.

The truck's grille hammered the rear of the Accord, knocking the car clockwise so that its right flank became wholly exposed. The truck driver desperately tried to avoid a collision. His truck, still hurtling forward, swerved left. Still the right corner of his hood struck the Accord, sending it, like a baseball off a bat, into the metal guardrail along the right side of the road.

The guardrail buckled, catapulting the Accord. Aglow in the head and taillights of the truck and the cars on Old Stamford Road, it rolled upside down before smashing, roof first, into the concrete highway overpass wall.

The impact nearly flattened the roof, so that it was flush with the hood and truck. The car dropped to the grassy roadside on its flank and remained still, until, at once, the hood erupted into flame, which swelled and engulfed the whole car, bringing much of Old Stamford Road to a glow. Then just as quickly it receded into nothing but ribbons of chalky smoke that blended into the dark sky and soon dissipated, returning the roadside to darkness.

The high grass swayed with the breeze. Otherwise nothing moved. Nothing at all.

BOOK THREE

A MESSAGE FROM YODELER

Published: July 4, 2015 2:15 A.M. *1,344 comments*

[Editors' note: We at the *Mighty Pen* received the following message from Yodeler, who also supplied the fuselage markings on the drone downed late last night by the NYPD. The FBI has verified the accuracy of this information, which has not been made public.]

Greetings, Citizens of New York:

I am, in the great scheme of things, your advocate against the Police State that has usurped control of our Democracy and co-opted our trust. The campaign of deception waged by these so-called authorities knows no bounds. The latest example came a few hours ago in the joint statement from the New York Police (ironically, a criminal organization) and the United States Marshals (glorified goons) that Mr. Merritt Verlyn met an accidental death. I do not believe a word of it, with the exception of "death." I believe that he is dead. Moreover, a great man is dead, a great and wonderful man who dared to stand in the way of the Police State's suppression of truth.

I shall exact a steep price forthwith.

—Yodeler

At four in the morning, Chay, Fisk, Evans, Weir, two executives from the Department's PR firm, and Dubin all crouched around the big computer monitor in the family room of the chief's lower Fifth Avenue apartment. Apparently Dubin's grand-daughter was the only member of the family who ever used the desktop computer, or the family room, for that matter. Evans held one of the little girl's Barbie dolls. Weir clutched the stuffed hippo he'd started to fling out of his way until Mrs. Dubin, bringing in the coffee tray, pointedly cleared her throat. Weir's exaggerated look of guilt, for the benefit of the others, might have provided a mea-sure of levity, but instead it served to emphasize the overall solemnity.

"I'd call this a total disaster, but that's not the half of it," said Dubin while pacing the Oriental carpet, the floorboards underneath whining with every step and resonating in the still of the night. From underneath his flannel robe peeked royal-blue pa-jamas with little white anchors, a gift from his wife or one of his daughters, Fisk would have bet. The chief stooped, as if beneath the weight of his pre-dicament. Rounding the antique floor globe on the far side of the room, he found Fisk's eyes and said, "I don't know how releasing Verlyn could have gone any worse, frankly."

Fisk was still trying to work the case, which, at the moment, felt like trying to stem the flow of the ocean. "What about the downed quadrocopter? Did we get anything useful?"

"It's on its way to Quantico," Evans said. "The preliminary wasn't encouraging, though. One of our techs hypothesized that to avoid leaving traces, Yodeler had used an industrial robot to remove the Specter from the factory case and to mount the rifle."

Weir added, "The guy is pitching a shutout."

"Could be a clue," Fisk said. "How many people have industrial robots?"

Evans checked a chart on his tablet. "One hundred and sixty-six thousand industrial robots manufactured in the United States in 2012, one hundred and sixty-eight in 2013, and I'm still waiting on a number for 2014."

Fisk was undeterred. "How about we check the customer lists against the drone-supplies customer list?"

Weir shook his head. "Fisk, after what you've seen, do you really think Yodeler would have been stupid enough to have a robotic arm delivered to his apartment?"

Fisk would have liked to punch the G-man. "Nothing to lose in checking, right? Speaking of which, what about his communication to the *Mighty Pen*? Maybe we can get metadata from that."

"Glad you asked." Weir turned to Evans. "You can tell him."

"The *Mighty Pen* was happy to cooperate with us, as long as we gave them an exclusive on the results." Evans checked his notes. "Yodeler used the comments box, like he did before on the *New York Times* site. This time he posted his comment from a location with a latitude of 35.843318 degrees north and a longitude of 14.384385 degrees east. Does that mean anything to you?"

Fisk shrugged.

Chay said, "Is it in southern Italy?"

"That's pretty good," Evans said. "It's close, in the Mediterranean Sea, just off the coast of Malta. An old Maltese temple called Gebel Gol-Bahar that wound up underwater after an earthquake."

"Okay?" Fisk waited for the punch line.

Weir snickered. "It's Atlantis."

"That's the speculation," Evans clarified. "This is based on some new research."

It sounded to Fisk as though Yodeler might have gotten a bit too clever with his counterfeit transmission locations. Everyone knew Loch Ness, but Gebel Gol-Bahar? "Good, this will make Yodeler easier to find."

"You gonna send a submarine down?" asked Weir.

Dubin wandered over to Fisk, eyes on the carpet. Fisk was reminded of a manager coming to the mound to take out his pitcher. "We need to talk next steps, kiddo," the chief said, nodding to Weir and the others.

As if having received their cue, they gathered up their things and said hasty good-byes. At the same time, Mrs. Dubin appeared and asked Chay to accompany her to the living room—which was at the other end of the apartment—"to give Jeremy and Barry a moment."

When everyone else was gone, Fisk said to Dubin, "I'll throw myself under the bus if I can stay on the case."

The chief plopped heavily into a leather wing chair, his lips pursed—he was clearly averse to saying what he had to say. "You know how politics work."

"Then have you considered pinning the blame

instead on whoever taught Verlyn escape and evasion? Or was it just that he watched too many Jason Bourne movies?"

"The perception is that everything you've tried on the case hasn't worked."

"Yet." Fisk refrained from smashing the lovely porcelain vase on the mantel, because it was undoubtedly Mrs. Dubin's.

"You're gonna get a promotion and a raise," Dubin said without joy. "The Department hopes you'll accept the position of chief of intel at our Tel Aviv office."

It smacked of PR, which explained why the PR people had been in the room. The Middle East was a vital front in the Department's intelligence efforts. The Tel Aviv job would get Fisk out of New York in a way that would satisfy those who wanted to punish him for what happened to Verlyn yet could be defended to those who supported him, assuming he had any defenders left, as a better and more targeted deployment of his abilities, or some such crap.

"Let me guess," Fisk said. "There's a case in progress with life-or-death stakes that I won't be able to turn down, the lawman's version of a puppy left on a doorstep?"

Dubin nodded. "As it happens, the Mossad has an al-Shabaab source. There's reason to believe al-Shabaab's planning a new op targeting New York. You speak Arabic, you know New York, you're a hell of an intelligence officer . . . Much as I hate to lose you, this is tailor-made for you."

Fisk's biggest objection to the move was that it would cost him Chay. Then again, distance could be surmounted. No, his biggest objection was that Yodeler's act would play on. "Are you offering me this 'promotion' or . . . ?"

"This is for your own good, too. The only usable evidence we pulled out of the maroon co-op across Centre Street from the old headquarters building was the prints, a whorl pattern, almost totally erased."

"So a Capecitabine user?"

"Gotta be."

Fisk understood this to mean that this wasn't any Cartel goon tasked with a hit, but someone enduring a harrowing treatment on top of the cost of four hundred dollars per day in pills. Generally, this was true of just two categories of people: cancer patients whose lives depended on it and elite criminals for whom fingerprints were an occupational hazard.

"What about video?"

"Same kind of hat he was wearing the other night on East Seventy-Fourth, plus makeup and light prosthetics . . ." In other words, he'd successfully taken steps to thwart the Domain Awareness system's Skin Texture Analytics and Linear Discriminate Analysis software.

"So not a cancer patient?" Fisk said.

Dubin shook his head. "The Federal Ministerial Police are looking for a serial liquidator who has no prints." He meant the Policía Federal Ministerial, Mexico's equivalent of the FBI.

"El Polvo?"

"Does that mean dust, something like that?"

"That's all they find of him."

Fisk knew of El Polvo from the Interpol alerts, an

assassin in the mold of the Venezuelan Ilich Ramírez Sánchez, aka Carlos the Jackal, but believed to be a European or American. The only clue police had was a trace amount of plaster dust at each of the crime scenes, a subtle calling card, it was thought.

"If we're talking about that guy," Dubin went on, "it'd be that much better for you to get out of Dodge."

"Unless you want to catch a serial liquidator."

"If he tried to get into Ben Gurion Airport, he'd be as good as caught. Apart from that, the Department wants you to embrace this assignment, publicly. Any mention of the Tel Aviv office is good PR."

"I need to take care of one thing first," Fisk said.

Dubin stiffened. "What?"

"Get me into F6."

"The Special Collection Service?"

"I want to see the wizard, yes."

Dubin shook his head. "You know that's impossible."

"Impossible for an NYPD Intel officer to access WIRESHARK on his own, sure," Fisk tried, "but not to look over the shoulder of a SIGINT Terminal Guidance jockey. You would just need to make a call to one of your buddies at Langley."

Dubin reddened. "No."

"Why not?"

"I've already made all the calls I can for you. If I hadn't, we'd be opening an office in Bumfuck, Alaska, for you to work at. And you wouldn't be the chief there, that's for damned sure."

"Just think about it, okay?" Fisk hoped reason would prevail. "Yodeler's first two messages appeared to originate from Loch Ness and Diego Garcia, both of which are notorious—"

Dubin cut in. "What's your point?"

Better than no, Fisk thought. "Loch Ness and Diego Garcia are both the subjects of hundreds of thousands of Internet searches every day. So even if Yodeler had looked online for their latitude and longitude to plug into whatever location-masking app he was running, we wouldn't be able to track him. But unless he just happened to know Gebel Gol-Bahar's latitude and longitude to the hundred-thousandth of a degree, he would have needed to look it up. And if he looked online, F6 would be able to give us our best lead on this case to date."

Dubin's expression of exasperation softened into one of appreciation. He looked at the ceiling. "Put it in your report. Weir and Evans can carry the ball."

Fisk locked eyes with him. "They'll fumble—you know that. This is why Intel exists."

Dubin shook his head. "I'm trying to keep Intel in existence. This case was supposed to make us look good, remember?"

What Fisk remembered was that Dubin remained conscious of Intel's public image to a fault. "Chief, do you really want to open the *New York Times* tomorrow and read about the consequences of Intel's decision to hand off the case to the Bureau?"

Clenching both fists, Dubin stomped toward the globe before turning back abruptly and grumbling, "Fuck you."

Which, Fisk knew, was the chief's way of saying yes to F6.

Dubin called and woke one of his old golf buddies, who now helmed the CIA's Directorate of Science and Technology. Within minutes, Fisk and Chay were climbing out of a taxi at Broadway and Fifty-Third Street. In order to access the Special Collection Service offices—listed in the building lobby as part of a cyber security firm that did government work—Fisk first had to leave Chay in the cyber-security-firm conference room kept under guard by Defense Security Service agents. Once inside the F6 suite, which looked like any other corporate suite, he had to check everything but the clothes on his back, then submit to two types of body scans.

After signing a series of waivers and demonstrating that his fingerprints, iris texture, face, and voice matched those in the Agency's database, he was escorted by a DSS guard into an area closer in appearance to a science-fiction movie starship than to any midtown office. The ceiling, comprised entirely of sleek lighting panels, glowed faintly, causing the metallic walls to shimmer a dull blue.

The air was kept so cool that Fisk was surprised to see no vapor when he exhaled. He figured that the temperature was for the benefit of the batteries of hard drives, unseen but responsible for a mechanical purr. At the end of the hallway, he underwent another round of eye and hand texture scans, the result of which was the snaps of bolts disengaging from locks within the wall. Although a heavyweight, the guard strained to push open the thick metal door.

This was what it had been like to use the Internet thirty years ago, Fisk had heard older intel hands recount. Then it was the ARPAnet, the first operational packet-switching network, created by the Defense Advanced Research Projects Agency. Maybe thirty years from now, he thought, data-mining programs like XKEYSCORE and WIRESHARK would be available as free apps.

The guard brought him into a terminal room, which was anticlimactic. A couple-million-dollar SCIF, sure, with an outer layer probably made of some space-age material, but inside it looked like any dimly lit copy room. The hard-drive arrays likely cost north of a million dollars apiece, but they were housed in a rolling pressboard rack that could have been left overnight on the curb outside of Fisk's new building in Hell's Kitchen without any takers.

The rack stood beside a basic round table with metallic legs, atop which sat a medium-size black-framed LCD monitor identical to the model Fisk had bought at a January clearance sale. From behind it, a doughy young woman—twenty years old at most—rose to meet him, her hand outstretched. She had a button nose framed by a round face and crowned by a chaotic mass of red curls. Oblong lenses magnified the fatigue in her eyes, which was understandable at four thirty in the morning. She was all alacrity, however, when she introduced herself as "Jean—sorry, can't give my last name, company policy."

After introducing himself and accepting the seat across the table from her, Fisk explained what he needed, a list of all Internet searches or input involving the words "Atlantis" or "Malta" or "Gebel Gol-Bahar" cross-checked against similar uses of "Loch Ness" and "Diego Garcia." When he'd finished, Jean said nothing. She sat and stared into her monitor. He peered around the monitor, wondering if perhaps she'd nodded off.

"Sorry, this can throw people," she said. "WIRE-SHARK was listening and transcribed everything you said, then transformed it to search terms. Here are the results." She tapped at the monitor, swiveling it so that it faced him. "In the past seven days, there were 447,332 search engine queries in the United States involving some permutation of 'Atlantis' in the context of the lost city, or 98,403 less than those for the Bahamian resort also called Atlantis; 27,548 users searching for the lost city also visited the Discovery Channel site's post about Gebel Gol-Bahar."

She had memorized the figures, Fisk realized. Unfortunately they were about a thousand times greater than he'd anticipated. "That's all?"

"It's actually not that many, given that in an average week, there are twenty million searches for Lady Gaga. And we haven't even gotten to page views of Gebel Gol-Bahar content via other means."

Given refined parameters, WIRESHARK reported that of the 183,783 IP addresses in the continental United States from which individuals demonstrated an interest in Gebel Gol-Bahar, 24,710 had also demonstrated an interest in Loch Ness. The two places were featured on myriad websites and forums. Diego Garcia had a similar cult following.

All three locations garnered the online attention of 8,540 unique users, of whom 990 were in New York City and an additional 661 were within a fifty-mile radius. Because those IP addresses included 234 public Wi-Fi locations, used by thousands of people, the suspect pool included a quarter of a million people. Which was a start.

Fisk could open leads on all of them. If he still had any control over the case and a couple of months to follow the leads, that is.

Jackson," said Chay.

"Who's that?" asked Fisk.

"Jackson, Mississippi."

She lay inches away in bed, also wearing nothing. Heat rose off her skin. Her breath was warm and pleasant against his neck. But she might as well have been miles away now. His mind was on the case, going around it and around it in search of a clue, and around it yet another time.

She poked him. "I thought you'd be dying to know, right?"

"Huh?"

"Where I'm from."

"Right."

"My father was a sculptor. Not the biggest art scene, though, in Jackson. Ever been there?"

The answer was within reach, he thought. But in which direction? Looking up at the ceiling, dark save for the occasional comet cast by headlights zipping past on Eighth Avenue, he replayed the night's events from the moment the escorting officer brought Verlyn into the administrative office to be processed out.

Chay cleared her throat. "Have you ever been to Jackson?"

"Oh, sorry. No."

"Most people are surprised that there's a city that

big in the middle of Mississippi: twenty-story buildings, nearly two hundred thousand people."

"Did you like it?" he asked. Another time he
would be interested. He wanted to know all about
her. But now he fell into pondering Yodeler's letter
to the editors of the *Mighty Pen*.

"Yes and no," she said.

A great man is dead, a great and wonderful man.
Yodeler was a bright guy. Why was he spouting sen-
timents instead of taking the singular opportunity
to make his case against the Police State?

Chay ran a fingertip down his jawline. "Hey,
don't you want to hear the 'no' part, the traumatic
childhood experience that spurred me to right society's wrongs?"

"I do, yeah. Of course."

"But you're at work now, right?"

Her tone told him there was no good answer. "I
feel like we're missing an obvious piece." He could
use her help.

She pulled away. And she was right to, he knew.
They'd all been right, all of them who'd said the
same thing about him, in so many words. He was
skilled at compartmentalizing, but that created too
many barriers. Now, that illuminated a contrast,
Fisk thought: Yodeler had exhibited no such flaw.
He cared about Merritt Verlyn, cared deeply. That's
why the *Mighty Pen* letter had thrown Fisk. Yodeler
didn't lament the loss of Verlyn's document cache,
the perpetuation of the Police State, nothing like
that—although, come to think of it, it was odd
that both Verlyn and Yodeler used the same dated
phrase. The key was, Yodeler had decried the loss

of a wonderful man. His effort wasn't ideological or political.

"Maybe it's personal," Fisk thought aloud.

"No shit," Chay said.

He'd half forgotten she was there. "I meant Yodeler's connection to Verlyn," he admitted, bracing for the latest take on his emotional unavailability.

To his delight, she said, full of intrigue, "Murdering innocents on a daily basis is rather extreme if all you want is to get some documents uploaded to the Internet." She sat up. "Why didn't we think of that before?"

Fisk shot out of bed, checked the F6 data on his phone, and felt like he'd hit pay dirt: "There's an IP in New Canaan, Connecticut, that someone used to look up both Diego Garcia and Gebel Gol-Bahar."

"But wouldn't Yodeler have to be in New York?"

"That's what everyone's assumed, but the entire point of an unmanned aerial vehicle is you can control it from far away."

They worked together, she researching the Connecticut chapters of Merritt Verlyn's life and he parsing the WIRESHARK metadata, leading to the discouraging discovery that the signal originated from a prepaid Southern New England Telephone cell phone, registered to a Dan Smith, no longer in use. A burner phone.

"Still, possibly a clue," Fisk said. "If you're in the market for anonymity, you would use the most common surname in the United States."

"Or you're in fact one of the country's two million or however many Smiths."

"And interested in Gebel Gol-Bahar in the same time frame Yodeler would have been?"

Chay said, "Where, physically, was Dan Smith?"

"A bowling alley called Nutmeg Lanes that has a popular video-game and pinball-machine arcade, which would be a great place to use your burner phone if you wanted to maintain your anonymity."

"Do they have security cameras?"

Fisk said, "Now you're a fan of security cameras?"

"Let's say I'm coming around."

"Not looking like this place is that modernized. Check out their website: the newest video game they have is Galaga."

"I love Galaga. What do you say to a drive to Connecticut, then?"

Fisk hoped she saw something he'd missed. "I know a place that has Galaga in Times Square."

Chay said, "Within walking distance from Nutmeg Lanes is a house that a Ms. Ellen Lee purchased in 1996 for two hundred and thirty thousand dollars from the estate of Bridger Verlyn, Merritt's father."

Nonspecific though it was, Yodeler's threat in his *Mighty Pen* piece to exact a steep price forthwith was enough for Governor Cuomo to declare a state of emergency—in Manhattan, the outer boroughs, and part of Long Island—allowing him to immediately contract Shane Poplowski's Lightning Factory.

The young company was immediately able to deliver eighteen working models to go with the prototype Poplowski had demonstrated in downing Yodeler's reconnaissance quadrocopter. And stepped-up production in the LightningWorks Portland, Oregon, facility would net an additional fifty-six per day. Unfortunately, a law enforcement officer or National Guardsman armed with a LightningRod and standing in an intersection could only cover the four blocks to his right, left, front, and back, and Manhattan alone had more than two thousand blocks. Likening the use of LightningRods to an ant farting in a windstorm, Mayor de Blasio ratcheted up the state of emergency, requesting businesses in the city to close and that citizens "shelter in place" if able, to keep safe from Yodeler, and to expedite the hunt for him.

But what exactly, New Yorkers asked, were all the tacticians and experts looking for? No one had a good answer. Meanwhile, the thumps of low-flying helicopters—magnified by the otherwise hushed city, then resounding in what amounted to empty canyons between buildings—seemed to echo the heartbeats of the terrified city.

Yodeler owned New York now.

Everything was closed, even the bodegas that never closed, not on Christmas, not on 9/11. Vehicular traffic was nil, save for Army trucks and law enforcement and emergency vehicles. What little movement Fisk and Chay witnessed, from inside the unmarked NYPD Dodge Ram he'd signed out, was oddly accelerated. Everyone approached activities like a walk down a sidewalk or getting into a car as potentially fatal.

The storybook summer morning and the Independence Day decorations—red, white, and blue Uncle Sam hats mounted on streetlight poles throughout the city—added layers of sad irony.

Driving toward the West Side Highway through the still life that Hell's Kitchen had become, Fisk's primary evidence that the bulk of the population hadn't already been wiped out was the quick and unnatural flickers at apartment windows—residents wrestling, he thought, with whether to look out for drones or to stay the hell away from the windows. After passing the Jacob Javits Convention Center, he turned right onto the West Side Highway and headed north, toward Connecticut, along the same route Merritt Verlyn had taken hours earlier.

"Find out anything about Ellen Lee?" he asked Chay, who was taking in the activity around them—or, rather the lack of it—with wide eyes.

She returned her attention to the car's tablet computer—now a standard feature in NYPD vehicles, offering proprietary links to the Department databases. "She was a teacher at a public school in Darien. Retired now. She lives alone at the old Verlyn family place on Maple Valley Lane."

"What happened to Verlyn's parents?"

"The mother ran off years earlier, and the father died of cancer the year before Ellen Lee bought the house. Merritt was seventeen that summer, but he'd been taking care of his little brother for well over a year after their father was incapacitated and eventually entered hospice care. In order to keep the brother out of a foster home, Merritt told caseworkers from Connecticut's Department of Children and Families that he was eighteen.

"The two of them continued to live in the house in New Canaan for almost an entire year before the Department of Children and Families figured out the truth. But by that time, Merritt *was* eighteen, and old enough to serve as his brother's legal guardian. So he took him along to MIT—the kid stayed in Merritt's dorm room and went to a high school in Cambridge. Merritt wouldn't have blamed his expulsion on his brother, but there's reason to believe that he didn't keep his grades up because he took the guardianship seriously, including washing dishes late every night in the dining hall."

"He had a good heart," Fisk said. Too bad, he thought, that the quality was negated by Verlyn's misplaced notions of national security interests.

They didn't see a single car on the West Side Highway for fifty blocks before passing an Army Humvee headed in the opposite direction. Then, well into Riverdale, no one else. Given how little he'd slept, Fisk might have found the drive interminable, mile after mile of empty asphalt, glinting rhythmically in the morning sun. Yet each curve that they rounded, yielding another stretch of empty highway, filled him with wonder: How long could this last? To what extent had one guy with a couple of five-hundred-buck drones paralyzed the world's most powerful city?

At the Connecticut border, traffic began as a trickle and increased to normal holiday-morning proportions. Suddenly the New York portion of the drive seemed to Fisk like it had been an eerie dream. In New Canaan, on what was an unqualified brilliant summer day, any one of the prim colonial homes—with their tidy yards and sparkling picket fences and Stars and Stripes flying for the holiday—appeared suitable for an American propaganda poster.

As Fisk and Chay continued their drive north, the houses grew farther apart and the woods thickened. At the end of Maple Valley Lane, he turned the Dodge up a long, steep driveway, entering a tunnel of tall overhanging boughs and hedges. He parked by a detached garage across from a majestic two-story brick colonial. As he stepped out of the car, his soles crunched into gravel. At the same time his senses were overwhelmed by the sweet scent of daisies, the rustling of branches in the light wind, and the trill of birds—or what a New Canaanite might have called silence. There was no hint of civilization other than the house.

Rounding the car, he gazed into the glass panels on the garage door, which were thick with dust. From the sunlit outdoors, the inside of the garage was almost completely dark, but he saw no cars. No tire prints in the gravel. Schoolteachers, especially retired ones, went on vacation during the summer. Fisk wondered if their drive out hadn't been premature—or at least if the investigator's instinct to surprise subjects had been foolhardy—when a woman called out, "Merritt?"

Ellen Lee appeared from the woods behind the house. She looked to be in her early fifties, but unless the Connecticut Department of Motor Vehicles records Chay had accessed were mistaken, she was sixty-six. She was trim, her features were sharp; her sea-glass-green eyes radiated intelligence. Both her sleek ski parka and her horse-riding breeches contributed to a windblown vitality. She looked as though she'd just finished a morning ride or hike.

Yet something was off. Fisk couldn't put his finger on it, beyond the parka—if in fact she were sixty-six, she wouldn't be the first senior citizen with circulatory issues. Maybe it was that, at the sight of strangers, she continued her approach without any sign of circumspection. Then again, this was rural Connecticut, where people still left their front doors unlocked.

If Lee were unaware of Merritt Verlyn's death, as context suggested, Fisk hoped to keep the news from her until after he'd learned what he could. Catching Chay's eye, he pointed to himself, intending to communicate, *I got this.* She nodded.

"Ms. Lee, I'm Detective Jeremy Fisk of the New York Police Department and this is Chay Maryland, a journalist who is reporting on an ongoing investigation."

Her eyes widened. "Well, that is not something I hear every day."

"We were hoping to ask you a few questions, just for background."

"That would be my pleasure." She came off as too eager. "Would you like to come inside the house?"

If Yodeler were waiting inside, Fisk thought, he could probably kill them several ways. Because of the distance from civilization, he could use one of his Colt AR-15 Sporter assault rifles and no one would be the wiser. On the other hand, Fisk had his own gun, and going inside promised additional information.

"That would be great," he said.

Lee led them around the house, past shutters that actually shut, installed back in the day when they were a defense against storms.

"Who was it that you were expecting?" Fisk asked.

"Oh, I wasn't expecting anyone." Lee climbed the slate steps to the back door. "Every once in a while, the previous residents come by."

They proceeded into the living room via the mud-room, old floorboards whining with each of their steps. The place was tidy, and done in the minimal New England rustic style—solid, simple pine furniture, framed nature watercolors of ducks, braided rugs—but it was oddly lacking in contemporary amenities like a microwave, TV, or air-conditioning.

Lot of nooks and crannies to hide in here, Fisk thought. He inched his hand closer to his holster.

Lee gestured them onto an antique Chesterfield sofa. The cushions spouted dust when they sat down. After they said thank you but no thank you to her offer of iced tea, she took the wing chair across from them.

"I can see why the previous residents come by," Chay said. "It's a lovely house."

"Thank you, dear. I do what I can."

Chay said to Fisk, "Don't let me sidetrack us, but I'm interested in this." She returned her focus to Lee. "It's not often that you hear of previous residents coming by."

"It's not often in life that you get to know such lovely boys," Lee said. "They're just wonderful."

Fisk and Chay discreetly shared a quick look that asked, *What the hell?*

Maybe Lee also didn't know that Boyden had died, he thought. "How often do you get to see them?" he asked her.

She smiled. "Every now and then. Sometimes they keep me company on the holidays—I used to think they just felt sorry for me that I had no one else, but over the years, I feel as though we've become like family. I bought this house from the estate of their father, who'd passed away, and they too had no one else."

"When was that?" Fisk asked, although he knew.

"Oh, a long time." Lee counted on her fingers. "Eleven or twelve years now."

Actually it was closing in on twenty years, Fisk thought. Dementia would explain a lot of things here. "When was the last time?" he tried.

"They come fairly often. It was a turnkey sale—the house came with most of the furniture and a good deal of their father's possessions. Mind you, nothing valuable—nothing with monetary value, I should say, but a good deal in terms of sentimental value. Merritt, the older one, loved to read the adventure novels from his father's boyhood collection that was still in the attic. And I was delighted to have his company."

"When was the last time you saw him?" Fisk asked.

"I haven't heard from him in a while—he said he was going away, but he hasn't written me. But he's involved in complex computer-science work for the government."

She seemed unaware that he'd recently been featured in every major publication in the United States, more often than not on the cover.

"Do you two e-mail?" Chay asked.

"I'm ashamed to admit that I've never made the transition to computers," Lee said. "Merritt has always been good about sending me postcards when he's traveled, though not this time. But Boyden was just here recently."

"How recently?" Fisk struggled to make it sound like just another question.

Lee paused to count again. "Last month."

"So June of this year?" Chay asked.

Lee nodded. "Boyden is such a dear; he made a trip over just to help me fix the shutters." She pointed toward the windows Fisk had noticed on the way in. "The rains this spring were particularly brutal, did a number on this old place."

Fisk thought back to the driving rain on the May night the Cartel team drove him out his apartment window. But what spring didn't have rain? Might she be remembering a particularly brutal spring a decade ago?

Chay said, "I wish I had someone to call when I need repairs."

She was angling, Fisk suspected, for the contact information for Boyden—or whoever was posing as him. The key was to get it in such a way that Lee wouldn't be spurred to call him and, effectively, warn him.

"I don't call him," Lee said.

It had been too much to hope for, Fisk thought.

Lee laughed. "I text him!" From her riding pants pocket, she drew a late-model iPhone. "The boys gave me this mobile phone for my birthday."

"Oh, is that the new iPhone?" Chay asked.

"Yes, it is," Lee said proudly, showing it to her.

Fisk rushed through the attic tour, the key features of which were a Verlyn family hope chest as well as their dresser, a Victrola record-player cabinet, four camelback steamer trunks brimming with documents and photo albums, and many more packed bookshelves than could be seen. It didn't help that the dusty attic was hot enough to roast a turkey, but Fisk had a strong feeling that Boyden Verlyn's death had been fabricated, and he wanted to act on it ten minutes ago.

As the Ram left Lee's house in the rearview, he said to Chay, "If Intel had instant access to phone records, it would be useful to have Ms. Lee's right now."

"I've never had any doubt about the utility of data. But I think you can get the number she believes is Boyden's."

"With an NSL, sure, we'll look at her call logs, but by the time we get it . . ."

"I just happened to get a look at the text when I was 'admiring' her phone."

She relayed the number to Fisk, who could have kissed her if he weren't turning the car out onto the road.

They drove five miles to downtown Norwalk while R2 ran the number Lee had entered in her contacts as *Boyden*.

When R2 called back, Fisk and Chay were waiting at Starbucks, sitting at an outside table, under an umbrella, nursing iced coffees—or, in Fisk's case, going through the motions of picking up a cup, sipping, and replacing the cup. His thoughts were on Boyden Verlyn.

"The phone belongs to a Darren Draco," came the tech's voice. Fisk put him on speaker. "Does the name Darren Draco mean anything to either of you?"

Chay's mouth fell open. Fisk thought he knew why. "Isn't Darren Draco the former Princeton student who's in an institution now?"

"Permanently brain-damaged as a result of Boyden's nerve-agent experiment," Chay said. "The institution is in New Mexico."

"Near Santa Fe," R2 chimed in. "According to the staff, he's there right now, and hasn't left once since his admission in 2009. But that evidently hasn't stopped him getting a Southern New England Telephone account, or taking up residency in Connecticut in 2010."

"Wasn't Boyden's suicide in 2010?" Chay asked.

"The empty rowboat with his suicide note taped to the bench was found in Long Island Sound on August third, 2010," R2 said. "That was three weeks to the day after the Connecticut Department of Motor Vehicles issued a driver's license to Darren Draco, or at least to someone who had successfully posed as Darren Draco."

In Fisk's experience, people who had been institutionalized with permanent brain damage were often targets of identity theft because they seldom complained. "I don't suppose we have the address on that Connecticut driver's license?"

"We do. It's 2308 Connecticut Avenue, which is just two blocks from where you are now. If you're going there, will you be wanting backup?"

"Why not?" Fisk was already on the move to the parking lot, with Chay behind him, her iced coffee in hand. He looked back, confirming that he'd left his on the table. Not worth going back for it, he thought as he clicked the Ram unlocked. He ripped the driver's door open and clambered in, still on the phone, then thrust the key into the ignition, twisted it, and started the car. Chay didn't immediately follow, her door not unlocking maybe?

"Did you somehow get Darren Draco's phone?" came R2's voice over the phone.

Fisk wondered if the tech had become distracted, uncharacteristically, as he simultaneously messaged the FBI and the Norwalk PD. "How would we have it?"

"That's weird," said R2. "I show you as having it in the Starbucks parking lot."

"Must be a glitch," said Fisk, reaching across the center console to manually unlock and open the passenger door for Chay, then realizing there had been no glitch.

Darren Draco's phone was indeed in the Starbucks parking lot. The man who'd assumed Draco's identity, Boyden Verlyn, was standing in the shadows of a tree on the grassy strip dividing the lot from the street, holding a pistol to Chay's head.

Mr. Verlyn, please don't shoot Chay," Fisk said through the Ram's tinted passenger window, largely for the benefit of R2, who was still on the phone. "Please put the gun down, Boyden."

A single Norwalk patrolman on the scene could tilt the scales in Chay's favor, Fisk thought. She appeared steeled, by adrenaline or otherwise. But that wouldn't help if Boyden snapped the trigger of what Fisk took for a Colt model 1911, with a glossy black barrel, wood-tone checkered grip, and .45 ACP bullets sufficient to take off a good deal of her head.

With his free hand, Boyden gestured for Fisk to roll down the passenger window. Fisk complied by toggling the window switch on the driver's-door console. With the tinted glass no longer between them, he saw Boyden's complexion as much paler, to the point of anemic. The onetime robust Princeton University chemist was also much, much thinner than in the most recent photos Fisk had seen. Of course those had been taken five years ago. Boyden appeared prematurely old beyond the scope of cosmetics. His face was drawn as though he'd just swigged lemon juice, with the frown lines of a man twice his age.

Boyden prodded Chay, moving them both sideways to place the tree trunk between himself and Fisk. Boyden said, "Now raise your right hand where I can see it, and use your left hand to toss the phone out the window, Detective." His was a nasal, higher-pitched version of Merritt's lilt, with, at least right now, an edge of hysteria.

Without disconnecting the call to R2, Fisk leaned across the seat, ready to drop the phone out of the car.

"Toss!" Boyden said, punctuating the command by drilling the muzzle into Chay, who swallowed a cry.

Fisk flicked his wrist and the phone flew out the window before landing with a crack on the asphalt two or three feet away. Boyden lowered his gun, meanwhile gathering the hair that fell down Chay's back and yanking it back with such force that, as her head followed, it was a wonder that her neck didn't snap. Her cry was devoured by an earsplitting blast from the Colt. The phone jumped like a frog, landing in two pieces, the faceplate detached. Possibly still transmitting, though.

Boyden fired twice more, two good shots, leaving the device in pieces. The third shot pinged off the sidewalk and cracked through the rear window of a station wagon hurriedly backing out of a parking spot behind Fisk's. The driver hit the brakes, sending the car rasping on the asphalt. Fisk thought he smelled burning rubber.

The driver's door opened, and a young woman jumped out, tears striping her mascara. "Please, please, don't shoot again!" She threw her hands in the air. "I have a baby in the backseat." Her claim was substantiated by the infant's wail heard over her idling engine.

"I won't shoot the baby," Boyden said. He raised

the gun, and keeping Chay in front of him—whether or not it was his intent, she was shielding him from Fisk—he snapped the trigger.

The Colt boomed, its barrel jumped, and the young mother dropped to the asphalt as though she'd been hit by a truck. If she were still alive, she didn't show it.

"What do you want, Boyden?" Fisk called out.

"For starters, for you to get out of your car, keeping your hands above the window line, where I can see them, at all times. If I so much as suspect you of trying anything, I will shoot Ms. Maryland in the head."

"Don't, Jeremy," Chay said, before doubling over from the impact of one of Boyden's sharp elbows to her jaw.

"It's going to be okay." Fisk kept his hands above the window line, working the door lever with his left elbow, opening it and rising slowly out of the car. Slowly was key. Because whatever Boyden wanted, delaying increased the likelihood of a better outcome.

With the barrel of his gun, Boyden gestured for Fisk to step in front of the hood of the car, over the tire curb, and onto the grass, where he would be completely exposed.

"Don't worry," Boyden said. "I want you to have a clean shot at me." Jerking Chay sideways, he stepped out from behind the tree.

Was he trying to commit suicide-by-cop? Suicidal individuals sometimes acted in a threatening way or harmed other people with the objective of provoking a lethal response from a law enforcement officer. In this instance, it made no sense to Fisk. None.

No matter. He wanted Boyden alive.

Delay.

"Why would you want to die now?" he asked Boyden. "You're not really suicidal."

The killer shook his head. "True, I faked it last time. This time, I imagine I won't get the opportunity. And as you've taken my brother, I don't want to live. Not that I have any intention of obtaining your blessing here. Just do what I say. Shoot me now, or I'll shoot her." He shook Chay for emphasis. She only gritted her teeth.

In the Ram's windshield, Fisk saw the reflection of a Norwalk policeman, blocked from Boyden's view by the Starbucks. The guy was muttering into a phone, probably a call for more assistance. Anyone else around, wisely, stayed out of sight.

"Boyden, is there any alternative?" Fisk asked. "Is there anything at all that you might want?"

"Just for you to move close enough that you won't miss."

There were twenty feet between them. Fisk could take him down now. Easy. He took a step forward to appease Boyden, a slow step, to prolong his life by that many seconds. Then another. "Let Chay walk now, and you'll get what you want."

"What I want is a bullet before I count to five. Otherwise she gets one."

"Let me just ask you one thing?"

"No. Draw your goddamned gun."

Fisk drew his Glock, keeping the barrel pointed at the ground.

"Just one question, regarding Ellen Lee?" Fisk didn't know what he'd ask, but hoped the topic would move Boyden enough to say something.

"One," Boyden said. "Two."

"Why Yodeler?"

"Random. Three."

But Fisk saw the beginnings of a grin. Boyden's ego remained intact.

Play it.

"How in the world did you make it seem you were posting from Loch Ness and—"

"Four." Boyden's finger tightened on the trigger.

He might have pointedly pressed the gun closer to Chay's head, again. Instead he backed away. To make sure of receiving a lethal shot, Fisk believed. He raised his own gun and fired. The round sent Boyden staggering backward. The tree trunk then batted him the opposite way. He crumpled onto the grass and lay still, eyes unblinking, a purple-black cavity between them.

The best part of Fisk's job was when a case closed. He liked the feeling. Loved it. Maybe lived for it. All at once the tension dissolved, and he looked forward to a good night's sleep for a change—but not right away.

Before sleeping, he wanted to savor the triumph, a win that he judged superior to that in any race, any hunt, or any puzzle: justice had been done. When a case closed, he liked to take the subway home. He would once more be any other New Yorker crammed onto the train, except he would be high on the satisfaction of having kept the rest of them safe.

He felt none of that today, though. Despite the best efforts of millions of New Yorkers. At the news of Yodeler's demise, they threw open windows and cheered. Fisk and Chay heard the isolated whoops of joy while they were driving across the Triborough Bridge. By the time they reached Manhattan, the whoops had increased in frequency, blending together to form one constant delirious roar. On every block, people were streaming into the streets, high-fiving strangers, kind to one another, buoyant to the point—it seemed—that they might take flight.

Times Square had become the site of a spontaneous street party, just like when the Yankees won the World Series, the crowd there responding with giddy ovations to each update that crawled across

the giant *New York Times* news ticker—NATIONAL
GUARD WITHDRAWS FROM NEW YORK CITY—and
each video clip shown on the Jumbotrons, for example the Iron Apple trucks rumbling across the
George Washington Bridge. On top of that, it was
Independence Day. 1010 WINS broadcast the live
announcement by a jubilant Mayor de Blasio: the
evening's fireworks show, which had been canceled,
he proclaimed, was now back—

Fisk snapped off the car radio.

"Don't like fireworks?" Chay said.

"I still can't get my head around the SBC."

"Suicide by Cop?"

"We had his home address, sure, but Boyden could
have just driven to Mexico, or even hitchhiked there,
and we would probably have been none the wiser."

Chay sat back in the passenger seat, puzzling
it over. "It would have been reasonable for him to
think that every road was blocked off. In any case,
trying to find a rational explanation for a suicide is
usually an exercise in chasing your tail."

"Maybe." Fisk wasn't satisfied. "The other thing
is, his apartment."

"What about it?"

The place had been sterile. No photos, no me-
mentos. Fisk asked Chay, "Did you see any quadrocopters there?"

She smiled. "On the way in, I'd expected that
the walls would be covered with Times clippings,
photos of the victims, and, I don't know, scrawled
quotations from *Catcher in the Rye*."

"It's never like that." Fisk turned off the West
Side Highway. "But there's usually *some* evidence."

"If Boyden were clever enough to keep all traces out of his apartment, isn't it reasonable to think he did his work somewhere else?"

"It would be good to know where."

Chay's warm hand fell onto his forearm. "Are you worried the machines are going to attack us on their own?" she asked.

He wanted to laugh. But couldn't. "I hadn't been thinking that the Yodeler drones would operate autonomously, but drones are certainly capable of that."

"Why would Boyden preprogram them?"

Fisk wished he knew. "What if he had a partner?"

"Isn't being a loner the trait most common to serial killers?"

"I think it's that they kill people. But, yeah, loner is a common trait, and if anyone fit that profile, it was Boyden. In which case . . ."

He dialed Evans. The call went to voice mail. Unusual for Evans not to pick up before the end of the first ring, he thought. He left a message asking Evans to toss the name Darren Draco to the group of FBI agents following up leads on unmanned aerial vehicles, parts, and related purchases.

As they turned onto Ninth Avenue, intending to skirt the crowds in Times Square, they heard the crowd break into a chant of "N-Y-P-D, N-Y-P-D."

"Why don't you let yourself enjoy this?" Chay asked.

He couldn't think of a good reason. "An old spook once told me that sometimes paranoia keeps you alive, and sometimes it keeps you from living."

She grinned. "Maybe you're casting about for a reason for us to continue our working relationship."

He wished it were that simple. "That's probably it."

"Well, as long as I'm a target of enemy spy agencies, I'd like to retain you."

He turned left onto West Fortieth. "Okay."

"There's just one thing I need to tell you."

"Okay?"

She said nothing.

He turned left again, onto Eighth Avenue. "Hit me," he said.

"It's about the documents." Whatever it was, she appeared to be wrestling over telling him.

"What about them?"

"I'm afraid they'll come between us."

He pulled the Ram up to the curb fronting the Times Tower. "Chay, your source is dead. Who are you protecting now by keeping the cache to yourself?"

"That's a good question," she said.

Fisk ventured, "If I were to somehow come into possession of the documents, the bull's-eye would be taken off your back."

"But then it would be on yours."

He shrugged. "There's already a bull's-eye there."

She leaned closer to him. "Can we speak off the police record?"

"Of course."

"I need immunity."

His stomach tightened. "Have you cooperated with a foreign intelligence service?"

"No, no, it's not like that."

He wasn't convinced. What else could this be? His inclination was to protect her regardless. Unless getting him to feel that way had been her objective in wrangling an invitation to his off-the-grid bed? Wouldn't be the first time in the annals of spying.

She said, "I need to keep fighting for the constitutional protection of the communications between journalist and source. Also, if I were to hand over or even discuss documents that Merritt showed me in confidence—that would betray his trust. Why would a source ever trust me again?"

"There's always an escape route."

"Except when you're trapped."

"We could work it so that a collection of the documents found its way onto the Internet. We would simply omit anything that jeopardized national security. Or better still, we could turn this into a counterintelligence coup by adding documents designed to mess with our enemies' heads. For instance, we include an Above Top Secret memorandum about our mole at the Chinese Ministry of State Security."

"That would work except for one part." She looked at the footwell. "I don't have the documents."

He figured he'd missed something. "What happened to them?"

"All of the material I ever had was excerpted in my story, the same documents Merritt simultaneously uploaded to WikiLeaks, which WikiLeaks posted a few hours after my story was published. I promised Merritt I wouldn't reveal what I'd seen and what I hadn't, for his protection, not until he'd uploaded everything he had."

"I thought you had terabytes sitting on a flash drive somewhere."

"Unfortunately, I perpetuated that notion."

"Why?"

"Simple. To get what every journalist wants. Access. Access to you, for instance. And that sure paid off. If I don't go up to my desk now and write a behind-the-scenes story of the Yodeler investigation that puts me on the Pulitzer short list, it will be because another enemy spy grabs me first." She looked up, her eyes rimmed red. "I'm sorry."

He drew her toward him, kissed her on the forehead. "As long as you're not in league with our enemies, we're good. Also, as confessions go, trust me . . . that's nothing."

At Intel, Weir and Evans, of all people, tried to convince Fisk that he'd done his job, done it well, and that the case could be closed. He'd run into them on his way in. As Weir put it, in his inimitable way, "I think you're fucking nuts, Fisk."

Evans quickly added, "Burt means that in a good way."

"He gets it, he gets it," said Weir, before turning back to Fisk. "I mean, here you've nailed this case closed, and you're still all OCD about clues—which I've come around on, by the way. It gets you thinking of stuff no one else does. With Yodeler, it made a life-and-death difference. I was totally wrong about you, man." He offered a beefy right hand.

Moved by his contrition, Fisk shook hands. "You're not all bad either," he said.

"As we just told Chief Dubin, we're going to submit you for the Director's Award for Excellence," Evans said.

The Director's Award for Excellence, Fisk knew, was given in recognition of FBI agents as well as outsiders judged to have made an outstanding contribution to the FBI and its mission. Agents who won considered it a career highlight. Fisk was humbled.

"But the Director's Award's just a trophy—looks just like the ones my kids win every year just for showing up to tee-ball practice," Weir said. "Which is why I want to give you FBI special agent Burt

Weir's Award for Excellence, which is whatever the hell you want at Old Town. Ev and I are heading there right now for the longest lunch of our careers."

Fisk knew that the Old Town Bar, just north of Union Square, had been an FBI-agent favorite for more than a century. His mouth watered at the thought of an Old Town burger—maybe the best of any pub's in the city—washed down by a Black and Tan.

"First let's cross Darren Draco off the bucket list," he said.

"His name turned up on one of our lists, but it turned out to have nothing to do with drones. So, Old Town?"

Fisk couldn't leave it at that. "Which list?"

Weir said to Evans, "Put our guest of honor's mind at ease, will you?"

Evans checked his phone. "Using the identity of Darren Draco, Boyden had a slew of part-time chemical-plant jobs, including, this week, at an industrial-cleaning-products manufacturer in Hoboken called Bantam Chemical. So his name went automatically onto our watch list."

"Why?" Fisk asked.

"Bantam bulk-orders a number of different chemicals that can be weaponized."

"Was Boyden making use of his doctorate in chemistry?"

"He's held similar jobs at other cleaning-supply companies and agricultural chemical plants all over Connecticut. Two weeks here, two weeks there, filling in for chemical-plant and systems officers who were out."

"Better cooking pesticide than meth," Weir chimed in while, pointedly, turning to go.

Fisk wondered aloud: "Hoboken's a haul from where Boyden lived, in Norwalk, isn't it?"

Evans waved away the concern. "Fifty miles, but he could have done the drive in just over an hour if he'd avoided traffic."

Stepping toward the elevators, Weir said, "That wacko probably was lucky to get work anywhere."

"I'll meet you guys over at Old Town," Fisk said. "I just have a couple of quick things to wrap up here." It would be a matter of minutes, he thought, to rule out any connection between the case and Boyden Verlyn's employment at a company that bought weaponizable chemicals in bulk. Hopefully, it wasn't the portent it seemed.

The two FBI agents headed off with the air of children on the last day of school. Fisk started toward his office, burning to research Bantam Chemical. Something was off. He didn't know what, but he felt it, like a splinter in his mind.

Dubin intercepted him and exclaimed, though no one was in earshot, "Here he is, ladies and gentlemen, the man of the hour." He pointed Fisk to the corner office. Following him, the chief added, "I'd say you hit a home run, Detective, but it's more than that. It's like you were due up to bat with the team trailing in the bottom of the ninth, with three outs, meaning the game was over. But you'd seen something on the last play, and you had the umpires look at the replay, then reverse the call, letting you bat. Then you smacked the ball out of the stadium."

"Thanks," Fisk said, wondering about Dubin's true agenda now. Or, rather, the PR team's agenda.

Dubin dropped onto the couch. He scowled when Fisk didn't immediately take one of the chairs across from him. Fisk sat, but at the edge of the cushion, poised to spring up and out.

"Need a Coke?" asked the chief. "Or a seltzer, maybe?"

"I'm good, thanks."

"How about lunch? You have lunch yet? Sally can order from El Quixote."

"Wish I had time."

"Got it." Dubin tugged his shirt cuffs into alignment. "Real quick, then, about the Tel Aviv gig . . ."

By necessity, Fisk had pushed the transfer to the back of his mind. "I haven't had a chance to think about it yet."

"That's okay. See, the other thing you accomplished with your game-winning home run was cause management to reassess sending you to Tel Aviv. They want you to stay, and the city needs you to stay. So how about it?"

Excellent, Fisk thought. He expected that there would be a price, though. "Maybe," he said.

"Also I'd gotten to thinking that David Rettenmund would be the man for Tel Aviv. We could send him there to pick up tech tips from the Israelis."

David Rettenmund—R2—was an excellent choice for Tel Aviv, Fisk thought. R2 was young and single, would kill for the opportunity to work abroad, and was probably uniquely suited to thrive in the tech-intensive Israeli environment. Fisk had doubts about Dubin's motivation in suggesting R2 as the man for the job, though. Was it because the chief, aware of Fisk's affinity for R2, sought to gain leverage?

Fisk feigned indifference. "Okay."

"The Department just needs you to do one small thing," Dubin said.

Huge surprise. "Use the city's box at Yankees games more often?"

"Close. I know this isn't your shtick, but Mayor de Blasio wants to present you with a key to the city in Riverside Park before the fireworks ceremony tonight."

A key to the city didn't sound that bad to Fisk. With it, he would be like a made man in New York—able even to cut through red tape.

But Dubin, shifting uncomfortably on the couch, had more. "There are just a few things they'd like you to say."

"Like what?"

Dubin went to his desk and snapped up a printed sheet of paper. "This just came by messenger. In light of current events, the PR folks are afraid of their e-mails being electronically intercepted, so now they've gone old school with the commo." He glanced at the document. "So what they want you to do is decry previous Intel policies."

"*Decry?*"

"Not my word." Dubin lowered himself into his desk chair, slipped on a pair of reading glasses, and scanned the memo. "They want you to quote from the Declaration of Independence as a way of condemning the spooky tactics and gadgets we've gotten flak for. Do you know the part where Thomas Jefferson talks about what happens when government becomes destructive of people's unalienable rights to life, liberty, and the pursuit of happiness?"

Fisk knew the opening of the Declaration of Independence by heart—unfortunately to the tune from the Broadway musical *1776*, of which his music teacher at the American School in Abu Dhabi had been the world's biggest fan. *Whenever any Form of Government becomes destructive of these ends, it is the Right of the People to alter or to abolish it, and to institute new Government.*

"My only problem with that is I don't think we're doing anything wrong," Fisk said. "I wish New Yorkers could leave their apartment doors and windows open when there are strangers in town. But until we can trust the strangers—"

Dubin raised a hand, like an ax, poised to cut him off. But he didn't. Instead he tugged at his own lip. Fisk had seen this before—albeit rarely. The chief was taking something he'd said into consideration.

"You know what?" Dubin said finally. "Why don't you say what you just said?"

"I wouldn't get the key."

Dubin rose with energy Fisk hadn't seen from him in a long time. He balled up the printout and jump-shot it at the corner wastepaper basket, missing badly. "The memo got lost. They should have e-mailed it. All you need to say is the Department's going to continue to protect people. We're fucking spies, not marketing executives."

Fisk was glad Dubin had come around. The sentiment was diluted, though, by his nascent theory of what Boyden Verlyn had been up to at Bantam Chemical.

Darren Draco is a terrific chemist," said Sol Bellinger, the silver-haired founder and longtime owner of Bantam Chemical. "He's a genius."

Bellinger had come to work at the Hoboken plant today so that his foreman could take his children to a July Fourth parade. Hearing that, Fisk liked Bellinger. Also there was an undeniable geniality etched between the seventy-year-old's jowls, which, like his ample belly, spoke of a predilection for comfort food. His sharp eyes were full of a certain reassuring gravitas.

Bellinger added, "I would do just about anything to get him to come to work here full-time."

Fisk saw no reason to explain why Darren Draco—aka Boyden Verlyn—would never be coming to work at the plant again. Purporting to be here as part of a routine security check, Fisk followed the old man out of an elevator and onto the uppermost of four tiers of catwalks circling a chemical mixing room that reminded him of a giant diesel truck engine. Glinting beneath dim fluorescents stood fuel and oil centrifuges, cylinder heads, alternators, air reservoirs, turbochargers, camshafts, crankcases, pumps—at least that's what Fisk thought Bellinger was saying. He could barely hear him over a gargantuan turbine that, in combination with the other machines, filled the air with the whine of thousands of vacuum cleaners gunning at once. Yet the air was stagnant, heavy with oil, and searing—easily 110 degrees. Fisk was relieved on several fronts when Bellinger led him into the vast soundproofed and air-conditioned control room overlooking the works.

Bellinger gestured to the bank of controls that were part late-twentieth-century computer and part World War II submarine. "This is where the magic happens."

"What exactly does Darren do?" Fisk asked.

"He's a chemical plant and systems officer, like Priscilla and Jim here." Bellinger gestured toward a man and a woman sitting at clusters of instruments and computers across the room. Each looked up from their monitors to exchange a quick greeting with Bellinger. Jim was a big, bearded, studious-looking African American man of about fifty, who wore a bow tie under his white lab coat. Priscilla was perhaps ten years younger, a trim and attractive redhead, making the dark circles under her eyes all the more jarring. She looked to Fisk like she'd been sleeping even less than he had lately.

Returning his attention to Fisk, Bellinger said, "Chemical plant and systems officers use all of these gauges and readouts to ensure that your chemicals are mixed in the right order, that the reaction rates, temperatures, and other variables are on target.

"Why?"

"Chemistry is science, of course, but on the industrial scale, it's an art, and like painters or sculptors, plant and systems officers need to know everything about their materials, especially how they react under all sorts of conditions. Take moisture content: it completely varies depending on the weather. Computers can help you, but in the end it comes down to the skill and judgment of the operator, and, in some cases, like Darren Draco, artistry. He's as good as they come."

"Why wouldn't he want full-time work?"

"Good chemists can make more in two days as a freelancer than they can in a week full-time, because of the union caps. If a plant and systems officer is going to be out, you have to replace them. Otherwise your operation comes to a standstill. When a plant and systems officer misses work unexpectedly, the subs have you over a barrel."

"Is that what happened last week?" Fisk asked.

"Well . . ." Bellinger hesitated.

"You don't need to tell me the specifics of Draco's contract."

"No, it's not that." Bellinger shot a quick glance at Priscilla, who appeared absorbed by her work. With a look of relief, he hurried to an exit door, pulled it open, allowing Fisk to pass through, then followed him into a tall concrete corridor with heavy acetic fumes like those in a hair salon. Pulling the door shut behind him, Bellinger explained, "Priscilla had to miss a few days because of her father's death. I told her to take all the time she wanted, but what she really wanted was to be back at work, to take her mind off it. Horrific business. Her father was Walter Doyle, one of the drone victims."

Shock buffeted Fisk. He tried to hide it. So, Yodeler/Boyden's claim that he would kill people in New York City at random had been a cover. And likely Boyden killed Walter Doyle with more in mind than getting a gig as a substitute chemical plant and systems officer.

Fisk asked, "Are there any chemicals you work with here that they wouldn't commonly have in plants in Connecticut?"

Bellinger offered a one-shouldered shrug as he gestured with his other arm for Fisk to precede him around the corner. "We make industrial cleaning fluids and sewage treatment products, so we don't have anything that's very sexy."

Fisk started down another corridor, wrought in bare concrete, leading to the supply room. "What about chemicals that can be weaponized?"

"What chemicals can't be weaponized? Your basic drain cleaner and rust remover contain nitric or sulfuric acid, like H_2SO_4, which is required to make the high-order explosive nitroglycerine. The little engines in the model rockets that my grandson's Boy Scout troop build run on nitro-methane, CH_3NO_2, which is a chemical with explosive properties greater than TNT, and when you mix it in with an oxidizing agent like a basic ammonium nitrate, NH_4NO_3, which many agricultural companies use in fertilizer products you can buy at any garden store, the explosive power is even greater." Bellinger stopped by the supply room door. Signs warned away unauthorized personnel. Opening the door required entering the proper code on the numeric keypad as well as a fingerprint scan. "Here we have a lot of concentrated hydrogen peroxide, H_2O_2, which we use in our sewage treatment products, and it's the same stuff my wife picks up at the drugstore to sanitize various things in our bathrooms and kitchen. However, as I'm sure you know, Detective, H_2O_2's gotten a bit of a bad rap in your world lately."

Al-Qaeda's favorite impromptu high explosive of late, triacetone triperoxide, or TATP, could be made using concentrated H_2O_2—hydrogen peroxide—which was available in most pharmacies and hardware stores. A small quantity of "Mother of Satan," as terrorists called it, could produce tremendous destructive force. It was famously used in 2001 on a transcontinental American Airlines flight by passenger Richard Reid, subsequently known as the Shoe Bomber. The ten ounces of the explosive he'd packed into his black suede sneakers could have taken down the plane. Fortunately a flight attendant first noticed Reid trying to light one of his sneakers with a match.

Fisk winced at the thought of the damage Boyden Verlyn could cause with a quadrocopter and a four-pound TATP payload if the quad were to land on a city street. Conservatively, everyone within 1,000 feet of the blast would be a potential casualty—the standard Manhattan city block was 264 feet long. The blast itself could cause eardrum damage and lung collapse and, of course, hurl people to more severe injuries or death. And high-velocity flying debris was the biggest threat in such explosions—shards of glass were responsible for 40 percent of the casualties in the Oklahoma City bombing.

Fisk asked Bellinger, "Does anyone here ever do the chemical plant equivalent of taking home office supplies?"

"Back in the day, sure, guys would take home some concentrated H_2O_2 or C_3H_6O, especially this time of year, to make their own firecrackers. But since 9/11, no one would dare. Not worth losing your livelihood over. Also, in compliance with the new federal regulations, it's kind of impossible." Bellinger typed in a code above the handle and pressed his thumb against the adjacent panel, which glowed red as it scanned. With a series of pops and hisses, the bolts sprang free of the jamb. He pushed down the levered handle and then heaved open the big metal door.

Fisk was hit by a wave of chilled air that smelled intensely like an indoor swimming pool. Bellinger swatted at a light-switch panel on the wall inside the door, illuminating fluorescent ceiling tubes protected by thick sheets of plastic and metal cages, stacks of drums, barrels, and industrial-size bottles in a surprising array of bright colors. If not for the stench, Fisk might have thought he was in the supply room of an ice cream or candy factory. The containers were labeled with the names of the chemicals Bellinger had been discussing, and many more Fisk hadn't heard of.

"Not that this happened," Fisk said, "but if someone did get in here and somehow snuck off with a drum full of concentrated hydrogen peroxide, would you know?"

"Yeah, six ways until Sunday. Every last one of these containers has an adhesive decal over the seal that's not only tamper-proof but contains a transponder that constantly transmits a radio signal. I can track the whereabouts of everything, in real time, using my mobile phone." He fished an iPhone out of his jeans pocket and clicked open an inventory app. "Let's take the concentrated hydrogen peroxide as an example. Currently we have seven of the Global Peroxygen brand fifty-six-point-eight-liter containers of standard grade seventy percent concentration." He looked up from the phone. "Right over here." He pointed to three royal-blue plastic containers, each the size and approximate shape of a beer keg, each with an identical container stacked on top of it.

Fisk counted six containers in total.

"Now this is very strange," Bellinger said.

The Connecticut coastline flew past, with the cerulean Long Island Sound making appearances in bursts in and around trees at their summertime lushest. Blackwell had just gone all the way out to Norwalk for nothing. Now he was driving back to the familiar confines of square one in New York. So he couldn't enjoy the view.

His phone trilled and he answered, "Freeman."

"A marvelous Independence Day to you, Mr. Freeman," came Segui's silky voice, with an excess of joy.

The Cartel man was overcompensating again, Blackwell thought. Meaning the day was about to get even less marvelous. "Back at you, bud. What's up?"

"Certain CNN viewers were displeased to see our prospective customer from Appleton on live television today, in the embrace of a beautiful young woman no less."

Blackwell decoded this as: Segui's Zeta bosses were watching TV—probably a news network other than CNN—and saw the coverage of the man from Appleton (New York), Detective Jeremy Fisk, rescuing Chay Maryland from the clutches of Yodeler.

The Cartel's problem with "live television" almost certainly referenced their dismay that Fisk remained alive. Once they'd put out a hit on someone, they tended to feel as though each hour the target continued to live cost them in clout. Whether or not that was true, each hour that Fisk lived certainly depleted Blackwell's clout, as well as his future earning potential, and, if he were to fail altogether, his future in general.

Segui offered him an out. "Listen, I know you've had bad luck on this sales trip."

Blackwell didn't need any sympathy. "Amigo, any fool can have bad luck. The art consists in exploiting it."

"Glad to hear it! Also, maybe F-dash-F-dash-33511-dash-5 will help."

A few minutes later, sitting inside a Wi-Fi–equipped roadside food court, laptop powered on, Blackwell opened the Tucson junkyard website and entered the middle six characters Segui had given him. F-33511 produced a listing for a 1974 BMW 3.0 CSI driver's-side chrome flag-shaped side mirror in good condition, $129.95 plus shipping.

Within pixel number 3,351 Segui had inserted his idea of help, or, more likely, that of his impatient superiors, who had determined that Fisk was impossible to find, but not to trap. So they'd gotten a message to Chay Maryland inviting her to an off-the-record interview with a Sinaloa Cartel representative bent on exposing the Zeta hit currently out on Jeremy Fisk. Their idea was to use a Zeta operative in the role of Sinaloa Cartel representative. That operative would kidnap Chay and use her to bait Fisk. The operative was to be none other than Blackwell.

Using Chay as bait had essentially been his own backup plan the other night on East Seventy-Fourth Street, in the event that Fisk hadn't been with her in the taxi. It had been a convoluted plan then, and it was worse now, because she would probably be on guard. Also she'd seen Blackwell, although it had only been a fleeting look in the dark.

The good news was that they'd gotten her to agree to the meeting.

Fisk stood on the roof of Bantam Chemical, looking out at the industrial landscape of Hoboken, and just across the Hudson River, Boyden Verlyn's probable target, Manhattan. In the waning sunlight, the skyscrapers and the harbor resembled molten copper. As much as anything, TATP was a security headache because of the difficulty in detecting it. The explosive defied most standard methods of chemical sensing: it didn't fluoresce, it didn't absorb ultraviolet light, you couldn't readily ionize it. Moreover, screening for TATP required cumbersome and expensive equipment, and even with the best machines, it took a ridiculous amount of time to prepare the samples for testing. Eventually, the NYPD invested in handheld colorimetric sensors. With a readout that changed colors based upon the TATP concentration in the air, the way litmus paper reacts to pH, the devices detected as few as two parts per billion. If Boyden had in fact made TATP and then snuck it elsewhere, thought Fisk, the Department would now need about five million sensors to track it.

Fisk had decided to come up here because Bantam's owner, Sol Bellinger, had told him that Darren Draco often came up here for cigarette breaks. Fisk saw no evidence of that now, no quadrocopter launch pad, nothing but gull shit, crumbling asphalt roof tiles, a road map of blemished ducts, and a water tower that looked ready to topple off its stilts as soon as a strong gust came along. On the elevator ride up, he had confided to Bellinger the truth about Boyden Verlyn in hopes of spurring him into additional recollection. Now Bellinger just paced in the shadow of the water tower, in stunned silence. The elevated corner of the roof supported a pair of giant air-conditioning units that spewed hot and chemical-laden air, the vapor slicking the wall of the wood-slatted water tank.

"Do you drink the water from that?" Fisk wondered aloud.

"Oh, God no," said Bellinger. "I'd have grown scales and five eyes by now. Thing's been dry since my father bought the place."

A couple of years ago at a party in Chelsea, Fisk and Krina had been handed an antique pocket watch by one of her friends, who instructed them to go to the top floor of the building, climb the fire escape to the roof, and then knock on the trapdoor at the base of the water tower there. How could they resist? Knocking on the trapdoor gained them admission to the Night Heron, a bar within the tower that was as exclusive as it was lawless, and due to the latter, was soon shuttered.

Fisk now tapped the rusty ladder running up the side of the Bantam tower. "Would it be okay if I have a look in there?" he asked Bellinger.

"Fine with me," the old man said, then, as if having thought better of it, hastened over and gripped the side rails. "I'd better hold on, just in case."

Fisk hoisted himself on the metal ladder, cold and wet on account of the discharge from the elevated cooling units, before he too had second thoughts. If Boyden had used the tower for any Yodeler-related business, it could be booby-trapped.

"You better stay back," he told Bellinger.

When the old man was out of harm's reach, Fisk continued to the top of the ladder. The rungs terminated at the pitched roof, a six-sided pyramid atop the barrel, which was once covered with tar paper. Now it was covered with scraps of tar paper and, mostly, more seagull crap. The point of entry was a square hatch on the nearest of the six triangular panels, wide enough to admit a man—or launch a Specter quadrocopter through.

Fisk leaned as far away as the ladder would allow, ducked his face so that the barrel shielded him, then reached the Pelican to the hatch and poked at the knob. The hatch, unlocked and already open, flew sideways, clattering against the roof panel.

"Everything okay?" Bellinger called up.

"So far," Fisk said.

He set the flashlight on full lumen blast and peered into the barrel. If he hadn't once visited the illicit nightclub, he would have been shocked by the structure's expanse. The air was stagnant, oven hot, and smelled like soil. The base was ringed with deposits of some sort, decayed leaves or dust or more droppings.

But the central part was oddly clean, as if the debris had been swept or pushed to the side. Before climbing down the interior ladder, rungs bolted to the inner wall, Fisk scoured the place with the flashlight, searching for a booby trap and then for a sign of weakness in the rungs. That was when the beam landed on a black rotor blade. At first glance it was identical to the Specter blades Fisk had seen. On closer look, he realized, it was twice their size. A bigger blade, meaning bigger rotors, meaning a bigger drone. Which you would want why? he thought. To carry a bigger payload? Like a bomb?

The bad news was that Chay Maryland was nobody's fool. A beefy pair of *New York Times* security guards accompanied her to the agreed-upon meeting spot beneath the Coca-Cola sign in Times Square.

The good news, Blackwell thought, was the impromptu street party: half a million in Times Square celebrating Yodeler's dirt nap or getting a head start on the July Fourth bash. If things went south, getting away would be cake.

And he was nobody's fool himself. He wore a black wig, fake 'stache, and gobs of bronzer—to mess with any skin-texture recognition software. Damned if he didn't look like the wetback he was pretending to be. He'd barely recognized himself in the Toys "R" Us men's room where he'd donned his disguise. He also had on a pair of wraparound mirror shades and a Band-Aid on the bridge of his nose—these things threw a wrench into the measurement-based stuff. And he'd packed a wad of Red Man between his cheek and gum. Another wrench, and good stuff. Still, the guards were reason enough to abort. She was supposed to have come alone.

Then again, she had legitimate security concerns apart from her Cartel reporting, he thought. And if this were a trap, an NYPD Intel or an FBI takedown, the ridiculously risk-averse cops and Feebs would never put her in jeopardy. Blackwell was further tempted to stay because he was running out of time. And with the holiday here now, who was to say that Fisk wouldn't spirit this honey away to the beach for a long weekend? *Shit, look at that body. He'd be crazy not to.* This, Blackwell thought, could be his last chance. Worse came to worst, he had at the ready, within his loose fisherman's vest, a slim and lightweight Ruger Mark III 22/45 capped with a Gemtech Outback II suppressor that reduced the report to a pop that, in this crowd, would be nothing. He could shoot both guards, as well as Chay, and be long gone before anyone was the wiser. Probably before their bodies hit the sidewalk too.

He unfolded the red Washington Nationals baseball cap from the back pocket of his cargo pants (loose-fitting clothing veiled his stature) and pulled it on. This was Chay's cue to ask him the time, to which he was to reply 3:34 even though it was a good four hours past that.

The guards stayed back as she weaved her way through a crowd lined up for a food cart. Coolly, she asked him the time, he said 3:34, and she hit him with "Are you El Polvo?"

He was shocked. "Where'd you get that?"

"My father was one of those sculptors who always had plaster dust on him, even after he took a bath." She didn't look him in the eye so much as look him over—reading him, looking for physical cues, he figured. She had guts, he had to give her that. "So I brought that to my investigation, which was mostly a fishing expedition, until I called the statuary in Chicago where I spoke to Franciszka."

This was bad, Blackwell thought, and it could get

a hell of a lot worse fast. Abort, he told himself, and get the hell out of here. Turning away, he said, "I don't know what you're talking about."

She made no attempt to follow. The guards too stayed put.

Immersing himself in the crowd, Blackwell cursed himself. He understood that when she'd asked *Are you El Polvo?* and he failed to deny it—or ask her what the hell she was talking about—he had confirmed it.

The unmarked Chevy Tahoe waited at the curb outside at the Christopher Street PATH train station, the first stop in Manhattan after Hoboken.

As Fisk hurried from the station to the SUV, the driver's door popped open. He heard Dubin's gruff voice from inside. "Don't worry about it, Luis, I got it." Then the chief reached across the backseat and punched the door open.

Fisk climbed in. As always, the chief's ride had a bouquet of cigar smoke and musky cologne and he had the a/c set to arctic, which he thought wasn't cold enough. He appeared especially uncomfortable in a crisp, double-breasted navy blazer, white slacks, and a red-white-and-blue-striped necktie. A matching handkerchief, folded with origami precision, spouted from his breast pocket. The problem was that, by nature, he was a sweats guy. Tossing Fisk a handled shopping bag from a trendy Chelsea men's store, he said, "Change."

"Hey, Chief, how are you?"

Dubin rapped the driver's headrest. "Come on, Luis, we need to be there five minutes ago."

As the SUV lurched uptown, Fisk looked in the bag, finding a navy blazer, white slacks, a matching dress shirt, and a Stars and Stripes–themed silk tie. When he had called from Bantam Chemical, the chief sounded more concerned about the toll that the descent into the water tower had taken on

Fisk's clothes than about Boyden Verlyn's plotting. Fisk asked now, "What happened to 'We're fucking spies, not suits in marketing'?"

"Ended when I was to serve as your valet tonight." Dubin squeezed his brow. "How the hell often are you awarded the key to the city?"

The more things change . . . "What'll it be worth if the city is blown up?"

"Not going to happen."

"Glad to hear that. How do you know?"

Dubin groaned. "Maybe you're right, maybe Boyden Verlyn was working on a bomber drone. I'll upgrade that from *maybe* he was to *probably*. But he's not blowing anything up with it tonight. Or ever. Not unless he rises from the dead."

"Drones can fly autonomously," Fisk reminded him. "Once you input their flight plans, setting them to launch at some point in the future isn't much harder than setting an alarm clock."

"I just don't get why he would have done that."

"Remember his threat to 'exact a steep price'? Setting a drone full of TATP in the right place, say, a tank full of liquefied natural gas . . ."

Dubin nodded. "Possible but unlikely. In any case, largely to humor you, I had the Airborne Division send up both of its Koalas and a couple of the Bell helicopters, all of them with their detectors set to TATP. Also we've got K9s out, our guys and gals on the street have been issued the five-hundred-however-many colorimetric sensors, and over in Jersey, the Port Authority PD's flying Sikorskys. Plus the Bureau ERTs are taking fine-tooth combs to Hoboken in search of missing drones or bombs or a big container of hydrogen peroxide. Same deal in Norwalk, Connecticut."

"Did you reach the National Geospatial-Intelligence Agency?"

"You're welcome. What's your guy at NGA's name again?"

"Roy Plummer."

"Plummer, right. He was on his way to watch the fireworks show. A cruiser's taking him down to his video games at the World Financial Center."

Fisk tipped the shopping bag upside down and let the contents fall on the seat between him and Dubin, then set to work unwrapping the oxford shirt and extracting the pins. The chief had done a hell of a job setting the defense, he thought. It troubled him, though, that they still had no inkling of what Boyden had in store.

He'd knotted the red-white-and-blue necktie, and on the third try, just as they reached Riverside Park, dimpled it to Dubin's satisfaction.

Blackwell ditched his disguise piece by piece—into a trash can here, down a sewer grate there—while making his way up Eighth Avenue, which was effectively closed to vehicular traffic due to the overflow of celebrants from Times Square. He dodged the July Fourth revelers, many of whom had apparently availed themselves of the special "Yodeler Shot!"—a shot glass full of vodka with blood-like red food coloring in it, for sale in so many of the area bars. And he tried to do what he always did: think positive.

He would find Fisk.

He would kill Fisk.

Then he would go home and buy an RFF 28 with the proceeds. He now imagined himself sitting in a captain's chair, rocketing across whitecaps at the powerboat's top speed of seventy-three knots. Damn if he didn't feel the sea spray cooling him now, on Eighth Avenue.

Then, as if the positive energy he'd generated had influenced the powers controlling the universe, he saw, on a TV above the bar, none other than Detective Jeremy Fisk, wearing a navy blazer and an American-flag tie. He was ascending the steps to a stage. LIVE FROM RIVERSIDE PARK, read the caption.

Then, after his promotion to the rank of detective, he served New York City courageously and selflessly," Mayor de Blasio told the full bleachers up and down Riverside Park. The park, the piers, the boat basin, and most of the western shore of Manhattan had become a viewing area for the fireworks show over the adjacent Hudson River, now golden in reflection of the sun descending over New Jersey.

The mayor went on, his words amplified by hundreds of speakers and reverberating off the water, "Detective Fisk single-handedly thwarted the assassination of President Obama . . ."

Waiting stage left to receive the key, Fisk wanted to enjoy this experience, he really did. He wished he could have notified family and friends. But seeing no need to do the Cartel any favors, he had done what he could to make sure that tonight's "surprise presentation" remained a surprise. He'd told only Chay, albeit via a last-minute text, and she texted back her regrets; she was caught up in investigating an El Polvo story. Only one other person knew: somehow Shane Poplowski, the LightningRod kid, had gotten wind of the presentation and wasted no time texting Fisk and asking for an assist in getting a VIP table for him and his buddies at Riverside Park's Boat Basin Café, which was within spitting distance of the stage.

The other reason that Fisk wasn't enjoying himself was that he couldn't turn off his apprehension. Where would the attack come from? About the only place that could be ruled out was the water tower in which he'd found the rotor blade.

". . . And today, once again, he has delivered our city from the clutches of a terrorist, restoring our independence on Independence Day . . ."

Could that be it? Could Boyden Verlyn, always a step ahead, have foreseen that his death would bring New Yorkers streaming out to celebrate Independence Day in record numbers? That would go a long way toward explaining today's precipitous suicide-by-cop. And if his plan had included getting law enforcement to drop its guard, he'd succeeded wildly: the Iron Apple, a temporary fix, had been dismantled entirely. The few National Guardsmen who had been equipped with LightningRods were gone too. Once again, there was no system in place to detect drones, let alone counter them.

Or was there?

Fisk dug his phone from his white slacks and,

cupping it in his hand for stealth, connected to the 360-degree cameras on an A-119 Koala helicopter sniffing for TATP. He wasn't stealthy enough, though. He felt Dubin's eyes go hot on him from the front row of seats. The Koala was circling Liberty Island, high above the Statue, offering a stunning—and stunningly sharp—view of New York Harbor, which looked like a sheet of silver gift wrap. The clarity of the feed notwithstanding, he thought, a drone would appear as no more than a dot. He might easily miss it. In all likelihood, he wouldn't see anything. He hoped and prayed that there was nothing to see.

He did see a bird, a gray-and-white seagull, flying past Lady Liberty's torch. To Fisk's surprise, he was able to make out the bird's eyes and beak set in a gentle expression.

". . . The first key to New York City was presented on June twenty-seventh, 1702, when Mayor Philip French awarded what was termed a 'Freedom of the City' to the Viscount Cornbury."

Fisk tapped into the feed from another of the Aviation Division helicopters, a Bell 412, which hovered over the Hudson directly above the Holland Tunnel. The tunnel consisted of a pair of tubes situated in the bedrock a hundred feet below the surface of the river. Every year, 35 million vehicles used it to go between New York and New Jersey. A terrorist target if there ever was one. Fisk saw only the river, free of boat traffic due to the fireworks. He also had a clear view of one of the Coast Guard Maritime Safety and Security Team's red twenty-five-foot Defender-class security boats maintaining the fireworks safety zone. He was able to read the white numbers on the Defender's bow: 91106.

"By the middle 1800s, it became the custom to bestow a key to the city as a symbol of New York City's intention that the recipient was free to come and go at will."

Fisk saw more of the same via the second Bell, which was flying over the Hudson just off River-side Park's dog run, just a couple of blocks from the stage. Looking up, he spotted the helicopter against a backdrop of purple clouds. He realized he'd been hearing the rhythmic thumps of its rotors throughout de Blasio's speech. The Bell's camera provided a view of one of the five fireworks barges bobbing with the current. And no drones. One of the Koalas, over Central Park, showed tens of thousands of people on the Great Lawn and on the Sheep Meadow. There could be fifty drones hovering over this hive, Fisk thought, and he wouldn't notice them. He was wrong: he was able to make out several helium balloons and Frisbees, a Nerf football, and two different Batman kites, and nothing hovering or zipping the way a quadrocopter would. Good. His preference was to be 100 percent wrong about an attack.

Switching to the camera aboard one of the Port Authority Police Department's Sikorskys, in the air above Union City—just north of Hoboken—his eye was drawn to movement between the roofs of two industrial buildings. Something about the size of a pizza box. He zoomed in. A quadrocopter. Although he couldn't read it, he could make out the shape of the sporty red Specter logo on the fuselage.

Fighting the inclination to jump from the shock, he tried to get a read on the drone's heading.

"It is my great honor to present a key to the city of New York on this July Fourth to a true American hero—"

"Thank you, Mayor de Blasio," Fisk said, advancing to center stage.

Surprised at the interruption and understandably indignant, de Blasio handed over the gleaming skeleton key in its leather case. Fisk accepted it—an afterthought. He needed to figure out a way to bring down the quadrocopter without sending millions of people into a panic in the process. Turning toward the Boat Basin Café, he said, "I want to thank Shane Poplowski. Where are you, Shane?"

A high-pitched whoop from within the crowd directed him to Shane's white-blond hair, above which his arms were raised. The kid had taken off his shirt, revealing uniformly burned skin. Fortunately he still had on the LightningRod in its scabbard.

"Shane, come up here, please?" The kid's cry of joy matched any game-show contestant's. If he only knew what was coming. "I also need the chief of NYPD Intel," Fisk said, looking for Dubin, finding him looking on, openmouthed. "Barry Dubin, please join me too—it's important."

Getting it, Dubin snapped into his commander mode and rocketed out of his seat. Fisk held his hands in front of him as if he were turning a steering wheel. Dubin nodded, message received.

Fisk continued, "These men represent the blend of state-of-the-art technology and shrewd old-school intelligence that makes our city as safe as anyplace on the planet." Handing the microphone to the mayor on his way off the stage, Fisk added, "And we need to get back to work."

The mayor said, "That's the spirit, ladies and gentle—" The ovation drowned him out. Leading the cheers were the two public relations executives who'd been at Dubin's apartment. Meanwhile the chief's Tahoe rolled to the end of the nearest asphalt walkway. Policemen fanned into grass on either side of it to keep spectators back.

Hurrying toward the Tahoe, Fisk corralled Poplowski. The kid was clearly befuddled, a function of the situation as well as, Fisk surmised from the skunklike scent, smoking something New York had yet to legalize.

"Is something up?" Shane asked between gasps.

"Nothing that we can't bring down," Fisk said. As he and Poplowski met Dubin and proceeded to the Tahoe, Fisk told them about the quadrocopter he'd seen headed across the Hudson River from Union City, probably laden with the explosive TATP. Barreling into the SUV, Dubin got on his radio, issuing intercept orders to the Aviation Division and Emergency Services.

The quadrocopter was flying slowly, just ten or fifteen miles per hour. Still, none of the three helicopters would be able to get within firing range before the drone reached Manhattan. The Air National Guard redirected two F-16s from their air patrols within fifty miles. Flying at their top speed of fifteen hundred miles per hour, the fighter jets would be in range within two minutes, which would put its arrival in Manhattan at about the same time as the quadrocopter's.

While trying to maintain a visual on the quadrocopter via his phone, Fisk directed Dubin's driver through the Riverside Park dog run. The SUV parked on the unpopulated cement shoulder of the Seventy-Second Street West Side Highway on-ramp, out of view of everyone except northbound drivers. The drone, flying at about fifty feet over the river and one hundred yards off the industrial pier at Fifty-Ninth Street and Twelfth Avenue, was beginning to blend in with the dusk.

Like Dubin, Fisk sprang out of the Tahoe. He ran to open the door for Poplowski, who slid out, meanwhile regarding the LightningRod readout panel with consternation.

"What is it?" Fisk asked.

Poplowski groaned. "The charge is wicked low."

Of course it is, thought Fisk. "How about you try it anyway?"

The drone was within fifty yards of the shore.

"We'll have one shot." The kid leveled the LightningRod at the quadrocopter and pressed an eye against the rear sight. "Maybe." He clicked a button on the wand.

A pale red beam shot from the device's mouth, reflecting on the quadrocopter, which was within twenty yards of them.

"The laser has a lock on the target system," Poplowski said. "Now compiling data on the target-system sensors."

"How long does that take?" asked Dubin, pacing frenetically.

"Done." The kid glanced at the readout on his phone, then tapped in a response. "Now adjusting the collimating lenses to generate sufficient infrared."

He again checked the readout and then input instructions accordingly. And again.

Dubin chewed a nail. "When will you shoot the thing?"

"It doesn't exactly work that way," Poplowski started to explain. "It's more like an arm wrestle is taking place between the UAV's system and the—"

He stopped himself short as the drone seemed to brake in midair, then dropped like a stone. It cracked the surface of the river and disappeared.

Poplowski jumped into a victory dance and whooped. As did Dubin, almost causing Fisk to miss the ring of his phone.

He eyed the readout: PLUMMER, ROY. He hit answer, and before he could say anything, the National Geospatial-Intelligence Agency man said, "I'm tracking three more quadrocopters launching from Union City."

Fisk iced up. "Heading?"

"Manhattan based on current trajectory, one is going toward Thirty-Fifth Street, give or take a block. One is angled toward the low Forties, one to around Fiftieth Street."

Fisk looked up. Dusk veiled any drones he might have been able to see before. "Empire State Building, Times Square, Rockefeller Center?"

"It's very probable that . . ." His voice trailed off.

"Roy?"

"Now there's more quadrocopters."

"How many?"

"Another fifteen, maybe twenty. Like vampire bats."

Fisk started to do the math in his head. Twenty TATP-bearing drones landing in crowded areas, where New Yorkers were currently massed to watch the fireworks, could mean casualties in the hundreds, maybe even thousands—

"And there are other aircraft trailing them," Plummer said with a gasp that quashed Fisk's hope that the new aircraft were a positive development.

"Not F-16s, I take it."

"No, UAVs, three of them. Octocopters."

"Drones with eight rotors?"

"*Huge* drones—fourteen, fifteen feet in diameter—with eight rotors."

This explained the big rotor blade at Bantam Chemical, Fisk thought. Bigger drones to deliver bigger bombs. "But what good would bigger drones do?"

"Good question," said Plummer. "They're more susceptible to conventional defenses—they'll be low-hanging fruit to the F-16—" He stopped abruptly.

Fisk saw the quadrocopters launch rockets of some sort. Incandescent orange baseballs, they looked like, hundreds of them, at least two dozen from each quadrocopter. On both sides of the Hudson, spectators let out cheers, no doubt believing the fireworks show was under way.

"The quads have released a hot-burning magnesium-based composition," Plummer said.

Fisk braced. "Meaning?"

"Decoy flares, evidently."

The flares didn't rise much higher than the quadrocopters, then began drifting back to the Hudson River. As the flares' luminescent trails gave each drone the appearance of having sprouted a pair of angel's wings, Boyden's plan became clear to Fisk: decoy flares were used by aircraft as a countermeasure against infrared homing missiles. The missiles sought out the heat signature from the flare, leaving the aircraft unscathed. Boyden meant these flares to neutralize the F-16s and helicopters protecting New York, clearing the way for the octocopters big enough to deliver payloads of TATP, in turn big enough to dwarf the casualty total of 9/11.

Plummer said, "Pray that the octocopters aren't packing bombs or anything like that."

A total of twenty-four quadrocopters, according to Plummer, had flown out of an apartment window in an empty three-story building in Union City that was scheduled for demolition. The quads preceded four octocopters that rose from the building's water tower, in which they'd been stacked. One of them quickly fell behind, Plummer reported, evidently experiencing technical difficulties. This offered Fisk no solace—the octocopter's TATP payload might still detonate in Union City, which had nearly seventy thousand citizens packed into just over a square mile.

The swarm of drones then began its way to the Hudson River, which now resembled a mosaic, flickering from black to white in reflection of the building lights on either side. Under ordinary circumstances, at their speed of between ten and fifteen miles per hour, the drones would cover the mile and a fifth to Manhattan in five minutes. The westerly wind now accelerated that, leaving Fisk with closer to four minutes to stop them.

First he needed to defeat the veritable obstacle course between the Seventy-Second Street on-ramp and the shore—an eight-foot chicken-wire fence, two medians, three sets of guardrails so far, and the speeding cars and trucks he had to dodge. He couldn't tell whether the moisture he felt was blood spurting from the wound in his hip, now reopened, or just perspiration. The pain said the former. But he didn't care. He didn't care about anything except getting to the NYPD Harbor Patrol boat Dubin had ordered. Getting to the edge of the water where the boat would meet them, that is. Meanwhile he dragged Poplowski along.

"So can this work?" Fisk asked. For the third time.

"I just don't know, man." The spindly kid, probably not much of an athlete on his best days, struggled to haul himself over the final West Side Highway guard wall before the water. "Theoretically, yeah, I guess so. The thing is, I've seen fireworks videos recorded by drones flying through the fireworks, so obviously those fireworks didn't do much to the sensors."

Fisk helped him down, onto the mucky roadside between the highway and the water. "Could it work if we sent up hundreds of fireworks?"

"Could, maybe, yeah."

Fisk was hoping for a stronger endorsement of his plan.

When the patrol boat was within ten feet, he ran and jumped the watery gap. Dubin, lagging behind, still on the highway median, waved Fisk ahead. Probably better he stay behind anyway, Fisk thought, so that he could oversee the other desperation measures, including distributing night-vision goggles to cops on the street so that they could take their best shots at the drones. Although unable to shoot down the octocopters, the F-16s could still aid in the defense of the city, ironically by use of their onboard pyrophoric flares, which ignited on contact with the air as soon as they were dropped, and, like the fireworks, might overwhelm the drones' sensors. One more line of defense for New York was Poplowski, who remained behind in hopes of recharging the LightningRod using the Tahoe battery. And perhaps the Emergency Services Unit would deploy the LightningRods they'd purchased from his company.

Such were the countermeasures that the city had been able to muster one minute into an attack that Boyden Verlyn, Fisk suspected, had had several days to plan.

"We've been briefed, Detective," the harbor cop in the boat's small wheelhouse said as Fisk came aboard. "Except which barge do you want to go to?"

"Good question." Fisk had counted five of the behemoths in a row along the center of the river, distributed evenly over the seventy or eighty blocks between Chelsea and Morningside Heights. "How about the one closest to Union City?"

The harbor cop spun the wheel, meanwhile flattening the throttle. The boat lurched out onto the river, the shore seeming to fly away. Fisk had to grab hold of a rail to remain standing. Noting the streetlights flickering like stars on the ink-black water, he might have believed the boat was in outer space if not for the repeated thumps of the bow.

In thirty seconds, the boat slowed alongside the barge, which was surprisingly large close up, bigger than a basketball court, yet rising and falling with the slightest wave. Fisk guessed three minutes had elapsed in total since the drones took off, meaning they were more than halfway to Manhattan.

Looking up, he discerned flashes from the gray

clouds overhead: whirling rotors. As the boat engines quieted, he heard the drones' whine.

He wasted no time, jumping from the bow and
onto the deck of the barge, which was almost entirely covered with wooden crates, each the size of
a child's desk, their open tops providing a view of
the sand filling them. The sand held in place cylindrical metal mortar tubes that launched the fireworks shells. Thousands of wires led from the crates
to a single control panel, where a chubby twenty-
something technician with a neck beard was sitting.
He was snacking on a bag of cheese curls, until,
seeing Fisk, he got up and brushed some of the
orange crumbs off his T-shirt. He asked, as people
always do when the police pull up, "Everything
okay?"

Fisk met him in the middle of the deck. "Can you
launch all the fireworks at the same time?"

The technician screwed up his face. "All the fireworks?"

"Yes."

"Why would I ever want to do that?" Clearly it
was the first he'd heard of this effort.

"To stop drones from killing people."

"*Drones?*"

Fisk pointed up.

The technician looked up at the solar system's
worth of flares, then quickly down again, now with
a wispy grin. "Dude, those are just flares."

Pointing up again, Fisk barked, "Listen!"

The technician cocked an ear. It sounded like
there was a swarm of giant bees overhead. Intermittently, the flares illuminated fuselages and rotors. If

that weren't enough to convince the technician, the wobbly octocopter bringing up the rear abruptly descended off the coast of Jersey City, tumbling end over end before splashing into the river beside the bow of a moored tugboat. The tug, rising and falling with the current, leaped into the air before disappearing in a ball of flame, a sun in miniature, accompanied by an earsplitting blast and a pillar of water like something out of a Bible story. A hot blast current buffeted the barge, nearly costing Fisk his balance again. The water and flames quickly shrank to nothing, having reduced the tugboat to smoking flotsam. Through the blaring whine in Fisk's ears came delirious roars from the spectators on shore.

He exchanged a knowing look with the technician, whose eyes bulged. He stammered, "I'm still going to need some, you know, authorization."

"How about my key to the city?" Fisk drew his Glock.

Raising his hands, the technician slowly backpedaled. Toward the control panel, fortunately.

Fisk followed. "What do you do? Just turn it on and then press the red buttons?"

The guy nodded.

Holstering his Glock, Fisk snapped the oversize toggle switch at the top of the panel into the on position, causing the red light beside it to dim and the green to illuminate. With both hands he swatted the red buttons—four rows of sixteen, the numbers beside each corresponding to crates, he supposed.

He turned to the technician to verify that he'd done it properly. Needlessly. Confirmation came in the form of a cannonlike blast from one of the mortars and a plume of flame that reached twice his height, sending a shell whistling into the darkness.

It appeared to be headed directly into the path of the drones. Two or three hundred feet overhead, Fisk estimated, the shell let out a gut-rattling boom and expanded into a sphere of yellow, red, and orange stars that drifted back down to earth with trails of sparks.

Meanwhile more blasts—hundreds of blasts up and down the barges—blended into a single roar, with the plumes of flame commingling to produce a reverse rain of shells, many bursting into neon comets that formed large tendrils, producing a palm-tree-like effect.

Other shells exploded at their apex into small stars that crisscrossed one another. Some generated a quick flash followed by a very loud report and then nothing but smoke. Each bang rattled Fisk from head to toe. He dug his thumbs into his ears to protect his hearing, and still his eardrums were pummeled.

Quickly it became impossible to distinguish one effect from the next, the airborne stars and candles and comets merging into a single giant multicolored sun. The conflagration gradually descended, engulfing the drones, which, like flies, dropped, one after the next.

They sliced into the Hudson River and sank slowly, their duct-tape-wrapped payloads shimmering in the reflection of what turned out to be the last shell to launch. It erupted into a cluster of stars that whizzed in all directions before forming a swaying American flag.

Amid a rain of sparks and ash and cumulus

smoke that tasted of cordite, Fisk heard the cheers on both sides of the river transform to confusion, everyone wondering no doubt why the hell all of the fireworks for the hour-long show went off in one twenty-second burst. He also heard his phone buzz with a text from Plummer of the NGA.

GOOD WORK! 4 OCTOS DOWN, 5 TO GO.

Swallowing hard, Fisk looked up through the thinning smoke, making out a brand-new set of octocopters preceded by another twenty or thirty quadrocopter escorts, most directly overhead, a few more than halfway to Manhattan. All he could do was draw his Glock and hope for unprecedented range and marksmanship.

At the same time, from the pier, Shane Poplowski managed to take out one of the octocopters with a recharged LightningRod—the drone fell like a twirling baton before knifing through the surface of the Hudson and disappearing unceremoniously. A Koala pilot proved a deadeye shot, taking down another of the octocopters with his Smith & Wesson 5906 service pistol at a hundred yards. Get that guy on the Olympic team, Fisk thought. Unfortunately, no other helicopter crew scored a hit, and on the city streets and rooftops on either side of the river, not a single sharpshooter got into position in time to expend a round.

As Fisk's own rounds disappeared into the night around them, the three remaining octocopters turned downriver. The smaller quadrocopters turned as well before taking the lead.

Fisk's mind played a feverish montage of downtown landmarks. Like One World Trade Center. Or how about the Stock Exchange? An explosion there would have the effect of crippling the economy. Or the Statue of Liberty—the TATP could take her head off. And then there was the High Line park, into which hundreds of thousands of New Yorkers—at least—were packed to watch fireworks.

Damnably, he could do nothing now but watch. Right away, however, he received a measure of hope: an F-16 flew over the barge and onto the scene, so fast that it seemed supernatural, the sonic boom dwarfing that of the explosions of the fireworks shells. The fighter plane released dozens of flares. The balls of yellow-green fire drifted down into the path of the drones.

Whether or not the flares did any good was difficult to say because, on instructions from Dubin, thousands of fireworks shells shot into the night from the four other barges. They rose past the drones and burst into a galaxy of stars before seemingly setting the sky ablaze, lighting New York City like noon.

The drones plummeted.

To a watery grave.

All of them.

And Fisk felt it at once: the mix of exhaustion and delirium and satisfaction. The one-of-a-kind buzz that accompanied a case truly closed.

He might have fallen to his knees and kissed the deck, or maybe embraced the technician. But then he would have missed the end of the fireworks. He enjoyed every last spark.

Fisk knew of no standard procedure that follows the downing of a fleet of drones. It was nine-something at night on a federal holiday. He got back onto the Harbor Patrol boat only because it seemed like the most expedient way to get off the river, and because going ashore seemed like a better idea than not.

When the harbor cop in the wheelhouse asked him where he wanted to be dropped, he needed to think about it. They could drop him anywhere, really, no big, the guy said. Where they'd picked him up was fine. He appreciated being able to make a low-stakes decision for a change.

They dropped him at the Riverside Park boat basin, because it was more accessible and extended far enough from shore that his disembarking wouldn't draw a crowd. In fact, no one seemed to notice.

Reaching the park, he walked between pools of dark shadows, unrecognized. He heard people, from their lawn chairs and picnic blankets, wondering if there were going to be more fireworks. Others were already packing up. Most stayed, enjoying the night. This was the best part, Fisk thought. Having kept them safe, free to enjoy sitting around in a park at night doing nothing, he felt like a superhero.

He thought he might go get a beer, maybe catch an inning or two on TV at a bar. When given the gift of time, it was hard to pass up a walk in New York. And since it meant prolonging the case-closed buzz, it was a no-brainer. He decided to walk the thirty-some blocks down to the Times Tower, in hopes that Chay had made sufficient progress in that El Polvo story and was able to get a nightcap. He cut through the dog run at the base of the park. Still deserted. Dogs and fireworks weren't a good mix, plus the trees blocked the view onto the river. The stout metal trash barrel smelled like it had worked overtime collecting bags of dog shit.

Accelerating past it caused his hip to hurt. Better to take a cab to the Times Tower, he thought. Fishing his phone out of his pocket in order to text Chay first, he saw that she had texted him twice. No surprise that he'd missed it between the detonation of the octocopters and all of the fireworks.

COMING 2 RIVERSIDE PK AFTER ALL, said the first message.

The second said only *EL POLVO IS*, ending abruptly.

As Fisk puzzled over their meaning, he heard a crunch of gravel behind him.

He spun around. The lone illuminated streetlamp silhouetted the man twenty feet away, leveling a Glock, the same model Fisk should have drawn, but capped with a sound suppressor. Fisk didn't recognize the guy, but figured from context it was the hit man from East Seventy-Fourth. Yeah, same cold eyes, and that misplaced grin. The dark, wavy hair was probably a wig, or maybe it was what had been underneath the wig the other night. What mattered was, Fisk was about to die.

There would be no discussion, no time for him to dive out of the way of bullets traveling at a thousand feet a second, certainly no time for him to draw his own Glock. What stood to be the last second of his life played out now in hundredths of a second.

The barrel glinted as the hit man tweaked his aim, exhaled, and tensed his trigger finger. Then he added his left hand to the base of the grip, steadying it—and in taking those extra few hundredths of a second, he remained in place for the rolling trash barrel—one of the metal city-park models that weighed a good fifty pounds when empty—to impact his calves and the backs of his ankles, taking his legs out from under him. In the shadows beneath the dense trees lining the dog run, someone must have tipped the barrel onto its side and pushed it toward him.

The hit man still got off a shot, and Fisk still instinctively dove and was hit—hit by gravel kicked up by the round. It ripped into his throat and face, but he'd happily take that over bullets. The hit man meanwhile landed on his side in the gravel, enabling Fisk to draw his gun and aim. But the guy rolled away, then sprang into a kneeling firing position, both arms extended in front of him, a firm hold on his pistol. He pivoted the barrel toward Fisk, pressing the trigger. At the same time Fisk's bullet boomed from his Glock and drilled through the hit man's neck, exiting along with a shimmering tail of gore and ringing against the base of the trash barrel before ricocheting into the night. The man fell sideways like a spent top and lay in the gravel, writhing.

"Thank you," Fisk said to Chay, who stepped out

of the patch of trees from which she'd rolled the trash barrel.

"Meet El Polvo," she said with a wave at the hit man. "He's wanted for seven murders, responsible for exponentially more business at the morgue, and if you believe his mistress—which I do—he's an even worse guy at home."

"How do you know this?"

"Some old-fashioned research, and some new-fashioned. After he took another crack at me in Times Square, I was able to track him using the Domain Awareness system feed on faa.gov."

Fisk was eager to hear more. "That's how you followed him here?"

She smiled. "The Domain Awareness system is amazing. I've come around on it now—" She was interrupted by a wail of pain from El Polvo.

Scrambling to his feet, Fisk said, "We should call Emergency Operations."

"Nine-one-one?"

He reached for his phone. "Yeah."

She put her hands on her hips. "Could really put a damper on the rest of our night."

Fisk smiled, shaking his head. He yelled to a passerby, "Hey, call 911, will you?"

What happened to Chay?" asked Ellen Lee, leading Fisk into her Norwalk house.

The sentencing had been all over the news three months ago. If the old woman didn't know by now that Chay had been jailed for contempt of court for her refusal to testify, Fisk thought, she would probably never be the wiser.

"She's away on business," he said.

Which was true. Chay was defending a journalistic principle, and he admired that, particularly since her sentence had been cut to five months. It didn't hurt that the minimum-security Federal Correction Institution in Otisville, New York, offered extended conjugal visits to inmates' boyfriends who happened to be New York cops.

He followed Lee up to the attic, where the bookcases had been emptied of Merritt Verlyn's collection. In front of them sat four stacks of three moving boxes.

"Are you sure you want to buy them?" she asked.

He held forth the check, which he'd made out to her before he left New York, because he thought this might happen, that she would hesitate, as she did now, keeping her hands at her sides, acting as though she didn't notice the check. Seller's remorse.

"What makes you want Merritt's book collection?" she asked. Not what *made* you, past tense, but what *makes* you, as if this were not in fact a done deal.

"I'd like to have a first edition of Camille Flammarion in my library," he said. "I've always been a fan of both Flammarion and R. A. Lafferty. I knew it was science fiction, but reading Lafferty in particular when I was a boy made me believe anything was possible."

The only truth in his answer was his desire to have the first-edition Flammarion, for work reasons. He'd never heard of either Flammarion or Lafferty before Ellen Lee's craigslist ad pinged on R2's computer in Tel Aviv. He didn't like deceiving Lee. But he was a spy, and sometimes doing the job effectively required operating in gray areas.

That evening, back at the apartment in Hell's Kitchen—he'd decided to keep the place because he liked life better off the grid—he cracked the first edition of Flammarion's *Lumen* and felt himself immediately engaged by the astronomer who was the novel's main character. But he wasn't looking for a good read tonight. He set the book aside, in favor of a hardcover edition of Orwell's *1984*. Probably where he should have started, he mused.

He was right. He found a secret compartment carved into the spine and then patched over with surgical precision using the original red cloth. Wedged into the compartment was a silvery micro 512-gigabyte USB 3.0 drive, about the size of a Chiclet, yet containing about 130,000 classified documents.

And a hell of a read. Before he knew it, the dark shapes outside the window became the water towers and chimneys and roofs across the alley and, with the first flecks of dawn, individual roof tiles. Another hour still and Fisk rose from his reading chair in possession of secrets that would be devastating to the careers of so many politicians and law enforcement and intelligence-agency officials—so many that he'd lost count. Several of the documents could bring down regimes. One in particular might result in anarchy in the United States.

He resolved to destroy Merritt Verlyn's micro drive immediately.

Then he thought better of it.

ACKNOWLEDGMENTS

To Chuck Hogan, for all his help and support, and for his enthusiasm for new technology.